Timeswept Passion...Timeless Love

A ROSE IS A ROSE

"Are you under the impression that there's some big romance going on here, Colt? I admit there's a physical attraction, but I have no intention of entering into an affair right now."

"Is that so? You were half in love with me before the end of the day yesterday."

"Why, you conceited lout! Are you going to take me back to Jackson or not?"

"I'll take you to Jackson Hole, Madison, but I can't do it now. It may not be for a few days, but don't worry I'll get you home."

"Can't someone else take me? Or I can go myself. I'll be okay."

"That's damn thoughtful of you, sugar—but no one else knows which rosebush is the magic one," he answered sarcastically. "And no, you're not going alone! This is 1878, and that is wild country out there. Jackson doesn't exist yet. More than likely what you'll find are Indians, hungry wolves, and, if you're really lucky, some degenerate outlaws who would just love to get a taste of you! Do you comprehend *that?*"

TIME OF THE ROSE

BONITA CLIFTON

LOVE SPELL NEW YORK CITY

For my husband, David, with love.
Thank you for telling everyone, especially me,
that I could.

LOVE SPELL®

January 1994

Published by

Dorchester Publishing Co., Inc.
276 Fifth Avenue
New York, NY 10001

Prologue

Wyoming Territory, 1878

Lightning serrated a silver lance through the blackened, churning storm clouds with inconceivable force, jolting the earth with its subsequent peal of tooth-rattling thunder. Squaring his shoulders, he snapped his head back. His brows furrowed over his eyes, and he puzzled at the gyrating vapor that emerged from nowhere, filling the skies. It seemed as if the heavens were colliding with the earth. Gigantic raindrops splattered his upturned face, cascading across his jaw in smooth rivulets.

Damn! Where in God's name had this storm come from? Colton Remington Chase stalked through the snarl of new spring grass toward a clearing. His hands resting on his hips, he stood among the graceful, silvery trunks of an aspen grove. Giant lodgepole pines backed him in dense stands, their feathery tops spreading over the ruggedness of the mountain and the canyon in soft, yellow-green waves. The cool air hung heavy with the crisp aroma of pine and rain, touched by the sweetness of wildflowers.

Colt remounted his gray stallion in a single powerful movement. Lifting the doeskin-colored Stetson from his head with a drawn-out sigh, he raked his fingers through his long hair.

It wouldn't do to head down the pass now, he rationalized. A downpour could trigger a flash flood. But then, he was a sitting duck for a strike of lightning on this open mound.

Confident astride the great horse, he wore a faded blue cotton pullover shirt with fine German silver engraved buttons, one side partially undone and draping down. A red bandanna was knotted loosely about his neck. His tan Levi trousers were well-worn and covered with a light coating of range dust. As was customary, buckskin had been sewn over the seat and down the inner thighs to keep them from wearing thin. His pantlegs hugged his thighs, tucked into Cuban-heeled leather boots that rested easily in the broad wooden stirrups.

His pale leather vest barely concealed the ornately embossed hideaway rig that housed twin Colt Peacemakers, and was always supplied with a bounty of ammunition. Each six-shooter was silver-plated, a single intricate rose carved into the ivory-handled grip. A cowhide boot attached to the saddle held a Henry .44 rifle, easily accessible to his right hand.

Colt twirled the peculiar rose by its thorny stem, contemplating its color. It may have bloomed a vivid crimson, but with the passage of time, it had paled, marbled with shades of mauve.

Intricately tangled branches of leaves were wrapped around the scabrous girth of a snow-bent spruce, forsaken beneath its sheltering boughs. Having been unable to resist its fascinating allure, he had pinched a blossoming bud from the misplaced rosebush. Now he pressed the flower to his nose, reveling in the rich, sweet fragrance. He'd always fancied the rose. Its silken petals were almost like the creamy skin of a beautiful woman, he mused, the corners of his mouth curving into a slow smile. He slipped the rosebud carefully into the suede pouch at his waist.

Lightning arced another blinding blue light of warning, the thunder rolling in waves throughout the fog-darkened valley. Suddenly, the air around the rider and his horse seemed to shimmer. The mist lowered, a swirling vortex threatening to swallow them up. The stallion stood atop the grassy ridge, his head into the wind—and he began to prance with uncharacteristic nervousness.

"Whoa there, boy. It's only a little storm brewing," Colt murmured to the huge animal, stroking the finely muscled horseflesh to deliver a reassuring pat. The gray wasn't one to be spooked easily. A hint of worry crossed Colt's face.

The gales strengthened, whipping larkspur into a frenzy around the horse's enormous black hooves. Colt deftly reached behind the cantle to loosen the leather ties that bound his rain slicker. Shaking it free, he shoved his arms into the stiff, unbending sleeves and pressed his hat firmly onto his head.

Despite the angry outburst from above, he felt strangely at peace. It was a good feeling, one he hadn't experienced in a long, long time, and he was relishing it. He sensed excitement, an urge to give in to some unknown force, pulling at him, beckoning him down into the meadow, into the fog. Elusive promises to forget his mission . . . to clear his head . . .

"What the hell! Let's go for a little ride," he muttered under his breath.

A thunderclap shook the heavens at the same instant he nudged the gray with spurred heels. Springing forth and down, they vanished into the murky haze.

With the flowing rhythm of a man and beast who know one another well, they moved as one. Colt lay low, giving the animal full rein. Like the wind, they raced into a full, sleek gallop. He was unable to get enough of the speed, the exhilaration. He felt free, free for the first time in ten years—all of those years of wandering, chasing after anything that might bring him closer to his goal. Right now he felt as if he could ride the massive steed forever, lose himself in the muscular power beneath him and ride into eternity. . . .

It was impossible to see. There was only the liquid motion and the rippling of long grass beneath the gray's shod hooves. Rain pelted Colt's face in a stinging deluge. He no longer pressed the stallion on, and yet the animal continued ever faster, breathing in harsh, lusty snorts.

The wind sung a deafening chorus against Colt's ears. Overwhelming dizziness enveloped him and rapidly turned to nausea. His senses reeled, and he couldn't help but envision the swirling cloud around him as an unfathomable tunnel, hurling him headlong into its gray, misty corridors.

A shrill ringing within his head became distorted, mutating into what sounded like human voices. Thousands upon thousands of them, drawn from eons of triumph and tragedy. Indecipherable. A calliope of sound—yet he could almost discern the fleeting rhythm of an Indian war chant, the resonance of an operatic baritone, melting into a delicate, tinkling feminine laughter that floated on the wind at his side. Intermixing, louder and louder the discord grew—until he thought he would surely be driven mad.

A final, blood-curdling scream was his own.

With all the power he could muster, he heaved in on the reins. Abruptly, the gray veered to a skidding halt, digging into the spongy soil with its sharp hooves.

Drawing in his breath deeply to quell the rising nausea, Colt leapt from the saddle, stumbling a few feet away, where he promptly lost his morning meal. The sickness passed quickly enough. He slowly straightened, swiping his sleeve across his brow to mop the dripping rainwater. He was panting. His hair hung in heavy, wet strands; a brisk shake sent the excess moisture flying in a shower of droplets.

The haunting mist curled, dissipating to reveal a luminous rainbow arching over the emerald valley. He walked to where the horse nibbled along a patch of sweet clover, scooping his hat from the ground and knocking it against his thigh. The sun was already warming the rain-chilled air. A songbird's repetitive chirp could be heard from the crest of distant pine.

The rugged, snow-capped Tetons reigned over Jackson Hole in all their glory. Glittering rivers twisted meanderously along a velvet green valley floor as far as the eye could see, connecting with yet larger rivers, then lakes, forming a complex maze. Early June wildflowers were coming into full bloom, interspersing tall spires of wheatgrass with dramatic spangles of vibrant color. An eagle cut the air above with powerful wings, soaring away to vanish into crystal azure skies.

Colt breathed deeply with inner satisfaction. Then, squinting to validate the accuracy of his vision, he stared in utter disbelief at the sight the lifting fog revealed.

Nestled at the base of the far range was a town—quite a large town by his standards. There hadn't been a trace of it before the storm, although the way he had been positioned could have obscured it from view, he reasoned. True, nearly a year had passed since he last rode up to this area, but how could a town of this size spring up so quickly? And why hadn't he at least heard about it?

Always curious and never one to recoil from a challenge, a spirit of adventure overtook him. What in tarnation were those carriages and wagons that moved up and down smooth, black streets without the assistance of horses? Everything was so shiny and colorful, the entire town glistening in the sunlight. An unfamiliar droning hum reverberated through and beyond far treetops, then was gone.

"Sonova—" he broke off in wonderment, craning his neck up. He shielded his eyes but was unable to see the source. Nothing but blue sky.

With the unthinking ease of experience, he hoisted himself back into the saddle and clicked the gray forward. He positioned the Stetson back onto his head, giving a slight downward tug on the front brim.

Book One

Book One

Chapter One

Jackson, Wyoming 1993
Old Town

The fiery intensity of the sun warmed Madison Calloway, even though the air still harbored a distinct chill. In the aftermath of an unexpected spring thunderstorm, Madison noted that Main Street was already crawling with sightseers engaged in shopping. Their shorts, tennis shoes, cameras, and cars disrupted the otherwise authentic 19th-century atmosphere of the turbulent Old West. The narrow street was lined with rows of gaudy saloons, cozy hotels, and a medley of shops and antique stores, which Madison had ducked in and out of, obsessively filling her slouchy shoulder bag with a variety of odd-sized purchases. An avowed lover of antiques, she beamed with the elation of having successfully bartered for a perfectly preserved flow-blue gravy boat to add to her collection back home.

The music of a rain-scented breeze catching windchimes drifted along the street, filling the air above with a delicately haunting melody. Glancing about for her companions, Madison increased her pace along the planked boardwalk, stopping before her own clear reflection in a large picture window.

"Rats . . . I knew I should have worn it up," she mumbled under her breath as she fiddled with a misplaced spiral of gold hair. Madison wrinkled her nose at the mess the wind had made of her hair. Despite the fact that she would soon be turning 31, she still sometimes felt like a little girl, and looked it, too, when her hair hung down past her shoulders as it did today. But she was glad that her almond-shaped teal eyes, which flashed sparks of bright green when she became excited or angry, were sparkliing and clear and that this morning her heart felt lighter than usual. The all-too-familiar lead weight that endlessly rested in the pit of her stomach wasn't there—yet. Maybe this little trip was precisely what she needed. After what she had been through in the past year, anything would be a welcome reprieve.

It was only a weekend excursion, provided to her own Calloway World Travel Agency in Colorado Springs by a local Jackson tour operator. She usually took several trips like this during a year's time, but lately she hadn't felt much like traveling. Instead she sent either her brother, Mark, or one of her travel agents while she stayed behind and buried herself in work at the office. But not this time. Today she was actually looking forward to the monotonous hotel inspections. Their return flight to Colorado Springs wouldn't depart until late Sunday, so there would be ample free time to do as she pleased tomorrow.

It wasn't typical of Madison to feel so old and hopelessly used up, as she had so often lately. After eight years as a travel agent, three of them running her own agency, she was a very successful businesswoman and proud of it. She had been immensely happy with her personal life as well, but all that had changed when her marriage of eleven years turned sour, threatening to shatter all she had worked for.

She had come so close to giving the agency up, so tempted to let it all go right along with him. After all, if it hadn't been for Jon's investment in her dream, it might never have materialized. But she had created this little empire all by herself, with the help of a small troupe of talented agents. Jon might have provided some of the much-needed financing, but it had been her hard work that had made it successful, and she had decided not to let it fall by the wayside. After all was said and done, her agency was like a thriving child, its clientele growing by leaps and bounds.

Jon Klein. Out of habit, Madison's thumb moved across her palm to toy with the gold band, finding only the soft skin of her finger instead. The lead weight returned, falling right into place at the base of her stomach. She still loved him, no use denying it and, that fact irked her. Did she have no pride at all? How could anyone continue to love a man like that? Despite the repetitive arguments that battled inside her head, the end result was invariably the same. Madison would probably always love him—she would just have to find a way to live with it.

Even though she tried not to dwell on it, questions and doubts about her failed marriage would sneak up on her, usually at the most inopportune times, bringing the familiar salty burn to her eyes. Why had Jon done it? Hadn't she been a good wife? Maybe she wasn't pretty enough. Maybe it was just his personality, always taking the elusive chance, living on the edge, attaining a much-sought-after goal only to feel cheated and demanding a higher one . . . never satisfied. His choice of careers certainly reflected that side of him. A fast-paced stockbroker, extremely intelligent—maybe too intelligent—his wheeling and dealing had sometimes led his ethics astray. In fact, Madison had suspected that the means by which he had obtained the money to invest in her agency hadn't been totally on the level. But he had denied any wrongdoing when she had asked him about it, insisting he'd been playing options and got lucky.

Jon was continually in pursuit of the almighty dollar, making it quite evident that nothing else mattered as much—except for, Madison discovered, women. Lots of different women.

"Earth to Maddie . . ."

Mark's voice sifted through her thoughts, and though Madison hadn't even heard his silent approach from behind her, she sent him the hint of a musing smile. His gentle hand kneaded the tension from her shoulders and she mindlessly turned back to gaze at the display of ghastly instruments exhibited in the dusty window of the Barber/Dentist.

"We should get a move on, Maddie! There's a hotel inspection in fifteen minutes at the Blue Lady. After that a bus tour of the ski resort and countryside, then back here for lunch. . . . Oh, I also managed to get a few tickets for the Wild West show this afternoon." His eyebrow cocked at her in triumph.

If anyone knew her, it was Mark. He recognized her every mood, and she guessed he knew right this minute what she had been thinking. If Mark hadn't been there to scrape her remains from the bottom of the pit of despair when her marriage had ended, she didn't see how she could have made it. Madison's eyes lifted to his, and she knew he detected the moisture that threatened to spill from her eyes. Madison's mood lightened. She knew his reminding her of their agenda was Mark's way of getting her mind off her problems and on to other things. Mark glanced at his watch.

"Good." Madison sighed absently. "It's that time already, huh? Where are Lanie and Gertie?"

"I was hoping you knew."

"I haven't seen them since breakfast. . . . Why don't you go on ahead? I'll round them up and be right behind you."

"Sure thing. Don't be too long." With an affectionate squeeze to her shoulder, her brother continued on toward the hotel, his long strides eating up the boardwalk.

Madison was extremely grateful to Mark for helping her to overcome the emotional setback of her divorce. Though they had some pretty hair-raising disagreements, she knew she couldn't have a better brother. They had always been close. Mark was four years her junior and the most cherished friend she had. When she wasn't contemplating how to murder him she was loving him to death. It was only natural to hire him as her agency manager once he'd graduated from the university in Colorado Springs. He was definitely the brainy type, something one wouldn't guess looking at him. He was the type of man women swooned over: tall, well-built, athletic, with a thick mop of dark blond wavy hair and eyes to die for. Of course, whenever Madison looked into those bright green orbs she could only see a reflection of the ornery little boy who used to drive her nuts.

Madison took a few more minutes to browse at her leisure, then, spotting her two travel agents in the distance, traversed the crowd to where Gertie and Lanie had stopped.

"Find something interesting?"

"Would you look at that, Maddie?" Gertie whispered in awe, pointing at a display behind the thick glass of a showcase window. She grimaced, pursing her lips until they were as round as her plump face. "Isn't that the most beautiful dress? So eloquent."

"Whoever wore it must have had a tiny waist!" Lanie added, her sunny nature as bright as the pale yellow of her hair.

A faded burgundy velvet gown was shown on a mannequin. Its snug bodice was held together with dozens of tiny pearl seed buttons extending down to a wasp waist. High, starched frills, yellowed with age, adorned the neck and wrists. Pointy-toed ankle boots peeked out from the bottom of the full, gathered skirt, a draped bustle accenting the back. A crooked wig supported a hat fashioned from the same burgundy velvet, black lace veiling the chipped face of the mannequin.

"Hmmmm-mmm, but just imagine how miserable that lady was in order to have that small a waist. I've heard about women's ribs being malformed because they wore their corsets so tightly laced, sometimes causing punctured lungs," Madison replied.

"That sounds absolutely horrid!" Lanie shivered.

"It certainly makes a person feel lucky to have been born in the twentieth century, that's for sure." Gertie wrinkled her pug nose in distaste, patting her short graying hair. "I can't tell you my relief at not having to wear a bustle with a butt the size of mine!"

An infectious giggle rolled from Gertie's throat and trailed behind her as she and Lanie continued on to the hotel. Maddie admired Gertie, who was the oldest agent in the office. She possessed a zest for life that most people half her age wouldn't understand.

Madison tarried a little longer at the store window, a wistful expression playing over her features. Despite the many hardships, life in the last century must have been very romantic. The layers of feminine clothing that had to be removed slowly, piece by frilly piece, during an impassioned moment between two lovers . . . it must have been very erotic.

Startled back to reality, Madison jumped at the intrusion of a shrill catcall from behind her and spun around without thinking. Her unsuspecting gaze met that of a seedy, unshaven drugstore-cowboy type. A nasty straw cowboy hat lay low, obscuring his eyes in its cryptic shadow.

"Nice ass," he smirked, revealing brown-stained teeth, a wad of tobacco stuffed into his cheek. He continued to appraise her, as if he actually expected a favorable reply.

Annoyed, Madison backed away, the flesh creeping along her spine. "Jerk," she muttered caustically.

A blind turn to her left landed her directly in the path of a passerby. Dodging him, she leaped off the boardwalk, managing to stop just in time to avoid a collision with the shoulder of the most enormous horse she'd ever seen in her life. It was certainly the largest she'd ever been this close to.

"Oh, my . . ." A little gasp tore from her throat as she quickly reversed her step again.

Charcoal-tipped ears twitched uneasily at her nearness, the round, liquid-black eyes wary. The horse was a most unusual

color of mottled gray. Its mane and forelock hung like sheets
of pale gray icicles. For just a sliver of a moment she realized
that, with concentration, she would be able to count each delicate
black lash that fringed that eye.

"Pardon me, ma'am . . . my fault."

The voice was smooth and richly timbred, and at first Madison
couldn't tell from where it came. The man moved away from the
opposite side of the gray stallion and hesitated briefly. His gaze
locked with hers, as if he thought he knew her; then, apparently
deciding he didn't, he touched the wide brim of his hat with a
gloved hand. A solemn nod and he moved on.

The seedy cowboy long forgotten, Madison stumbled back
onto the boardwalk and continued distractedly down the street.
But curiosity gnawed at her. She stopped, turning back again
to watch the old cowboy's progress. The sight of him was so
authentic, typical and yet somehow unusual. Certainly no tourist,
she reasoned. Could it be he was a performer in the Wild West
show? He was such an antiquity; yet he walked—no, ambled was
the word—with the spirit of a much younger man.

A full-length tarpaulin rain slicker, slit up the back, drifted
behind the old cowboy as he preceded the huge horse cautiously
up the street. He passed some parallel-parked cars, slowing, staring unashamedly, oblivious to the stares he was drawing himself.
He peered inside one of them as if he was looking for something
in particular.

Those eyes . . . she couldn't put those eyes out of her mind!
Like a soft, compassionate, golden brown caress, so clear and
alert. His hair was a shimmering silver; almost white, flowing
past his shoulders from beneath a tan hat adorned with a snake-
skin band. His quiet demeanor made him appear unapproachable,
suggesting wariness to the casual stranger.

A yellow Jeep sped recklessly along Main Street, going too
fast considering the number of gadding pedestrians. Madison
found herself holding her breath as the old cowboy bounded
in exaggerated haste toward the safety of the boardwalk, the
horse shimmying nervously behind him. Several people halted
their activities just to watch. An attractive woman in shorts casually sprinted across the street. Dismissing the speeding Jeep, he
watched her with open interest.

Madison finally caught up to Mark and Lanie outside the Blue
Lady Saloon and Hotel.

"Did you see that old guy?" Madison motioned in the direction in which she'd last seen him, but he had vanished and the crowd had resumed its activities.

"The one with the horse? They must pay him to walk up and down the street for effect. He looked older than most of these buildings around here." Mark shoved a bag of popcorn in front of her; he didn't seem to share her enthusiasm for the cowboy.

"Did you see the arsenal he was packing under his coat?" Lanie reported excitedly. "He had enough ammunition to wage war on a small country—and win. I just hope he's a legitimate performer in that show and not some looney with a vendetta for tourists. . . ." She walked inside.

"You watch too much TV." Mark caught the door after her and, turning back to Madison, asked, "You coming?"

"You know," she said softly, absently chewing a long fingernail, "the way he jumped away from every car that passed—it was like he was scared to death! I don't think he's used to being around so many people. He was staring at everything, and everyone." Then, remembering Mark was waiting, she said, "Be there in just a sec."

At that moment Gertie rolled out of a gap in the steady stream of people, latching onto the door and following Mark inside.

Madison remained outside, continuing to scan the swarm of faces, hoping to catch another glimpse of the old man and the horse.

Chapter Two

Wrenching a dead limb from the low branch of a monolithic cottonwood, Colt hurled it with a spin across the trickling creek, where it landed in a spread of white-flowered hawthorn. With a heavy sigh of frustration, he lowered himself to his haunches, resting his forearms on his knees, contemplating the meager flow of rancid spring water that gurgled past him. He knew it was rancid because of the generous mouthful he had tried to drink from his cupped hands. Grimacing, he had spat the foul-tasting liquid over his shoulder, feeling as though he might lose his breakfast all over again. Wasn't it just a few hours ago that this very creek, swollen with a wealth of spring runoff, surged from its source at the mouth of the canyon, nearly overflowing the high banks?

Colt slowly shook his head in utter confusion, squinting toward the dilapidated ranch house, backed by the serenity of pine-clad foothills. His house. Barely standing, its windowpanes were either missing or broken, the shutters dangling hopelessly. The dirty yellow paint was peeling horribly, revealing the gray and splintered boards beneath. Planks were totally missing from the wraparound porch, and it sagged wearily under the stress of its own weight. The entire house appeared to be crumbling before his very eyes.

When he had first ridden up, certain he was dreaming, he angrily strode to a dust-coated window and peered inside.

Devoid of all furnishings, the room's faded wallpaper had peeled away, the plaster beneath severely watermarked. He had leapt up the broad porch steps, nearly breaking a leg when one of them collapsed under him with a resounding crunch. The slightly askew solid oak door had squeaked loudly in protest when he pushed it fully open and stepped inside.

Upon viewing the interior he had decided not to advance any farther. In places the once polished hardwood floor was rotted, having long since caved in. Looking up, he had seen through the broken rafters into the bedroom. A bird's nest rested on the ragged edge of another hole in the ceiling there, amid years of accummulated pine needles. Emptiness had torn at Colt's heart, twisting with a wicked spite.

Now, his apathetic eyes focused in the direction in which his horse happily munched along the giant clumps of wheatgrass that overran the front yard. Old Cinder must figure he's done gone to horse heaven, Colt mused dryly.

This was the land where he had been born, the Triple Bar C—he had been only six when the big house was built. He felt a part of him slowly die as he looked at the deteriorating remains of what used to be. What had been an enchanting rose garden, meticulously groomed, was now nothing more than a dried-up, unrecognizable, tangled mess of rot. A sludgy, stagnating pond occupied the very spot where the white gazebo had stood, built by his father for his mother.

Colt tiredly lifted his gaze out and over the rolling pastures. The bunkhouses, the old homestead, the barns as he remembered them—all gone. Nothing was the same. A suffocating blanket of helplessness settled over him. He fought it, desperately wanting to wake up, to be greeted by all the familiar surroundings.

A cruel trick indeed—but whose trick was it? For the first time in his life he felt self-conscious, embarrassed just to exist. He knew he didn't belong. Maybe he'd died during that wicked storm; but if so, where was he now? Purgatory? He dug the heels of his hands into his eyes in an effort to suppress the burning wetness.

Colt remembered how his father had admonished him for crying, even at the age of ten. "Men don't cry! Be a man, son! Your mama cries; you gonna be a mama someday?"

"Be easy on him, Charles," his mother had coaxed. "He's a sensitive boy. There's nothing wrong with crying."

His father's reply had been gruff, even though Colt had easily seen through the brusqueness to the tender man beneath. "You're gonna turn him into a mama's boy, Katie! Nothing but a whiny mama's boy, sidling up to your skirts for protection." Yet he had glimpsed Charles crying many times, though his father never knew Colt had seen. The time his mother had nearly died from the ague—oh, how his father had cried then, hadn't even tried to hide it. Colt smiled at the memory.

If only his father had lived. Charles would be proud to know his eldest son was in no danger of being considered a mama's boy. The tumultuous life Colt led would testify to that. All he had to do to clear any main street was to walk down it. How ironic, he thought. Never killed a man or initiated a fight, but just the same he possessed a reputation that would send the bravest men running for cover at the mere mention of his name.

It had all started ten years ago, not long after the brutal murders of Charles and Katherine Chase. Colt had sworn an undying vengeance on the murderer, Red Eagle, a half-breed Cherokee renegade from Texas who led a band of thieving, cattle-rustling butchers. Colt had left the ranch, determined to introduce the culprit to the hangman's noose—personally.

One warm summer evening at dusk in the little southern Colorado town of Rosita, Colt had been practicing his draw behind a saloon, blowing rusted tins from the angled surface of an old fence post. He had been at it awhile when he heard a cough. He had turned—and damn, if the entire town wasn't lined up as far as he could see, men, women, children, all watching the show. Mistaking their curiosity for annoyance, he had swiftly holstered his weapons and silently brushed past the gawkers with a sheepish grin.

What Colt hadn't realized at the time was that a powerful seed had been planted. Truth and rumors—some favorable, some not—grew, blossomed, branching out in every direction imaginable. Thus, a legend was born. Colton Chase, the wandering, charismatic, pistol-slinging stranger, became shrouded in a cloak of mystery. The gossip had compounded the myth, truth woven intricately with tall tales of daunting feats, creating a hero for some and a deadly nightmare for others. To Red Eagle, Colt was a nightmare, always hot on his trail, breathing down his neck—yet never close enough to destroy.

At one point, Colt was rumored to have killed upwards of thirty men, downing two with a single bullet. How he was supposed to have done that, he never could figure out. Nonetheless, hearsay continued to precede him into every town he passed through on his search.

Irritatingly, Colt had found himself confronted by every gun-wielding ruffian he happened to meet. Some were worth the bull they spoke; others were green around the gills and had no business challenging anyone. The gunfights quickly became a nuisance, only succeeding in detering him from the business at hand—finding Red Eagle.

As time passed, he simply took on the attitude of boredom. In a challenge he would ideally aim to blow the pistol clean out of his opponent's hand, sometimes before it even cleared leather. It never sat right with him to kill an opponent, though some said he would have been justified if he had. A man obsessed with the notion of proving his self-worth by means of a fast draw, in Colt's opinion, certainly didn't deserve to die.

Eventually, he was merely regarded with breathless awe, rarely being challenged at all. He managed to maintain his reputation by always practicing his deadly skill in public—where any potential contenders could look on.

Those early days had been roisterous. Flirting with danger at every turn, not only was the young pistoleer bound to uphold his lasting vendetta, but he took advantage of every opportunity to sow some wild oats while he was at it.

It was during this time, while dipping as far south as Fort Worth, that he had met Bat Masterson. Four years younger than Colt, Bat was a talented shootist with upright ethics, amassing his own extraordinary reputation. The two got on remarkably, riding together on and off over the next several years.

Colt remembered well the innocent havoc they had unleashed on an unsuspecting community when they rode into town. Not only were the local bad boys intimidated into shaping up under the close scrutiny of two such illustrious characters, but the ladies snapped to attention as well. Their carousing and debauchery was legendary in itself. It wasn't uncommon for a pretty young thing to be hauled away from their spellbinding charm by a raging parent, determined to preserve their beloved offspring's honor. Still, there were those who managed to escape the notice of any objecting entity, and one or both of the men would enjoy the company of a warm and willing woman for the night.

Trips back to the ranch had been few and far between during the past ten years, and Colt had mellowed, looking forward to the day he could retire his guns, marry a good woman, and call himself a cattle baron, exclusively and for good. But for the time being his younger brother, Garrett, and Bud, the foreman, were managing ranch operations, which worked out well for every one concerned. Colt's traveling gave him the freedom to conduct cattle negotiations and other aspects of ranch business from afar.

Now the sun was overhead and Colt sat, leaning back against the thick trunk of the cottonwood, chewing on a long blade of grass. It was much easier to reflect on the past instead of worrying about his uncertain future.

He thought of his father, a marksman in his own right, easing Colt into training with firearms when he was just a youngster. Colt's fascination grew with his knowledge, his skills ranging from a French repeating airgun to an American Arms 12-gauge, all from his father's prestigious collection. But the most important lesson he had learned from Charles was the immeasurable value of human life, and that a weapon was never to be used to kill unless it was for food or self-defense.

Garrett had never expressed much interest in the hobby, but Colt ate it up as if he was starving. By the time he turned sixteen he was an awe-inspiring sight to behold—and the chief source of entertainment for the ranch hands, as well. So swift, the men swore they hadn't seen him draw his double pistols until they saw the flash of firing and the inevitable trailing ball of gray smoke. Wherever there was a cluster of frisky cowboys and the noise of yelps and hollers, one could be fairly certain Colt was the source of the commotion.

His father's reminder often echoed inside his head: "Speed's fine, son—but accuracy's final. Always remember that."

Colt had—deciding the only answer was to perfect both.

A gust of wind grabbed at the drooping branches, sending a flurry of white tufts to drift over Colt's shoulders. Heart-shaped leaves as big as saucers fluttered and spun above his head. He got to his feet with a groan.

Suddenly he bolted back toward the house. With long, smooth strides, his boots skidded over loose gravel as he came to a halt at the edge of the porch. Colt's eyes lit expectantly as he examined the weathered support beam. There they were. His own initials: C R C—nearly faded away, covered with layer upon layer of paint. The sight of something personal anchored him; a touch of reality. He had carved those letters not long after the house was built, and had felt the sting of the switch for that little prank.

Loneliness hovered in the wind and sifted through the lofty treetops, finding its way to him, seeping into his very soul. He had lost his mother and father long ago—but now there wasn't anyone: Garrett, Bud, Rosannah, Emmy . . . Could he even call the ranch his own anymore? Furiously, he slammed an open palm against the timber, causing it to groan with the strain. He backed away, half expecting the frail structure to come crashing down around him.

What in God's name was happening?

Sliding his hand into his vest pocket, he pulled out a piece of paper, unfolding it carefully. He'd only glanced at it briefly after ripping it off a bulletin board in that crazy town. PUBLIC AUCTION . . . *date pending until further notification . . . Triple Bar C Ranch . . . Posting date, May 14, 1993* . . .

Colt only skimmed through the key words, his mouth falling open at the date—1993?

For a moment he forgot to inhale, then urgently gasped for air. A scowl marred his handsome features as he crumbled the paper and tossed it angrily into the swaying grass.

"This is *my goddammed ranch—my lifeblood!*" the words were pure agony, bouncing eerily between the canyons and plateaus, spreading over the vast openness of the prairie, then fading into nothingness.

Colt truly thought he had lost his mind.

"Bud! Rosannah!" Twirling on a boot heel, he shouted repeatedly until his throat ached. A tear coursed a wet trail down his smoothly shaven cheek—he figured he deserved that one. Stomping over to retrieve his hat, he mounted Cinder with an abruptness that startled even the animal.

"Well, boy," he muttered vehemently, "maybe this is what Ma was talking about when she said little boys should go to church every Sunday . . . or else. Could be this has something to do with the 'or else' she was referring to. If this isn't something Godly, I sure as hell don't know what is." He spurred Cinder into a comfortable trot back in the direction of the mountain trail.

"Lord," he continued, "I've never been much on prayer, and I haven't spoken to you in one heckuva long time. But I think I need to now. Please grant me the patience and wisdom to get out of this mess. . . ."

As horse and rider once again began their ascent, Colt scrolled in his mind the morning's events: the wicked storm that had come from nowhere, the odd rose, the town that had sprung out of an empty meadow . . . not to mention the motorized wagons and the strange way the people dressed, with their arms and legs bared. Now that he thought about it, he couldn't recall a single man carrying a weapon, and everyone was staring . . . at him!

Utterly fantastic. Could he truly be existing in the year 1993?

Colt's mood lightened considerably as he thought of the chance he'd been given, the possibilities that lay before him. With amusement he remembered the woman who had nearly run headlong into his horse, jumping back with a look of horror, as if she'd never seen such an animal before. Ah, yes, but she was handsome, despite—or maybe because of—her wide-eyed shock. A man could certainly fall into those bottomless pools of green without a single thought of rescue. Green with flecks of blue, if he wasn't mistaken, creating an intriguing aqua. And her hair—like threads of sunshine through honey. The wild way those honey-colored tresses tumbled over her shoulders and down her back made a man's mind wander. The times he'd seen a woman with her hair so shamelessly unbridled—well, she was either in a bawdy stage show or in his bed. The sight of her walking away had warmed his blood, too. With pleasure he recalled stealing a quick glance back to watch her feminine curves, finely displayed in man's breeches, her long legs not hidden under yards of concealing material.

Then there was that other woman who had raced across the street in front of him, half-dressed, her hair cut short like a boy's. She certainly didn't resemble a boy otherwise, for a fact.

Colt stretched his arms toward the sky with a groan. The day was still young, he mused. Going back to that queersome town just might be the wisest thing to do. Strike up a few conversations, gather some information. He'd never backed away from a challenge yet, and he didn't plan on starting now. Granted, he had been gawked at, but he didn't think anyone knew who he was. If they did, there wouldn't have been a soul left on the street. What the hell, he might even catch a peek at that honey-haired darling again.

He steered Cinder sharply away from the unstable edges of a washout, loping to a gentler hillside and onward.

Chapter Three

"Hey, Old-Timer! What can I do ya for?" Ernie Hawkins extended a welcoming hand to the silver-haired cowboy who leaned against a shadowed beam at the entrance to the arena.

Colt leisurely rolled a long stem of grass between his teeth, his gloved hands resting over the rifle propped in front of him. His eyes shifted curiously over the hordes of spectators arriving for a performance of the Wild West show.

"If'n you're lookin' for a job," the man continued, "I reckon I'd be the one ta talk to. Ernie Hawkins is the name—I run the show here."

Colt hesitated just long enough to gauge the stranger who stood next to him. "Colton Chase. Pleased to make your acquaintance, Ernie." Colt accepted the tanned and leathery hand in a firm handshake. "Can't say I'm looking for work. Just taking a look at the scenery is all."

To Colt, Ernie Hawkins seemed the epitome of western hospitality. Cobalt blue eyes squinted in the midday brightness. A battered, sweat-stained hat sat atop his salt-and-pepper hair; the unshaven, deeply lined face spoke of many days in the hot mountain sun. His pot belly hung in abundance over faded, dirty blue jeans, straining at the pearlized buttons of the plaid shirt.

"Don't get many gents strollin' in with their guns strapped

29

on," he said, chuckling good-naturedly while appraising Colt from head to toe with discernible interest. "So when I spotted ya over here, naturally I figured ya'd be lookin' for work. Mighty impressive pieces ya have there. Look like the gen-u-ine articles. Know how ta use 'em?"

Colt had to wonder at the boldness of a man who would bluntly ask another if he knew how to shoot his own guns. He knew of honest men who had been shot for lesser insults than that. But instinct told him that Ernie meant no harm. "I think I do a pretty fair job. And they are 'gen-u-ine,' " he replied, mimicking the drawl with a wink and the flash of a white smile.

Ernie laughed, his belly shaking comically. "Are ya serious, Old-Timer?" He scraped his chin in deep thought, then shook his head. "They must be worth a fortune. And in excellent condition, too. . . . Let me see, this here must be what? A Henry . . . say 'bout 18 . . . 90 or so? Don't know a lot 'bout antique guns, but I know a fair amount."

Ernie reached for the rifle to get a better look, and Colt released his grip with a wise measure of caution. Ernie held it up, admiring the polish of the wood along the butt, the lustrous blue steel of the barrel. A low whistle sounded from his lips.

"1860," Colt responded, absorbing Ernie's reaction with mounting interest, one eyebrow cocked.

"No kiddin'? This is somethin' all right. . . . Looks almost new." He handed the rifle back to Colt with the utmost care, motioning toward the holster partially hidden beneath his vest. "Got another goody hidden in there?"

Ernie's eyes were sparkling with curiosity and Colt couldn't help but like the man. In fact, he reminded him a lot of Bud, and Bud had been like a father to him over the years. Colt's hand disappeared into his vest. reappearing with his usual mannerism, a fluent spin that stopped with the butt presented to Ernie. "Peacemaker. '73," he answered the question before it was asked.

While Ernie admired the gun, Colt casually leaned his shoulder into the post, gazing toward a golden flicker that caught his eye in the crowd. The stairstep seating was full of people. A military-style horn blast sounded from somewhere inside the arena, followed by a barrage of men on horseback, making their entrance from two opposite sides. They were clothed in form-fitting Union blue, and at full speed they charged the center ring, flags flying, sabres drawn, rolling back just in time to avoid a collision. Led by the men who carried the flags, they fell in line to circle, one regal horse proudly prancing after the other. Three shots echoed in the distance. The crowd applauded their noisy approval. The show had begun, but Colt wasn't paying attention. Instead, his eyes were riveted to a blond woman sitting high above the arena, surrounded by an abstract of nondescript faces.

Ernie ran a calloused thumb over the engraved rose in the ivory grip, amazement glowing on his face. "Unbelievable . . ." he sighed, handing it back to Colt. "I'd guard them things with my life. 'Course, ya look like ya can handle yourself all right. Sure would like ta see them puppies in action. Got a shootin' range out back where the boys do their practicin'. I don't s'pose you'd be interested in givin' a little demonstration?" He glanced up toward Colt, the high hopes in his eyes barely concealed.

"Beg pardon . . . what was that you said?" It was only a split second, but the way her hair cascaded over her shoulders, Colt thought for sure he had spotted the honey-haired woman. A longer scrutiny proved him wrong, though, and he quickly lost interest, the loud cheering beginning to grate on his nerves.

"I said . . ." Ernie shouted, " . . . out back there's a shootin' range. Ya can do some shootin' if ya like."

"Lead the way, Ernie. I'm not much on public events, if you know what I mean."

"I can certainly appreciate that. Follow me if ya will. . . ." Ernie was as jubilant as a child with a new toy as he hurriedly led Colt through an employees-only doorway, then down a long corridor.

A most heavenly aroma hung in the balmy atmosphere of the hallway. Colt's stomach began to churn mercilessly, and for the first time all day he became preoccupied with the thought of food. As they neared its origin, the smell became heavier and more tempting. A spattering noise, like something frying, emitted from an open doorway. In stride with Ernie up to this point, he paused just long enough to peek inside. He glimpsed a glass case with scores of skewered sausages, the grease bubbling from their shiny casings. On the other side, a young girl fried several round steaks on a flat black surface. Tearing himself away, Colt ducked back into the hallway.

Ernie snickered knowingly. "Kind of gets to the ol' taste buds, don't it? Ya hungry, Old-Timer? C'mon, it's on me—what'll ya have?" He backtracked, clapping his new friend on the back.

Nodding gratefully, Colton wondered why Ernie kept referring to him as Old-Timer.

"That's right friendly of you, Ernie. Don't mind if I do. Haven't eaten since morning. I sure do appreciate your kindness." Colt stuck his head back into the doorway, wondering if it would be rude if he asked for a little of everything.

"No problem! Hot dog? Hamburger? French fries?"

Colt had no idea what Ernie had just said, so he looked at him and shrugged. "Everything . . . sounds just fine."

Ernie grinned with a disbelieving shake of his head. "Betty, fill up a bag with a little of everything. My friend here is packin' a powerful appetite." A moment later, a grease-stained paper bag was delivered into Colt's waiting hands, along with a cold drink.

Ernie chattered endlessly as they wound their way through the hallway and out into the daylight again. Colt simply grunted an occasional acknowledgment in between bites.

"Ya know," Ernie said, "when I was young a kid's idols were Roy Rogers, the Lone Ranger . . . ah, hell, Jesse James was one of mine! Nowadays, ya got Batman and those green turtle thingamajigs. I tell ya, it's sad. There's an art to slingin' them guns—but it's a lost art, I'm afraid. Sure could use somebody who knew what they was doin'. I get lots a young'uns comin' in here thinkin' they're somethin' special. Probably never touched a gun until they decided they needed a job; then they practice a day or two and come here." He shook his head sadly.

Colt wasn't all that sure what Ernie was talking about. The only name he recognized was Jesse James. He'd met up with his brother, Frank, outside of Denver a while back but thought it wouldn't be wise to mention it. He was puzzled, though, why children in the twentieth century would have turtles and something called a batman for idols. Colt's idol had always been his father.

Ernie stopped inside a large fenced area outside the arena. Hay-stuffed targets lined the far border. Across from them were rows of tiny log shacks that Colt assumed were bunkhouses for the performers. In the center courtyard milled dozens of men and women, apparently in costume, and a few tacked horses tethered here and there.

"Wow, I'd say ya was a little hungry!" Ernie pointed to the near-empty bag Colt clutched in one hand.

Colt shoved the last bite of hamburger into his mouth. He couldn't recall ever having food like this before, but it sure did taste good. He wouldn't mind having another sausage, but he didn't want to impose. He brought the drink to his lips, stopping short as his eyes first crossed, then focused on a long stick that protruded from the lid. Perplexed, he just smiled.

"Don't like them straws? Me neither. Betty just assumes everybody has to have one—ya know how kids are." Ernie took the liberty of removing the straw and disposing of it.

Just then a slim, wiry cowboy swaggered slowly past, his narrowed eyes devouring Colt, not missing a detail. He was dressed entirely in black leather, silver studs adorning the inseam of his pants and his hat and belt. His gunbelt rode low on his hips and his eyes glinted like chips of gray ice. His hair was of the same steely gray, giving him an overall appearance of menace. Stopping when he reached the tall split-log fence, he propped a foot and leaned back to watch.

Colt found it hard not to laugh; he'd never seen such a motley group of milksop cowboys in his life. They looked like a bunch of Eastern city slickers who came out west just to play cowboy—and they weren't doing a very good job of it. Take for instance the one in black who wore his holster low. Didn't he realize a low holster made it impossible to draw a fast pistol? A shapely woman brushed past him, her light brown hair in two long braids. She was dressed in a skintight buckskin-fringed dress, her face painted like a porcelain doll. He couldn't recall ever seeing an Indian squaw who looked like *that*. Poor Ernie—Colt supposed he didn't know what a farce this Wild West show really was. If he was aiming for authenticity, he'd missed the target.

Colt examined the lid on his drink with a serious frown and then pried it off, downing a huge gulp of the ice-cold soda. Immediately, his eyes watered, growing big right along with the fizz. He struggled to maintain a straight face as the carbonation snaked its way up into his nose.

"What . . ." he managed to croak, " . . . is this?" He wiped his mouth along his sleeve.

"Why, it's Coke, I imagine." Ernie looked at Colt a little strangely, then said, "If'n ya wanna use them targets over yonder, help yourself. Sure would like to see what ya can do with them treasures." Ernie began to shoo away any stragglers from the shooting area.

"That's not necessary . . . I don't miss."

Colt sauntered over to set his cup and bag on a bale of hay, pulling a sprig of it free and placing it between his teeth. He strolled back, purposefully bending to scoop a handful of fine dirt from the ground and holding it up to sift into the wind. He removed his gloves.

Outwardly, he knew he appeared calm and relaxed. But inside his every muscle was tensed, every nerve as taut as the strings on a fiddle.

Colt widened his stance. Ever so slightly, he felt a muscle in his cheek twitch just as the rifle spun around and up in one fluid motion. Cocking the rifle with one successive twirl after another, he repeatedly fired while strolling confidently up and down the line of targets. By the time he finished the black circles were totally obliterated.

"Hot damn," Ernie mumbled in astonishment, squinting in an effort to see the mangled bull's-eyes. "Where on earth did ya learn to shoot like 'at?"

Colt just smiled.

The performers began to gather closer, whispering among themselves in the abnormal quietness. The gunfighter in black also advanced, his demeanor changing from self-absorption to amazement and respect, his jaw slightly agape.

Colt lifted his hat just enough to wipe the sweat from his brow, then set the rifle aside. He ran his tongue over his lips to moisten them. Slowly, he began to pace back and forth, like a predatory cat, gauging his target. His arms held wide, he flexed his fingers. If this was a real showdown, he would wait, wait in motion for the other man to make a move.

Facing the bull's-eye, he dropped to one knee, both arms crossing over his chest to slide each pistol from its place in its holster. Then, a sort of mating between flesh and metal took place as the pistols twirled and spun, barely visible until he stopped them to fire. Six accurately trained explosions from each pistol made their marks on the bull's-eye.

Another blinding spin and the weapons were once again holstered. Colt rose with a sigh, pushing his hat back with one finger. One by one the performers began to clap until there was unanimous, thundering applause.

When the acrid gray smoke began to clear something prompted Colt to glance around. Then all of his attention was riveted to the arched gateway of the arena.

There she stood—watching. No doubt about it this time; it was the woman with the honey-colored hair. And her eyes were on him. He had to admit his thoughts were untimely, but what he wouldn't give to run his fingers through that golden mane of wanton ringlets. He pulled the sprig of hay from the corner of his mouth and broke into a broad grin. If he could draw her closer with just his gaze, he certainly would . . .

Madison was looking for the snack bar, where she could buy a drink. The pandemonium of the Wild West show had given her a monster of a headache. In her search she happened upon a doorway and couldn't help but notice the assembled crowd, obviously enthralled. She naturally hesitated, straining to see what the commotion was all about.

A break in the wall of people produced a sight she couldn't resist. It was him! The old silver-haired cowboy—the one she had seen on Main Street that morning. Thunderstruck, she watched the private backyard demonstration, doubly impressed with his abilities in contrast with those in the actual show. It amused her greatly to see that some of the actors were as entranced as she.

So, she had been right. He must be a performer—but why wasn't he in the show?

Madison had just been entertained by some very good actors portraying such historical figures as Buffalo Bill, Annie Oakley, and Sitting Bull. They had demonstrated exceptional horsemanship and proficiency with firearms. Gunfighters shot it out in the center of the arena; mountain men rendered impressive performances with their hatchet throwing . . . and yet none of those acts seized her imagination with such intensity as did this solitary man.

She pondered the nagging questions: Who was this old cowboy? Who was he supposed to be? He seemed so at home in his costume. Could it be that it wasn't a costume at all?

Madison was hypnotized by his movements—so lithe, so full of masculine grace. Not overly muscle-bound, but there was just enough there to reveal a sculptured strain against the confines of his shirt and pants when he spun his guns. Definitely not the body or moves of an older man—and yet the long silver hair, the lines on his face—who could he be?

As she watched this man's achievements, he somehow struck Madison as all-wise, all-knowing, almost immortal . . . some sort of sovereign being. Then she flushed at the outrageous thought. A pagan deity, she mused, barely suppressing a giggle—that's it, a very old pagan deity. My, but he must have been something in his younger years. . . .

The cloud of thick, black smoke thinned, an odor of sulfur burning her nose. Good Lord, his eyes were resting on *her!* She could feel goosebumps popping out, one by one, over her flesh. Even at this distance she thought she saw the golden lights in his eyes dance. Such a dazzling smile—at her? Uncertain, Madison glanced over her shoulder, and when she saw no one else, turned back. The other performers were beginning to notice her presence as they followed his intense gaze to the archway. She smiled self-consciously before backing away from the doorway and into the safety of the shadows.

Madison passed the snack bar twice before she remembered exactly why she was roaming around in the first place.

Chapter Four

It was approaching 10 P.M. on a Saturday night, and the Blue Lady Saloon was bustling with activity. The enormous, highly polished mahogany bar was lined with locals and tourists alike; a dozen tables were occupied already. Dancers scooted the two-step to the beat of a country band jamming on an elevated stage. Cigarette smoke hung in a blanketing haze within the confines of the large room, the only reprieve when the double doors were swung open, encouraging a cool breeze to drift through.

Madison, Mark, and the other agents were piled at a corner table, having finished their hotel-hosted dinner at the Shady Oak a few hours before. Madison wore a slim-fitting denim skirt that reached down to mid-calf, a bright red camp shirt, and sandles. The sides of her hair were lifted by silver barrettes that matched the western design of her belt buckle.

She nursed a frothy mug of ice-cold beer, still defending her obsession with the old cowboy. While still at the Wild West show that afternoon, Madison had animatedly described what she had seen through the gateway that exited to the back of the arena, insisting to Mark and the others that the silver-haired cowboy was the highlight of the entire show.

"Well, if he's so good, why wasn't he in the show?" Mark had reasoned at the time.

Madison had wondered the same thing. Maybe he had been auditioning. Everyone had certainly watched him as if they'd never seen anyone like him.

Now, Madison's mood was ebullient. She still couldn't shake him from her musings. She'd become enamored with many antique pieces in her life, but never had she taken a fancy to one that was *alive*.

"Face it, Maddie. You've got the hots for a real, live gunfighter—only couldn't you have picked one a little closer to your own age?"

Mark's grin was irresistible, his teasing constant since they had sat down at this little table. In spite of his nagging encouragement, not to mention her mother's, there were no men of any kind in Madison's life. Not that there wasn't plenty of opportunity. It was just too soon. She wanted nothing to do with men, not romantically—not yet. The pain was still too intense. Everytime she met a man's gaze head on, she couldn't help but imagine how many times that guy had cheated on a woman—wondering if he was cheating right then and there, with her.

Madison's own pessimistic attitude scared her. Could this be the beginning of a lifelong hatred of men? She'd known women like that, virtual man-haters. They were like vipers lurking in the grass, hissing at every man who happened a little too close. More than anything she didn't want to end up like that. But for now, she felt she hadn't just divorced Jon, she'd divorced herself from men entirely. She honestly didn't know if she could ever let her guard down again.

"Oh, please!" Despite herself, Madison blushed. "I *do not* have the hots for that old guy. I simply find him interesting, don't you? If you had seen him do what I saw him do . . . why, he made the others look like children playing!"

"I just knew he was somebody special when I saw him walking down the street with all those guns," Lanie interjected, her chin resting in her palm. "Wouldn't it be something if he really was some famous gunfighter in his younger days!"

"Well, here's your chance to find out. Your antique friend just mosied on in." Mark nodded toward the swinging double doors.

Lanie and Gertie followed his gaze, their jaws hanging slack.

Madison watched as the silver-haired cowboy slowly meandered toward the bar, curiously taking in the surroundings, a furrow etching his brow. The crowd parted, making room as he sidled in. There were a few inquisitive stares from people but then they resumed their conversations.

Madison's heart lurched at the sight of the stark white shirt accenting his sun-bronzed, leathered skin. The highlights in his hair were more gorgeous than she had remembered, giving him an almost ethereal look. His brown eyes lifted, scanning the crowd. When his gaze skimmed past the travel agents' table it slowed, then stopped, locking onto Madison in a most unsettling manner. She inhaled sharply before averting her eyes, embarrassed that he had caught her staring, and even more irritated that he intimidated her so.

"Wow! Did you see that?" Gertie whispered loudly. "He's looking over here. Did you get to meet him today, Maddie?"

"No! Of course not!" Madison shot back with a quickness that surprised even her. "He did smile at me, though. At least I think it was me."

Mark started laughing, slapping his knee. "It looks like that old guy has a hankering for you, honey! This is great! I think you should go introduce yourself properly."

"Stop it, Mark—all of you. You're being ridiculous."

"No, seriously, Maddie." Gertie's eyes were as round as marbles as she absently shoved pretzels into her mouth while she spoke. "Go find out who he is, then come back here and fill us in."

"Sounds like a great idea to me!" Lanie added.

"Would you guys listen to yourselves?" Madison shook her head at the absurdity. "I think I'd feel a little silly—what in the world would I say?"

"Simple. Just say what you're thinking. You saw him at the show today; where did he learn to shoot . . . there you go, a perfect opening line." Mark tipped his mug in a long draught, emptying it. He motioned to the waitress for another round, then continued, "C'mon, Maddie! Since when have you been shy? He's probably just some old rancher from around here. Looks like he could use the company."

He did look lonely, Maddie thought, all by himself at that crowded bar.

"Go on!" Lanie prodded, "we're dying to know who he is. He may be rich. Could be a good prospect for your mother, or maybe even Gertie!" She smiled brightly, circling her arm around the older woman's shoulder.

"Thanks a lot," Gertie replied with a frown. "I may be old, but I think I've got a ways to go before I catch up with him."

Madison couldn't suppress a smile. His hair certainly matched her mother's. And she'd been a widow for some time now. . . . Madison was beginning to feel the effects of the single beer she'd just drunk, which somehow made the idea of approaching him that much more appealing.

"Ohhhh, all right. . . . It'll be fun, eh?" Madison pushed her chair back and stood up, smoothing her skirt and fluffing her hair.

"All right, sis! That's the Maddie I know and love." Mark smiled his encouragement.

Lanie and Gertie gave her the thumbs up. Madison walked away, her heart palpitating, excusing her way through the congested mob of people.

Colt leaned his elbow on the bar, one boot propped on the brass foot rest.

"What'll it be?"

Colt looked up at the barkeep, who barely hesitated as he passed.

"A bottle of your best rotgut."

"What?" the barkeep asked crankily, his lip curled into a snarl.

"Nah . . . on second thought, just pass me down a few jolts." The last thing Colt needed right now was to get stinking drunk. After the harrowing day he'd been through it was mighty tempting to drown his troubles, but for obvious reasons it wouldn't be the wisest thing to do.

The barkeep stood rooted to the floor, gaping at him like he'd never heard of whiskey before.

"*Whiskey!*" Colt clarified.

"Yessir," the young man mumbled, glancing dubiously over his shoulder as he walked away. Returning, he planted a fat shot glass on the bar and filled it from a bottle of Jack Daniels. Before he had the chance to leave, the shot glass was emptied and waiting for a refill. Staring first at the glass, then at the old cowboy, he obliged. "That'll be five bucks, mister."

His heavy-lidded gaze never wavering, Colt slid two fingers into the suede poke at his waist, pulling a bill free and slapping it down on the bar. He downed the second glass of whiskey. "Highway robbery . . ." he breathed, relishing the burn as the liquid gold slid soothingly down his parched throat. The bill was snatched up and the barkeep left.

Colt wasn't in the best of moods. Things had begun to look up when Ernie had offered a seemly place to hang his hat for the night. He had been able to wash and could look forward to a soft bed tonight. But water squirting down on his head was a poor substitute for the therapeutic soak of a bath. At least the water had been hot.

But his troubles had begun earlier, when he'd ventured into a store for a change of clothes. Picking out only the bare necessities, a pair of indigo Levi's and a white linen shirt, he had thought he might pass out cold when he heard the price. Then the shopkeeper had refused his coin. He was sent across the street to the bank, where more problems had cropped up. Eventually, the bank manager had replaced some of his gold coins for paper money, even more than he'd started out with, which had made him a little happier. He was able to go back to the clothing store and make his purchases.

Unfortunately, his spirits had been squashed again when he'd strolled up the boardwalk that evening, marveling at the brilliance of the hundreds of lamps that shone from windows and storefront signs. He had seen a fair belle approaching from the opposite direction. She was so scantily clad that her bosom had nearly heaved free of the short red dress that clung indecently to her abundant curves. Colt had merely inquired if she was free for the evening. Her pleasant expression had instantly turned ugly, her verbal response even worse: "Go to hell, you dirty old man!" Old man? He'd spun around and stared after her, pondering her strange remark for a full minute.

Now, as he stood at the bar, it all fell together with a solid click. Ernie had called him "Old-Timer." That woman had called him a dirty old man. Could it be that he'd been hurtled forward more than a hundred years and been robbed of his youth as well? Usually the hurdy girls were after *him* instead of the other way around. Now it appeared he couldn't get one if his life depended on it. Not that he was in desperate need. It had just seemed like a good idea at the time—maybe relieve a little ill-borne tension.

Funny, though, he thought, observing his own reflection in the ornate mirror that decorated the length of the wall behind the bar. He looked as dapper as ever. His hair might be in need of a good cut. He wore it long during the winter months to protect his ears, neck, and face from the frigid prairie winds. Besides, it seemed to gain favor with the noble red man, an advantage he was happy to have. But he supposed it wouldn't hurt to get it cut—the weather was warm now. Still, he didn't look a day older than his twenty-eight years. This town was even crazier than he'd originally thought!

Shaking his head, he spotted her in the mirror. The honey-haired beauty. He was barely able to stifle a groan of frustration as she walked up behind him. Surely he appeared old in her eyes, too, and he wasn't about to risk being called a dirty old man again. If the tables were turned and she had been on his home ground, he knew exactly what he would do. There was nary a female who could resist his charms once he decided to employ them.

"Excuse me. . . . Hi, I'm Maddie Calloway. I saw you at the Wild West show today and I couldn't help but notice your shooting skills. You're very good, but I'm sure you hear that all the time."

Not believing his good fortune, Colt slowly turned his head toward the melodic voice, his eyes fiercely locking onto her aqua ones. They were like the ocean, only twice as deep, and he was lost momentarily. Her face was so smooth, as if begging to be touched, framed by a bounty of soft golden curls. She looked like an angel of mercy. His concentration shaken, he'd barely heard what she'd said.

"Ma'am." He nodded politely, touching the brim of his hat. Straightening to his full height, he turned to face her. " . . . appreciate the compliment. I do hear that quite frequently, but usually not from such a fine lady." Colt's eyes slid down her body with undisguised appreciation.

Madison was mesmerized by the warmth in his eyes as he took her extended hand in his and, in place of a handshake, brought her fingers to his lips. Taken aback by his gallantry, Madison smiled weakly, glancing toward her table in mute supplication. Gertie and Lanie gaped, looking as dumbfounded as she felt. She was speechless.

"Colt Chase is the name," he continued, his eyes not letting go of hers. "My father taught me to shoot, starting from when I was knee-high to a grasshopper. Had a collection of weapons you wouldn't believe. Maddie, did you say? Pretty name. I like it."

"Thank you." Madison felt herself flush hotly, though she wasn't sure why. "It's short for Madison—but most everyone calls me Maddie."

"I see. Very pleased to make your acquaintance . . . Madison." Colt broke into a charming, lopsided grin.

Madison should have anticipated his response. Naturally this man wasn't "most everyone." She was astounded at the velvety smoothness of his voice. Not at all what you'd expect from someone so old. And his teeth were so white, and almost perfectly straight. Madison was surprised; he wasn't as tall as she originally had perceived, just broad-shouldered and solid—solid as a rock. He smelled pleasantly of soap and leather. She couldn't help but notice that beneath the butter-soft tan vest he still wore his holster and guns, complete with a neat line of extra bullets fastened into brown leather slots.

His eyes—Madison recalled how his eyes had stirred something inside of her when she first saw him that morning, but she still couldn't pinpoint the reason. Such an uncommon color: a warm golden brown with just a hint of amber. They were staring down at her when she suddenly realized he had spoken.

"I'm sorry . . . what was that?"

"Could I get you something to drink?" he repeated.

"Oh, thanks for asking, but I've got something back at my table . . . over there." She absently motioned behind herself. "I won't bother you any longer; I just wanted to meet you. I was so impressed by your talent."

"No bother. I've been craving some company. Are you sure you can't stay for a spell?"

Colt lifted his hand to her shoulder in a sincere gesture of welcome, and Madison was shocked at the heat that emanated from his touch. It was like an electric charge that penetrated to the bone. Colt's words struck a chord deep inside her, and she simply couldn't refuse his request. Something about the way he said it—forlorn, like a lost puppy. She somehow felt sorry for him. Maybe he was all alone in life, didn't have anyone for company. She wondered how old he was. It was hard to tell from his face, so deeply creased from years of an unforgiving sun.

"Of course I will. I'd love to stay for a bit."

"What'll it be?" The barkeep stood in front of Colt again, and he cast her an expectant glance.

"Draft, please."

Colt only had to place his hand on the shot glass and it was filled again with the dark amber liquid. He downed it in one smooth swallow. "Are you from around here?" he asked, turning back to Madison.

"No, I have a travel agency in Colorado Springs. I'm here with some of my agents. We're just educating ourselves on the area.

And you?" She stepped in close to the bar, clasping her hand around the frosty mug of beer as it was slid in front of her.

Colt pulled another bill from his pouch and laid it down. "Ahhh, Colorado Springs. I'm very familiar with the Pikes Peak area; it's beautiful there. You said you own a travel agency?"

Madison nodded. "Ummm-mmm. It's a small one, but all mine."

"Sounds intriguing. . . ." Colt enjoyed the way her mouth moved when she spoke, the lush fullness and the sexy dimple right in the center of her lower lip. And especially the way her whole face lit up when she smiled. It was difficult keeping his mind on what she said rather than on how she was saying it. "I have the Triple Bar C, not far from here." The words caught in his throat, ringing with an air of untruth. Could he even say the ranch was his any longer?

"A ranch!" she exclaimed, "I've always been fascinated by ranches. I don't know much about that life-style—but how exciting! All those cows and horses! Ever since I was a little girl I've had this fantasy of living on a ranch. I guess the faraway and unattainable always seems the most glamorous."

Colt grinned, charmed by her. With amusement he remembered her expression when she'd almost run into Cinder that morning. "It's certainly not all fun and games, but it's the life I love."

"I bet you've had a wealth of experiences up here in this beautiful wilderness . . . ranching and all. Have you lived here all your life?"

"Born here. With the exception of the last ten years, my life has been on the ranch." He chuckled, toying with the squat glass in his hand. "I suppose you could say I've had some experiences . . . hair-raising and otherwise."

"Oh? And what have you been up to the last ten years, if you don't mind my asking?"

Colt contemplated telling her the truth—for about five seconds. He wondered how quick she'd hightail it out of there, thinking him a crazy coot. "Guess you could say I've been wandering. A little traveling, like you're doing."

"That's great! Got the travel bug, eh? You're a lucky man—a little of both worlds. Have you traveled internationally?" Madison noticed the sadness that lingered behind his brown eyes. What was he thinking that he wasn't saying?

"Nothing quite so fascinating, I'm afraid. Texas, Colorado, Arizona, California for a time."

"That's sounds plenty exciting to me."

Silence hung over them, and when Madison looked up, his eyes seared into her like red-hot branding irons. Unable to stand the heat, her gaze flitted down, then back to her table, where it appeared the others were preparing to leave. But she wasn't ready to go—not yet. Rather than appeasing her curiosity, talking to this Colt Chase had only stirred it, and she was dying to know more. She couldn't explain it, even to herself; something about him was . . . familiar, and she wouldn't be satisfied until she knew *why*.

"Maddie? We're heading out." Mark touched her shoulder.

"Mark! I'd like you to meet Colt Chase. Mr. Chase, this is my brother, Mark."

The two men exchanged pleasantries, shaking hands.

"I'll catch up with you in a little while, okay?" Madison asked.

"Are you sure?" Mark raised his eyebrows, like a doting father, and she smiled. "Okay, we're stopping in at the other saloon down the street for a while," he informed her. Then, looking back at Colt, he added, "It was nice meeting you."

Mark mussed the top of Madison's hair affectionately before he left, Gertie and Lanie close behind, trying not to gawk as they passed.

Mr. Chase. She'd called him Mr. Chase. The formality awakened a distant loneliness that had become all too familiar that day and only confirmed what he had suspected. He looked old to her, too. One good note in all of this was that at least Mark was her brother and not her husband, and that delighted him immensely.

"Please, call me Colt, if you will."

"Sure . . . Colt." Madison smiled, fluffing the hair from her neck in an effort to ease the cloying, humid heat that was gathering in the saloon. "I sure could use a cool breeze. Would you like to sit outside with me?"

"Best idea I've heard all night." Cold had been ready to suggest that very same thing, as the crowd became thicker, clamoring around the bar.

The two pushed through the barrier of people and out the swinging doors. Spellbound, he couldn't take his eyes off her naked legs and ankles as she moved in front of him. Her feet were tantalizingly exposed, the leather-strap shoes she wore anything but modest. And her toenails were painted a delicious shade of pink. Outside, the cool breeze caught her intoxicating scent, carrying it to him: a spicy, woodsy fragrance, with just a hint of rose. Extremely vexed, he rolled his eyes upward and mentally cursed the gods above. Why on earth did he have to look to everyone's eyes but his own like he was a hundred years old?

Madison took a seat on a wooden bench next to the brick building, smoothing her skirt. "So tell me, why do you wear your guns all the time?"

Colt sat down beside her, latching his elbow over the back of the bench. "Never go anywhere without my pieces," he said, thinking to himself that there was one place, but he just couldn't say it. Guns. Madison referred to his six-shooters as guns, just as Ernie had. It was a term he hadn't heard before today.

"Not anywhere? Oh, c'mon!" she exclaimed, "surely you don't where them out to dinner, the grocery store, church?"

"Out to dinner? Sure do. The other two I don't do much."

"So level with me, Colt . . . did you used to be a gunfighter? I know you're not old enough to have mingled with Jesse James or the like." Madison laughed at her own preposterousness. " . . . but there were gunfighters well into the twentieth century, right?"

Colt laughed along with her, but for a slightly different reason. There was that name again. Ol' Jesse apparently had left quite a legacy in his wake.

With a drawn-out sigh, he extracted a pouch of tobacco and some papers from his poke. Expertly rolling a cigarette, he licked and pressed the seal, placing it between his lips. He struck a match on the heel of his boot, then held the dancing flame to the tip of the cigarette, drawing in deeply and then exhaling the aromatic smoke. Colt could feel the weight of Madison's stare. She watched with intense interest, almost frowning. Damn but she was a beauty. She just made him want to pull her into his arms and hug the stuffing right out of her.

"No, guess it would be impossible for me to have mingled with the likes of Jesse. Did strike up an acquaintance with his brother Frank, though." Colt slanted his gaze slowly toward her, winking with a curt nod.

Madison just watched in awe, not sure whether to laugh at his dry humor or not.

He continued, "To answer your question—yes, Madison, I'm what is commonly known as a professional shootist. Rumor has it I've killed many men." He hesitated for effect.

Madison's eyes widened and she opened her mouth to speak.

"But I must confess, those particular rumors have no truth."

"Well," she sighed, "*that's* nice to know." Now her interest was really piqued. She fervently hoped he wasn't tiring of her questions. Colt brought the cigarette to his lips, his eyes shifting to her as he inhaled. The end pulsed a red glow into the night. A tingle surprised her, running along her arms and up her spine to the base of her skull. If she didn't know better, she'd swear there was something almost sexual in his eyes, some tension. Now, if he were fifty years younger, maybe she could fathom the idea. It had to be something else, only she couldn't quite put her finger on it.

"Laramie—quite a few years back . . . I was just passing through." He paused. "Are you sure you want to hear this?"

"Yes! Please go on."

"Well, I was confronted by three local roughnecks. Had that town at their beck and call for some time. Bullies are what they were—and they had this notion that they were pretty fast with a pistol. I didn't want any trouble, just wanted to be on my way, but they wouldn't hear of it. Insisted I meet all three of 'em at the edge of town."

"Three against one? Doesn't sound fair to me." Madison drew one leg under her, rotating her body toward him.

"Fair? No, but I wasn't too worried about numbers. You see, I knew exactly what I would do. They knew me, my reputation. Already had one strike against them. I met 'em precisely where they specified. I was waiting when they showed up. All three of 'em, advancing slowly, hands ready for the draw. When they started walking so did I. Only difference was, they were scared. I wasn't."

"So?" Madison interrupted excitedly. "What happened?"

"I'm here, aren't I?"

Colt grinned mischievously, rubbing the fire from his cigarette on his boot heel. Madison gasped, playfully poking his arm, urging him to go on.

"They drew their pistols. I didn't. They began to shoot, their panic rising with every shot. It was a beautiful sight—all three of 'em shooting for all they were worth, none of their pitiful bullets making their mark. After I'd counted eighteen shots I casually drew my revolver—only needed one. Then I watched 'em weep."

A slow, rumbling laugh emanated from deep within his chest, and Madison laughed, too. "Then what?"

"I took aim and blew the pistols out of their hands. Only when I got to the third, he'd already tossed his into the air and was running like hell. I don't think that little group caused much trouble in Laramie after that, at least not when I was around."

"But I don't understand—weren't you afraid of being hit by one of those eighteen bullets?"

Colt gazed at her with a cocky air of self-confidence, half smiling. "No."

"Why not?" she urged, laughing. "And how did you know to count eighteen bullets?"

"Three six-shooters. Any brains at all and they would have had their pieces fully loaded. Eighteen bullets. A six-shooter is virtually worthless after so many yards; a man's considered proficient if he can hit his aim at fifteen. Knowing the kind of yellow-belly characters they were, I pretty much figured they would panic and use all of their ammunition before I even got into range. I was right."

Madison clapped her hands together with delight. "That's great! Don't stop, tell me more. Was there ever a time when you were *really* afraid?"

This woman astounded him. He usually met with disinterest or scolding scorn from the women he elected to relate his escapades to. Madison was not only interested but in her own way seemed to approve. From all appearances, she genuinely liked and accepted him for who he was.

Madison noticed his face light up and his eyes dance with animation as he nodded in response to her question.

"The most terrifying opponent by far was not a man at all. Down in southern Colorado, a little too much whiskey, one thing led to another and before I knew it, I had accepted my most formidable challenge yet. Seems the ranchers in the area were having problems with an old grizzly who'd developed a taste for cattle . . . and man, too. He'd been terrorizing everyone for a good two years and no one had been able to take him down. His tough hide was riddled with the bullets of those who tried—some never returning to tell the tale. They called him Old Bones, named for the cadaverous remains he'd left behind."

Madison wrinkled her nose at the gruesome thought, scooting to the edge of the bench, anxious for him to continue.

"I've never reneged once I've committed—so the next day I headed out with plenty of ammunition and food for several days. It took two of those days just to track the old buzzard down. But I found him, high atop a stacked bluff amid a thick grove of junipers. That monster must have stood ten feet tall on his hind feet." Colt whistled at the memory, "I'll never forget how the drool hung in long strings from his floppy jowls—the huge yellow fangs when he turned his open mouth to the heavens in a screaming roar. It was the most devilish sound you'd ever care to hear."

Madison shivered, rubbing goose bumps.

Colt continued. "My horse and I were caught off guard. Cisco reared in terror; I made a grab for my rifle just as a paw the size of a dinner platter knocked me from my horse. I pumped that monster with so much lead, by all rights he should have been dead . . . but he only got madder and madder. I was on the ground when another swipe caught Cisco across the head, two-inch claws slicing into her neck. She never had a chance."

"Oh, my God," Madison moaned, "your horse was killed?"

"Yeah, she was a brave one. Saved my life. For that I'll always be thankful. Old Bones was preoccupied with finishing the job on Cisco. I was smart enough to crawl away while I still had the chance. I wasn't in any mood to be a hero, let alone a dead one, so I headed back without food or a horse. It took me a while on foot, but I made it. Old Bones . . . he reigned in those parts for many months before finally meeting his doom at the hands of some local rancher. I understand his hide hangs in that man's home."

"I certainly don't think I'd want that thing's hide in *my* house." She shuddered, then started to laugh. "I bet a person could see daylight pretty well with all those bullet holes."

Colt chimed in until they were both laughing so hard they had tears in their eyes.

When they sobered she asked, "Were you hurt?"

"Got a few scars—nothing too terrible."

Madison begged him to tell her more, thoroughly fascinated by the life this man had led.

Lightening the mood, he told her funny stories involving the annual rodeos that were held at his ranch. He told her about the stinky old billy goat he had had as a pet when he was a child, and how he had insisted on naming it Bob just to be different. They laughed until their sides threatened to split.

Turning serious, Madison asked if he'd ever been married. When he said he hadn't she felt bad for him. Colt looked at her for a long time, a thoughtful expression on his face. She wished she knew what he was thinking.

"Your brother is going to be wondering where you are," he finally said, a trace of reluctance in his voice.

"That's true. I should be heading back to the hotel. I've enjoyed our conversation so much!" Madison rose to leave, and he stood up, too.

"May I escort you back to your hotel?"

"That would be nice," she answered, impressed at his chivalry. If only men were so considerate of women today as they must have been in his day.

"Thank you for your company, Madison—maybe we'll meet again," he said as they arrived at her hotel.

The richness of his voice caressed her like velvet, and she smiled her thanks before he turned and slowly ambled back up the boardwalk, the rowels of his spurs jangling in double time.

Madison blinked twice. Then three times, sure her contact lenses were playing tricks on her vision. His hair didn't look silver anymore! It must be the light, or rather the lack of it. It appeared to be more of a deep brown. How could that be possible? She watched until he disappeared back into the saloon. The sway of his slim, compact hips, those muscular shoulders . . . he looked old, and yet, somehow, not so old. . . .

Sighing, she opened the door of the hotel and went inside.

Chapter Five

Tightening the cap on a bottle of pink fingernail polish, Madison dropped it back into her leather shoulder bag. A knock sounded on her hotel-room door, causing her to start. She wasn't expecting anyone. In fact, she still wore a short terry bathrobe, her long blond hair piled haphazardly atop her head in a thick, fluffy ponytail. Snatching her watch from the nightstand, she saw it was only eight o'clock. Confident it must be either Mark or one of the girls, she flung the door open, careful not to smudge a wet fingernail.

Madison stared directly into the smiling golden brown eyes of Colt Chase. At least she *thought* it was Colt. His hair! . . . and his face . . . ! Boy, did he ever look different in the light of day. Come to think of it, she had seen him yesterday morning and he hadn't looked quite like *this*. His hair wasn't totally silver anymore. Now it was mostly a rich, burnished brown, with only a few silver highlights. If she didn't know better, she would swear he had had a facelift overnight.

"Er . . . hi! Gee, I . . . I wasn't expecting anyone." She instinctively pulled the robe closer to her neck, while kicking aside a heap of clothing piled just inside the door. That was the nice thing about having your own room. A person could be as slobby as she wanted to be and nobody knew—that is, until somebody dropped by unexpectedly.

"Good morning," he replied in that velvet voice, obviously amused at finding her in such a state of dishabille. He removed his hat, the corners of his eyes crinkling as his mouth moved in a slow grin. "I hope I'm not bothering you. Just thought you might like to accompany me on a Sunday picnic." Colt dangled a brown paper bag in front of her, eyeing it like he wasn't quite sure what it might contain. "There's a horse downstairs that would very much like to meet you and show you the finer points of horsemanship. Her name is Cinnabar. I think she's taken a fancy to Cinder—so even if you should decide not to go, I have a feeling she will, anyway." He grinned lopsidedly.

Madison laughed. "Oh, she will, huh? Seriously . . . it sounds wonderful, but I'm accountable to my agents. It wouldn't be very professional of me to up and leave them alone."

"I'm sure they'll be fine left to their own devices for a few hours. I know a beautiful place." Casually leaning against the doorjamb, he looked down at his boots as he spoke, then lifted his eyes with a sly grin. "Lush, green meadows, birds chirping, bees buzzing, warm sunshine . . ."

Colt pulled his other hand from behind his back and presented Madison with a single rose in the most unusual color she had ever seen. It was marbled, reminding her of her favorite raspberry swirl ice cream.

"Oh, my," she sighed, "this is lovely—thank you! She touched the soft petals to her nose, inhaling the gentle sweetness. "It all sounds fabulous, really. But I can't. Thanks for asking. I hope you understand."

Madison felt bad for turning him down. He was getting that lost-puppy look again. But what could she do? She was the agency owner. She couldn't just take off on a picnic with a strange man she'd just met, deserting her employees. Colt unwillingly pushed his weight from the doorway with a sigh of disappointment, and Madison didn't miss the silent challenge he issued with his eyes.

"I understand. But you'll be sorry. I'm sure whatever is in this bag is awfully good. . . ."

He was starting back down the hallway and Madison had to stick her head out to see him.

"I *am* sorry!" she called after him, charmed by his dramatics. "'Bye . . ."

She shut the door and felt like a total fool. Worse, her heart felt as if it had dropped clean down to her toes. She leaned back against the door and stared at the ceiling, and it suddenly occurred to her that Lanie and Gertie were probably already off doing their own thing. After all, this was to be a free day. Surely Mark could handle the last hotel inspection without her.

Twirling around quickly, she jerked open the heavy oak door and ran out into the hallway, expecting to have to chase after him. But Colt stood at the far end of the corridor, one foot propped against the wall, his arms folded across his chest. He dangled the paper bag again, raising his eyebrows.

"One second; let me grab my purse." Madison dashed back into her room and then back out in a quick reversal. " . . . Uhmm, guess I'd better get dressed while I'm at it," she added with a sheepish shrug of her shoulders. "Wait for me?"

"Sure thing." Colt nodded. If hell froze over, he'd still be waiting.

Madison made a hasty phone call to Mark's room to let him know where she'd be for the day. Then she raced around the room getting dressed—hopping about as she shoved first one leg and then the other into a comfortable pair of faded jeans, then slipping into riding boots and a rosy pink T-shirt. Madison removed the band from her hair, combing it out and fluffing it around her face. She applied a little makeup, then snatched her purse and was out the door.

The bright warmth of the June sunshine was a shocking reception, in contrast to the cool dimness of the hotel. Colt watched Madison curiously when she dug a pair of sunglasses from her purse and put them on.

"What?" she asked, smiling as they made their way up the boardwalk to the only hitching post for blocks, which Madison had thought was just for decoration. Nonetheless, Colt had tethered both horses there, in between two cars.

"Nothing," he replied. "You look very nice." He handed her Cinnabar's reins. "We'll need to walk the horses off this black road and away from all these . . ." At a loss for words, he indicated the passing vehicles with a wave of his arm.

"Cars," she finished for him, preoccupied with the pretty red mare.

"Blow softly into her nostril and let her get your scent."

"Oh! Is that how you do it?" She smoothed her hand affectionately over the velvet muzzle, cooing softly, "You're such a pretty girl."

"So, do you have one?" he called back to her as he headed down the street.

"One what?" she asked as she hurried to catch up to him and the horses.

"What you said—cars." Colt stopped at the edge of town, offering Madison a step up onto her horse.

"Do I have a car? Of course," she said, laughing, "don't you?"

"No."

"Really? Why not?" She placed her booted foot in his hands and he hoisted her up. Then he looked at her, his hand casually resting on her knee. A rousing heat radiated from his touch; she thought it might burn a hole right through to her skin. Madison fidgeted in the creaky saddle to get comfortable.

"Just old-fashioned, I guess," he answered.

"Nothing wrong with that. Do you realize how long it's been since I've ridden a horse?"

"Tell me."

He was still touching her, the breeze blowing a long strand of hair over his cheek. Madison wished he wouldn't stand so close. It wasn't that he repelled her. Quite the contrary; she actually found his touch pleasant—but it was all wrong. This man was old enough to be her . . . well, grandfather. Or at least she had thought that when she first met him. Now, she wasn't sure what to think. He didn't appear nearly as old. When she tried to conjure the memory of what he had looked like last night, she drew a blank. But that wasn't the issue at all, was it? It scared her to have any man close enough to her to touch, especially one who evoked such a mixture of feelings. All she wanted was to push away.

She sighed. "I haven't ridden in years, and even then I didn't ride very well."

"Well, we'll just have to teach you, won't we, Cinnabar?"

Colt winked, squeezing her knee before walking away. He mounted his horse with such lissome grace that she at once felt totally incompetent. He nudged Cinder into a slow walk and Madison followed suit.

"Where did you get Cinnabar?"

"Ernie Hawkins—the old guy who runs the Wild West show. He was nice enough to let me borrow her for the day. She's very gentle," he said as Madison pulled up alongside.

They proceeded into the undulating waves of grass, away from town and toward the mountains. The warm, sweetly scented breeze tickled Madison's nose as they drew in close to the Snake River and rode the riverbank. The intimidating splendor of the Teton range loomed at her side, a thick woodsy base spiraling toward the sky to point with jagged, snow-crested pinnacles. On her left were acres and acres of gentle, sage-dotted hills. Tamer mountains in the foreground were lush with dense forest vegetation, an impenetrable wilderness that made her imagination run wild and her skin tingle. The man who rode next to her suited the scenery so well, it was almost too real, too perfect.

The lonely music of the wind filtering through the trees recaptured a different period of time for Madison. She and Mark had grown up in an environment just like this, and Madison was just now recognizing how much she missed it, and what pleasant memories she possessed.

Raised in Colorado by two high-school history teachers, Angela and Lee Calloway, Madison had spent almost every weekend with her family, digging into the state's colorful past. Armed with only a four-wheel-drive vehicle or dirt bikes and backpacks, they set out on what was always an adventure, searching for lost ghost towns or exploring ancient homesteads. Madison came to know Colorado's history as well as she knew her own name. Though, at the time she and Mark were only interested in riding the bikes or creating a rowdy game of hide and seek, recklessly dashing through deteriorated buildings that were in grave danger of collapsing at any moment.

Madison smiled when she thought of her parents—amateur archaeologists, eternal packrats, cleaning up and saving everything they found, whether it be just a pretty rock or a genuine artifact. She had a vivid memory of her mother, pickax in hand, squealing exaltedly as she pulled a completely intact antique bottle or dish from the ground around some old homestead. Over the years these treasures were displayed with impeccable taste throughout their house.

Madison never had to wonder where she developed her love of antiques. Back then she had become bored with the endless outings on which her mother and father had forced her to accompany them, but only because she was a teenager and more interested in boys than anything else. The sweet thrill of discovery had never deserted her, though.

Sadly, the adventures had ceased when her father had passed away just after she was graduated from high school. Then Madison got married, Mark discovered girls, and Angela was content with hitting antique shows, auctions, and stores on a regular basis. And Madison still loved to go along with her whenever her hectic schedule allowed.

Riding next to Colt reminded her so much of those days—the atmosphere, the crisp smells. She studied him as he rode just a few paces ahead. He looked as if he'd just stepped out of a John Wayne western, his hat casting shadows over his face, armed to the teeth. Why in the world would he wear those guns all the time? Surely they must be awfully heavy.

Madison was wondering if his guns were antiques when Cinnabar jolted into an energetic trot, ignoring her weak jerks at the reins. A squeal erupted from her lips as she passed Colt, the backward glance a mute plea for help. If anything, the mare went faster despite Madison's efforts to stop her.

"Uhhhh . . . Colt . . . help me here, please. I thought . . . you . . . said . . . she . . . was gentle. . . ." Her bottom bouncing horribly in the saddle, Madison's words were nothing but a helpless staccato.

"She is!" Colt answered, unable to repress a burst of hearty laughter. "We're close to the meadow. She smells the bluegrass and she's hungry. Pull back on the reins . . . hard!"

"I am!"

He was tempted not to lend a helping hand at all. Madison's shapely backside looked much too enticing moving up and down in the saddle as it was. Those tight denims she wore did quite a bit to facilitate the imagination. He considered just sitting back and enjoy the view, but Madison shot a fiery glance backwards in between bounces.

On second thought, he pulled abreast and reached across like an old pro, yanking the reins and bringing Cinnabar to a dead halt. Colt adjusted Madison's grip over the thick straps of leather, closing a warm hand over hers and squeezing it as he spoke.

"You've got to let her know who's boss. If she senses she has the upper hand, you'd better believe she'll take advantage. When you ride, just relax. Bend your knees. Find her rhythm and move with it."

When Colt released her hand Madison immediately felt bereft, but quickly recovered when he spurred Cinder into a graceful gallop toward the open meadow. Not far behind, Madison stopped on a small mound to watch the stunning spectacle.

The sight of man and beast melding as one with nature tugged at her emotions. It was like nothing she had ever seen. Cinder raced proudly over the grass and flower-covered floor of the crater, his muscled flanks undulating, his long mane floating in the wind. Colt merged with the animal in perfectly orchestrated harmony. They came to a stop at the other side, Cinder shaking his head and sidestepping with cocky vigor. Colt motioned for her to follow.

Madison took a deep breath, and with a cry of elation she nudged Cinnabar with her heels. They tore down into the meadow as fast as she dared, if not as fast as the horse wanted to go. She held on for dear life, bending her legs and squeezing her thighs, while trying to remember all Colt had said.

"Very good!" Colt's praises flowed freely as she reined in next to him, the two horses brushing muzzles.

Invigorated, Madison turned to him, her face flushed as she smiled with a rush of excitement. Colt's expression suddenly became serious, his brown eyes smoking with an intensity she didn't understand. Before she could speak, he was gone, dismounting beneath a lone spruce tree several yards away. Madison wondered if she had done something wrong.

"What are you doing?" Joining him beneath the tree, she tried to make light conversation, but he seemed oddly preoccupied. "Oh, look. A rosebush all the way up here—how about that! And the same color as the one you gave me." Following his gaze, she bent down on one knee and touched a delicate bud.

"Don't!" Colt fairly leaped to stop her, grabbing her hand away from the flower. "Please. Don't touch those. . . ."

Madison frowned in bewilderment, rising slowly to her feet. "Why not? Tell me what's wrong—why can't I touch a flower?"

Colt riveted his gaze to hers, then briskly turned away. Maybe he should let her pick one. Why not? For all he knew, those damn roses had nothing to do with his predicament. But what if they did? It was all too eerie for his comprehension. But . . . what if? Would he be launched backwards in time—would he be home again? More importantly, would she be with him? The thought of her by his side in his own time was enough to send his mind reeling. Colt had never met a woman like her before and likely never would again. She made him feel alive; he could actually feel his blood coursing through his veins when she was near. And he knew it wasn't just the fact that she was the loveliest creature he'd ever laid eyes on—no, it ran far deeper than that. More than he could understand, it was as if she had always been an intrinsic part of him, and the removal of that part, now that he had found her, would result in a slow and agonizing death. Madison saw him differently, too . . . he could tell by her manner.

"Colt?" Madison broke into his thoughts like a slap of harsh reality. She stood, hands on hips, her head tilted inquisitively. "Is there something you want to tell me? Colt, why is your hair . . . well, darker than it was yesterday?"

"My hair? It's darker?" What in the world was she talking about? Colt just stared, squinting against the bright sunlight.

Madison nodded.

"What about my face?" he asked hesitantly.

She frowned. How did he know she was, at that very moment, puzzling at the disappearing creases on his face?

"Madison," Colt added, wanting to tell her, needing to tell *someone*. " . . . In truth, I don't know. And you'd think I was nuts if I tried to explain."

"No, I wouldn't. Why don't you try me?" When Colt didn't answer she said, "Tell me about the rosebush. Why did you grab my hand like that?" He looked so lost. She felt an overwhelming desire to reach out and touch his shoulder, to comfort him.

"Would you like to ride down to the ranch? It's not too far." Colt spoke with renewed zest. "The trail's a little more overgrown than it . . . er . . . used to be, but we'll go slow. You'll be fine."

"Not far, huh? Well, I do have a plane to catch tonight, but okay I'd love to see your ranch. Let's go."

This man piqued her curiosity even more now than when she had first seen him. He was creating more questions than he was answering. What *was* his story? Logically, Madison thought she should be more wary of Colt than she felt. For all she knew, he could be an ax murderer waiting to get her alone, but instinctively, she felt as safe with him as she did with Mark.

"Better get a move on." Colt flashed her a smile, helping her to mount the mare.

Astride the gray, he led her beyond the darkened shelter of the towering evergreens to a winding and rocky trail.

Chapter Six

They were surrounded by impenetrable stands of aspens, the silver-dollar leaves fluttering in tenuous whispers. Most of the sunlight was blocked by lofty treetops, only shining through in a few precious life-giving rays. The atmosphere became instantly cooler, a pungent, mossy scent hanging in the air.

At times she was so cold her teeth chattered. But Madison didn't care. The visual beauty overshadowed any mild discomforts she might have to endure. As they circled down, and still farther down, every tortuous curve of the trail held a pleasant surprise for her. Firs were covered with sinuous shrouds of hanging lichen. The combination of yellow leaves with bright red spikes at the end and red-orange blossoms gave the appearance of a flaming spire. The forest throbbed with an abundance of life: Colorful birds flitted from branch to branch, squirrels scampered along tree trunks, their tails twitching, and there was the droning buzz of insects swooping overhead.

Colt and Madison stopped only long enough to water the horses in a frigid creek. Nearing the base of the mountain, the grade of the trail eased, leveling into low hills and arroyos with the vast grazing lands emerging before them. Scattered junipers and sagebrush surplanted the pines, and once again they pulled in close to a trickling stream and followed it the rest of the way down. A lanky jackrabbit jumped from a thicket, dashing in front of Cinnabar before disappearing into the plains.

A house materialized in the distance, along with other deserted structures. It was surrounded by a large grove of spreading elms and balsam poplars, bright red blossoms in full bloom. The closer they drew, the deeper the frown became over Madison's brow. This huge country ranchhouse was obviously very old and in shambles! The once-grand front porch tilted to one side. The house was Gothic-style, with three front gables, the center one with French doors and an elaborate veranda. The ground-story porch wrapped around the entire structure and was supported by massive Tuscan columns.

Colt stopped at the front of the house beneath the welcome shade of an oak, the drop in elevation having heightened the temperature substantially. Dismounting, he walked to Madison, offering her assistance. It was after she swung her leg over the mare's head that she realized she might have done it backwards. Her anchoring heel slipped from the stirrup, causing her body to fall against his, sliding downward. Reflexively, Colt gripped her waist in order to stop her fall, his hands lingering just a little longer than absolutely necessary.

Pressed against him, Madison felt his hard muscular chest, his strong, wide shoulders as her hands grasped his faded blue shirt. He smelled good, of heat and leather. His lips were mere inches from hers. She knew he was looking at her, could feel his half-lidded gaze burning down into her soul.

"It gets easier with practice."

The words were deep vibrations, emanating from his chest and into hers. At first she wasn't sure of his meaning. Colt released her abruptly, tethering the animals to a nearby hitching post. Ruffled and embarrassed, Madison smoothed her hair and clothes before starting for the house.

"I wouldn't go up there . . . it's rotted." His back to her, Colt called out as if he had read her mind.

"Oh, it's okay. . . . I've been around plenty of rickety buildings, mine shafts, that sort of thing. I grew up in Colorado, you know. I'll be careful."

She mounted the porch steps, mindful to avoid the rotten and broken-through places. A familiar spirit of adventure soaring within her, she pushed open the front door. It creaked with resistance, and she stepped inside.

Colt watched her protectively. He hung his hat on the pommel, tore a long sprig of grass and placed it in his mouth, then followed her inside. Avoiding fallen plaster and splintered wood strewn about in haphazard piles, he crossed the room and stood next to her before the rock fireplace.

Madison ran her fingers along the cool roughness of the moss rock then raised her eyes to his. "Were you born in this house?"

"I was six when my father built this house. I was born in the old house down by the . . ." he answered tightly, suddenly remembering it no longer stood. " . . . Er . . . well, it's not there anymore."

"How long ago?" Madison desperately needed to know his age—not that it made any significant difference, but it was a question that had nagged at her since morning.

Colt was tiring of the age issue. It wasn't her fault, but was he supposed to say that he was born a hundred and forty-three years ago?

"One hell of a long time ago," he responded bitterly, picking up a rock and chucking it through a broken window.

"That's no answer," she pushed. "I really want to know." It was obvious something was bothering him ever since the rosebush incident. Now his demeanor was even worse, his expression laced with a scowl.

Colt veered to face her, cocking one eyebrow. "How old do I look, Madison?"

Madison flinched. "That's not fair. If I'm wrong, I could offend you, and I don't want to offend you."

"*Who* the hell cares about offending *me?*" he snarled.

Madison awkwardly looked away, unable to endure the depth of his glower.

"I'm sorry, I didn't mean to lash out at you." He sighed raggedly, thrusting his fingers through his hair.

Colt took a step toward her, not knowing what to do. The longing to pull her into his arms was overpowering, to hold her close, inhale her fragrance. But that was impossible, wasn't it? Her perception of him was as an old man. Unless, just maybe, she was beginning to see him as he truly was. There was her remark about his hair being darker . . . Besides, what difference did age make when two people genuinely cared for each other? If he was sure, and he thought he was, that she felt as drawn to him as he was to her . . . then why not?

Colt tore the blade of grass from his mouth and tossed it aside. He reached for her, running his fingers up along the smooth skin of her arm, gently grasping, bringing her close. Then his arms embraced her. His hands moved gently over her back and deeply into her hair, masterfully, the heat of her body searing into his.

Inhaling sharply, Madison's first reaction was to push her palms against his chest, to move away, but she felt as if all her strength had been drained from her body. Her arms and legs trembled uselessly. He hugged her tightly, nuzzling closer until, sighing, she felt his warm lips brush the sensitive skin along the column of her neck. Slowly, Colt trailed deliberate, sensuous kisses down, then up again to linger at her earlobe. She was like warm honey in his arms, melting, dripping into him with all her being.

Madison wasn't even aware exactly when her arms circled his neck tenderly and her fingers threaded through the long hair at his nape, clutching. The exquisite warmth of his breathy kisses traveled along her jawline. She tilted her head back, her entire body atingle from his powerful hands massaging her back.

Her eyes met his golden brown ones and she opened her mouth to speak, to say anything to stop this. It must stop. . . . But his mouth slanted boldly over hers, stifling her objections, and her heart leapt wildly at the intrusion. For a moment she had lost all coherent thought, abandoning herself, opening up to him. Her tongue tangled with his needfully, the taste of him indescribably sweet.

Faint moans brought her to her senses, and she was shocked to discover that they were her own. Her eyes snapped open and she frantically pushed against him with all her might. When Colt loosened his hold, Madison backed away, her world reeling with the headiness of unexplored emotions. Grasping for a diversion, she pretended interest once again in their immediate surroundings. "Uhh . . . er . . . I . . . I'd like to see the upstairs."

Madison's legs were truly numb, but they managed to take her to the foot of the stairs as casually as possible.

"That wouldn't be wise," he spoke deeply, his voice gravelly with desire.

"You're right—we shouldn't."

Misunderstanding his meaning, she headed for the front door. With long, determined strides, she hurriedly trotted down the stairs and across the yard.

Reality struck her like a bolt of lightning. My God, she thought, what was wrong with her? She had been virtually out of control in there! Never before had she lost control—or enjoyed a kiss quite as much, for that matter. It unnerved and frightened her. Who *was* this Colt Chase, anyway? Last night the long, delightful conversation with an 80-ish-year-old man seemed like light years away, another lifetime, another *planet*. That hadn't been the kiss of an elderly man just now, and that definitely wasn't the body of one either.

A balmy breeze, tinged with the subtle essence of cedar and wild flowers, invigorated her, easing her tension. Her arms folded, Madison strolled toward a thick stand of poplars that ran alongside the house. Overgrown with years of tangled underbrush, it appeared inaccessible. She started to turn back when an unnatural whiteness against the landscape caught her eye. Above and beyond the trees, atop a swelling mound, stood the broken remnants of a white picket fence. Because it seemed out of place, her curiosity got the better of her. Madison fought the thick growth, propelling herself through, heading up the hill.

At the first glimpse of a stout granite cross in the waving grass, she knew it was a tiny cemetery. Gently swinging the brittle gate open just far enough to step inside, she hesitated, worried that Colt might not want her here. A quick look back toward the house produced no sight of him, and Madison continued inside.

There were two identical markers side by side, elaborately connected by a common base. Madison knelt, sweeping the weeds aside and examining the inscriptions on each: *Charles Willum Chase and Katherine Mae Chase. Died August 3, 1868. Joined In Life—Together Forever In Eternity.*

Touched, she moved to the next marker. It was of a much simpler design: *Rosannah Bartlett Tipsword; born in 1832, died in 1888.*

There were several more: *Joseph Daniel "Bud" Tipsword, born in 1826; died in 1882.* Next to that was a cross that was crumbling and unreadable. What looked to be a newer monument stood apart from the rest: *Emily Anne Bartlett, born in 1863; died on her birthday in 1968.* Fascinated by the dates on this particular marker, Madison noted that she had died on her 105th birthday! It was as if she'd set a goal for herself, attaining it, then letting go. . . .

Wistfully, Madison started to leave. On her way out she ran across two tiny wooden crosses side by side, almost hidden beneath the layers of matted grass, any inscription long since faded. Either infants or small children, judging by the size of the crosses, she thought. A sad smile and a tear springing to her eye, she turned, startled to run into Colt, standing rigid at the crooked gate.

His fingers were shoved into his jeans pockets, his face a stony mask as he stared long and hard at the markers, as if he were seeing them for the first time. A twitch pulsed along the firm line of his jaw. At first, Madison was afraid he was angry at her for coming here. Then she realized he seemed completely impervious to her presence, absorbed by his own thoughts.

Dabbing at a tear that had run its course along her cheek, Madison squeezed past him through the gate.

"Long-lost relatives?" she asked softly.

"You could say that. My folks . . ." he replied, indicating the fancy headstone, "killed by a renegade rustler. Shot while they slept." Colt's gaze shifted to the others, speaking more to himself than to her. "Rosie, Emmy . . . Bud . . ."

"That's terrible. Your folks, did you say? You mean great-grandparents, something like that?"

"I mean *folks*—as in my Ma and Pa. Rosannah was like a second mother to me. Emmy, just like a kid sister. And overprotective Bud." Colt sighed, shaking his head. "Even worse than Pa was. He and Garrett took over the ranch when I had to leave."

Suddenly, he grabbed her hand and unexpectedly started back down the hill, pulling her behind. "I'm hungry—let's eat."

Having no choice but to follow, her long legs stumbled into rapid motion behind him. Madison's brow bunched in confusion. She opened her mouth to speak, but thought better of it. She needed every ounce of concentration she possessed just to keep up with his strides without falling flat on her face.

Chapter Seven

"Don't drink that water; it's tainted." Colt inclined his head toward the gurgling creek with a look of dead seriousness.

They sat below the spreading limbs of the great cottonwood, looking out toward the open prairie as they ate their lunch. The brown bag contained two submarine sandwiches, two bags of potato chips, and two cans of Coke, wrapped in foil to keep them cool. Colt's sandwich was nearly gone. Madison had barely begun to eat hers.

Amused, initially she thought he must be joking. Surely he didn't really think she might try to drink from that abominable creek that barely seeped through squashy mud. "Don't worry, I won't," she answered, her eyes sparkling. She saw he was eyeing her sandwich just as seriously. "Still hungry? Here, take half of mine, I'll never be able to finish it."

"Are you sure?"

"Positive." Madison handed him the sandwich and he scarfed it down like he hadn't had food in days. "I take it you're pretty fond of submarine sandwiches."

"Is that what you call it?" he asked between mouthfuls, wiping his palms along his pant legs.

"Don't tell me you've never had one before? Where did you get them?"

"No, I haven't. A little different than what I'm used to, but it's not bad. Just went into the store next to the saloon and told the lady behind the counter to fix me up a lunch for two. I didn't even know what she was going to put in it."

"Aren't you going to drink your soda?"

Madison rolled the cans from the foil as Colt watched intently. When she popped the tab, a fountain of foam sprayed into the air, raining down on them both. Colt jumped to his feet in a mad rush. Madison laughed. "It's okay—a little sugary syrup never hurt anyone."

Colt slowly sat back down, taking the can from her hand. He examined it closely before taking a big swig. His eyes watered. A moment later, he issued a loud burp, grinning at her sheepishly.

"Pardon me . . . stuff kind of grows on a person, don't it?" He took two more long draughts, emptying the can.

Madison smiled in response, still finding it difficult to maintain eye contact. She studied the deep, furrowed creases across his forehead, the wrinkles forever etched along his eyes—despite these, he was a very attractive man. Because of that, and what had transpired between them only an hour before, he unnerved her. On the one hand, she felt the undeniable urge to mother him as if he were a lost little boy—yet on the other, she was stricken with the fervent desire to make delirious love to him. Her very sensibility was jolted by this outrageous admission, even if it was only made to herself.

"Colt?"

"Hmmmmm?" He toyed with the wrinkled sheet of aluminum foil, first smoothing it out perfectly on his leg and folding it into a precise square, then repeating the process. It fascinated him.

"I don't understand what you meant by those graves up there being your mother and father. They were very old. The dates were in the 1800s. . . ."

Actually hearing the words spoken substantiated her worst fear: that Colt might be suffering from senility. Last night that might have been easy for her to accept, but today was different. Somehow he just didn't seem that old to her anymore—at least not as old as she had first thought. Good heavens, it was all so confusing.

"What do you call this?" He was still engrossed in the foil, apparently not having heard a word she said.

Madison frowned. "Foil. Aluminum foil, of course."

"Let's talk about you. All we've talked about is me. Don't know much about you, except that you own a business in Colorado Springs."

"Yes," she sighed in resignation, "I started it several years ago with financial help from my husband—"

Colt shot her a startled look and she quickly amended her statement. "Ex-husband, now, of course. Mark graduated from the University of Colorado along about that time and he joined me as my manager. We get along well. All in all, things have been good, except for my marriage—that was a mess. I travel a lot, or at least I did when I was married. This last year hasn't been the best. I've been just about everywhere, though, at least once. Europe, the Orient, Australia, South America, cruises, safaris. I've done it all."

Madison hugged her knees to her chest, rocking back and forth as she spoke, the bittersweet memories flooding back without her meaning for them to. Jon had accompanied her on most of her trips; the remembrance was painful, yet in some obscure way, blissfully warm.

"Did your husband die?" Colt asked, concerned.

"Er . . . no, we were divorced." She watched his reaction carefully. He simply nodded, continuing to stare out toward the horizon. "Gee, what else can I tell you?"

"Tell me about your family."

"My mother is a widow—my father died several years ago. They were both schoolteachers. My mother is a real pistol, let me tell you. She always has a million things on the burner at full boil. The crazy thing about her is, she never shows a single sign of stress. Now me, one thing goes haywire and I'm a basket case!"

Colton laughed. "Admirable profession . . . schoolteacher," he said, nodding his approval. "How old are you?"

"Well now, as I recall, you wouldn't divulge your age." With a disconcerted smile she recalled what happened the last time she asked that question. "Really, it's okay if you'd rather not say. I'm 30."

Colt's eyes glimmered—he must have remembered, too. Madison wondered if he'd ever tell her.

"Do you miss your husband?"

He sure has a way of getting right to the point, she thought, opening wounds that had barely begun to heal.

"I do—but only in a certain way, the way it used to be before . . ." she cut herself short, not wanting to tell him why

Jon had left her. Somehow hearing herself say it made it even more painful. Her whole life had come crashing down around her the day she found out about Amanda, Jon's coworker, being pregnant with his child. And Jon was more than eager to seek a divorce and marry Amanda.

Madison had suspected Jon of dallying in a few affairs during their marriage; she had just refused to acknowledge that fact to herself. What a dunce she felt like sometimes. Jon must have thought she was a total idiot. Then it had all caught up to both of them, a pregnancy and a truth she had no choice but to accept. He wanted a divorce. What an ironic slap in the face! It should have been she who made that demand. Slick-witted and sharp-tongued, in all their years of marriage Jon had outdone her in every disagreement. She had never stood a chance. And finally, he'd even gotten in the last word when it came to ending their marriage. She thought that probably hurt worse than anything, her self-esteem plummeting to an abysmal low when he delivered that crushing blow.

Their divorce was final now. Jon had a son. Madison wondered if he had started messing around behind Amanda's back yet. There were rumors. . . . She almost felt sorry for Amanda, guessing that must be a good sign, signaling her own imminent recovery. Amanda had left behind a career for Jon, and Madison had come close to doing the very same thing. Thankfully, she had caught herself before committing the last inexcusable blunder.

"Did he hurt you very much?" Colt eyed her perceptively, twirling a blade of grass over his teeth.

It was forever before she could choke the words out, her own voice sounding strange when she did. " . . . yes, very much."

It wasn't a great achievement for him to detect the torment behind those aqua eyes, even before she had admitted it. She was far too special—such a beautiful, warm, caring person—to be treated with such disregard—and by her own husband, at that. Although Colt didn't know the details, her brief statement irked him. Her eyes were haunted . . . and he wished he could exorcise the demons that lurked within those aqua depths. Colt wanted to try. Extending his hand toward her, he lifted her chin with his forefinger.

"I'm no expert, by far, but I know that the pain will fade . . . in time. The hurt somehow transforms itself into a valuable wisdom that you wouldn't trade for the world. Don't try to forget; it only prolongs the inevitable. Just accept."

A slow smile curved her full, sensuous lips, lighting up her entire face. For the first time he noticed how her nose turned up just a little at the end, giving her a cute, impish look.

A whirring vibration sounded from above. Colt's head jerked up, and he recalled a time when he had heard that noise before. He bounded to his feet, this time determined to catch a glimpse of whatever made that annoying disturbance. It was akin to the buzzing of an extremely large bee.

Madison stared after him, resting her chin dreamily on her knees. The way he walked, the swivel of his slim hips, she wondered about his muscled thighs beneath the blue denim . . . then, fiercely, she chastised herself for the direction her thoughts had insisted upon taking her.

"*What* in God's name is *that?*" Colt shouted, shielding his eyes from the blinding sun as he gawked toward the heavens.

He shot an astonished glance toward Madison as if he had just made some profound discovery. She got up to join him, half expecting to see some sort of alien spaceship.

"It's only a plane, silly." She started back toward her place beneath the tree when he grabbed for her arm.

"Are there people in that thing?"

It hit her like a slap in the face—she couldn't disregard his odd behavior any longer. "Colt . . . what is going on with you?" her voice quivered despite herself. "Tell me why you act so . . . unusual sometimes."

"Are there *people* in there?" he repeated impatiently.

"Yes! C'mon, is this some kind of a joke? Don't tell me you don't know what a plane is!" Madison stamped her foot in frustration.

"Is that what you meant when you said you had to catch a plane? Are you planning on flying inside one of *those?* This is absolutely unbelievable!"

He hadn't heard a word she said. Without giving her a chance to respond he took off, running to get a better view of the disappearing aircraft. Madison waited with her arms folded across her chest until he returned. His eyes were wide with a childlike exuberance.

"Tell me about planes. What makes them fly like that?"

Was this a taste of a very warped sense of humor, or could it be possible he'd never seen a plane before? Skeptical, she decided to answer him seriously. "That one flies with propellers. *That* one," she said, pointing at a barely visible dot trailed by a cloud of white, "is a jet . . . Colt! *Now* where are you going?"

He took off again. Throwing her hands into the air, Madison followed him farther out into the clearing.

"You mean *that? There?*" he said excitedly, pointing upward. "You wouldn't be giving me a bum steer, now would you? There can't be people all the way up there!"

"A few hundred, I'm willing to bet," she answered tiredly.

"How do they breathe?"

He looked very concerned, and taking hold of his arm, she tried to direct him back toward the stand of trees, but he wouldn't budge. For someone who wasn't overly tall—she estimated him to be just under six feet, judging by her own five-and-a-half-foot frame—he was sturdy as an ox. It was a little like trying to move a house, she mused. Clasping two hands around a bulging biceps, she tugged and tugged.

"C'mon, Colt . . . let's talk. . . . I want to know where you've been for the last eighty years or so."

Finally, he planted his hand over hers and, laughing, said, "You wouldn't be trying to catch my attention, now would you?" Then, seriously, he added "Let's talk, Madison, if you're absolutely sure you want to hear what I have to say."

"Yes! I'm very interested in you. Er . . . I mean your life." Even as she said it, the words rang truer than she cared to admit.

Sublime pleasure settled over his features, a scintillating glow from his golden brown eyes pouring down over her. The creases along his eyes and cheeks visibly relaxed, but then his face became a blurry haze. Madison blinked several times, sure her contact lenses were playing tricks again. Colt's visage seemed to waver before her eyes, offering but a brief glimmer of smooth, wrinkle-free skin. Young skin. Just as quickly as it appeared, the vision was gone in a flash, like a mirage in the scorching heat of the desert. Aghast, she could only stare.

Colt touched her cheek. "Madison, what's wrong?"

"Huh? Oh, nothing. It's just your face . . . and your hair . . ." The sun played over the copper highlights of rich chestnut hair. His eyelashes were obscenely long. Why was it that men were always the ones blessed with the long lashes?

"What's wrong with my face and hair?" Tremendously pleased, he was having trouble suppressing a wild burst of laughter. Finally! This was it, he was certain. She was beginning to see him as he really was. Was she the only one? he wondered. Maybe that was the key . . . she was developing an affection for the man he was on the inside, regardless of his physical appearance.

"Ohhhhh, nothing." Madison threw her arms up in exasperation, stomping a few feet away. "You have very nice hair for a man. I mean, not that a man shouldn't have pretty hair; it's just that yours is a lot darker than it was before! Excuse me while I lose my mind. . . ." She shook her head.

Colt led her back toward the inviting shade tree. Twirling about in midstride, he began to walk backward. Triumphantly, he gushed, "You're not losing your mind. Your mind is beautiful. And as long as we're dishing out compliments, so's your hair. And you've the loveliest face I've ever seen. . . . That is, of course, with the exception of the painting of a nude that hangs above a bar in Laramie." He gave her a teasing wink.

"You're funny!" Madison giggled, totally swept into the charm of his boyishly lopsided grin. "Are you absolutely sure it's the nude's *face* you're referring to?"

With a growl he picked her up by the waist and swung her around twice, and her giggles were transformed to shrieks of surprise. Setting her down, he bent so that his eyes were level with hers. Grasping her firmly by the shoulders, he said, "I'm going to bare my soul to you, Madison Calloway. You've given me my youth back. By God, if you're losing your mind, then I certainly am, too. C'mere."

He placed her beneath the tree.

"What in the world are you talking about? I don't understand."

"You will soon enough. Just promise me one thing?"

"What's that?"

Colt lowered himself onto the cool cushion of grass, leaning back, his weight resting on his elbows. "Promise me you won't say a word until I've finished?" He was quite serious now.

"Well, sure, I guess." Madison crossed her legs Indian-style.

Satisfied, he began. "I was born the first son to Charles and Katherine Chase, August 16, 1850."

"You can't mean . . ."

"Ah-ah-ah," he wagged a scolding finger, "not a word!"

Madison clamped her mouth shut and listened.

"There were two children after me. Both boys who died soon after birth. The doctor told my mother that if she bore any more children, it would kill her. I have an adopted brother, Garrett. My folks brought him home when he was only a few months old. I was barely two. There was a Shoshone uprising on the ranch, and Garrett's natural parents were murdered. His mother was a Sioux, his father white. They were among the first ranch hands we had—it was only a small spread at the time. My folks being the caring people they were, they took Garrett in and raised him as their own.

"When I was eighteen my folks were brutally murdered, in that bedroom right up there." He nodded toward the verandah. "It was the dead of night. I found them. They both took shotgun blasts to the chest. The big barn was engulfed in flames—I'll never forget the reflection the flames made in the diamond earrings my mother always wore. She lay crumpled by the window, my father hovered over her protectively. When I left their room that night I found Garrett cowering in the corner of the hallway, his eyes cold and vacant. He was never quite the same after that. But then, I suppose none of us were. I know my life changed forever."

Madison listened intently as Colt spoke, his voice low and smooth. It was as if she could almost see the amber flames dance in his eyes as he described that awful night.

"A note, scribbled in blood, was left skewered to the bedroom wall with an arrow. 'Only with just cause . . . ' was all it said, but the arrow was the personal signature of Red Eagle, a notorious murderer and cattle rustler. Not three months later I gave up the life I'd always known, pledging to track down that lowlife scum. It's been a long time. I've come so close, Madison. But it's been ten years. I won't admit defeat, though. I'll search that monster out even if it takes 'til I'm an old man. . . ." Colt glanced at her with an air of irony.

"I've been wandering ever since. Occasionally I return to the ranch—bring supplies, cut a few deals, take care of pressing business—then I'm gone again. I'd only been home for a couple of days when I rode up to Jackson Hole yesterday morning. I like it up there. Gives me my peace of mind back." He sighed, leaning his head back to gaze up pensively through the ceiling of leafy branches. "I guess you could say I harbor a weakness for roses. I don't know why, but I was inclined to pinch a bud from the rosebush we saw earlier. I don't understand what happened"— he shook his head—"but a lightning storm encompassed me, out of nowhere, with a fury like I've never seen before. When I rode out of it, soaking wet and sick as a dog, the clouds lifted, and there before me was a town that hadn't existed a few minutes before. Madison, I swear to you, a day and a half ago I was in the year 1878—this ranch was alive and well. Correct me if I'm wrong, but now I seem to be in the year 1993. I realize this sounds impossible, but you might take a moment to look at it from my point of view."

Finally, he dared to seek her eyes with his own, afraid of the disbelief he was sure he would find.

Madison just gaped, her mind backtracking furiously over the events of yesterday and today. If this was some sort of joke, he sure stayed in character. He'd have to be one hell of a good actor. *What was she thinking?* What he was implying was unimaginable . . . impossible. And yet, the way he seemed to be regressing in age right before her eyes—*that* was crazy, too. And what about when she had first seen him, leading Cinder up Main Street, terrified of every car that passed—and he hadn't even known her then. It sure would explain his utter fascination with airplanes. But she must be crazy herself even to consider his story as truth.

"Please don't think that I've gone mad," he pleaded.

His soft brown eyes tugged at her mothering instincts again. "Of course I don't think you're mad! It's just that there has to be a rational explanation. It's not possible," she said, her voice low.

Madison wished she didn't have to return to Colorado Springs so soon. How could she leave him here alone in this state of mind? She enjoyed Colt's company and considered him a friend. A poignant empathy welled from the center of her soul. Such a proud man, with so many wonderful qualities. If only there were time to find out his true origin and exactly how long he had been plagued by these delusions, been in this state of mind.

"Isn't there someone who lives in the Jackson area, a relative maybe, who could help?"

Colt's sarcastic smirk cut her short.

"Madison, just about everybody I know is buried in that graveyard up there. Most were alive and well when I saw them yesterday. . . . So you tell me!" Any glimmer of hope he had had that she might believe him was snuffed out like a flame from a candle.

"Where do you live? I mean, where have you been staying?"

"Ernie Hawkins was hospitable enough to take me in last night. Suppose I'll just spread my bedroll out somewhere tonight. Madison, I know you're thinking I'm as crazy as a loon, and I can't blame you on that score—but I don't know what else to say. That's my house, and yesterday it was more than livable." Shaking his head hopelessly, Colt pulled the tobacco pouch from his vest and casually rolled a cigarette. He lit it, exhaling the smoke into the wind.

"Smoking causes cancer, you know." She didn't know why she said it—maybe it was just the need to break the silence.

"Pardon me?"

"Lung cancer. It kills you. Cigarettes cause it."

"Oh."

He didn't seem too worried, and she knew it was useless trying to convince him.

"Tell me about the ranch, Colt. You said it was alive and well. What was it like?"

She noticed that he visibly relaxed as he spoke of the familiar. He told her of the old ranch house down the hill, the one his family homesteaded before the big one was built. He told her of the unspoiled splendor of this land, the cowboys, the roundups. He recounted the big house in such vivid detail that she was salivating at the image of such a treasury of antiques under one roof. At last, he told her of the notice he had pulled from the bulletin board back in Jackson—the imminent auction of the Triple Bar C. Madison empathized with the tremendous melancholy she saw in his eyes.

Glancing at her watch, Madison reluctantly got to her feet and stretched, brushing the grass from her jeans. "I have a plane to catch," she reminded him, smiling warmly as she headed for the horses.

"So you said. You'd have to kill me first to get me that far off the ground." Colt was right behind her.

"I bet I could get you on one—it's my job."

"Maybe one of these days I'll get the chance to prove you wrong."

He delivered another one of those charismatic winks before helping her to mount Cinnabar and she smiled at him.

Neither spoke much on the ride back up the pass. There didn't seem to be much need. There was an odd sort of comfort just being in one another's presence. It was something they both seemed to feel but lacked the means to explain.

When Colt dropped her at the Shady Oak Madison dismounted and handed him Cinnabar's reins with heartfelt thanks for such a pleasant day. Hating good-byes, she didn't know what else to say. She watched sadly as he touched the brim of his Stetson with his finger, nodding. Turning around, he slowly led Cinnabar back toward Ernie's.

"Farewell, pretty lady."

The breeze carried his velvet voice to her ears, his words tearing at her insides with a cold finality. Because, deep down, she knew that he meant it.

Chapter Eight

Madison joined Mark at the hotel front desk. He had been in the process of checking the group out just as she was returning from her outing with Colt.

Mark was brimming with curiosity, not having spoken to Madison since that morning. He wanted to know everything about the mysterious old cowboy. Madison briefly filled him in as they waited for the desk manager to complete the checkout. She carefully left out the part about Colt claiming to come from the previous century, and also the way he appeared so much younger today than he had yesterday. Somehow just voicing such crazy notions made her feel . . . well, unstable.

"So now it's 'Colt,' huh? Sounds like you two are becoming quite close." Mark's eyebrows rose knowingly.

"Close friends, if even that. Don't turn it into something it isn't, Mark."

Mark just grinned in response.

Sore and tired, all Madison wanted to do was to climb into a steaming tub. The last thing she was looking forward to was fighting the airport crowds, arriving home late, and getting up early for work the following morning.

"You know, I think I'll sell the agency, buy the Triple Bar C, become a recluse, and raise cows. What do you think of that?"

Madison leaned her weight against the glossy pine counter, her chin propped lazily in her palm. She stared dreamily past him.

"I think Mr. Chase made quite an impression. Why is his ranch going up for auction, anyhow? Isn't there anything he can do to save it?"

"I really don't know. . . . Apparently not." She sighed. "I feel sorry for him. He's such a nice man, but he's got a lot of problems."

"Don't we all?"

"Not like what he's facing. There's something major going on with him and it's affecting everything in his life. I haven't quite figured out if it's mental or something else."

"He's losing his ranch—that's a major problem. I hear the Triple Bar C is one of the largest spreads in the area."

"No, I think it's more than that." A lot more than that, Madison thought, but she didn't dare divulge the whole story.

The desk manager appeared in front of them again, separating the charge form. She was a middle-aged woman with a mantle of unnaturally Titian-red hair in tight ringlets over her head. Enormous blue eyes looked out over the bifocals perched on the tip of her nose. "Couldn't help but hear you two talking," she said. "The Triple Bar C has quite a colorful past!"

"You don't say?" Madison instantly perked up.

"Ohhh, yes!" the lady continued. "It hasn't been active since Old Lady Bartlett died back in '68. Quite an empire while she was living—went to hell in a handbasket after she died, though. There were problems with the will, I hear, and it lingered in probate for years after her death. It's just now being pushed through the final process. Rumor is, if they don't get top dollar for it, the government will turn it into National Forest land. You thinking of buying it?"

Mark and Madison glanced at one another, their eyes reflecting the same thoughts. No mention was made of Colt Chase. Had all he had claimed about the ranch been an outright lie? It was Madison who spoke. "No . . . I was just wishing out loud, is all. Who was Old Lady Bartlett, anyway?"

"Emmy Bartlett—some say she was well over a hundred when she finally kicked the bucket. A spry one, she was. Would get out there and ride them horses clear up to the end. 'Course, she was always an eccentric old soul. Lived there all her life—I believe she was born there. Never married, though. People say," the woman leaned in close and whispered, "had the love of her life snatched away when she was but a young girl, never found another who could fill his boots, so she just ended up an old maid. 'Course, can't believe everything you hear."

"Hmmmm, interesting." Madison nodded, recalling the latest headstone at the ranch cemetery. "You wouldn't happen to know Colt Chase, would you? I rode out to the ranch with him today. He claims he's the owner."

The red-haired woman frowned pensively.

"He's the old guy who's been wandering the streets the past two days—wears his guns all the time. He did some demonstration at the Wild West show yesterday," Mark added, hoping to jog her memory.

Madison found herself praying the woman would know about Colt, and therefore shed some light on this mystery. Possibly her worst fear was finding out that her nagging thoughts were indeed true . . . that he was suffering from senility.

"Ah-hah! Got it!" The desk manager slapped her palm down onto the counter, startling Mark and Madison both. "No, no, that's not possible! The Colt Chase I've heard of has been dead for quite some time. He was a gunfighter in these parts. Quite a famous character in our local history. Here, you may enjoy reading this." She reached across the counter and pulled a thin paperback book from a wire rack, sliding it in front of them. "This is just a short history of the area. There's a chapter on the Triple Bar C, and quite a bit on Colt Chase, if memory serves me correctly. He was a very dashing fellow—a charmer with the ladies, if ya catch my meaning." She blinked a big blue eye in Madison's direction.

Mark and Madison glanced at one another simultaneously, his eyes growing wide as he began to hum the theme from "The Twilight Zone." Madison delivered a swift kick to his leg beneath the counter, while smiling at the woman. Snatching open the book, she began to thumb through its pages.

"Could this gunfighter have had any descendants who remained in the area? Maybe that's who I met."

"Doubt it. At least not legitimate descendants," she said, snickering. "I believe he was a bachelor and was killed at an early age."

Madison located the chapter entitled "Legend Of The Triple Bar C." Turning a page, her heart began to thump erratically at what she saw. A picture of two boys, seemingly in their mid-teens. The youngest had dark skin and eyes, his expression sour. The taller boy stood stiffly next to him, his hands resting on a propped rifle.

His hat was low on his forehead, which made it difficult to see his features clearly. Even so, the somber expression held a familiar quality. The caption below it read:

COLTON AND GARRETT CHASE—THE EARLY YEARS
Colton disappeared 13 years after this photograph was taken. Legend has it he was murdered at the hands of a cowardly sniper in Abilene, Kansas, while on a mission of vengeance for his family's murder, though no marked grave has ever been found. Some say Garrett was hanged not long after for various crimes, including cattle rustling, but this is not substantiated by any known facts.

Madison swallowed hard at the dry lump that had formed in her throat, suddenly feeling sick to her stomach. Confusion mounted, magnified by the intense concern she already felt for Colt's situation. It seemed the more she learned, the more bizarre everything became. Madison closed the book with a weak smile, clutching it to her chest. "I'll take the book. What do I owe you?"

"Oh, you can have it. It's on us. It's always a pleasure to serve the travel agencies. You bring your agents back any ol' time. We enjoyed having you."

They said their final thank you's, and Madison blindly headed for the stairs in the lobby.

"Where are you off to in such a hurry?" Mark asked, though he already knew.

"Upstairs . . . to pack." As she lifted her foot to the first step she grimaced, rubbing a hipbone. The soreness was beginning to settle in but good.

"And to memorize that book."

"So? What's wrong with that?"

"I think you've been duped, Maddie! Your friend's hero is obviously the infamous Colton Chase—the *real* one. That guy is just some senile old man who took on the Chase dude's identity."

"Could be, but you haven't talked to him like I have. You didn't see the way he used those guns of his." Her brows arched in challenge.

"Practice, that's all. What else could it be? Hey, unless you've just spent the day with a . . . a . . . ghost!" Mark's mouth fell open in mock fear.

"Oh, stop it. I'll meet you and the others back here in the lobby in time to catch the bus to the airport, okay?"

"Sure thing. Have fun!"

Madison brushed him off with a wave of her hand before she stiffly mounted the stairs, the muscles in her thighs talking to her the entire way. Mark happily strolled from the lobby, whistling.

In her room, she flopped across the bed and immediately began to read, not stopping until she was sure she'd gleaned every drop of pertinent information from its pages. Madison rolled onto her back, holding the book overhead, memorizing a second picture of Colton Chase, during his gunfighting heyday. The resemblance to the man she had just spent the day with was uncanny.

In the picture he sat on an ornate chair, a gunbelt crossed over his chest beneath a light-colored vest, a rifle propped at his side. His demeanor was somber. The hair was cut short, but the eyes, the mouth, were *same*. Madison shivered, rubbing the goosebumps that popped out along her arm. Next to him stood a woman, her hand resting affectionately on his shoulder. Her hair was dark and piled into a loose coil on top of her head. She was slim, buxom, and pretty. The caption read: *Colton Chase and unknown woman, South Pass City, 1875.*

A heavy sigh and the book was slammed shut, tossed aside as if it had burned her. Madison closed her eyes. Maybe Mark wasn't all that far off with his ghost theory, after all. Everything Colt had revealed to her today had been authenticated in that history book. He would have had to commit all that to memory to come up with his story, which was, indeed, possible. The inexplicable factor was, how come he looked so much like the original Colton Chase? Not just his manner of dress, but his face, his build . . .

The book claimed he had died in July 1878. What had Colt told her? She thought she remembered him saying it was June 1878 when the storm brought him forward in time. Groaning, she pressed her fingertips to her temples. She must be daft. Now he had *her* trying to analyze his absurd delusions. No doubt she'd just spent the day with a descendant of *the* Colton Chase, a senile old man with the notion that he was the gunfighter himself. The resemblance was the evidence.

A deafening crack of thunder rattled the windowpanes of the tiny hotel room, causing her heart to leap into her throat. The skies had been perfectly blue when Colt dropped her off less than an hour ago. She bounded from the bed just as the first pelting raindrops hit the glass. The skies were smothered with black, churning storm clouds.

Recalling her earlier conversation with Colt, she grabbed her shoulderbag and dug through it. She pulled out the faded rosebud, twirling it gingerly between two fingers. It still looked fresh. Just a little bit of black edged the swirled silken petals.

He was out in this storm; she felt it! Madison's heart ached when she pictured him, wet and cold, maybe disoriented. Another bolt of lightning set the darkened room aglow, and she cringed at its intensity. Colt didn't stand a chance in this storm. He could be struck by lightning or catch pneumonia at the very least! The question was, could she find him and get him back to the safety of town before she had to catch their bus to the airport?

At a frantic pace, she threw her clothes into her suitcase and slammed it shut. Paraphernalia atop the sink was raked into her shoulderbag, the rose tucked back safely into a side pocket. Snatching up her belongings, she was out the door, her luggage deposited at the front desk for safekeeping until she returned.

Chapter Nine

Blowing rain stung Madison's face and hands like sharp little daggers as she rode the cinnamon mare into the foothills. At least she had possessed the presence of mind to wear a jacket, though it obviously wasn't waterproof. Her leather shoulderbag, now sopping wet, was strapped behind the saddle the way she had seen Colt do. Her hair clung to her cheeks in soggy, cloying strands, and she struggled to brush it from her eyes while concentrating on staying astride the trotting horse. She didn't dare encourage the mare to go any faster; the pain in her pelvis was almost more than she could stand now, an agony with every step.

Finding a horse had been no easy task. She had recalled that Colt had borrowed Cinnabar from Ernie Hawkins at the Wild West show, and so that was where she had gone. Madison had suspected that Ernie thought she must be cracked, wanting to ride out in this weather. But by that time she hadn't cared. First, she had inquired about borrowing a horse, and when he apologetically refused, she had asked to rent one for a few hours. He couldn't do that, either. Increasingly desperate as the storm raged on, she had begged, explaining that she feared for Colt's safety.

They had finally arrived at a mutual agreement. Madison had bought Cinnabar. It was a good thing Ernie took credit cards. Not believing what she had done, and for a virtual stranger's benefit, she rationalized to herself that she *had* become quite attached to Cinnabar. And she'd always wanted a horse. . . .

Madison had no earthly idea what she would do with the mare once this little mission of mercy was completed. She mused that she could always ride her to work—wouldn't that be a sight? Maybe if she was lucky, ol' Ernie would buy Cinnabar back when she returned. Oh, well, she really *had* always wanted a horse.

Colt damn well better appreciate her efforts to help him. She could have turned her back and flown home, never giving him another thought. But she had felt him to be a wonderful friend and sincerely wanted to help him overcome his problem.

The damp air was becoming more and more frigid, the skies gray. Madison halfway expected it to start snowing. The rain was slowing down to a weeping drizzle, and Cinnabar's hooves sank deeply into the spongy soil. At least the crisp fragrance of the freshly washed meadow was pleasant—the tang of moist sagebrush and cedar mixed with a sweetness of cowslips and buttercups.

The daylight faded fast under the influence of thick, swirling clouds, and it occurred to her that she hadn't left a message for Mark as to her whereabouts. If she were to encounter some sort of trouble, nobody would know where to find her—only Ernie, and all he knew was that she had barged into his office insisting that she had to have a horse.

Where was that elusive meadow? She thought she knew, but now she was beginning to wonder.

Jumpy, Madison found herself scrutinizing every shadowy movement, unsure of what animals, if any, she might run into. Recalling Colt's frightening account of Old Bones made a chill run up her spine. Hastily, she pushed the memory away and tried to concentrate on something a little more cheerful.

Thunder clapped around her with earth-jarring force, and Cinnabar shied dramatically. Then there was an illuminating flash of lightning, and on the crest of the next ridge was a man on horseback, brilliantly silhouetted against the eeriness of the dusky light. He looked majestic, ethereal, reminding her of a painting she had once seen of a single cowboy riding watch over his herd in the ghostly light of a full moon.

Madison knew she'd find him! She didn't know how she knew, but it was as if it were written on her soul. Poor Colt; what he must be going through right now! Did he really believe he was from another century? More importantly, did he really expect this storm to take him back?

"Colt!" she called through her cupped hands, her voice all but drowned out by nature's upheaval. "Collll-tonnn!" She tried again, louder this time, nudging Cinnabar into a faster trot. Madison thought she saw him turn but couldn't be sure. As they ascended the hill, a gust of wind whipped her hair into a frenzy. She frantically brushed it away, her other hand gripping the reins for dear life.

"No . . . ! Madison, go back!" She heard him shout, and there could be no mistaking the baritone velvet of that voice.

Didn't he know she couldn't make her horse turn around even if she wanted to? The animal was as mesmerized by Cinder as she was by his rider. The two animals brushed their muzzles together in greeting.

"Dammit, Madison, I told you to *go back!*" he growled in a blaze of temper. Jerking around to face her, his face was bathed in the luminescence of gray-blue light.

Madison gasped. She must have made a horrible mistake. This wasn't Colt! But he had called her by name. . . .

For what seemed an eternity, unable to speak, she stared into his dark, scowling features. Gone were the furrows and creases along his cheeks and eyes; his skin now was smooth and firm. As if chiseled from granite, the lines of his jaw were straight and square. His brows were heavy over that smoky, intense gaze. Damp strands of sun-lightened chestnut hair blew across his cheek, floating in the wind. Madison shuddered. This was possibly the handsomest man she had ever seen in her life.

The storm continued on in a heedless frenzy around them, as if they were alone, suspended in time. The air hung heavy between them, charged, an electric vibration humming in her ears.

"Colt . . . ?" Her voice was barely an audible squeak, her eyes wide.

"Do you understand English? *I said* I don't want you here!" he grit out between clenched teeth, pointing a gloved finger to enunciate each word as if she were a child. Cinder pranced impatiently.

The scathing words jolted her. Madison bit back a sarcastic reply, persuading herself that despite his appearance, this was a deranged man, consumed within a fantasy world he believed to be real.

"Come back to town with me. The lightning . . . you'll be struck for sure on this hill! Please! Listen to me. . . ."

"Don't worry about me. Just take care of yourself."

Colt forced himself to say those words to her. More than anything, he wanted to scoop her into his arms, sitting her on the gray
stallion in front of him, and take her back . . . home. He stared.
He wanted to memorize this vision, knowing he'd never see
her again. God, but she was beautiful—the dripping-wet golden
curls framing her heart-shaped face, the moisture beading over
her pouting lips, those fathomless aqua eyes, pleading with him.

An icy wind penetrated to her very bones and a shiver overtook
her, causing her teeth to chatter uncontrollably. His countenance
softening just a little, Colt reached over and tugged her jacket.

"Is this what you call a coat?" he asked incredulously. "You'll
catch your death. Here . . ." He removed a bundle from behind
his saddle and held it up for her.

Automatically, Madison extended her arms one at a time, slipping them into the fringed suede jacket. She closed her eyes with
relish, luxuriating in the heavenly warmth and musky aroma of
worn, comfortable leather . . . and him.

"Thank you."

Clutching the oversized coat close about her neck, her eyes
lifted demurely to his. Perplexed, she was still trying to understand
this visible change in him. Something deep down inside told her
it was Colt, something she couldn't put in words. The familiar
timbre of his voice, the way he sat astride Cinder, his clothes . . .
no doubt it was he. Even so, how could he be a young man
now, when last night he was practically prehistoric? Earlier this
afternoon he seemed somehow younger—yet older than he did
now. How was it possible? This man had regressed right before
her eyes.

Colt drew her from her thoughts with another rose, identical to
the first, holding it in front of her. His golden brown eyes spoke a
final farewell. Madison slowly raised her hand, taking it haltingly.
With that, he spurred the gray stallion into action and bolted down
into the valley below, vanishing beyond the whirling mist of rain
and clouds.

Cinnabar snorted, tossing her head forward and then back again,
dancing in an effort to break free. Unprepared for this sudden
change of events, the reins slipped free of Madison's cold, stiff
fingers. A yelp tore from her throat as the mare jerked forward,
lumbering downward—and she knew, in one cataclysmic second,
that she had lost all control.

"Ohhhh nooooo . . ."

Every sore muscle in her body tensed. She grappled to reestablish her hold, finally heaving back on the reins with a sobbing groan—but to no avail. Cinnabar was moving fast, ignoring the bit in her mouth.

Amid the turbulence of the lurching ride, Madison gathered the courage to open her eyes, quickly finding she was unable to see anything. The drizzle beat at her face. Thick fog obscured her vision. With a moan of desperation, she ducked as low as possible over Cinnabar's back, afraid of being knocked to the ground by low-hanging branches. Her hands ached. Her body was rudely jostled. A sick dizziness reeled within her head, causing her stomach to pitch.

The throb inside her head was becoming so extreme she thought surely it would burst with the pressure. A heavy blanket of electricity surrounded her, pulsing an eerie vibration. The friction escalated to a full-blown ringing, voices fading in and out, the harmony of a harp combined with her father's words of comfort, all so unbearably loud. . . .

"Sto-o-o-o-p-p!" she wailed at last, as much to the ringing as to her galloping horse. Wide-eyed, the mare skidded to a impetuous halt, catapulting the novice rider over its head and into the dense shrubbery with a sickening thud.

Chapter Ten

Colt slid wearily from the saddle. He stroked a tanned hand over the velvety muzzle of the gray. "Well, Cinder ol' boy, I think we made it." He felt nauseous but managed to keep the bile down. He was getting pretty good at this time travel thing, he mused.

His hands reaching toward the sky, he groaned with a satisfying stretch. The clouds were clearing, making way for a beautiful dusk. Then, sure his eyes were playing tricks, he stopped breathing, staring aghast at the red horse, the reins hanging loose as it nibbled at the grass beneath a tall pine not twenty feet away.

"Damn . . . !" he muttered, breaking into a run. How had Cinnabar gotten here? Unless, maybe it hadn't worked after all. Maybe he was still in the future! Or . . . my God, the horse could have somehow been sucked into the time warp. But if that was the case, where was Madison?

A soft moan from the other side of the tree answered his question. Colt hurried to the source and dropped to his knees beside her. Madison lay in a crumpled heap at the center of a hazelnut bush, a small amount of blood oozing from a cut on her forehead. Her eyes were closed and she rolled her head from side to side, mumbling incomprehensibly.

"Ohhh, sugar! What have I done to you? Don't try to talk; just lie still."

After pulling her free of the tangle of branches, Colt quickly shucked the slicker, tossing it aside. He removed his shirt and tore it into strips, blotting at a rivulet of blood that rolled down her cheek. He gently bound her wound with the remaining strips of cloth and secured them with a tidy knot. When he was finished he cradled her head in his lap, lightly caressing her cheek with his thumb.

Madison's eyes fluttered open, crossing when she tried to focus on the blurry face above. Colt . . . ? No! What was he doing in her bed, anyway? Her thoughts a disheveled mess, she tried to push herself up, but her battered body screamed in protest. Flopping back down, a garbled moan escaped from her lips.

Thinking she might have broken bones, Colt eased out from beneath her and lay her down cautiously. He began to examine the rest of her. With great care he slid his hands up and down her extremities, checking for any irregularities or signs of pain. It wasn't easy for him to ignore the soft, feminine curves, but he did his best. Satisfied that her limbs were intact, he spread his hands over her rib cage, gently and thoroughly examining her until her entire body was shaking. Puzzled, he jerked his head up to look at her face. She was laughing—a deep belly laugh.

"Stop! Please . . . you're killing me!" she moaned with a giggle, tossing her head.

Colt grinned, sighing with relief. It appeared she hadn't broken anything, but there was one thing he knew for sure—she was very ticklish. He leaned his face in close to hers. "Madison . . . talk to me, sugar."

"Ohhhhh . . . Colt," she breathed sexily, her lips curving into a slow smile, "what are you doing here? Whatever it is, don't stop . . . Colt . . ."

Her eyes closed, her lashes were dark smudges against her cheeks. He thought she must be dreaming or delirious—maybe both.

" . . . Kiss me . . ." she whispered.

His thick eyebrows shot up in amusement. "I will, sugar. I will, just as soon as you're feeling better." It would have pleased him much more if she had possessed all of her wits when she said that, but given their obvious plight, there would be plenty of time for that.

Madison opened her eyes. She concentrated on a patch of lavender snapdragons dangling over her shoulder, then upwards, slowly, aware of the fading daylight as it reflected into a weighty raindrop suspended perilously from the tip of a pine needle. Her hand instinctively moved to touch her aching head.

"My head hurts—what happened? Jeez, my *whole body* hurts." She groaned, laboriously pushing herself up with Colt's help. Her head was swimming. "I think I'm gonna . . . throw up."

Rolling to her hands and knees, she rapidly crawled away, relieving her sick stomach near the first handy bush. Done, she leaned back on her heels to gaze thoughtfully at the pink glow behind the mountainous horizon. Her memory a paralyzed collection of splintered fragments, it took a moment to gather her senses.

"Feel better now?"

The velvet voice was a reminder of his presence.

"Yeah . . . all except for this." She rubbed the makeshift bandage, wincing. "Guess I'm wearing your shirt on my head, huh?" Madison's gaze flitted sheepishly over his naked chest, and she tried not to gawk.

Colt got to his feet, an odd expression playing over his features. He stood at the edge of the clearing with his back to her, his fingers shoved into his pockets. It was evident something grievous weighed on his mind.

"You took a pretty good blow to the head. Do you remember anything about what happened?" he called back over his shoulder.

Madison heard the words, but her mind took an alternate route. Leisurely, her gaze, traveling over the length of chestnut hair spread over his brawny shoulders, skimmed lower to the hard leanness of his waist. She admired his slim hips, his powerful thighs, as he shifted his weight to one leg. His back was perfectly smooth, unblemished, except for three symmetrical scars running down the middle, slightly paler than the rest of his tawny skin. "Old Bones . . ." she mumbled, snapping her jaw quickly shut when he swiveled around and came toward her, then on past to retrieve his canteen.

He stood before her, offering a drink from the canteen. Madison was allowed the luxury of gaping unabashedly at his back; now she longed for the liberty of doing the same to his front. His gaze bore down on her. Suddenly feeling very shy, she brought her eyes to his, sighing. My God, she thought, struggling to swallow the dry lump in her throat. Seemingly of their own accord, her fingers slid numbly around the leather canteen. She took a sip of the cool water and handed it back. "Thank you."

He smiled.

If ever there was a question as to what a Greek god might look like, the answer stood right before her. Light-colored hair trailed over his well-formed pectoral muscles, extending downward over his flat stomach and disappearing in a thin line beneath his denims. Long gone were any recollections of the old man who used to be. Madison absorbed all that was right now, every detail of his face. His nose was crooked, slightly bent—probably from a break, but it did lend him a certain charm. His cheekbones were high and his brows straight and heavy over his beguiling golden brown gaze. His mouth was perfectly sculptured, and when he smiled lopsidedly, his entire face lit up, a dimple appearing on his right cheek. He probably hadn't shaved since that morning, for there was a slight stubble on his cheeks.

Colt tilted his head back, taking a long draught from the canteen. She watched a single drop of water course down over his jaw, where he caught it with his forearm. He snapped his fingers in front of her face.

"Are you sure you're all right?" he said, lowering to one knee.

"Hmmmmm?" Yanked unwillingly back into reality, Madison flushed, certain he knew what she was thinking. " . . . Sorry, just not myself yet, I guess. . . ."

"Do you remember what happened?" he repeated the question.

"Only that I came to find you. I was worried about the storm. It seems like a faraway dream, now. I lost control of the damn horse. The same horse *you* said was gentle, by the way."

The old man seemed light years away; she was having trouble connecting the two.

Colt smiled again. "She is gentle; she just got spooked by the storm, I reckon."

"So now that I'm half-dead, are you willing to forget about going back to 'your time,' and come back to town with me? I've got a plane to catch."

"Madison . . ."

"Don't interrupt," she insisted. "There's nothing to be ashamed of; you're just a little confused is all. It happens to the best of us. I'll—"

"Madison . . ."

"What?" She sighed impatiently.

"We *are* in my time . . . the year is 1878. At least I hope it is. I know this is hard to digest, but you're going to have to trust me on this one."

"Trust . . . you? You, the man who keeps transforming his appearance?" She vented an ironic laugh.

"C'mon." He surprised her by grabbing her arm, pulling her to her feet, and leading her toward a rise. "Look over there, through those trees. What do you see?"

"Nothing. A meadow. So what?"

"Exactly. That's where Jackson is, or should I say *will* be—in a hundred years or so. It's getting dark. You should be able to at least see the bright lights sparkling in the distance, don't you think?" He studied her reaction closely.

It was true; rolling hills butting up to the overwhelming Teton Range were all she saw. Of course, it was dusk and hard to see anything at all . . . but he was right; where were the lights? She pried his fingers from her arm and began walking in stiff determination toward her horse.

"As much as I hate to get back on that lovely horse over there, I'm going to, and I'm riding back to town. It's got to be out there somewhere. You coming?" She hobbled up to Cinnabar and, despite the pain, managed to pull herself into the saddle with a lengthy groan.

Colt wasn't far behind her. "I can't let you ride out alone. This is certainly no place for a woman at night."

"Then come with me." She stared down at him in all seriousness.

"Come back to the ranch with me. I'll have to sneak you in the house. I'm in no mood to explain a woman to Rosie and Garrett tonight. That can wait until tomorrow. You'll have a warm bed and we'll figure this mess out tomorrow. Deal?"

Surely he didn't mean *the* Garrett who was supposed to have been hanged for cattle rustling! Who was Rosie? And could he possibly be referring to the dilapidated ranch house he had taken her to earlier? Surely not—it was absurd, unless he was a lot farther gone than she had originally thought.

"A warm bed, huh?" she asked in a tone laced with sarcasm. Madison shook her head. "Well, I have to admit, that's a new one. I've never been seduced with that approach before."

"Don't flatter yourself too much; you may be disappointed."

With long, deliberate strides, he went to his horse and jerked another shirt free from the roll behind the saddle. He threw it on, then, gathering the slicker that still lay in a heap, rolled it tightly and secured it behind the cantle. Madison watched in puzzlement as he grasped Cinnabar's reins, mounted Cinder, and began to lead them from the valley—and away from town.

"Hey! Wait just a minute! There's a real good chance I'm going to miss my plane as it is." Madison moved the cumbersome sleeve of her jacket away from her watch, frowning when she discovered it had stopped, the time still reading 7:05. It had to be at least 8:00 or 8:30 by now. "You've got no right to do this to me, I was just trying to help you," she ranted.

"For one thing, sugar, this plane you keep referring to . . . I seriously doubt you're going to find one in 1878. Secondly, you're in no condition to be wandering around the countryside trying to analyze the philosophy of life tonight. Get my meaning? You need some doctoring. Let's get you to feeling better, then we'll have this conversation."

Madison was seething, but when she attempted to give him a piece of her mind, a horrendous pain shot through her head, from one temple to the other. Whimpering, she grabbed her head, almost losing her balance with the onset of dizziness. Colt was at her side in a flash.

"Let's go," he commanded, securing her arms around his neck and lifting her down. "You're riding with me."

Words of protest wouldn't come, the pain consuming all of what energy she had left. Effortlessly, he lifted her onto the stallion's back and positioned himself behind her. A strong, bracing arm slid around her waist, his other hand taking Cinnabar's reins, pulling the horse behind them. Colt's body was her cushion of cozy warmth. She hadn't realized until now just how cold she was. A murky fog blanketed her senses, choking the objections that popped randomly into her head. Despite herself, Madison eventually relaxed, letting her weight press into him, her head leaning back against his sturdy shoulder. She was so very tired. . . .

Colt, however, was feeling anything but relaxed. The pressure of her shapely backside against his loins, combined with the rolling gait of the horse, were almost too much to bear. The sweet fragrance of her damp hair, the swell of her full breast brushing next to his arm were like good whiskey—intoxicating and *very* addictive.

The horses slowly plodded around the corner of the ranch house, circling to stop close by the kitchen door. The windows were dark except for a dim light in the study. Good, Colt thought. It looked as if most everyone had retired for the evening. That would make it easier to get Madison inside the house and upstairs to the guest room without being seen.

It was sheer luck that they had gotten this far without being spotted by one of the line riders. He made a mental note to speak to Bud about that tomorrow; nobody should gain access to the house without being seen and checked out first.

Colt had caught himself holding his breath several times as they neared their destination, fearing a recurrence of his worst nightmare: arriving at the main house and finding it in the same crumbling condition as he had in the future.

But it was just as he had left it and home had never looked so good. In spite of the impressive advancements in 1993, he much preferred to remain right where he was, in his own time. But there was one good thing he had gained from his journey, and she was sitting asleep in front of him. Madison was just the affirmation he had needed to prove to himself that he wasn't crazy, somehow imagining the entire episode. Though she was here through no fault of his, Colt was apprehensive about her reaction once she was fully rested and feeling like herself again.

Another concern gnawed at his gut, too. How was he going to explain her presence?

Chapter Eleven

A cheery spray of midday sunlight filtered through white lacy curtains, forming intricate little patterns that danced over the blue-and-gold-flowered wallpaper. Curtains puffed from the warm breeze that filled the room with the fresh, sweet scent of green grass, hay, lilacs, and . . . and horse manure?

Madison wrinkled her nose, her prone form cozily tucked beneath a frayed patchwork quilt that covered a feather tick mattress. Her eyes shifted around the tiny room. Furiously, she tried to recall exactly where she was, her memory nothing but a befuddled mess.

The heavy brass bed took up a good part of the room. To her right was a simple oak washstand, a fresh display of linen neatly folded over the top rung and an ironstone bowl and pitcher occupying the top. Along the far wall was a matching kneehole dressing table and a deep red velvet upholstered seat. To her left was a shiny black Singer sewing machine in a lovely dark stained-oak cabinet, its condition absolutely perfect. With a sigh of appreciation, Madison pushed herself up to a sitting position to get a closer look, only to have the room begin a maddening spin around her. Her hand flew to the source of the painful throb, brushing over the gauzy bandage in surprise.

"Good Lord, where am I?" she mumbled to herself. "And what happened to my head?"

Glancing down, she noticed that she wore a full-length, thin white cotton gown; a garment she knew she didn't own. Just then, footsteps sounded from the hall, followed by a soft knock on her door. In last-minute desperation she grappled to collect her thoughts—to remember something, anything at all! She opened her mouth to speak, but nothing came out.

The knob rotated and the door swung gently open. In stepped a very short round woman. Her hair was black, with strands of silver intermixed, braided and coiled into a chignon at her nape. Her kindly raven eyes grew wide in pleasant surprise to see that Madison sat up in bed, soft crinkles feathering at the corners of them when she smiled brightly. The woman wore an ankle-length brown gathered skirt and a white blouse that buttoned up to her neck. A yellow bib apron was tied neatly around her chunky waist.

"Madison, dear, you're awake!" she gasped. "I heard about that nasty fall you took. How are you feeling?" The woman moved to the bedside, reaching out to adjust the bandage in a caring and motherly fashion.

"I'm not too sure," Madison answered truthfully. "Where am I?"

"Well, now, isn't that terribly rude of me, dear! I'm so sorry. . . . I'm Rosannah." She fiddled with a lock of Madison's hair, gently running her fingers through the tangles as she spoke. "I've been with the Chase family practically since the dawn of time." She chuckled. "Indeed, I assisted Colt's ma when he came into this world. Oh, and that there is my daughter, Emmy—Emmy, get in here and introduce yourself proper!" Rosannah energetically waved at the slight figure hovering in the doorway.

A thin girl bashfully slid inside the room, her hands positioned behind her as she leaned against the safety of the wall. She was a full head taller than her mother, and her light brown hair was also parted down the middle and pulled back into the same sort of tight knot. Her round hazel eyes scrutinized Madison carefully. She gave a curt nod in acknowledgment, her smile obligatory.

Madison responded warmly even though she couldn't help but feel this young girl who appeared to be in her mid-teens, harbored some sort of resentment—whether it was directed toward her, she wasn't sure.

"Now, Madison." Rosannah stood at the washstand, dipping a cloth into the water she poured from the pitcher. She came to the bed and bathed Madison's face and smoothed her hair.

"You're home now—one of the family. Emmy and I are here to help with whatever you may need. Bud, Garrett, and I are more grateful than you know. You've brought our Colt home to stay. He's a good man, Madison. Of course, I'm sure you know that. If you're wondering where he's off to, he's been out on the range since dawn. 'Spect him back anytime now."

Madison gave the little round woman an inane look. How did she know Madison's name and what in the world was she talking about? So far, Colt's name was the only one she recognized. The last thing she remembered was the picnic—was that yesterday? The ride into the mountains, then down to his ranch . . . no wait, later, much later she had ridden into that rainstorm to find him. She bought a horse—where was her horse?

Disjointed images flitted through her mind in rapid spurts, none making much sense. A sensuous kiss, amazing golden brown eyes, and a face sprung into her mind. Unable to grasp the full depth of its features, she frowned, looking down at her hands laying across her lap.

Madison touched the bodice of her gown, "Where . . . I mean, who . . ."

Rosannah gave her a knowing smile. "Emmy and I undressed you early this morning. Your old clothes will be laundered. Why ever a pretty young thing like you was wearing men's clothes is beyond me . . . but I'm sure that's your business, not mine." Rosannah prattled on as she busied herself about the cozy room. Opening a cedar trunk at the foot of the bed, she dug through its contents, removing a stack of clothing. Her head popped above the lid just as it slammed shut with a loud thud.

"Colt didn't bother to explain why you didn't bring any other clothes with you. Maybe this happening was as much a surprise to you two kids as it was to us! In any case, there's plenty of extra clothing in this trunk to get you by, and more besides, should you need it. If you feel up to a bath, I'll have one brought up right away. We'll get you moved into Colt's room before dinner—"

Enough time had lapsed since Rosannah first entered to allow Madison to rid her mind of the lingering cobwebs. Well, at least she now knew that Colt had told this woman who Madison was, but that last sentence hung in the air like a foul stench. She broke in, "I'm sorry, Rosannah, I still don't quite understand. Colt's room, did you say? I won't be staying. I do need to call my brother, though, if I could use your phone. He'll be terribly worried by this time."

Rosannah positioned her hands over her fleshy hips, a pitiful expression spreading over her face. "Sweetie, I understand your shyness, believe me I do . . . but it's best to get it over with. Once you do, there's no place you'd rather be than with your husband."

"My husband?" Madison questioned, more baffled than ever. How in the world did this woman know about Jon? And what was it she needed to get over with?

Rosannah's smile did little to comfort her as she dolefully glanced at Emmy, then back.

"I really do need to get home," Madison continued, her voice trailing off to nothing, then added, " . . . when could I speak to Colt?"

In a crush of dawning realization, the memory of gravestones creeped into Madison's head. The names . . . Rosannah, Emmy, there was even a Bud . . . and she remembered how Colt spoke of them later on. . . . Oh, how she needed a familiar face right now!

"What you need is more rest. That knock on your head is going to cause a world of grief if you don't take care of yourself. I applied a fresh poultice before you woke." Rosannah touched Madison's cheek affectionately, "You're such a pretty thing—Colt is a lucky man."

"Really, I don't want to rest, I feel fine."

Madison flipped the covers back to demonstrate, swiveling her legs over the edge of the bed. Ignoring the intensifying throb in her temples, she stretched her toes until they touched the rag rug, forcing herself to stand up. Dizzy at first, she hesitated, then turned. "See? Everything's fine. I think I'll take you up on that bath, but then I'll need to find Colt."

Rosannah smiled helplessly, shrugging. "Emmy, run and get Zak to bring up the tub."

Emmy obediently slid away, just as silently as she had entered.

Rosannah rested benevolent eyes on Madison. "I'm sure Colt will check on you when he returns for the noon meal. I'll keep some food warm for you, dear."

"Bring up the tub . . . ? I'm afraid I don't understand." Madison fully expected Rosannah to begin laughing in jest.

"Why, yes. There's much more privacy up here for a lady. You wouldn't want to have your bath downstairs. I've laid out your clothes, and the pot is down at the foot of the bed. Everything here is yours, so please make yourself at home. If you need anything, just let Emmy or me know."

Rosannah squeezed Madison's hand warmly before she left the room in a swirl of skirts, closing the door softly.

Madison didn't waste any time. Her body a cluster of aches and pains, she gingerly crossed the cool floorboards toward the half-open window. Holding the sheer curtains apart, she devoured the scene below. Familiar, but she wasn't quite able to place it. A full-blown and bustling cattle ranch was laid out before her, as far as she could see in any direction. Rolling green grasslands, mottled with sagebrush and pine-veiled foothills, completed the vista. Dozens of barns and other structures were strategically scattered along the far landscape—hundreds of cattle leisurely grazed along the open range. A swollen brook happily bubbled its way around the house, a mixture of saplings systematically planted along its banks.

A horses's nickering drew her attention directly below her window, where half a dozen men, some standing and some on horseback, talked and laughed among themselves. A pair of horses were hitched to an old-fashioned buggy, their tails swishing at the flies in what seemed a choreographed rhythm. The men were all dressed cowboy-style, with hats, except for the man in the buggy. He wore a black frock coat and trousers, a white shirt, black string tie, and a derby.

In a quandary, Madison regarded the cowboys again. A group of dusty, trail-worn characters, she noticed they all wore guns in holsters at their hips, except for one who stood out from the others. Rich brown hair hung long beneath his hat. Broader in the shoulders and more strapping than the rest, he exuded an air of authority and self-assurance. He stood in conversation with a coffee cup in his hand. Something was said, and they all broke out into loud guffaws.

At the same moment a loud commotion came from the hallway, followed by a brisk rapping at her door. Hastily, Madison wrenched the quilt from the bed and wrapped it around her lightly clad form.

"Come in."

The knob turned and the door was shoved open with a boot, revealing a tall, gangly cowboy bearing a big copper tub. None too gently, it was dropped with a clatter at the corner of the bed. Clearly embarrassed, the cowboy averted his gaze, refusing to make eye contact with her. As he hurriedly exited the room, two more dusty cowboys tramped in, lugging two buckets of steaming water apiece. When those two left the first was back again with two buckets. Rooted to her spot by the window, Madison watched, dumbstruck, as the men paraded in and out of the room, carrying the water.

Finally, the last cowboy left, tipping his hat and muttering, "Ma'am."

Madison pressed her palm to her sore head, staring as the steam rose from the quaint old tub. "I don't believe this." She smiled in disbelief, slowly shaking her head, convinced that some sort of enormous joke was being orchestrated at her expense. Who was responsible for this? Colt? Whoever it was, they were good—everything was so authentic! Maybe it was Mark. It would be just like him to pull something like this, knowing her love of history. Better yet, it was probably Mark and Colt together.

These thoughts rattled around in her head in no particular order. She dropped the quilt and slipped the gown from her shoulders. A bar of lavender-scented soap was next to the bowl and pitcher; she snatched it up, along with her shoulderbag, which sat at the edge of the dressing table. Dumping the contents on the bed, she rummaged through the cluttered pile in search of something she might use for her toilette. She fished out a miniature bottle of shampoo, her toothbrush, a tube of mascara and some blush, her comb, and a lipstick.

Setting them aside, she lowered herself into the welcoming warmth of the water. This was exactly what her aching muscles needed, she thought, leaning back against the cushioned headrest. Careful to avoid soaking the fresh bandage, Madison ducked far enough down to wet her hair for a quick shampoo. Then she worked the bar of soap between her palms to create a billowy lather, smoothing it over her face and body.

As she bathed, she worried anxiously over the chain of events that had led her here. Though she tried, the details eluded her. Exactly how had she injured her head? She recalled embarking on a search for Colt. Had she found him? She *thought* she had, as she vaguely remembered an argument with somebody. Had it been with him?

With a drawn-out sigh, she pushed herself up and stepped from the tub. She pulled a flannel cloth from the washstand and wrapped it around herself, then gazed despondently at her reflection in the beveled mirror above the dressing table. Her face was a mess. The purplish bruise on her forehead extended past the whiteness of the bandage, her pallor a ghostly gray. Picking up the comb, she tugged at the snarls in her hair, desperately wishing she had brought some conditioner.

Madison felt as though she was dressing for a masquerade when she began to put on the clothes Rosannah had left for her. First, she drew on a pair of black silky stockings, followed by a volumous pair of white pantalettes and a thin white cotton chemise. She held up a long white underskirt with eyelet lace trim around the flounced hem. Positive it would be too hot, she hesitated, finally deciding to put it on anyway. Next, she dangled a boned silk and ribbon corset between two fingers. "They've got to be kidding," she murmured, shaking her head skeptically.

The corset was tossed back into the trunk before she donned the dress. It was a little worn but was made from the loveliest material: a soft blue calico with tiny pink buds. Delicate white lace was sewn into the seams that ran parallel down each side of the bodice, then extending to a deep *V* at the front. A line of tiny pearlized buttons started at the high neck and ran to the waist. The gathered skirt fell to her ankles, a modest bustle decorating the back.

Dressed, she once again surveyed her appearance in the mirror, this time with approval. Everything seemed to have been made for her. Considering the era of the clothing, she looked rather good. Even without the corset her waist was amazingly trim, and an expression of self-satisfaction crossed her face.

Ever curious, Madison began to inventory the interesting items that lined the top of the dressing table. At one side was a rawhide-and-leather storage box with a red flannel inset and lined in blue velvet. There were two matching heart-shaped porcelain boxes with tiny handpainted little girls on each. A silver repousse dresser set, a button hook, a nail file, and a letter opener were arranged next to that. On the wall next to the mirror hung a hand-made cross made from tin and blue glass.

Once her hair was mostly dry, she arranged it into a loose knot with a ribbon and some hairpins she found in her purse, bringing a few wispy tendrils out around her face. She brushed her teeth as well as she could without toothpaste and then applied a little makeup.

Looking down at her stocking feet, Madison realized she still lacked shoes. On the corner of the bed lay a pair of soft black leather high-heeled ankle boots. Incredibly small, it would be a futile effort even to try to fit her size 8s in those shoes. The boots she had worn yesterday stood neatly in the corner, but they certainly wouldn't work with a dress. Madison decided to forget the shoes for the time being.

At last she began to rake the scattered items from the bed back into her purse, when she noticed the marbled rosebud. The black edges she remembered were gone. It now looked as fresh as a newly picked rose, its petals firm and moist. Nonplussed at the flower's apparent immortality, she touched it to her nose, breathing in the heady scent before placing it carefully on the dresser.

The sweet scent triggered an anarchy of impetuous memories; the shadowed face of a young man, a wicked storm, an old cowboy whom she knew to be Colt, the rose . . . How were they connected? Was Colt Chase even real, or had she dreamt the entire episode? Her jaw set, she was determined to find the answers to all that plagued her. It was now or never. With a preparatory sigh she headed for the door, a sense of excitement gripping her.

Madison quietly tiptoed down a winding staircase that was protected by a floral runner in tones of burgundy and gold. Everything was unnaturally quiet; not a soul was in sight. The rhythmic ticking of a cherry wood Shaker tall clock echoed throughout a myriad of small rooms. Her eyes feasted upon the richness of the decor; how she would love the chance to explore at her leisure! Madison stepped inside the hallowed silence of the parlor. A maroon velvet upholstered sofa was flush against one entire wall, the wide-paned window above it screened with ivory lace curtains and the walls lined with books. Just like walking into the past, she mused with irony.

As she turned to leave, a papier-mâché table with a marble top caught her eye, and she moved in for a closer look. Atop it was a massive Bible, red with ornate Victorian tooling; next to it was a small, brown-toned picture in a gilded oval frame. Madison carefully picked it up, running her fingertip over the cool glass. Her heart began to thump almost painfully, feeling as though it were being crushed. She had seen this picture before! It was the same as the one in the little paperback history book she had gotten at the hotel. No doubt, this was a picture of Colton and Garrett Chase. To her annoyance, her hand trembled when she set it back down. She scoffed at herself for spooking so easily, deciding she needed to lighten up and have some fun with this charade.

There was a low rumble of baritone laughter. Madison jerked her gaze toward the double doorway at the far end of the dimly lit hallway. Conscious of the unfamiliar feeling of swirling skirts around her legs, she ventured toward the voices. Inching closer to the open doorway, she paused, peering around the corner with extreme caution lest she be seen.

It appeared to be the same group of men she had seen from her window, shrouded within a cloud of cigar smoke. Not wanting to be noticed yet, she stepped back, pivoting to leave.

"Madison!"

She stopped cold at the unmistakably timbered voice. It was like liquid velvet to her ears. Colt. Spinning around, she flushed hot when she saw that every eye in the room rested on her. The noisy conversation abated, and she fervently wished for a convenient hole in which to crawl. Normally a roomful of people didn't faze her, but today wasn't exactly normal.

A man rose from a leather chair behind the imposing mahogany desk. His features were unclear in the smoky haze. He didn't hesitate to excuse his way through the congestion to get to her. Colt? No, it couldn't be; this man was far too young—but there was a remarkable resemblance. No, an uncanny resemblance. To whom? . . . the Colt she knew or the picture? Ohhhh, it was all so confusing! Her head was beginning to pound again.

He was rakishly handsome, a few strands of hair hanging over his forehead, the tan shirt fitting exquisitely over his finely muscled torso. As he neared, a golden brown gaze swept over her appreciatively. She shivered. His lips parted as if he was going to say something monumental. Those eyes—Colt's eyes!

Madison's heart pumped furiously as he approached, his arm encircling her shoulders protectively. He pressed her close to his side. Stunned at the intimacy he displayed, she discreetly tried to move away. His embrace only tightened.

"Madison," his voice was gentle but firm, "I'd like you to meet some friends and business associates of mine."

She looked up at him with the intention of speaking, but something in his forbidding expression made her think twice. He went around the room with his introductions, Madison obediently smiling at the cluster of rough-looking cowboys and then the man in the black frock coat.

" . . . and this ornery character over here is our foreman, Bud," Colt continued.

Madison nodded politely at the pleasant-faced cowboy with thinning white hair and ice-blue eyes.

" . . . my brother, Garrett . . ." Colt added.

Garrett bit the end off a cheroot, spitting it into the corner, while openly appraising Madison with black, solemn eyes. He was a pudgy sort, dark complected with black hair. He didn't smile, his cold stare sending an unwelcome chill up Madison's spine. All the men rose from their chairs, politely expressing individual greetings—that is, except for Garrett.

Madison couldn't help but glance up into his face, this man who held her so familiarly, sure this was all an elaborate joke. So he was supposed to be Colt? And that was Garrett? She would have to be insane to fall for any of this!

But before Madison could gather her wits to utter a single word to the man who gazed down at her so seriously, he continued, "Gentlemen, I'd like for you to meet . . . my wife, Madison."

Chapter Twelve

Her aqua eyes widened in disbelief as her jaw fell open. "What . . . ?"

Colt whisked Madison down the hallway before she could complete the sentence, but not before making a brief excuse to the roomful of men about her feeling a trifle under the weather. With a firm grip to her upper arm, he quickly ushered her into the privacy of the empty kitchen, as a stream of enraged demands spilled from her mouth.

"Why in the *hell* did you say *that?* What is going on here, anyway? You told those men I was your *wife?* C'mon, I'm no idiot, where is Colt? I demand to see him, *now!*"

Colt stopped, spinning her around to face him. His fingers dug into the fleshy part of her shoulders and he leveled his gaze with hers.

"I don't believe this! Let me go, dammit!" Madison shrieked, struggling ferociously against his hold.

"Keep your voice down; everyone will hear!" he whispered harshly.

"Maybe everyone should hear!" She deliberately raised her tone a notch, "You have no right to touch me—let me go!"

"If you will just listen, I can explain everything." His patience was wearing treacherously thin.

"Look, I'm forced to put on nineteenth-century clothing, my

head feels like its been run over by a truck, and now you announce that I'm your wife?" she hissed, her fists clenched rigidly at her sides, her chest heaving with every angry breath.

"Madison, calm down—"

"I'm not—"

Colt's mouth came recklessly down on hers with the initial intention of silencing her. His powerful arms crushed her body to his in order to restrain her increasingly wild struggles.

Her eyes open wide with shock, Madison pushed vehemently at his hard chest with open palms—with no consequence. She then tried to scream against his mouth, but his embrace only tightened, becoming more painful.

His soft, pliant lips were all too familiar, and Madison's body seemed instinctively to know what her mind and eyes refused to admit. Her head reeled with the masculine scent of shaving soap and leather, the taste of his mouth. The stormy tension in her body liquified, dripping down to her toes, evaporating.

Colt sensed the change in her, feeling the truth radiating from deep within her heart. His mouth began to move sensuously over hers. Madison's arms hesitantly creeped up, coiling about his neck, her slender fingers toying with the long strands of his chestnut hair. He groaned, gently nipping at the fullness of her lower lip with his teeth. His hands moved over her back, caressing upwards to cradle her head as his mouth slanted over hers with a new softness. His tongue teased and she responded in kind, a breathy moan of pleasure sounding from deep within her.

Madison's honest arousal nearly drove Colt to the limits of his endurance, and irritation gave way to an insatiable desire. His hands slid lower, stroking her in slow circles until he gently grasped her firm, ripe backside, bringing the softness of her body against the hardness of his.

She was lifted with the demanding pressure, until only the tips of her toes brushed the cool floorboards. Enveloped in a sensual loftiness, she was aware of only the deliciously searching kisses trailing across from her mouth to her cheek, her jaw, then wetly along the length of her throat. Her eyes closed, Madison leaned her head back, succumbing to a swirling vortex of emotion.

Colt broke free from their embrace at the very same instant the chimes sounded from the tall clock in the parlor, the resonating tones bouncing through the twisting corridors.

The spell rudely broken, Madison stumbled back, mortified at her own behavior. Colt's hand remained at her elbow to steady her. She jerked it free, acutely embarrassed that it had been he who had put an end to a kiss that should never have happened in the first place.

Clamoring for a shred of sensibility, her first impulse was to slap the living daylights out of him. Even as she thought it, her hand rose, only to be stopped in midair, mere inches from his face. Colt's fingers locked tightly around her wrist in a steady grip.

"Don't be a hypocrite, Madison—you enjoyed it as much as I did," he drawled.

Angry, her cheeks burned as she frantically searched for a derisive remark. It was frustrating enough that he was right, but she wasn't going to let him worsen matters by forcing her to admit it. Her eyes narrowed and her chest heaved in indignation.

Footsteps on the back porch stopped Madison's reply, causing them both to jerk around to face the opening door. In scurried Rosannah, slapping two plucked chickens onto the countertop, the screen door slamming shut loudly. Colt immediately released Madison's wrist—but she wasn't free. He wove his fingers lovingly through hers and brought her hand down securely at his side. Though she squirmed to escape, he was just too strong and wasn't about to let her go.

"Oh! I didn't know you kids were in here. Madison, how are you feeling, dear?" Rosannah's lilting voice was bright and cheery as she glanced at them.

A deluge of responses instantly filled Madison's head. *This man just attacked me! I'm not anybody's wife, let alone* his! *Please, help me go home!*

"Madison is feeling much better, though she's gone and worn herself out by coming downstairs. I think it would be best if she lay down for a while, don't you, sugar?" Colt took the liberty of answering for her, squeezing her hand steadily as he gazed down at her through heavy-lidded eyes.

Madison delivered a scathing look, biting back the response that clawed to get out. The fury was building up inside her nearly to the point of explosion. Yet it wasn't right to drag Rosannah into this mess—whatever was going on, she was sure it was no one's fault except for this impudent stud who stood by her side.

"Wouldn't you like something to eat? You must be fairly starved." Rosannah frowned with concern. She wiped her hands along her apron and then retrieved the butcher knife to begin hacking at the chickens.

"Er . . . I . . . I think I'll just get something a little later. I appreciate the thought, Rosannah."

Oh, why was she letting this man intimidate her? Colt was the recipient of her murderous glance.

"Take care of her, Colt. That bump on her head worries me, you know," Rosannah said.

"Don't fret, Rosie. I guard this little lady with my life."

Colt shot a deep scowl right back at Madison before leading her stiff form from the kitchen and down the hallway, not stopping until they reached the foot of the stairs. He finally released her and she haughtily stood before him, arms akimbo.

"You've got some heavy-duty explaining to do, mister! No, on second thought, I don't care what you have to say, or who you are. Thanks for the hospitality, but this is a looney bin and I'm getting the hell out of here!" With that, she dismissed him by swiveling around to lift her stockinged foot to the first step. He stopped her by placing a hand on her shoulder.

"My room is right next to yours. Meet me there in ten minutes; we need to talk. But first I need to conclude my business with these gentlemen."

She watched over her shoulder as he disappeared down the hallway, his spurs jangling in the quietness. That walk. Those eyes. *That heady kiss*—it was Colt! But how could that possibly be? Was she indeed losing her mind? Colt was an *old* man!

Grabbing her skirts, Madison briskly marched up the stairs, intending to grab her purse and leave. Did he really expect her to be waiting when he came upstairs? She wasn't even going to hang around long enough to get her own clothes back. All she had to do was find Cinnabar—and she would be gone.

At the top of the landing Madison turned to her right, slowing when she arrived at the specified doorway. The door was slightly ajar. Curiosity gnawed at her, for she could just imagine what antique treasures might lie beyond that door. What harm would it do just to take a quick peek? Five minutes at the most . . . plenty of time to hightail it out of there before he arrived.

She touched the thick crystal doorknob and gave a little shove, the door creaking as it swung open. Reluctant, she stepped inside. Madison was immediately taken with the masculine coziness of the room, at least three times the size of hers. A mammoth mahogany bed with eight-foot columns occupied the far wall, its canopy adorned with homemade evergreen-colored cotton hangings. A deep burgundy-and-evergreen-plaid comforter was spread smoothly over the bed and decorated with several needlepoint pillows.

Opposite was a rock fireplace, only slightly smaller than the one she had glimpsed downstairs. Catty-cornered across from it was an early-Victorian-style armoire in mahogany; a matching wig dresser stood next to that. The darkly stained hardwood floors were scattered with hook rugs, the largest laid out before the neatly curtained French doors. Walking over to look outside, she saw that the doors led to a wide verandah that overlooked a generous sweep of the ranch.

She turned back to the hearth, running her fingers over the smooth deep green leather of a well-worn easy chair. There were sparsely scattered personal effects: a chocolate brown Stetson hung on a peg by the door, a holster and gun next to it. As she slowly passed the washstand, the scent of shaving soap assaulted her already battered senses, causing her heartbeat to quicken.

Just as Madison approached the door to leave, to her horror she spotted her very own purse and boots placed neatly over a black domed trunk! She was astounded that her belongings had been switched to this room so quickly. Hurriedly, she seized them to her chest and twirled to bolt from the room.

With a breathy gasp of astonishment, Madison found herself nose to shoulder with *him*.

Chapter Thirteen

"I'm sorry if I startled you. Leaving so soon?" Colt's gaze dipped to the items cradled in her arms.

"Of course," she replied tightly. "Surely you don't expect me to hang around." Absently, she backed up a few steps to put some distance between them.

"Once you hear what I have to say, you may change your mind."

His voice was smooth and controlled, irritating Madison. He gave the door a shove and it clicked shut. He regarded her lazily as he rolled a sprig of hay between his strong white teeth. His thumbs hooked into his waistband, he took two steps toward her.

"Somehow I doubt that. But, since I'm here, why don't you say your piece so I can be on my way." Madison put her possessions down with a sigh of inconvenience, moving away from him again, this time pausing by the fireplace.

Colt followed, advancing ever closer.

"About this marriage situation. I'm sorry I shocked you that way in front of those men. I'm sure you were very uncomfortable. But it was necessary, and I feel I handled it the only way I could have at the time. The consequences if I hadn't made that excuse could be far worse."

He lifted his arm, bracing himself against the rocks just above her head. Those eyes bore into her, breaking down her composure. Madison ducked beneath his arms and again took flight, this time standing before the French doors. He was toying with her and she didn't like it, not one little bit.

"I *still* don't understand! Don't you see?" She waved her arms in exasperation. "You're supposed to be Colt, but you're not the Colton I know! *Where is he?*"

She felt stupid just saying it. Yes, this was Colt. She didn't know why he didn't look the same—why he was so young. The memory of a young face floated into her mind, a face hovering over her with concern etched into its features. Other memories of tender hands brushing her damp hair from her face, a voice of velvet asking if she was all right, a man ripping a shirt to shreds to bandage the wound on her head, flooded her mind. One and the same—Colton Chase.

"*I am* Colton Chase!" He jabbed a finger into his chest for emphasis as he approached her once again. "I am twenty-eight years old. The story I told you yesterday was the honest truth. I don't know why I appeared to be old in your time—"

"*My* time? Please, don't insult my intelligence!" In a twinkling, the information from the past two days came tumbling down over her in an avalanche of awareness. She must now deal with a man who claimed to have transcended the barriers of time. And the fact that he was an incredibly handsome man certainly didn't help matters any. A very close, irresistible man . . .

Madison tried to retreat again, but her heel bumped the french door. "Ouch," she whined, bending back to rub it, wondering which hurt worse, her head or her foot.

A smile played over Colt's lips. "Careful. I wouldn't be making you nervous, would I?" Amused, he knew he ought not to be teasing her like this, but she was just so damn cute—he couldn't resist.

"Don't be ridiculous. I just happen to think better when I walk, that's all." Trying not to act as flustered as she felt, she took flight again. Damn him for making her feel so helpless.

He caught her arm. "Well, stop it. You're making *me* nervous."

Releasing her, he plopped himself down into the plush green chair. He looked up at her with the enormous eyes of a mischievous little boy.

Madison felt silly, as if she didn't belong. How rude that he hadn't even offered the chair to her first! She folded her arms across her chest, shifted her weight to one foot, and began chewing her lip.

"You must realize none of this makes any sense. Let's forget how you managed to make yourself appear old—explain why you said I was your wife? What consequences could there possibly be?"

"What kind of man would I be to leave you alone in the mountains, an injured woman? But what was I to tell everyone in the household when I returned after an unexplained absence of two days with a gorgeous woman on my arm? You would have been looked down upon, no matter how clever a justification. Nothing would have overshadowed the fact that we were unmarried, traveling together, and staying in this house together. Regardless of where you slept or what the true circumstances were, people would talk. Once the hands got wind of the 'strange' woman I brought home, you would have been labeled a . . . well, a . . ."

"Slut?" Madison finished tiredly.

Colt laughed. A lopsided grin flashed across his face in a most charming way as he nodded in earnest. "Yes, exactly! You have such a colorful way with words. Now, as my 'wife' you're treated well, Rosie and Emmy are at your beck and call, and the cowhands will treat you with the utmost respect."

He seemed immensely pleased with himself and Madison hated to burst his bubble. It was too bad the circumstances weren't a little different—she thought she might like to get to know him a little better. He was the most fascinating person she'd ever met, despite his outlandish allegations. It was all for the best, she reasoned. The last thing she needed right now was another relationship.

"Okay . . . prove it was you I was with yesterday—and the night before." Madison was going to figure out this mystery if it was the last thing she ever did.

Colt nodded thoughtfully, his eyes circling the room in consideration. "Let me see. . . . It was you who approached me at the saloon; we shared a few laughs afterward, outside, beneath the stars. I invited you for a picnic the following morning, and you looked quite fetching when you answered the door in nothing but your dressing gown—I believe the color was pink. And the way your behind bounced in the saddle when Cinnabar got away from you. I liked that."

He paused for effect, enjoying the sudden flush in her cheeks. "I stopped you just in time before you picked a rose; I saw a tear in your eye at the cemetery; you tried to explode a tin of sarsaparilla in my face." Colt smiled at the memory.

"Coke . . ." Madison couldn't suppress the laugh. "It was Coke."

"And you explained the concept of people flying around in machines called airplanes; and when I kissed you, downstairs, by the fireplace, I could tell you were a very warm, open, and caring person." His voice lowered, his gaze smoldering.

Madison chewed a long fingernail. Then the fire rose to her cheeks and she went to stand by the small window at the other side of the room. She wasn't sure why, but she thought she might cry. The lump in her throat was working its way up, and she fought against it. A warm, caring person . . . Why couldn't a certain other person have seen that? Jon's unwelcome face popped into her mind, and she closed her eyes tightly to ward it off.

"You're very pretty when you blush." Colt pulled the sprig of hay from his mouth and tossed it into the fireplace, then moved to stand behind her. He suspected the truth was just now beginning to sink in—and he knew firsthand the helpless feeling that realization brought with it.

"Colt?" Madison wiped her eyes before she faced him.

"Yes?"

"Would you take me back to Jackson—right away?"

"You still don't comprehend the situation, do you?"

"What's there to comprehend?" she cried. "I just want to go home!"

"We'll never see each other again," he declared, much like he was handing down a death sentence. He'd only known her for two days, but to him, she represented everything good in life. In some fantastic way she filled a void that he hadn't even known existed. When she wasn't with him the summer breezes never smelled quite so sweet, the sunshine never so warm. . . . Suddenly, life without her seemed awfully bleak. Something inside told him not to let her go.

"I imagine that's true. Are you under the impression that there's some big romance going on here?" Madison pointed to herself and then to him, her expression incredulous. "I admit, there's a physical attraction, but I have no intention of entering into an affair right now. Besides, this is all just too . . . weird."

Colt brushed a stray curl that had fallen over her eye, the touch of his hand like an electrical charge coursing through her.

"Is that so?" Gazing on past her and out the window, his brow furrowed in deep concentration. "You were half in love with me before the end of the day yesterday."

A challenging gaze of smug confidence darted back to meet hers, infuriating her. "Why . . . why, you crazy, conceited lout! Are you going to take me back to Jackson or not? If not, show me the way to my horse and I'll be on my way." She brushed past him to retrieve her belongings, but Colt dogged her heels.

"*You* were the one who approached *me* in the saloon, then risked your own life to rescue me from a storm!"

Madison whirled around. "Excuse me! I happen to *like* antiques! . . . and the Old West! and history!"

"That's real good, because you're living it!"

"Do you really expect me to fall for that?" She clenched her fists in exasperation.

"You damn well better." Colt raked his hand through his hair and began to pace back and forth. He stopped, pointing at her sternly, ignoring the anger in her eyes. "No, there was more to it than that, Madison, and you know it! You were drawn to me, just as I was to you. And even though I appeared as old as the hills, you still couldn't resist me, could you? Just as I couldn't resist searching the crowds for a glimpse of you. As affection grew, you began to see me as I truly am. Do you deny that you saw me as I am today, yesterday during the storm? You did. It was in your eyes. Be honest with yourself."

Madison was rendered speechless, entranced by the tic in his jaw. His golden brown eyes shot amber sparks into the air, a heady charge seeming to occupy the space between them.

With a weighty sigh he tore his eyes from hers and went to the washstand to pour water from the pitcher, splashing his face several times. He didn't speak again until after reaching for a cloth to wipe his face.

"I'll take you back up to Jackson Hole, but I can't do it now. I've got scores of calves out there that need to be rounded up for branding—and even more bulls awaiting castration. The boys are working long into the night as it is; they need all the help they can get. Don't worry, it may not be for a few days, but I'll get you home. Mark my words . . ." With that, he tossed the cloth aside and jerked open the door.

Madison lunged a few steps forward. "But . . . wait—"

Colt turned, his eyebrow cocked impatiently.

"Er . . . isn't there someone else who could take me? Or I can go myself. I'll be okay. It's just that I'm sure my brother and my friends are worried sick. I imagine they've called the police by this time."

"That's damn thoughtful of you, sugar—but no, I don't think anyone else would know which rosebush is the magic one," he answered sarcastically. "And no, again, you're not going alone! This is 1878, and that country out there is wild. Jackson doesn't exist yet. More than likely what you'll find are Indians, hungry wolves, and, if you're *real* lucky, some degenerate outlaw who would just love to get a taste of you! Anything else?"

"Yes." Madison raised her chin defiantly, her hands resting on her hips.

"Well?"

"Our sleeping arrangements. We're supposed to be married, remember?"

"What would you have me do?"

"You're certainly not sleeping in here with me."

Her aqua eyes glistened, daring him to offer resistance. Colt leaned against the doorjamb, leisurely propping his foot up and folding his arms. "This is the way I see it, sugar. This is my room and that's my bed. When I'm not home I pretty much have to sleep wherever I can—and most of the time, that's in a bedroll on hard, rocky ground. When I'm surrounded by the comforts of home I intend to use them. But I'm an easy man to get along with. Seeing as how neither of us are necessarily at fault here, I think we can compromise. You take the bed. I'll throw my bedroll on the verandah."

Assuming the issue was settled, he levered his weight from the wall and started to leave. "And don't worry. I'm no animal. I won't bother you."

Colt studied Madison intently, taking careful note as her expression evolved from mere annoyance to the critical point of explosion. Just as her eyes narrowed, glazing over with pure contempt, he ducked out of the room. The loud whack against the wall behind him told him he had left just in time.

"Ohhhhh!" Madison stomped to recover her boot, calling after him before she slammed the door. "Don't rush back on my account. The home fires *won't* be burning!"

Colt sprinted lightheartedly down the stairs, a smile on his lips. By the time he reached the office to fetch his hat and holster, he was laughing. As he made his way to the barn, he sensed her eyes upon him. But he wouldn't chance looking back. If she saw him turn, and she would, everything would be ruined. Madison possessed a rare spirit, kindred to his. As sure as the grass was green and bees made honey, she'd be in his arms within a few days—he was ready to bet his life on it. The tricky part was going to be getting her to stay. . . .

Whistling a jaunty tune, he disappeared into the barn in search of a horse with a whole lotta cow sense. He had work to do.

Madison came inside, letting the verandah doors click softly shut behind her. She sank into the security of the big green chair, a little stunned and tremendously bewildered. How could someone she had only known for two days have the ability to make her so fighting mad? Especially when everything started out so amicable. This was absolutely ridiculous! How could she be stuck here? Never had she allowed someone to dictate what she could and couldn't do—with the exception of Jon, and she'd learned her lesson on that score.

Colt might be a raving maniac for all she knew. No way was she going to accept his word that they had somehow passed through a portal of time into the year 1878. The idea was totally preposterous. Deciding to explore the situation for herself, she rose from the chair. Thanks to Colt, her head throbbed much more than it had before. Madison dug a few aspirins from her purse before heading downstairs.

Chapter Fourteen

The heat of the rectangular cooking area was oppressive, a heavenly aroma of fried chicken hanging in the air. Madison stood in the doorway, taking the time to study the room.

One entire wall consisted of a soot-blackened rock fireplace, an iron cookstove to its side. Rows of cupboards lined the walls, constructed from planked boards and painted a festive red. The countertop struck her as odd despite the fact that it was taken up with distinctly useful provisions: a red wooden sugar bucket, a cheese box, yelloware pottery for storage, and a red cast-iron water pump jutting up from the center. That was it, Madison mused. Where there should be a sink, there was none. A heavy wooden bucket sat in its stead.

The far wall was decorated with flower-sprigged wallpaper, and cast-iron utensils hung from giant suspended hooks. Shelves provided a commodious haven for a wire egg basket, wooden butter molds, an egg beater, food choppers, and several other supplies—some of which Madison had no idea what they even were. A tall wooden butter churn stood in the corner beside a wood-grained ice box.

Amazed, Madison observed Rosannah and Emmy bustle about the kitchen in their haste to prepare the evening meal. Black and silver strands had loosened from Rosannah's chignon, wisping around her face, a light sheen of perspiration on her forehead.

Rosannah caught sight of Madison and a bright smile spread over her face in spite of her apparent exhaustion. "Madison, dear! Feeling better after your nap?"

"Nap?" she answered distractedly. Then, remembering Colt's feeble excuse, she said, "Oh, yes, I feel much more rested."

"Good for you! Here." Rosannah plucked a roll from the cooling pan and handed it to Madison. "This will tide you over until suppertime."

Madison took it gratefully, her mouth watering from the medley of appetizing aromas. "Thank you so much. Could I bother you for a glass of water?"

Rosannah briskly motioned toward the bucket as she rushed by to pull the lid from the huge fry pan. She expertly rotated the spattering chicken, grease rising in a steamy spray.

Madison crossed to the bucket and dipped some cool water. She popped the aspirins into her mouth and drank. "Is there anything I can help with?" Ironic, but with all of Madison's modern knowledge, there were probably few of these utensils she would be able to figure out how to use.

"Oh! No, no, no! You go on outside and get some fresh air. Emmy and I do the cooking 'round here. Even when Colt's mama was living, bless her soul, I never let her set foot in the kitchen," Rosannah said emphatically, replacing the lid on the fry pan.

Emmy listened to the exchange in silence. Then she slanted a melancholy glance toward Madison, brushing past her to dash from the kitchen.

"Don't mind her." Rosannah waved her off with a shake of her head. "She's at that age. You know how it goes."

Madison smiled. "Yes, I think I do. If you don't mind, I'll just go outside and take a look around."

"You go right ahead. You'll hear the dinner bell—just don't get yourself caught up in the stampede for the door."

Madison laughed, hopelessly charmed by Rosannah's unending zest. Outside, she followed the porch around to the front of the house. Oh my God, she thought, what if it was true? What if Colt was right, and she had been trapped with him in a time warp? *Could the year possibly be 1878?* The whole idea was mind-boggling, exciting, and terrifying at the same time.

Madison stayed on the worn pathways when she left the porch. The dry earth was warm and the grass prickled beneath her stocking feet. She stepped carefully, stopping when she gained the creek. She spun around to face the house. It was as if her heartbeat skidded to a grinding halt.

Agog, her eyes absorbed the gothic beauty of the ranch house. It was the same house, she was sure. And this was the very spot where she had lunched with Colt only yesterday. The massive cottonwood was now only a thin sapling, offering no shade at all.

The old-world charm reminded her of a larger-than-life gingerbread house: pale yellow with white trim, three front gables proud and straight. Mammoth columns along the extended front porch were a glistening white, not chipped and gray like the day before. The grounds were perfectly manicured, voluminous lilac bushes neatly arranged along the anterior. Hence the sweet smell through her window this morning, she thought.

The outlook over the rolling pastures was empty, except for the milling herds of cattle. A few horses frolicked playfully inside the confines of the corral. Aside from that, she didn't see a single soul. The view was different, but she supposed it was only because of the change in growth patterns of the trees and shrubs; the actual landscape was exactly the same.

The buildings were inconsistent, though. Where a modern steel barn had stood, it was now empty land. But there was a big red clapboard barn and farther down were two smaller barns and another corral. Four rows of long, rectangular structures were constructed of rough-hewn logs. It made her think of a military barracks. Must be bunkhouses, she reasoned. Several smaller buildings were interspersed throughout. Set apart was a rambling ranch house constructed from the same rough logs. She wondered if that was the original homestead.

A snort and a yip caused Madison to turn around just in time to receive the rambunctious greeting of two identical golden retrievers. Both bounded directly for her, lunging at her skirts friskily. Madison laughed as she tried to push them down, vigorously scratching their soft heads, careful to pay special attention to behind their ears. Their slobbering tongues hung over the sides of their mouths, panting a hearty approval. As quickly as the dogs arrived, they were gone, cutting capers through the green pasture.

Madison smiled with pleasure as she headed back toward the porch. A revelation struck and she turned, a sudden shiver raising gooseflesh on her arms. Hugging herself, she moved to the side of the house, where the dense stand of poplars had been so overgrown before. Now, it was barely covered with a few small saplings and a vegetable garden. Rows of herbs and spices grew in the most advantageous spot to capture the mountain sunlight, and the crisp fragrance of mint wafted toward her.

To her left, Madison spotted a rock-lined path, winding around the hillside, disappearing over its crest. The cemetery. Just where she wanted to go.

At the pinnacle she paused to look down. Below, to the rear of the house was the most beautiful rose garden she had ever laid eyes on. It was a luscious grotto where roses grew in exuberance; riotous flushes of color spilling over trestles, vining around in a tangled web of rich green stems. In the center stood a quaint gazebo and a colossal birdhouse. This paradise was totally obscured by tall privet hedges, faultlessly trimmed. The heady, distinct perfume of the roses impressed her senses even way up there on the hillside.

By this time Madison wasn't surprised to discover that the tiny cemetery was so well cared for . . . and empty. Stepping past the white picket gate, she searched the entire area for the other graves she had seen only yesterday, but there were only five. Exactly as she remembered were the graves of Charles and Katherine Chase. Alongside were the miniature infant crosses. There was one she didn't recognize—then she decided it must be the one that had all but disintegrated before. Thomas Bartlett, it read, Died: 1870, RIP.

Madison stood beside the double cross, running her fingertips over the cold, rough-edged granite. Unexpectedly weak, she bent to sit, almost falling next to it. What was happening? Was she losing her mind?—or was she to believe that the Rosannah and Emmy inside that house were indeed the same people who occupied the graves she had seen here only yesterday?

Unable to hold back her tears any longer, they sprung loose and coursed down her cheeks in tiny rivers. Frightened, she leaned forward, burying her face in her skirts, sobbing until she just couldn't sob any longer. *Oh, Mark,* she thought, *what must you be thinking? I've disappeared from the face of the earth as you know it, and ended up in another century.* Frantically, she prayed Mark would somehow hear her words—that he would know she was all right and not to worry. And then there was her mother. With any luck at all, Madison would be home before Mark had the chance to break the news to her—but she seriously doubted it. The police had probably been notified, and more than likely were at this moment searching the suitcase she'd left behind for any clues to her disappearance.

Despondent, Madison wished Colt would find her there and sit down by her side and give her words of comfort. Funny how she desired the company of the one person who irritated the life out of her. He hadn't bothered her before, only since this morning— and only since she'd seen him as a young man. Madison refused to make any kind of connection.

The distant clang of the dinner bell, followed by boots clumping on wood, jolted her back to the present. Drying her eyes with the hem of her skirt, she got up and peered over the edge of the hill. Bud and Garrett were approaching the back door, removing their hats and knocking away the dust before they entered. Well, it must be dinner time. Sucking in a huge gulp of air, she set her sights back down the pathway. Her nerves chattered as she anticipated Colt's presence at the dinner table.

Madison was careful not to let her disappointment show. Least of all did she want to admit it to herself. After all, it was she who had told Colt to stay away from her for as long as possible— that she didn't care for his company. Didn't he know sarcasm when he heard it? He sure could dish it out when he wanted to. How dare he leave her to dine alone with his family—her first evening there! It was he who had concocted that ridiculous story of an impromptu marriage, and now he had left her to bear the burden of it at the dinner table, looking like a jilted newlywed. The more she thought about his humiliating her, the more livid she became.

"Have more potatoes, dear—you have to grab while you can at this table. It doesn't last long."

Rosannah held out a nearly empty ironstone bowl toward Madison, and she didn't hesitate. "Thank you . . . everything is so delicious, Rosannah and Emmy. I guess I didn't realize how famished I was." Madison dished up another generous helping, dousing the potatoes with a rich, creamy gravy. She had never experienced such delectable homestyle cooking as this: chicken so moist and juicy flaking away from the bone; sweet and spicy baked beans; fresh peas flavored with tiny pearl onions.

Rosannah beamed at the compliment—but when Emmy met Madison's smile through thick lashes, she simply looked away in quiet dismissal. Madison decided at that moment that she would wait for the right time to find out what Emmy's problem was.

"Bud, where in heaven's name is Colt? It's not often he misses a meal here at the house."

Rosannah and Bud had exchanged glances all through dinner, and Madison knew it was only a matter of time before the subject was raised.

Bud leaned back in his chair with a growl, patting his gut. "Now how am I supposed to know that, Rosie? I've been out on the north range most of the day. Colt's been over tendin' the brandin' fires."

Bud's blue eyes shifted back and forth between Madison and Rosannah, and Madison suspected he knew more than he had let on. She was thankful he didn't spill his guts in front of everyone, causing her further embarrassment.

"Oh, he told me not to worry," Madison lied. "He said he wouldn't be back until late. Something about a heavy workload . . ."

"Ain't that the God's honest truth. That time of year again." Bud's chair scraped back across the floor. "Well, think I'll head on out to the fires and see if I can find the boy. Gotta rub it in what a plum larrapin' supper he done missed." Bud delivered a wink of camaraderie to Madison before he lifted his hat from the peg and left through the kitchen.

Garrett soon followed, much to Madison's relief. During the entire meal his foreboding countenance had clouded the dining room with gloom. She likened his eyes to glistening black marbles, and they had rested on her endlessly. Not once had he spoken to Rosannah or the others, and no one had seemed to notice or care. Maybe it was just his way, Madison surmised, and everyone was used to his odd behavior. Whatever the circumstances, Madison despised the way he had continually stared at her. She recalled Colt's description of their parents' murders and how Garrett had been affected. Could that alone account for his dark demeanor?

Madison helped to clear the supper dishes, though Rosannah attempted to shoo her away several times. "Please let me help, Rosannah. I need to earn my keep somehow."

"You'll earn your keep just fine, dear—trust me on that one. You're the ranch's mistress now, and with that comes other, more important responsibilities. Colt is looking forward to many children. 'Course, I'm sure he's told you that."

Rosannah slanted a decorous smile over her shoulder as she carried an armload of dishes to the kitchen. Madison followed with a load of her own.

"Lots of children, huh? No, he's never mentioned that to me."

To her surprise Madison felt a little wistful as the picture of life on a sprawling ranch in Wyoming, children, and a husband like Colt entered her mind. It didn't seem half bad. Something deep inside her, unidentifiable, stirred.

"Well," Rosannah sighed with a chuckle, "I'm sure he'll make his wishes known soon enough. Is that what you'd like, too?"

"Me? Sure . . . I suppose, that would be nice," Madison answered.

Wasn't that a little like the fantasy she'd always envisioned, that fairy tale of a knight on a dashing white steed carrying her away to his castle in the sky? Colt fit the part—so did this ranch, for that matter. Shaking away the outrageous daydreams, she thought it would be best to change the subject, for any discussion of children reminded her of the harsh reality she had had to accept. She had never been able to become pregnant during her marriage—and now Amanda was going to have Jon's child.

"You know, these are lovely dishes." Madison held up a blue-and-white dinner plate as she dried it.

"Those old things?" Rosannah wrinkled her nose. "They're all chipped up and quite a mess. But if you like these, you should see the set inside the hutch."

Madison's interest was instantly piqued. "The hutch?" she asked quickly. "I'd love to see them! I love antiques. . . . I mean, dishes of all kinds. I collect them," she stumbled awkwardly over her words as she dutifully followed Rosannah back into the dining area.

"Right in there. Help yourself if you like." Rosannah pointed to the tall cherry wood corner hutch, moving to gather more dirty dishes from the table. "Colt's grandma on his mama's side brought them from back east. They came out west, settling in St. Louis when Colt's mama was just a young girl. Katie cherished them; only used them for special occasions."

Madison let out a little gasp of delight when she peered inside the glass-enclosed cabinet. She didn't know how she could have missed seeing them before. Inside were stacks and rows of flow blue china, the very kind she adored.

"Colt didn't tell us much about you. Just that you two got married sudden-like. Where are you from, Madison?"

She was so busy admiring the collection, she scarcely heard what Rosannah had said. "I'm sorry—where am I from?" Madison cringed, knowing she'd have to answer very carefully. "Er . . . well, Colorado Springs."

"Ahhhh, Colorado. It's lovely there, I hear." Rosannah exited, then came back with a wet cloth to mop the table. "Did you two know one another long?"

"Uhmmm, well, not too long," Madison stammered.

"When were you married? Colt didn't say a word about having a wife when he first returned from down south. I think, now, that he was just waiting for you to arrive so he could surprise us!"

"Yes! I'm sure that was it," Madison stalled, making a mental note to shoot Colt just as soon as he returned; either that or beat him to a pulp. "We . . . er . . . we were married a while back." It suddenly dawned on Madison that Rosannah was under the impression that she was virginal and afraid of Colt's bed, " . . . but not that long ago."

Rosannah frowned in confusion.

" . . . I believe it was maybe a week ago. My memory is so fuzzy since this bump on my head."

"Why, yes, poor thing." She shook her head with a sympathetic cluck of her tongue, disappearing once again into the kitchen.

Rolling her eyes and breathing a sigh of relief, Madison considered telling Rosannah the truth. Anything would be better than these lies. Then again, would she believe her? Madison strongly doubted it. With this knot on her head and barely knowing her in the first place, surely Rosannah would think Colt's new wife was a nut case. Dismissing the fleeting notion, she went back into the kitchen to finish drying the dishes.

"Emmy usually dries. I have to apologize for her; I don't know what's gotten into that girl lately. No doubt she's off moping in some dark corner."

"Would you mind if I talked to her, Rosannah?"

The older woman placed a work-worn hand warmly over Madison's smooth one. "Ya know, I think she would like that very much."

Later, alone upstairs, Madison lingered on the verandah. In the dusky light of the purple sunset, she watched as dozens of cowboys straggled into the red barn, then beyond to the bunkhouses. Far-off lights glowed dimly within small square windows. Night sounds pulsed in the air—crickets' chirping in a musical cacophony, a cow's distant bawling, a horse's occasional nicker.

Gently knocking, Emmy entered the bedroom. She carried a stack of fresh linens and a tin candle lantern. The flame flickered ghostly shadows over her face, her round hazel eyes wide in the darkened room.

"Why, Emmy, you frightened me. I didn't know anyone was in here." Madison stepped inside, leaving the French door open for fresh air.

"I'm sorry—I brought you these," Emmy said softly, setting the neatly folded stack atop the washstand.

Madison watched as she moved about the room to light the lamps, bathing the spacious room in an orange luster.

"I appreciate that, Emmy. Would you like to stay and talk with me awhile? It's lonely up here by myself."

"I shouldn't. . . . Mama's expectin' me downstairs."

Emmy fiddled with her skirt while staring at the tips of her toes.

"She won't mind if you keep me company for a bit. What do you say?" Madison smiled warmly, patting the edge of the bed for her to sit.

Emmy lifted shy eyes. She set the candle lantern on the bedside table before finally coming to sit across from Madison on the huge four-poster bed. She folded her hands primly in her lap.

"I thought it might be nice to get to know one another. There doesn't appear to be many women on the ranch. We have to stick together, you know. How old are you, Emmy?"

"Fifteen . . . but I'll be sixteen come September."

"I remember when I was sixteen." Madison drew her legs up under her skirt, Indian-style. "I got my first car . . . er . . . I mean horse." She laughed awkwardly, hoping Emmy hadn't noticed the blunder.

"You were my age before you had a horse?"

Showing interest at last, Emmy swiveled around to better face Madison.

"Uhhhh, yes . . . you see, we were city dwellers, didn't have animals like you do here on the ranch." Madison thought she'd better divert the conversation before she really stuck her foot in her mouth. "That's why I don't ride too well," she said, pointing to the bandage on her head. "But I love to ride. Do you ride much?"

"Nah . . . Mama keeps me too busy 'round here. She tries to work my fingers to the bone—says it builds character. I say it builds calluses. Ain't no man worth havin' gonna want some old, rough workhorse like me for a wife. Probably end up bein' an old maid." Emmy smiled bashfully, looking up quickly, then back to her lap. "You're so pretty, though. I bet your mama didn't work you to death."

"*Au contraire!*" Madison's brows shot up in emphasis. "I used to think she was a slave driver! All I ever wanted to do was to be with my friends—but no, there were chores I was expected to do every day, and I couldn't go out until they were done. I used to think she was so unfair. Looking back, well . . . she was right. And your mama is, too. You're a beautiful girl, Emmy. No doubt you'll meet some handsome cowboy here at the ranch who'll sweep you off your feet. In a few years, of course." Madison couldn't help but think of what the hotel manager said of Emmy's fate. She had, indeed, become an old maid, never marrying, never able to forget that one, lost love. . . .

Emmy screwed up her face with distaste. "Don't want no cowboy. I want to marry a rancher . . . somebody important. Somebody who'll take me travelin' with him. I want to see the world!" She shrugged her shoulders, gazing toward the ceiling, lost in her fantasy.

"Sounds wonderful! Have anyone special in mind?"

Emmy's fanciful smile vanished, and she once again stared into her lap, wringing her fingers. "Uhmmm . . . I used to. But he got married to someone else."

"Oh, I'm sorry to hear that. But there's a lot of fish in the sea, so don't lose hope."

Suddenly brightening, she said, "Colt told me you've traveled the world! Tell me about Europe . . . please!"

"Colt told you that, huh? How . . . revealing of him," Madison replied tightly, taking a deep breath and hoping she'd be able to muddle through this one. "What would you like to know?"

"Oh, everything! Tell me about Paris . . . and London. I've read lots of books about London."

Madison managed to highlight the historical landmarks without any trouble, and Emmy seemed immensely satisfied when she finished, a wistful expression on her face. An idea brought Madison to her feet, and she crossed the room to the mirrored dresser. Pulling around a stool, she motioned for Emmy to take the seat.

"What are we doing?" Emmy giggled when she sat down.

"Girl stuff. Do you mind if I take your hair down?" Madison began removing the tortoiseshell hairpins from Emmy's milk-chocolate-colored hair, until it cascaded well below the girl's waist.

"Ohhhh, make me beautiful . . . just like you, Madison!"

Madison snorted. "Emmy, you're already gorgeous. I'm just going to practice a hairstyle on you. You have the loveliest hair I've ever seen."

She grasped the silver-handled hairbrush and ran it through the young girl's long hair until it shone in the lamplight. Then, starting at the top of Emmy's head, she weaved an intricate French braid, which was no easy task considering its length. When she finished Madison dug a ribbon from her purse and tied off the end. She handed Emmy the silver mirror. A tiny squeal told Madison of the teenager's immense pleasure at the outcome.

"Now, let's play with some makeup." Madison rummaged through her bag for her blush and mascara.

Emmy was a model pupil, sitting rigidly on the stool, her eyes focused intently on the mirror. Finished, Madison stood back to critique the end result, a wide smile of approval encompassing her face.

"Ohhhh, Madison . . . I really *am* beautiful!" Emmy rose, leaning in close to the mirror in wonder.

"You certainly are. Now, do you distrust your ability to marry some rich rancher?"

Emmy giggled, startling Madison as she jumped up, her arms wrapped tightly around her in an ardent hug.

Both women were caught laughing, their faces flushed brightly, when the door swung open in a rush of air. Colt's form took up the better part of the doorway, a deep scowl etched into his features as he glowered at them.

"Uh-oh." Madison leaned in to whisper in Emmy's ear, her mouth barely moving, "Looks like the lord of the manor is home . . . and boy, does he look as mad as a hornet."

At that, they both dissolved into peals of laughter, struggling to regain their composure as Colt strode purposefully into the room.

Chapter Fifteen

Colt removed his hat and holster and hung them on the peg by the door, his eyes never wavering from the two females. His face was coated with a fine layer of dust, as brown as his shirt and pants.

Emmy squeezed Madison's hand in good-bye and edged toward the door. Her gaze lifted to Colt, and she smiled shyly as she passed.

"Emmy?" Colt pivoted on his heel. When she glanced back he said, "You look . . . very nice."

Emmy beamed. Blushing furiously, she dashed to retrieve the candle lantern and then disappeared down the hall.

Madison busied herself with straightening the clutter on the dresser. Colt passed behind her several times, never saying a word. She heard his boots thump to the floor, one at a time, then the sound of his footsteps in the hall and down the stairs. Moments later he returned, a brass tub in hand, dropping it with a clatter to the floor at the end of the bed.

"What are you doing?" Madison watched, her weight resting back against the dresser.

He regarded her solemnly before he spoke, "I'm going to have a bath—do you mind?"

His eyebrows shot up with the question, and she knew he still harbored a grudge from that afternoon.

127

"Well . . . yes. I mean, no, I'll just step out for a while." Madison started for the door.

"Wait."

She turned back.

"I need you to do something for me, if you would."

"Yes?"

Colt removed a giant pair of wrought steel shears from the washstand drawer, handing them to her. "Cut my hair."

"My lord," she responded, taking hold of them with care, "do you also prune the hedges with these things?"

Colt battled the smile that tugged at the corner of his mouth, determined to maintain his stern demeanor. Without answering, he unbuttoned his shirt and slid the bandanna from around his neck.

"Is this a wifely duty type of thing?" she questioned derisively.

"More or less."

Colt wasn't angry, but he was mesmerized by this woman who had swept into his life and had taken him by utter surprise. Nonetheless, he felt that fate had thrown them together. Madison stirred such deep emotions inside him that he wasn't able to understand their meaning. It was if a charged vibration, a powerful undercurrent linked their very souls. He strongly suspected she had been touched by it, too. And even though she wouldn't admit to it, and she claimed to be so anxious to go back to her time, he was sorely tempted to convince her to stay. But, ultimately, it would have to be her decision—she would have to be the one to come to him.

Tossing his shirt on the floor, he left the room and began to lug buckets of hot water up the stairs. When the tub was nearly full he popped open the buttons on his pants.

"Can't we cut your hair before you bathe?" Madison asked quickly, a little more breathlessly than she had hoped. The sight of his half-naked torso was unnerving enough—she wasn't about to let him go any further. The golden glow of the lamplight flickered playfully over his tawny skin, and she found it terribly difficult to remain focused on his face. Instead, for just a moment, she elected to admire his perfectly sculptured muscles, watching as his every move triggered a very slight tantalizing ripple. Lust clawed at her insides, stunning her, and she drew in a ragged breath to tame it.

"Whatever you prefer," he replied. Nonchalantly, he positioned himself on the stool before her and waited patiently.

Madison reached with hesitant hands to lift a lock of his hair, running a comb through. A radiating warmth exuded from his closeness, and she could swear she detected a subtle pulsation traveling up her arms. "It's caked with dirt and dust," she said with a grimace.

"That could be why I was going to take a bath. I knew there must have been a reason." He cast her a fleeting glance of sarcasm.

"You smell like campfires and burnt hair."

"Imagine that," he replied dryly. "Let me sink into the tub while it's hot—you can cut while I soak. I'll retain my modesty if that's what you're worried about."

"Oh, I'm not worried," she lied. "Go ahead." Madison presented her back to him, and he rose from the stool and proceeded to strip.

Once in the tub, Colt sank in over his head to wet his hair, rising with an invigorated sputter. He draped a small cloth over his midsection and leaned back against the headrest, closing his eyes. "Ready, sugar. Come work your magic."

Madison sat down on the stool and dolloped a generous portion of her shampoo onto his head, building it into a fine lather. She kneaded his scalp sensuously, concentrating on his temples.

A long, low groan of pleasure emanated from deep within his throat. "You have very talented hands, sugar."

Madison dug her fingers into his scalp with increasing pressure, hoping to relieve his tension and leaning in closer until she practically panted over him. As if remembering her mission, she suddenly straightened, dipping her hands to rinse them.

"Okay," she said, the tone of her voice extraordinarily high, "rinse."

He obeyed with a wet splash.

"How short?" she inquired.

"How short would *you* like it?" he drawled.

"It's your head. You tell me."

"Cut it away from my neck—just don't scalp me."

Feeling impulsively mischievous, Madison thought she might take care of a little business first. A wicked smile touched her lips, and she moved her tongue across them to wet them. She dangled the silver blades, trailing them lightly over the springy hairs along his chest, then up toward his neck.

"I want to apologize for throwing a boot at your head this afternoon. I shouldn't have done that. None of this is your fault;

I realize that now. It's all pretty unreal to me. I feel as though I'm in a dream and I can't wake up." Madison sighed. "All of that aside, I'd also like to express my irritation at your absence from the dinner table. Not only was it embarrassing when you didn't show up, but I was confronted with a barrage of questions I had no idea how to answer. *Then* I learn you've enlightened your family about me—I wish you would have let me know, in advance, what you had planned on telling them. In light of all that, I suppose it's a good thing I have a sense of humor, considering my advantage."

She continued to move the ominous blades, tracing a ticklish path along his skin. She noticed that Colt's eyes had remained closed throughout her monologue, his dark lashes fanning out, almost touching his high cheekbones. But now, abruptly, his eyes snapped open, his thick brows drawing low. A strong tanned arm slid up so fast she barely saw it coming. She felt the grip at the back of her neck, his hand pulling her face within mere inches of his. The warmth of his breath, the movement of his lips hypnotized her when he spoke, low and even.

"Apology accepted. However, you made yourself quite clear this afternoon. There's nothing between us. We're not married, only biding our time until you return home. All I've done for you has been out of compassion for your situation—you seem to forget that I was there, too. Only I didn't have anyone to turn to. I was simply some hundred-year-old man wandering around like a fish out of water. You're an intelligent woman. I get the feeling you'd be able to take care of yourself no matter what. Now, if you would like the benefit of my company, I think you need to change your attitude—and you know *my* feelings on that score."

Colt's heavy-lidded gaze dipped to the shiny blades. "If you plan on using those shears for something other than cutting hair, get it over with. I need some shut-eye. I've got one hell of a long day tomorrow." He released her just as quickly.

Madison bounced into an upright position, flabbergasted. Her tongue felt so thick in her mouth, she doubted it would operate even if she could think of a clever retort. She smoothed the wet marks he had made on her dress. Of all the nerve! *He had just dismissed her!* She had anticipated a kiss and got nothing more than a—a lecture. Had she *wanted* a kiss? No! She simply had wanted him to know . . . What? Her feelings? And just what were her feelings?

A blazing wash of hot temper raced through her veins, directly replaced by acute abashment. Damn him! He was right, *again!* After all, what did he owe her? It wasn't his fault she was here; at least not totally. Why was it she couldn't get near him without remembering what it felt like to be in his arms . . . craving his touch, wanting to return that touch. Why would she even think that way when she didn't trust him any more than any other man? He was self-centered, egotistical, probably had women waiting throughout the entire countryside. Oh, no, she hoped not. . . .

"I guess that means I won't be returning home tomorrow." Mechanically, Madison's fingers separated sections of his hair, cutting.

"Not tomorrow, sugar."

The words of finality didn't upset her. Quite the opposite. She felt strangely comforted, making the excuse to herself that it only gave her more time to explore her surroundings. The floor was soon blanketed with the drying locks of his chestnut hair. A guttural growl hauled her back to reality as Colt yawned, stretching his arms high above his head, his muscles bunching with the movement.

"Finished?" he asked tiredly.

Madison's answer was the sound of the shears clattering onto the top of the dresser. Why was she cutting his hair for him, anyway? She should have insisted he get someone else . . . Emmy, maybe. Madison told herself she hadn't cut it just because he'd asked her to; she'd cut it because she'd wanted to. If anyone was responsible for that luscious crop of hair, she wanted it to be her. At least she knew how to put a little style into it. It had turned out well, she mused, running her fingers through his hair one last time. It feathered back partly over his ears, not too short, tapering nicely at his nape.

Colt vigorously scrubbed his face and body, seemingly oblivious to her ministrations. Madison strolled away from the tub, still plagued by her tumultuous thoughts. Gone were the long tresses that had graced his broad, masculine shoulders. He would no longer have the aura of a heavenly Greek god.

She heard the splatter of water. Colt had risen from the tub, and Madison caught the briefest glimpse of water shimmering over his tanned skin as he wrapped the meager cloth about his waist. With an inward groan she went to the bed and dropped onto the feather mattress, burying her face in the soft escape of a pillow. My lord—she was wrong! He looked more like a Greek God than ever.

It wasn't long before sleep overtook her senses, her mind relieved, temporarily, of the tortuous contemplations that sparred within her head.

Chapter Sixteen

Colt sat behind the mahogany desk, his work-worn frame slouched into the wingback leather chair. His elbow was propped on the armrest and he rubbed his eyes wearily. "I don't understand how two hundred head of cattle can vanish overnight. It's the third time this year—and the third time without anyone seeing anything. It doesn't make sense. Don't the boys have clear instructions to ride the line the entire night?" Colt laced his fingers, leaning forward over the desk, regarding his younger brother on the opposite side. "When I rode in two nights ago there wasn't a line guard to be seen—"

"There are more than enough line guards, Colt. Too many have the night shift as it is. It leaves too few hands to complete the day work. I just wanted you to know the situation; I've got everything under control. This is the first chance I've had to speak privately with you since you returned. Relax; there's nothing we can do now."

Garrett sat at ease, his legs crossed. Though the black eyes met Colt's level gaze, they quickly shifted away when he spoke, his face otherwise showing no emotion. He chewed habitually at the stubby cheroot that seemed to be constantly clamped at the corner of his mouth.

Colt sighed heavily. "Relax? Garrett, that's not the answer! We can't afford any more losses. Sounds to me like we need more hands."

"We're about fifty shy from what we had this time last year," Garrett interjected defensively. "Fitch and Crandell hired the seasonals right out from underneath us this year. Somethin' about better pay. I put out the word in town that we were hiring, but so far we haven't had much luck."

"Well, pay 'em more, dammit!" Colt banged his clenched fist on the desk. "Them boys deserve every penny! Especially the old-timers who have remained faithful over the years. If we weren't losing so many head, we could afford to pay *better* than Fitch and Crandell! Speaking of the other ranchers, have they had the same rustling problems?"

"Baylor lost a hundred or so head last month."

Colt watched Garrett closely as the younger man rolled his eyes around the room distractedly, obviously bored with the conversation. Colt was worried about his brother. Recently, Garrett had become far too disinterested in the ranch's welfare—and now with the increased rustling, it was apparent Garrett couldn't handle it alone. There was always Bud, and he had been a godsend. If it hadn't been for him taking Garrett under his wing and teaching him all he knew, Colt would never have been able to leave the ranch at all in his search for Red Eagle. But Bud was older now, and he needed help.

Colt knew it wasn't fair of him to heap this tremendous responsibility on Garrett and Bud. He should have tried to remain home more often over the past ten years. But it wasn't too late. He would stay home for a while even if it did mean forgetting about Red Eagle for the time being.

"Well?" Garrett said dispassionately, "what do you want me to do?"

Colt rubbed his chin in grave concentration. "Nothing. You need a break. I'll handle it. You've virtually been running things since you were sixteen, wheeling and dealing right along with the big boys. Time off for good behavior, little brother."

Garrett's eyes grew wide, his lips moving soundlessly as he searched for the right words of protest.

Colt smiled tiredly, and continued, "I think it's high time to invest in barbed-wire fencing, and I'm going to be home more often than not for a change. As we speak, there are twelve hundred head of longhorn being driven up from Texas, scheduled to arrive anytime now. I can't take any chances they'll be rustled."

"No! We don't need barbed-wire fencing. I've heard plenty of horror stories about that stuff . . . animals getting caught up in it, dying a slow death. It's no good, Colt, just a passing fancy. I don't like it at all," Garrett babbled, moving to the edge of his chair.

"I disagree." Colt frowned at Garrett's agitation. He hadn't seen his brother show this much excitement over anything in years. "Fencing would significantly cut down the number of line guards, and I'm willing to bet our losses would stop. I think barbed wire is the way to go, Garrett. In fact, I'm taking Madison into South Pass with me tomorrow. I'll put the order in while I'm there." Colt rolled the chair back and started to leave when an envelope caught his eye. It was almost covered up on the littered desk. Colt's name was handwritten on the front of it in an elaborately slanted script. "What's this?" he asked as he pulled it from beneath the pile of papers.

"Oh, that . . . I forgot to give it to you. It's nothing important."

Garrett shifted uncomfortably in his seat, his black eyes darting around the room. Finally he stood, holding his hand out to take it. Instead of handing it to him, Colt eyed Garrett gravely while pulling the contents from the already torn envelope.

"This is from Sheriff Townsend in South Pass. . . . He wants to see me as soon as possible. Garrett, this is dated a week ago! Why didn't you give this to me first thing this morning?" Colt glared at him again before cramming the slip of paper into his pocket and heading for the door.

"I told you, Colt, I forgot. Townsend's always jumping to conclusions about one thing or another. It's probably nothing."

"Regardless, I need to know about these things. I expect it's a good thing I was planning on going to town tomorrow. I'll have to add this to my list of chores." Colt patted his pocket for emphasis as he left the office, leaving Garrett standing at the door, watching him go.

An hour later, Garrett still remained behind closed doors. He sat in the wingbacked chair that Colt had occupied earlier, the dim light of the kerosene lamp spraying an eerie glow over the desktop. A clap of thunder rumbled in the distance as a wash of raindrops splattered the ground outside the window. Silently, he cursed at his own carelessness, all the while nervously chewing his fingernails to the quick.

Now that Colt had found that blasted note from the sheriff, he'd surely be talking with the man tomorrow, possibly opening a can of worms that Garrett didn't want to deal with right now. All the rustling going on in the county was probably the reason the sheriff wanted to see Colt. Townsend knew well the designs Colt had on Red Eagle, and maybe he suspected Red Eagle was responsible for the stolen heads. That damn sheriff was notorious for working well beyond the call of duty. But what could he possibly want Colt to do? Unless . . . he had new information to give to Colt about Red Eagle. The more Garrett pondered, the more irritated he became.

On top of that, Colt announced he'd be staying home at least for a while. And where exactly did that leave Garrett? He seethed at the thought of the way his brother came and went, assuming charge whenever he pleased. Now he would be home and God knew for how long. You could bet that cursed woman was to blame for this! Colt certainly wouldn't remain on the ranch for any length of time unless he had taken a wife in earnest—or was planning to. Something about that situation just didn't sit right with him. Garrett didn't believe Madison was truly Colt's wife. So then, who was she and why was she here?

In a single movement, Garrett got up, angrily kicking aside the chair with a clatter. The hour was late, and he'd developed a mighty thirst from all of his brain work. Flinging open the cabinet door, he retrieved a half-empty green whiskey bottle. He clenched the cork between his teeth, wrenching it free and spitting it across the room. He blew out the lamp, exiting, the door slamming shut behind him.

Chapter Seventeen

The sun was but a pink promise in the far-off horizon when Madison descended the staircase on the third morning after her arrival. She treaded lightly in order to preserve the hallowed silence of the parlor, dim with the blue light of dawn. The only sound was the even ticking of the tall clock.

She was filled with anticipation and excitement about the forthcoming trip to town. After two full days of Colt avoiding her the thought of spending a day with him made her extremely happy. She told herself that the opportunity to get a look at an authentic western town, firsthand, was just too tempting to ignore. Plus, Madison had to pin him down to a discussion on his plans for getting her home.

Colt hadn't even needed to awaken her—she had woken with his first movements about the room. As soon as he left the bedroom, she had leapt from the cocoon of quilts to begin her toilette. Earlier that morning, after donning a lightweight white blouse and a teal calico skirt, she'd taken a little extra time to weave her hair into a French braid, securing the end with a white lacy ribbon. Then she'd fixed her face with what little makeup she had. Her bruise was improving, though it was still an angry yellow-blue. Unable to locate the buttonhook, she had finally given up and had come downstairs with her shoes unbuttoned. Luckily, Emmy had given her a pair of shoes that fit.

Now, as Madison entered the cozy dining room, her face broke into a wide smile as familiar golden brown eyes sparkled in greeting. Her heart thumped in its usual wild way whenever she saw him, continually amazing her with the effect his rugged-yet-boyish good looks had on her. It bothered her immensely to think that she might never feel this tremendous rush, this utter joy, ever again—the way she felt right at that moment when her gaze met his. His eyes swept boldly over her slender form, making no effort to conceal a distinct appreciation.

Colt leaned back on two legs of a Shaker chair, boots crossed, his legs extended to rest on the edge of the dining-room table. His holster and hat were neatly arranged on the sideboard. He wore a muted red chambray shirt, tan denims, and suspenders. A few strands of chestnut hair fell rakishly over his forehead, and if Madison had been about to say something, she promptly lost the words as all rational thought flew out of her head.

Colt dropped his feet to the floor and stood. "Care for coffee? I'm warning you, though. It kicks up in the middle and carries double—unlike the belly wash they call coffee in your time."

"Sounds too intriguing to pass up. Don't mind if I do." Madison pulled out a chair and sat down, waiting until Colt fetched two steaming ironstone mugs full of the black brew. She whitened it with cream and, closing her hand around the pleasant warmth of the cup, brought it to her lips. Surprise lit her face at the first sip, unprepared for such stoic bitterness. Colt tilted his head back and laughed.

"You're right," she choked, "this stuff could have walked out here by itself."

"Told you."

Colt was having trouble tearing his eyes away from her. She looked positively stunning, the green of her skirt a near match to her eyes. He suddenly had an incredible urge to pull the ribbon from her hair and run his fingers through the silken waves, loosening them wantonly about her shoulders. Her lips seemed extra full, almost pouting—and he found himself imagining their softness beneath his, the feel of tender bites . . .

"Oh, I almost forgot," Madison said, setting her cup down, "these shoes. Emmy found them for me and I've apparently misplaced the buttonhook. Is there another I could use?" Without thinking, she hoisted her skirt up to her knee, propping her foot on the chair that occupied the space between them.

The buttons gaped open on the black high-heeled ankle boot, and Colt's eyes traveled from the tip of the pointed toe, up over a shapely calf, lifting to rest on hers.

Madison knew well the meaning of that smoldering look, but it took a minute before she caught on to what had provoked it. To her own irritation, she blushed furiously. It occurred to her that a man in the year 1878 didn't readily get glimpses of a lady's legs—unless he was in a dancehall, perhaps. Never mind that her legs were covered with sheer black stockings that she realized only added to their allure. She knew he'd seen her legs before in Jackson, but that was another century, a lifetime ago. It was different now.

Hastily, she threw her skirt down and tried to cover her blunder with idle chit-chat. Meanwhile, Colt rummaged through the drawer in the sideboard, producing another buttonhook. Before she knew it, he was positioned in front of her, slipping a warm hand under her skirt to grasp her ankle, lifting her foot to rest between his spraddled legs. Her heart tripped at the hotness of his touch; her skin burned. It was a struggle just to keep her breathing on an even keel.

Supporting her leg, he snatched each tiny loop with the hook and brought it over to catch a button, a little slower than absolutely necessary. He repeated the process several times, his eyes occasionally raising to steal long, penetrating glances at her. Tenderly squeezing her calf, he said, "There . . . would you like me to do the other?" he asked, his voice low.

"Other?" she quavered, the meaning of his words escaping her. The perfect lines of his mouth were all she was able to focus on, his lips slightly parted, so close . . . "Other? No, I can manage. Thank you." Madison forced a frail smile.

Colt handed her the buttonhook, his touch lingering in a brief caress. "I'll wait outside," he murmured.

He fastened his holster and pressed the Stetson onto his head. Grabbing a cloth bundle from the table, he left the screen door slapping shut after him.

Madison took a deep breath, wondering if this was the wisest thing she could be doing this day. Why did she have to dissolve into a mass of trembling jelly whenever he was near? It just wasn't like her. It almost made her angry at him for causing this reaction. He scared her. How could a man threaten to cause her loss of control . . . her! Madison Calloway! After her divorce she had promised herself she'd always be in control of her own emotions. There might be times she'd let loose, consciously, always knowing she had a built-in safety net—that solid core deep within herself that never let her down. But with Colt—well, it was as if that sturdy net had been cut away, drifting down, into a vast bottomless void—and she was falling with it, deeper and deeper. . . .

The other shoe done, Madison gathered her wits and joined Colt outside. A cool morning breeze rushed into her face with a gentle reminder of reality. The air smelled of last evening's rain, crisp and clean, a sheen of moisture clinging to each blade of grass. From around the corner the matching pair of golden retrievers came bounding to greet her. Madison squealed in delight, bending to pat their soft heads. Wet tongues lapped at her cheeks, a cold nose pressing affectionately into her ear. Madison giggled, crooning to each one, their heads tilting as if they understood every word.

Colt watched her as he made last-minute adjustments to the horse's bridle, a swell growing inside his chest. God, but she was gorgeous, an expression of sheer joy on her face as the raucous animals threatened to knock her off balance in their jubilation. He broke into a hearty laugh right along with her.

"Sage! Brush! Run along, git! Go on . . ." Colt clapped his hands together sharply. Both dogs dashed headlong toward the pasture, barking and nipping at one another's heels.

Madison brushed the paw prints from her skirt. "Sage . . . and Brush?" she questioned dubiously, grinning. "Who's responsible for those names?" She was still laughing when Colt lifted her into the waiting black phaeton.

"Search me. Someone with a limited imagination, no doubt," he answered with a laugh.

He jumped up onto the opposite side, grasping the reins to give them a robust shake. The vehicle lurched forward, its large spoke wheels creaking in protest as they lumbered down the rutted pathway.

In the early morning stillness Madison could hear the clip-clop of hooves, a scattered bawling of calves in the distance, and the yips of the riders who urged them on. She ran her fingers over the worn and cracked finish of the black leather tufted seat. An intense awareness enveloped her senses and she wished her mother and her brother could be here with her to enjoy all she was about to experience. They rounded a sharp curve to enter the main road, which was nothing more than dirt with a center strip of grass.

"It's all right to sit back now. You look as if you're about ready to leap off the seat." Colt grinned.

Without an inkling of the feelings her touch invoked, she casually braced a hand on his knee when she scooted back into a comfortable position. "Isn't it absolutely wonderful in the mornings, Colt? I hate getting up early, but once I'm up I love it—it's like a whole new world." She brushed away a loose strand of hair that blew across her face.

Colt nodded his agreement, finding it difficult to keep his eyes off her. He marveled that her simple touch sent a jolt of raw heat beating through his veins, his very being. He wanted her, at the break of dawn or any other time. He wanted to make long, slow love to her—but he also wanted *her,* all of her. Never before had he desired a woman's companionship all the time, especially when he wasn't in a loving mood. With Madison, everything was different. He desired her presence all the time; even while working he could think of nothing else. It was almost as if he hadn't existed until a few days ago when he first laid eyes on her.

Several times since last night Colt had questioned his own sanity at asking her to come along to the howling boomtown of South Pass City. Full of genteel businessmen as well as a slew of brawling ruffians, he knew the arrival of a never-before-seen beauty such as Madison would cause no small stir. And he also knew if anyone so much as thought about laying a hand on her, he would kill for such a trespass. What frightened him the most was that he sensed a change in himself, and he wasn't at all sure if he liked it. One thing was certain. He couldn't live without it.

The thought arose that possibly the time warp that shot him into the future and brought them both back, wouldn't work again. She might be here for good. Colt's spirits lifted considerably at the idea. But then he envisioned the despair that would fill those aqua eyes, liquid with unshed tears, if that proved true, and he knew he couldn't endure her pain if she remained here without the desire to stay. He only wanted what would make her happy. But what *would* make her happy? he wondered.

Madison sat rigidly on the bench seat, bumping and lurching with the jars of the washboard road. Colt seemed untroubled by the roughness of the ride; probably used to it, she surmised. But her bottom was already turning numb and she was almost certain a vital part of her anatomy would rattle loose with the incessant shaking.

"Tell me more about the twentieth century." Colt's voice boomed above the plodding hooves.

Madison looked up at him with a sigh. The sun was climbing ever higher in the serene blue sky, and he gazed at her beneath the shadow of his hat.

"That's a tall order. Let me see . . . there has been so much medical technology in a hundred years. People rarely die from everyday illness as they do now, here. Doctors are able to transplant a heart or a kidney, even eyes, from a dead or dying person so that someone may live a better life. There have been two world wars, and there's been the threat of a third one since the onset of the nuclear age."

Madison attempted to explain the concept of the atom bomb to Colt, and with a mixture of shock and amazement he became totally enthralled.

"It's all so unbelievable, Madison . . . society must live in terror." Colt shook his head.

"Well, people do, on a certain level. But I suppose every age has its terrors and triumphs. For me, the incivility of the Old West holds its own apprehensions. I can't fathom being stuck here without someone like you for protection."

Madison's laugh died out when she felt the weight of his gaze upon her, only for some reason she couldn't force herself to meet it. Instead, she continued, relating how rockets filled with astronauts could shoot to the moon and circle the earth in space. She told him of world hunger and the war on drugs. Turning to lighter subjects such as television and movies, they laughed, talking continuously for well over an hour. Colt was like a dry sponge, taking in all the information she could possibly offer.

Before they knew it the sun was high, its rays burning intensely through the atmosphere of the mountain elevation, making it seem that much hotter.

"I think it's time for some chow—what d'ye say, sugar?"

"Sounds heavenly." Just the mention of food made her stomach rumble.

"Whoa, there . . ."

The buggy came to a halt beside a grove of ancient willows, graceful silhouettes in varying shades of green standing out against the drying prairie. A gurgling creek created a welcoming oasis. Colt leapt down and began to unhitch the horses in order to water them.

Madison busied herself with spreading a blanket and unpacking the bundle of food. There was leftover fried chicken, jerked beef, dried apples, sourdough biscuits, and two cans of tomatoes. Madison wondered why the tomatoes, then quickly forgot them when her attention was drawn to the creek bank. Fumbling, she gasped in annoyance as biscuits rolled this way and that across the blanket.

Colt knelt at the water's edge, his shirt thrown over a diamond willow bush. His muscles flexed beneath his smooth, tawny skin as he scooped a hat full of cool water, dumping it unceremoniously over his head. A waterfall gushed over the expanse of his bronzed back, coursing in rills, glistening like prisms in the sun. He splashed his face, taking a long draught from his cupped hands. When he stood he hesitated, his hands on his slim hips, his suspenders hanging limply at his sides. He shook his head to free it of the excess water.

Madison barely breathed, watching with admiring eyes, finally forcing herself to stop gawking long enough to gather the wayward biscuits. She brushed her palms along her skirt, then raised her head to call Colt, but no sound would come. He sauntered directly toward her, not ten feet away. He carried his holster; his shirt was open, flapping in the warm summer breeze. Madison could see the beads of moisture as they clung to his light brown chest hair and his hardened nipples.

"Are you feeling well?" Colt's first concern was the bump on her head. It seemed there were times she simply stared, not acting like herself at all. He plopped down at her side, snagging a chicken leg and tearing at it ravenously.

"Hmmmm? What . . . oh, I was just . . . daydreaming, is all," she replied. She reached for a piece of chicken with a trembling hand.

"Anything you'd like to share?"

There's plenty I'd like to share with you, if only I could, she mused to herself.

"Share? Nothing interesting, really."

Madison nibbled on the chicken, not tasting it, absently taking minuscule bites, as thoughts of the future filled her mind. She didn't want to go through life never to feel this way again! Despite her protests, she wanted him to push her back onto the cushion of long grass and make mad, passionate love to her. There wasn't much time left. She could feel it! Who knew what other chances they might have to be together. Some women might be able to seduce him, asking for what they wanted, but she couldn't, she just couldn't. He was making her crazy! Couldn't he see it?

"Well, maybe not to you. But I'd like to know. What does a woman from the twentieth century daydream about, anyway?" He leaned over on his elbow, his leg bent up as he began to polish off the biscuits, one after another.

"Boy, it sure is hot today, isn't it? I think I could use a splash or two of that water myself." Madison's skin was on fire. She jumped to her feet, practically running to the bank of the creek.

Colt stopped chewing, perplexed at her odd behavior. Shrugging, he tossed a clean chicken bone into a nearby bush and reached for another piece.

Madison pulled the hem of her skirt up so it wouldn't drag over the muddy edge. Squatting, she scooped water from the creek and dashed it soothingly over her scorched skin. She undid the top button of her blouse, letting the refreshing water trickle down. Her eyes closed blissfully, she tilted her head back with relief.

When she opened her eyes it took a moment for her to focus— her first thought was that she was seeing things. In a crush of realization, Madison knew that this was no mirage. Standing before her on the opposite side of the shallow creek was a full-fledged, authentic Indian! Dressed entirely in buckskins, he was rather short and hefty, his blue-black hair hanging past his shoulders in loose, rawhide-wrapped queues and several dangling feathers. His dark brown face was round, its features flat. His black eyes stared, emotionless, inquisitive.

A tentative movement caught her eye, and she jerked a glance up and past the Indian, only to spot another one on horseback behind the dense shrubbery. Her heart somersaulted, its pounding deafening in her ears.

Spinning around, Madison clawed her way back up the moist bank, slipping as the black earth crumbled beneath her feet. A strangled shriek erupted from deep inside her throat.

Chapter Eighteen

Her scream brought Colt to his feet. Pistol in hand, he made a mad dash for the creek. Madison met him halfway, flinging her body into his arms, her words spilling forth in broken sentences.

"Colt!" she gasped frantically, motioning back, "there! Indians! Two . . . staring at me . . . !"

Madison's body was shaking and she breathed convulsively. Colt gripped her shoulders and held her away, gazing intently into her enormous aqua eyes.

"Madison. Calm yourself. It's very important that you remain calm."

"In-di-ans!" she repeated tightly, sure he didn't understand the gravity of the situation.

"I know, sugar. You mustn't show fear. Be very cool, walk slowly over to the blanket, and wait. I'll take care of it."

The smooth surety in his voice eased her somewhat, but she continued to eye him skeptically.

"Go on . . ." he urged, releasing her with a gentle push toward the huge willow.

Though she obeyed, a pulse hammered at her temples. Cold sweat popped out on her brow. Madison fought the frightening images that clamored for space inside her head: all of the western

145

movies she'd ever seen, the books she'd read that recounted scalp-
ings, tortures, women kidnapped and used for who knew what
purpose. Good God, what if they tied her and Colt to an anthill
somewhere? She shuddered. Whatever happened, she decided—
if the Indians harbored evil motives, she'd fight them tooth and
nail . . . to the end.

An idea struck her. Inhaling deeply for courage, Madison
detoured toward the buggy. She retrieved Colt's rifle from the
gun boot, stealing a glance behind her before creeping silently to
wait beneath the tree. Madison was patient, her jaw set, the rifle
cradled carefully in her arms.

Colt stood at the creek's edge. He carried his pistol in a
casual manner, pointing downward, though Madison could see
his finger brushing over the trigger in readiness. She nervously chewed a long fingernail, grappling to understand the ensu-
ing conversation. The words were foreign to her ears, but Colt
seemed to have no problem communicating. His voice was earnest and commanding, the language uttered in an odd staccato
rhythm.

It wasn't long before Colt strolled back up the hill, his gaze
lowering to the rifle in her arms, then up again with a glow of
admiration in his brown eyes.

"We're trading them food," he said, kneeling down to sort it.
"This is for us." He shoved a portion toward her. The remainder he
packaged together, carrying it down to where the Indians waited
by the creek. When he returned he casually tossed something to
her, and she automatically raised her hand to catch it. Bewildered,
she propped the rifle against the tree and watched him sit back
down on the blanket.

"A little souvenir, sugar." A smile eased over his face. He felt
immensely proud that Madison possessed the gumption to arm
herself without having to be told. This woman had spunk—he
liked that. Colt felt through the suede pouch and began to roll
a cigarette. "Maybe you'll look at that in years to come, say a
hundred or two, and remember me." He winked.

Madison sunk to her knees at his side, examining the crude
necklace she cupped in her hand. It was crafted from an assort-
ment of brown, blue, and red imperfectly rounded seeds of some
sort. Interspersed between them were very large animal claws.
Madison raised questioning eyes.

"Bear claws," Colt answered her thought.

"I don't understand."

Colt drew deeply from the freshly lit cigarette, exhaling into the breeze. "A small band of Crow are camped just beyond that far bluff over there. Those two by the creek were scouts sent by the others to find food. I spotted them a ways back—they've been following us. I didn't want to mention it and risk frightening you. Looks like I didn't save you much grief. Anyhow, they're hungry. They have families to feed—"

"Oh . . . Colt! I feel terrible. They needed food? If I'd only known!"

"No, you did good. Just because they were hungry doesn't mean they weren't dangerous. You can't just go and donate food, even though it may seem the humane thing to do. To them, that would be a sign of vulnerability—and believe me, you don't want that. Best to treat it in a businesslike manner; offer a trade. That way, everybody's happy, and everyone's dignity stays intact. They get food . . ." Colt hesitated, his eyes resting on her meaningfully, "and we get to keep our scalps."

The little smile dropped from Madison's lips. Then he did something she wasn't at all expecting. Crushing the cigarette out under the heel of his boot, he leaned toward her, lifting her jaw with his forefinger. Colt's mouth came to hers in an achingly sweet kiss. He tasted of aromatic tobacco, and she kissed him back eagerly. The embers that burned readily somewhere deep down inside her soul were stirred, until she thought she just might swoon. He released her, much too soon.

"I was teasing—silly." Adopting her expression, he broke into a wonderfully lopsided grin, chucked her chin affectionately, and pushed to his feet.

Dreamily, Madison leaned back onto her heels and regarded him, loving every move he made as he hitched the horses— loving the way he walked, loving the way he crooned softly to the animals, loving him . . .

Madison wondered how in the world she could feel so ecstatically happy and so full of such despair, all at the same time.

Rounding an isolated headland, they circled west through mountainous foothills. Utah junipers were scattered over hills and arroyos. It was obvious they were nearing the northern fringes of South Pass City.

The once beautiful landscape was dredged up into monstrous piles of waste rock along played-out mines. Trains of rusted iron ore cars were lined perfectly along tracks, as if the miners

were expected back at any time. Madison's eyes sought out
the dark, foreboding entrances to abandoned mine tunnels, a
ghostly feeling of emptiness hovering over her as they drove
slowly by.

Some of the lateral shafts were boarded, and Colt told her
they were still used for sheltering women and children should an
Indian or outlaw rampage occur. Other mines trickled with a few
bedraggled souls, ducking in and out of black embouchements.
The occasional clink of a pick ax hitting rock echoed from deep
within the earth. Miners briefly ceased activities, curious eyes
watching as the buggy rolled past.

Her mood lifted as the gravel road grew wider, crude clapboard
buildings lining each side of the city street. This must be the main
avenue, Madison thought. Modest dwellings became closer and
closer together, tiny front yards enclosed with either wrought-iron
or white picket fences, small windows adorned with white lacy
curtains. As far as Madison could see, small log cabin homesteads
were scattered over the surrounding hills. A quaint metropolis
loomed ahead, and Madison thought what a shame it was that
the countryside was so cruelly marred by the yellowed waste
rock. Then again, she suspected, if it weren't for the bygone
prosperity of those mines, the town of South Pass City probably
wouldn't exist.

Road traffic increased; they were being passed by buckboards
and single riders traveling in the opposite direction. Low-fronted
stores with colorful signs filled the street before them, butting up
to one another. People strolled on the railed boardwalks. Men
were dressed in black coats and derby hats, some accompanied
by very elegant women in long, flowing dresses and towering,
befeathered hats. More common, though, was the cowboy-type
Madison was used to seeing on the ranch—most filthy, their
clothes worn. She fidgeted in her seat, craning her neck to see
everything there was to see.

Colt and Madison trotted on past a parked road wagon. A
plain-faced woman sat rigidly on the bench seat, her head covered
with a threadbare sun bonnet. Three dirty-faced children played
rambunctiously in the back of the wagon, suddenly jumping to
the ground to engage in a game of tag. Madison beamed brightly
at the solemn-faced woman when they passed. Bewildered at first,
the woman's mouth slowly curved upward in response.

"Ohhhh, look! Is that a real stagecoach up there?" Madison
frantically slapped Colt's thigh with the back of her hand, pointing

with the other, her voice high with excitement.

"Yes, sugar, I do believe that is a real stagecoach." Colt laughed, enjoying her exhilaration.

Madison stared in wonderment as they drove by, studying two burly men as they heaved a variety of trunks onto the top of the coach. One grumbled a few foul expletives just as they passed. Glancing up at Madison, his face was transformed to a deep crimson.

It seemed as though all eyes rested on them when Colt finally pulled in on the reins, bringing the buggy to a halt. Madison pondered the throng of curious stares. Some passersby actually quickened their pace, disappearing into doorways, but not before sending a last glimpse backward.

Colt seemed oblivious, jumping down and walking around to help her down. She placed her hands on his shoulders and he lifted her to the ground.

"Why are so many people looking at us?" Madison watched over Colt's shoulder as one young boy sprinted down the street, turning to break out into a full-fledged run.

"Because this is probably the first time in their lives they've laid eyes on such a lovely honey-haired woman," Colt answered.

"Seriously, Colt."

"I am serious. In fact, I question the wisdom of leaving you alone while I take care of some pressing business."

"No problem. I can occupy myself with some pretty intense antique shopping here, don't you think?" Madison grinned.

Colt regarded her, deep in thought. "Don't go anywhere except the mercantile. Understand? Stay inside until I come back to get you. By the way, I get this reaction whenever I come to town. People are going to be wondering who this gorgeous woman is that I'm with—so be prepared. I'll be just across the street inside the sheriff's office, then next door to make a few purchases. Will you all right?"

His expression was so serious. Madison couldn't fathom this little town being *that* unsafe. If she had managed to survive the subways of New York City, how hard could this be? Nodding her head, she showed him that she understood.

Colt walked her to the doorway of Butler's Mercantile Co. and tilted his hat to the little gray-haired woman behind the counter before he squeezed Madison's hand and left. Madison whirled around and went inside, smiling brightly at the woman, whose gray hair was parted in perfectly symmetrical waves, and drawn back into a tight knot. Her deep blue eyes sparkled, and she nodded kindly.

The mercantile was dim in comparison to the brightness of the outdoors. It smelled of plug tobacco, leather, and freshly ground coffee. Madison walked slowly, her eyes circling the tiny store with interest, attempting to take in the conglomeration of items for sale. Every nook and cranny was occupied. The rafters were hung with hams, slabs of bacon, and iron cooking pots. Barrels were brimming with flour, sugar, and even vinegar. Baskets, bolts of cloth, kerosene lanterns and lamps, candles and canned goods lined crude shelves. A huge coffee grinder sat bolted to a countertop. Half-full glass jars held licorice and colorful sticks of hard candy.

Madison browsed at a glass case, peering inside at the variety of items for sale. Bloomer girls smiled prettily from packages and bottles of everything from liniments to snake oils to remedies for baldness. The stern face of a mustachioed man, his hair parted in the middle, endorsed shaving cream.

Close by, gold chains and baubles sparkled in the gloomy light. She sighed in admiration when she spotted a tiny cameo on a delicate gold chain. Oh, how she would love to have that! She'd always been fond of cameos—and no question about it, this would definitely be an antique in her time!

Lucinda Beak squinted against the onslaught of glaring sunlight as she gaped, looking down from her window at the street, making her already pinched face appear even more so. A riotous shout from the saloon below had echoed the name "Chase" and, being the nosy person she was, she hadn't hesitated a moment to catapault her skinny form from the bed and to the window. Her thin lips spread into a grin, exposing discolored teeth.

"Aaahhh, if it isn't Colt Chase," she mumbled to herself, just like she always did.

Stretching her neck this way and that, she gawked, struggling to get a better view from the grimy window. She scrutinized the black phaeton as it came to a stop. Her pale blue eyes needy and lustful, she watched as Colt stepped down and went to the other side and helped a blond woman from the buggy. She frowned when she saw how he held her, so close, so intimate. Lucinda wasn't stupid. She knew what a man wanted when he stood that close to a woman. Lucinda was a professional when it came to men, and a damn good one at that. That blonde couldn't give Colt nearly the pleasure she could, Lucinda thought with a sneering smugness. Why, she knew of things that would drive a man half out of his mind with pleasure. She just needed the inspiration of a real man like Colton to try them on. To hell with these sleaze buckets around here. They couldn't pay her enough to do those kinds of things with them. But Colt Chase . . . now, that was a different story.

For years now, Lucinda had tried and tried to make a customer out of Colt, ever since she had come to this backwater town with that no-good husband of hers. She had married the old coot back east, not wanting him, just wanting the ticket out west—a ticket to wealth. She had heard the stories of rich cattle barons, of miners who struck it rich, all just starving for the love of a woman. Her husband had been a good twenty years older than she, but she hadn't cared as long as he got her out west in one piece. She'd planned on dumping him anyway, so what had it mattered? Then she would find a young, preferably handsome, definitely rich man to marry.

They had been on a wagon train traveling the Oregon Trail, ultimately heading for California. How they had ended up in this trashy town in Wyoming Territory she'd never know. Something about waiting for a new wagonmaster to take over the train. All she had known for sure was that her husband had up and got himself shot and killed nary a week after they had arrived. Lucinda had been left high and dry, whatever money they had gambled away.

Forced to stay behind, she had eventually become a sportin' gal in order to support herself. She certainly wasn't going to drag herself back home, her tail between her legs, to face a drunken father and snooty stepmother.

Things weren't so bad—or so she told herself on the good days. She had her health, and she believed that someday she'd find the man who would take her away from all this.

Lucinda also knew that if she got Colt into her bed—hell, she wouldn't even charge him—he would be hooked. She already had Garrett as a paying customer, and though he wasn't a shabby prospect for a husband, Colt suited her tastes far more. Much, much more. He wouldn't even have to marry her. No, she would happily consent to be his privately kept mistress if that's all he wanted. It didn't matter a hill of beans to her, just as long as she got him.

And now, six months since Lucinda had last seen him around these parts, he had shown up with some lousy blonde. Her thin lips curled into a devilish grin as she nurtured a budding idea. It wouldn't take much doing to find out just who this woman was, and how much she actually meant to Colt. . . . Her sparce eyebrows raised in consideration.

With the soiled green taffeta of her gown rustling, Lucinda left her room, slamming the door behind her. Bounding down the plank staircase, she bolted outside and directly into the Grecian Bend. Her hands on her hips, she surveyed the customers sprinkled about the smoky saloon.

Her pale blue eyes lit up eagerly when she spotted the one person she was looking for.

Chapter Nineteen

"Colt Chase! Well, if this don't beat all! Been waitin' for you to come waltzin' through that door for 'bout a week now! How have ya been?" Lloyd Townsend's voice boomed across the confines of the tiny office as he reached for Colt's hand across his scarred oak desk, delivering a robust handshake.

"Can't complain, Lloyd. How about yourself?" Colt removed his hat and placed it on the corner of the desk before he sat down opposite the sheriff.

"Fine 'n dandy. Mary and I are expectin' another young'un any day now—things are goin' right good." Lloyd flashed a cheerful smile beneath a black handlebar mustache. He rocked his weight back in his chair with a resistant creak.

"Congratulations. Number ten is it?" Colt returned cleverly, knowing Lloyd and his wife loved children and wanted as many as they could possibly have.

Lloyd's laughter nearly shook the rafters in the modest jail-house, and when he sobered, he said, "Damn close! Number eight, countin' the twins. Speakin' of young'uns, Colt, when do you plan on snaggin' yourself a pretty woman and raisin' up a brood of your own? Got to think 'bout the future, son. Who's gonna take over that spread of yours when you're too old to give a damn?" Lloyd smiled wryly, regarding Colt with hooded eyes.

"I don't suppose you caught sight of a particular pretty young woman I rode in with, now did you?" Colt asked, suspecting what Lloyd was leading up to.

"'Course I did! Not much goes on in this little town without my knowin' 'bout it."

Colt relaxed back into the chair, folding his arms over his chest in thought. "Well," he said finally, "consider yourself the first one in town to know that the lady's already made an honest man out of me. Her name is Madison . . . and she's my wife." That was the second time Colt had had to say it, and damn if he wasn't beginning to like the sound of it. The fact that he liked it was starting to bother him.

Another boom of laughter shook the walls. "Well, of all people . . . Sounds like congratulations are in order for you, too, son!" Lloyd straightened halfway out of his chair and delivered another vigorous handshake. As he took his seat, a shadow passed over his face and he paused with a heavy sigh. "That little bit of news sure makes me loathe to give you this." He pulled open the top drawer of his desk and removed a slip of paper, sliding it across to Colt. His bushy brows furrowed with heartfelt concern and he twiddled his mustache while waiting for Colt to read it.

Colt unfolded the paper and read the handwritten telegram:

Sheriff—South Pass City, Wyoming—
For Colton R. Chase—
Need help—Rustling/Murders—
Suspect Red Eagle—Left his mark—
Respond to—Your friend and Marshal—
Ford County, Kansas—Bat Masterson—

Colt put the paper down. He raised hesitant eyes to Lloyd, a troubled smile crossing his face. "I'll be damned. Haven't heard from Bat since I taught him a few shooting tricks down in Colorado a few years back. Sounds like he's doing pretty good for himself."

Lloyd wasn't falling for the small talk. "Bat's good. Real good. But I don't need to tell you that, do I? The point being, he can handle matters himself, Colt. He's got his brother Jim to help; he's the sheriff there in Abilene. Don't go runnin' off on no wild goose chase, boy. Ain't nothin' says it's Red Eagle down in Kansas. There's rumors flyin' around 'bout his whereabouts from Montana to Mexico—he can't be everywhere at once."

"That's true." Colt pushed forward and leaned over the desk. "But he's left his mark. Therefore, if it's not him, it's his gang. Through his boys I can get a direct line to him. It may take a little creativity, but I've never had a problem gaining the cooperation of a man with a six-shooter shoved down his throat." His voice rang low, a menacing quality to it.

"I don't doubt that one bit. Red Eagle and his gang are out there plying their trade, and if anyone can nab 'em, it's you." Lloyd shook his head. "But dammit, that half-breed's got a mean streak in him a mile long. He's always known you were on his trail."

"Like piss on a sow."

"Exactly, but one of these days, when you're least expectin' it, he's gonna turn around and fight." Colt opened his mouth to speak, but Lloyd held a hand up to silence him. "I know you can handle your own, but you've always been like a son to me, 'specially since your ma and pa died. Sure would hate to see anything happen to you. I guess you could say I've taken it upon myself to watch after you boys."

"I can appreciate that, but you've got to realize that I haven't surrendered ten years of my life to give up now. Red Eagle *will* pay for what he did. I despise the fact that it's taken this long already. He deserves to hang, and I'm going to see that he does, mark my words." Colt gazed straight into the older man's eyes, deadly serious.

Lloyd sighed, barely concealing the glint of admiration in his dark eyes. "Can't blame me for tryin', now can ya? That's why I refused to have a rider deliver this here telegram. Wanted you to come into town for it. Thought maybe then I'd have a chance to convince you to stay at the ranch, settle down, leave Red Eagle for the law. Good God, you've got a wife to think of now!"

Colt nodded. "Soon, Lloyd. Soon. Fact is, I told Garrett just last night that I would be around the ranch quite a bit from here on out. I suppose you've heard about the cattle we lost."

"Yup. You and 'bout eight or ten other ranches in the area. It's becomin' an epidemic. That's why I said you just can't be too sure where Red Eagle is hidin' out."

"Where there's people getting murdered, you can bet he's behind it."

"Yeah, but hell, there's sheep farmers out there squawkin' that the cattle ranchers are killin' off their sheep—the ranchers say it's the sheep farmers doin' the rustlin'. I just don't know.

Somethin' got to be done, or we're gonna have an all-out war on our hands."

"All I know is that I'm expecting twelve hundred head of Longhorn. They're already overdue. Kansas is a hot spot for intercepting the long drives up from Texas. It wouldn't take much at all to rustle a good part of a herd. I understand they're driving up as many as thirty-five hundred head at a time, Lloyd. It's rustlers' heaven down there! Not only is the possibility very good that I could stop Red Eagle once and for all, but I have a personal stake in my Longhorns. I see no other way—I've got to go to Abilene."

"I get your point, Colt. Though I'd still be a happier man if you decided not to."

"Garrett's just going to have to hold down the fort for a few more months. Hopefully when I return, I can get on with my life. . . ." Colt ended on a sad note, thinking dismally of his apparent future. Lately he couldn't seem to get excited about anything unless Madison was involved in it—and right now that didn't look too promising.

"Speakin' of Garrett." Lloyd twisted his mustache in concentration. "I'm a little worried about his carryin' on. It's been twice this month I've had to break up a brawl inside the Grecian Bend, only to find Garrett the instigator. I don't suppose you know he spent a night right here in my jail. I realize he's never been a real personable type of feller, but it's gotten worse lately. He's bitter . . . maybe hostile is a better word."

"I get your point." Colt rubbed the weariness from his eyes. "I'll have a chat with him . . . again. Sometimes I feel like I'm talking to a wall. But I'm confident his irresponsibility will end once I'm back at the ranch to stay."

"Can I get you some coffee, Colt?" Lloyd rose and advanced to the potbelly stove, the coffeepot bubbling on top.

Colt pressed his hat back onto his head, standing to leave. "Wish I could, but I've got a few other errands to tend to."

"Give that wife of yours my best wishes," Lloyd replied with warm sincerity shining in his eyes.

"Surely will." Colt grinned, extending his hand to the older man. "As always, it's been a pleasure, Lloyd."

The sheriff shook his hand warmly, wishing him and his new bride luck, and Colt stepped outside into warm beams of sunshine.

He glanced across the street to the mercantile. Just a quick scan to make sure all was well. At ease, he walked up the boardwalk a few doors and ducked into the telegraph office. As soon as he finished sending a positive response to Marshal Bat Masterson in Ford County, Kansas, his plan was to stop by Frye & Co. and put in an order for some barbed-wire fencing.

Lucinda swayed her boyish hips as she strolled over to the poker table in the center of the room. She came to stand behind a giant of a man commonly referred to as Three-toed Pete, aptly named for the fact that he'd blown part of his own foot off during a drunken brawl. Long black hair hung in greasy strands down his back. He wore a misshapen black hat that was nearly as dirty. At the touch of Lucinda's hand, he jerked around to face her. His facial features were as grotesquely oversized as his body; a drawn-out scar ran from the corner of his left eye and down his cheek. When he saw it was only Lucy he turned his back to her with a grunt.

"Hi, honey," Lucinda cooed as seductively as she could. "In the mood for a little fun?" She kneaded his thick, fleshy shoulders with her bony hands, the bodice of her ill-fitting gown gaping with the movement and practically exposing her small breasts.

"What's the matter? You horny for a change?" Pete rasped with a chuckle. The other scraggly-looking characters at the table snickered at his wit.

Lucy's mouth pursed into a wrinkled bow of disapproval, and she struggled to hold on to her temper. It wouldn't do to anger Pete, not when she needed his assistance. On the other hand, the others could all go straight to hell. Her beady eyes flashing, she sneered across the table. The snickering quickly died out.

"Pete, honey," she replied, the words dripping with insincere sweetness, "I wasn't referring to myself this time. No, I just happened by my window upstairs when I spotted a—" she frowned with distaste, "a most lovely lady with hair as yellow as a dandelion. You do love *yellow* hair, don't you, Pete?"

Pete stared down at the cards in his hand, appearing unaware that she was even behind him.

"I can't say I *know* the woman, personally that is, but I know of her," Lucinda lied, "and if memory serves me, she's quite the little tart—if you get my meaning? Now, I'm only thinking of you, Pete honey. I would much rather have you all to myself, but I've been so . . . tired lately." She sighed audibly, her skinny fingers fluttering to her brow. "I'm sure that woman would love to have a big bear of a man such as you to teach her some rare pleasures. She *does* have yellow hair . . ." Lucinda glared down over the sharp plane of her hawklike nose, her voice rising on the last sentence.

Pete pivoted in his chair, slowly looking up. His huge face was masked by a suspicious scowl. "What the hell are you up to, Lucy? Since when do you arrange my lovelife?"

"Ohhh nooo, I must be daffy. I shouldn't have said a word. If you get a taste of her, you may never want me again." She rolled her eyes skyward, feigning distress. "I only thought to make you happy, honey." Her eyes downcast, she started to walk away, a pout on her face.

"Wait! Git yer skinny ass back over here!" he thundered.

Disguising a smile of satisfaction, she veered back around in a swirl of taffeta. "Yes?" she replied sweetly.

"So . . . tell me more. Who is this dame? Where is she?" Pete picked up a stubby cigar from the edge of the table, biting down on the slimy end.

Lucinda briskly pulled a chair close, the lies rolling from her lips. Naturally, she left out the part about the blonde being with Colt Chase. That would ruin everything. Nobody, but nobody would mess with a woman in the company of Colt Chase, unless they had a death wish. Simple fact was, nobody messed with Colt Chase—*period*.

"Now listen," Lucinda continued swiftly, "let me go see her first. I'll put in a few good words for ya, honey. Would you like that? If she's interested, she'll meet you on down past the livery. You wait there. When she comes you two can get to know one another real good. How does that sound, hmmmmm?"

Lucinda knew Pete's interest was definitely piqued. He regarded her with bloodshot eyes, finally grunting an approval. Three-toed Pete had never been an overly bright individual. One of these days that fact was going to get him killed.

"Don't dawdle, now!" Her heels slapping loudly, Lucinda darted from the saloon, pushing through the swinging doors and on across the street. She slowed at the entrance of Butler's Mercantile Co. There she smoothed her dress and hair before strolling inside.

Chapter Twenty

Madison held the cameo up by its gleaming gold chain, desire shining in her eyes. The prim, gray-haired woman stood behind the glass counter, a demure smile curving the corners of her mouth.

"It is lovely, isn't it? We don't get many treasures like that, at least not often. That arrived straight from New York less than a week ago. 'Course, I believe it came from Europe before that."

Madison smiled, nodding her head in acknowledgment. "It is gorgeous. Maybe I'll get the chance to come back for it." She gave the delicate piece of jewelry to the woman, who placed it back inside the glass case. Madison twirled around at the sound of the door opening, expecting to see Colt.

What she saw was a far cry from what she had expected. A skin-and-bones, pale-faced woman approached her, not stopping until she was uncomfortably close. She was several inches shorter than Madison, and the woman's eyes traveled up and down her body in brash perusal. Her thin, mousy-brown hair was pasted into a careless roll at the back of her head, stiff tendrils snaking down around her pointed face. Her cheeks were garishly rouged into two pink circles. The purplish paint she'd applied to what lips she had did nothing to improve the appearance of her ashen complexion. This caricature of a woman was encased in an unbecoming dress of metal-green.

159

Her pale blue eyes narrowed with envy as they peered into the blonde's wide aqua ones. Even though she was swimming in jealousy, Lucinda managed to drag her lips over her teeth in what she hoped to be a pleasant smile. Up close, she found this woman to be even more beautiful than she had originally thought—and it angered her.

"Hello. I'm Miss Beak." She paused to flutter her eyes over the woman, giving her a chance to speak, to introduce herself . . . to say *something.* " . . . And you are?" she coaxed.

"Er . . . my . . . I'm—" Madison croaked, her train of thought totally shattered by this horrendous-looking woman. She cleared her throat. "Madison . . . Calloway. May I help you?" She waited politely for Miss Beak to continue, having no idea why she had barged into the store and approached her so abruptly. It could be this was just the way they greeted strangers around here, but she highly doubted it.

A loud harumph sounded from behind her. Having almost forgotten the presence of the shopkeeper, Madison turned. The woman behind the counter was glaring down her nose at Miss Beak with open disgust, her eyes sharp and beady.

"Relax, Grandma. I've got just as much right to frequent this store as this lady, here. Actually, I don't know why I would want to. All that's in here is crap!" Lucinda raged, her hands propped at her hips, her face squinching comically.

"Well! I never . . . !" The older woman held a hand delicately atop her heaving bosom, her eyes wide in shock.

"That's right, you never have. Maybe if you *had,* you wouldn't be so cranky." With that, Lucinda riveted her attention back to Madison. Her demeanor was instantly transformed to one of pleasantness.

The initial astonishment having faded, Madison quietly stepped to the side, pretending interest in the bolts of fine lace at the end of the counter. She yearned to disengage herself from the conversation; but more so, was finding it extremely difficult to suppress the giggle that insisted on bubbling up into her throat.

Lucinda sidled in close to her again.

"Well, now, where were we? Ahhhh, yes. Your name is Mad . . . uh . . . whatever, it doesn't matter, I suppose. I couldn't help but notice your entrance into town with Mr. Chase. I wouldn't normally be so bothersome, you see, but I *am* a good friend of his. A *very* good friend, and I've never seen you around here before," she pried, her tone clipped, as if she possessed the epitome of social grace. It didn't take long for her to realize that this woman wasn't going to part with any information as to who she was and why she was with Colt. In fact, she seemed to be too stunned to say anything. Lucinda knew she had to hurry it up if this little scheme was going to work.

"Doesn't make no nevermind," she chuckled amicably, inspecting her fingernails. "I just ran into Colt a few moments ago. He was down at the Bend. We had ourselves a little chat and . . ." She hesitated when Madison's eyebrows shot up. *Good,* she thought, *finally I've got a rise out of her!* " . . . and he asked if I would mind letting you know that his plans have changed, and he'll be meeting you on down past the livery. Do you know where that is? I'll show you. . . ."

In a flash, Lucinda was at the window, pointing a bony finger. "Right down there at the very end of the street. He had some last-minute business to tend to. I told him, naw! wouldn't mind at all comin' over here to tell you! He should be there by this time. You may want to get going." Her arms folded, her toe tapped impatiently on the boarded floor.

"Colt asked *you* to come and tell me that?"

Madison was very skeptical. Not only because it was strange that he hadn't come to get her himself, but also because she was having a hard time believing Colt knew this woman—let alone kept company with her.

"Yes! Yes! Not more than a few minutes ago. You'd better git!" Lucinda screeched in a most annoying tone, her skinny arms flapping as she shooed Madison toward the door.

Madison frowned dubiously, glancing back. The older woman simply shrugged and shook her head. This was very bizarre. But then, Colt had done other things she hadn't understood at the time. The picture in her mind of Colt and this atrocious woman together was almost too much to fathom. What ulterior motive could Miss Beak possibly have?

As she stepped outside, a gust of wind caught the fullness of her skirts. She paused to smooth them down and to get her bearings. Lucinda once again pointed down the street, fluttering her fingers in farewell.

Madison managed a weak smile, heading toward the weathered brown, barnlike building at the far end of the street. In white letters the words LIVERY STABLE were painted on the side. It stood by itself, located at the edge of town, where the buildings were few and far between.

As Madison neared the livery, she noticed that seedy degen-
erates loitered on the boardwalk, leaning lazily against support
beams and doorways. They were dirty and smelled, and Madison
shrank as far away from them as possible as she passed. Watery,
bloodshot eyes rested on her lustfully. She squared her shoulders,
increasing her pace. Rowdy shouts and the noxious odor of old
liquor emitted from a darkened doorway. It was becoming all the
more unbelievable that Colt would ask her to meet him down here,
and she was beginning to feel ridiculous for giving Miss Beak the
time of day.

With an irritated sigh, more at herself than anyone, she stepped
off the end of the boardwalk, thrusting her hands on her hips as
she looked around. It seemed deserted. No sign whatsoever of
Colt. Shaking her head at her own gullibility, she decided to return
to the mercantile. Just then, an inhuman sort of grunt from behind
her prompted Madison to turn.

The business at hand completed, Colt left the office of Frye and
Co. He sprinted across the street, dodging several slow-moving
wagons. With a rush of air he entered the mercantile, the jingling
of spurs signaling his arrival. The gray-haired lady swiveled
around, smiling in recognition.

"Hello again, Mr. Chase."

"Good afternoon, Mrs. Butler." He grinned good-naturedly,
leaning over the counter to peer inside. Colt naturally assumed
Madison was still in the store—he had no reason to think otherwise. He'd given her strict instructions. Probably browsing in the
back, he reasoned logically. He purposefully lowered his voice so
Madison wouldn't hear. "Is there anything the lady was especially
fond of?"

Mrs. Butler gave him a conspiratorial smile, reaching beneath
the glass to retrieve the cameo. She held it up for Colt's inspection.

Impressed, he nodded his approval. "I suspect we'd best wrap
it up." Colt charmed her with another smile. As he paid for his
purchase, he began to look around the store, searching for that
glimpse of striking gold hair amid the clutter. "Throw some
licorice in there, too. . . . Where is she, anyway?"

"The lady? Oh, she left a while ago."

"She what? Left?" His tone elevated harshly, causing the mild
woman to nearly jump out of her skin.

"Why, yes . . . that little trollop from across the street came and gave her a message—from you, I believe." Mrs. Butler's eyes were round with confusion, hesitantly handing him the brown package.

"Not from me! Thanks."

Colt swiftly grabbed it and was out the door. The package was stored beneath the buggy seat before he turned around to survey the dusty street, his features a mask of angry determination. First one direction and then the other; he saw no sign of her. Damn! Why in the world would she leave when he had specifically told her to stay put? He recalled Mrs. Butler's words, "a little trollop . . ." What interest could one of the whores possibly have in Madison?

Running back across the street, he burst through the swinging doors of the Grecian Bend Saloon. A hush fell over the dismal interior as the patrons rotated in their chairs to gawk.

"Where are the gals?" It was a demand. Nobody answered, the silence so concentrated it could have been cut with a knife. Colt sent intimidating eyes to the barkeep. The man merely shrugged his shoulders, dumbfounded. Impatiently, Colt spun around and was back out the door like a shot out of hell.

With horror, Madison found herself staring straight into the barrel chest of an enormous man. Her eyes were on a level with his shirt buttons. Gasping, her gaze inched up, past the thickness of his neck, directly into his swollen, leathery face. An involuntary whimper of panic escaped from her constricted throat. She stumbled backward, her hands grappling for anything to steady her.

A big, hot hand clamped tightly around her slim wrist, jerking her roughly. Before comprehension took hold, her legs were forced into ungraceful motion as he dragged her behind him. The huge man headed for the side of the building, out of the view of passers-by.

It wasn't but a moment before Madison found her voice. She screamed and screamed again, attempting to wrench her arm free of his evil grip.

"Let me go, you—you big bumble-headed gorilla!"

The grotesque man limped onward, and when he shot a glance at her, his eyes were narrowed slits. For the first time she got a good look at him. His skin was olive-toned and pitted; his long black hair hung like a shroud from beneath his bashed-in hat. His mouth grimaced in a snarl.

Madison's eyes grew huge and her mouth flew open to scream again. Like a wild woman, she began to kick at legs that reminded her of petrified tree trunks, her free hand pummeling his chest. He stopped. None too gently, she was shoved up against the planked wall, her head banging ruthlessly as his oversized hand pressed suffocatingly over her mouth.

"Shut up!" he grit out. "Why do females have such big mouths?" He studied her, then began to laugh, a satanic rumble from deep inside him. "Well, well, well . . . Lucy was right for a change. You are a beauty."

Madison tried a rebuttal into his sweaty palm, but he flattened her even harder against the building. She winced with pain when a loosened board dug into the small of her back.

"What's the matter?" he breathed thickly. "Does my size frighten you? You're probably wonderin' if I'm this big all over. Most women do." He snickered. "It hurts the ladies at first. But don't worry your pretty head, they all end up likin' it."

His voice was raspy, as if he had a terminal case of laryngitis, his breath foul as he panted into her face.

"Where would you care to go for a little fun, eh? I'll take my hand away if you promise not to start that blasted screamin' again. Promise? Eh?"

Madison nodded as best she could, her eyes pleading over the spread of his hand. Slowly, he eased his hand away, although the girth of his frame still held her very much captive.

"C-O-L-T . . . !" Her piercing cry shattered the otherwise peaceful quietude, echoing throughout the alleyway. The man's face turned red in his fury. He raised a massive arm above his head, readying to crash it down with deadly force across her face. Madison blinked, then squeezed her eyes shut with a squeak.

The ominous click of steel hammers secured control of the moment, freezing him in midstrike. Her assailant's body tensed, his small eyes shifting rapidly to either side.

The afternoon sun was blinding. Madison couldn't make out the shaded figure that loomed behind the big man, only the silver glimmer of a pistol gouging deeply under the bony part of his jaw. She wheezed frantically, gasping for air, the sheer weight of him crushing her.

"Unless you want what little brains you have blown all over that wall, I suggest you back away from the lady. Nice and slow." Just the tone of the voice issued a threat all its own. Menacing. Smooth as velvet.

The man hobbled back slowly. A tremendous relief flowed through Madison, like the rush of a rapid river. Greedily, she breathed again in huge gulps. Her legs were acting like overcooked noodles, and she feared she might slide down the wall and collapse right then and there.

Colt. Oh, thank God . . .

Colt replaced one revolver, keeping the barrel of the remaining one crammed into the man's neck. "I'm only going to say this once. If I ever see your ugly ass again, you'll be missing a set of real important equipment—*then* I'll kill you. Get my meaning, son?" He ground the pistol deeper into tender flesh.

The other man snarled his compliance, shuffling his gigantic frame around, his gimpy foot scraping noisily over the gravel. Then, just as he began to hobble away, his meaty arm was flung back impulsively, accompanied by an unearthly banshee yowl. It caught Colt's pistol, sending it into a sliding bounce across rocks and dirt.

"*Colt!*" Madison shrieked as she hurled outstretched arms into the huge man's fleshy side, hoping to knock him off balance. It only served to anger him more. He threw his other arm out and toward the man who had interfered in his business.

With lightning speed, Colt ducked the reeling appendage, lunging his shoulders directly into the thick legs. The lumbering attacker's eyes grew large as he crashed headlong into the dirt, his hat sailing into the air. Promptly rolling to his back, the man clamped Colt into a crushing, scissorslike hold between his legs. Colt endeavored to pull the remaining pistol from his holster, but due to his ungainly position, it was impossible.

Battling for the upper hand, the men squirmed amid a gathering cloud of dust. At a virtual impasse, both momentarily halted. Their heavy breathing dominated the silent alleyway.

Madison bounced in extreme agitation, her eyes darting this way and that for something she could pick up. *Anything.* A stack of firewood was piled in an orderly fashion beside the livery wall. Without hesitation, she ran to grasp a sturdy piece of kindling.

On her return she neglected to see the remnants of a broken and discarded wooden bucket in her path. As if they were made for one another, her foot slid neatly into the bucket, holding her fast, then causing her to trip. She stumbled about awkwardly— recovered, then managed to free herself with an energetic kick accompanied by a few unladylike expletives.

Madison danced around the writhing combatants, waiting for

just the right moment to strike. Aiming, she elevated the wood straight above her head. Thick fingers locked painfully around her ankle. Her eyes flashed the panic she felt when she looked down into the giant's face. The man smiled in satisfaction, apparently enjoying the way she squirmed.

Squeezing her eyes shut, she brought the stick down squarely across his forehead. The wood broke in half. The next thing she knew, her foot was rudely jerked from beneath her and she crashed down onto the heap of man flesh.

The hold on her ankle relaxed. In a blustery tangle of skirts, arms, and legs—mostly hers and Colt's—and a few muttered curses besides, they each promptly rolled off to either side, jumping to their feet. She ran to snatch the six-shooter, and with both hands trained it on the lifeless form. The gun was so much heavier than she might have guessed and Madison prayed she wouldn't need to use it. The large man's eyes spun in his head, then closed, a trickle of blood flowing from a jagged cut along his temple.

Colt stood over the giant, his pistol drawn, his chest heaving. Just as the man began to come to, Colt thrust a boot mercilessly across his neck. His black eyes rolled back into his head, then bulged, his arms and legs floundering like fish out of water. Grotesque choking sounds gurgled from his throat. He gazed up into Colt's face in a silent plea for mercy.

Madison grimaced at the scene before her. It was nearly incomprehensible what her own stupidity had caused. She watched as Colt smirked down at the ugly man, his boot slowly twisting, digging further in. Pure confidence dominated Colt's features when he spoke.

"Smart move, dumb-ass," he drawled. "Anything else you'd like to try while we're at it?"

The man could only squirm under the agonizing pressure, drool bubbling from his lips.

"Get the hell out of here before I change my mind and finish you off," Colt spat out disgustedly, delivering a swift kick to his adversary's hefty torso to get him moving. The man turned over with a grunt, pausing on his hands and knees to gasp for air. He reached for his hat and began the long climb to his feet.

"She's mine . . . arranged it myself," he mumbled with a cough, hobbling away as fast as his crippled foot would allow. " . . . gonna wring Lucy's scrawny neck."

No worse for the wear, Colt looked at Madison, his weight casually resting on one foot. He looked positively rakish with his hair tousled and dirt smudging his face. Groaning, he bent to retrieve his hat and knocked it against his thigh. Madison attempted to calculate his mood, unsure if he was truly angry or not. Although it was doubtlessly the most wretched experience of her life, she felt oddly invigorated, as if she had just pulled off a tremendously successful bank robbery—or maybe she was just happy to be alive. But Colt didn't seem to share her jubilation at their victory.

"Are you all right?" he asked with a frown.

"Fine. You?" Madison hesitantly handed him the six-shooter. He grabbed it, flipping open the cylinder with a spin to check the ammunition, then holstering it.

"Why did you leave the mercantile?" he asked sternly, ignoring her query.

He acted as if he were addressing a small child who had disobeyed. It was as Madison had suspected. He was definitely angry. Madison sighed for courage. "A woman gave me a message; she said it was from you . . . a very weird woman." She hated how naive she must seem to him now.

"Do you always do what weird people tell you to do?"

Madison willed herself not to cry. No, she *wasn't* going to cry. Instead, she busied herself with brushing the dust from her clothes, smoothing a small tear in her blouse. Her jaw tensed. "Ok, Colt, I get the hint. I screwed up. I'm sorry."

"All this may be a game to you, Madison, but it's not to me. This is real life for me. If you were to get hurt or killed, I couldn't live with myself."

"This isn't a game to me! I said I was sorry. I made a mistake— don't you ever make one?"

She glared at him as she pushed past him and marched back up Main Street. She moved as fast as she could, feeling his presence behind her all the way. Without any help she managed to climb into the buggy, where she waited stiffly, her hands folded in her lap.

As soon as Pete had disappeared from sight, Lucinda crept from her hiding spot beneath the back stairway of the brothel. She had witnessed the entire episode and was cackling with mischievous glee as she scampered through the alley and up the back stairs to her room.

"Colt, Colt, Colt," she mused out loud, "you're really taken with that sissified cream puff, ain't ya? Spend a night with me.

That's all it would take . . . one night. You'll forget all about Miss Priss, whoever she is."

Bounding up the stairs two at a time, Lucinda vanished into her room, careful to bolt the door. She was convinced she would need to remain hidden for the evening, or at least until Pete cooled off.

Falling back onto the lumpy mattress, she persisted with the fantasies that had ruled her every thought since she'd seen Colt that afternoon. The feel of his lips on hers, his body plunging into her . . . With a swoon she rolled to her stomach, propping her chin in her hands.

"Ahhh, Miss Priss . . . what are we going to do about you, hmmmmm?"

Chapter Twenty-One

At the outskirts of town Madison saw a commonplace one-room schoolhouse, lonely and isolated. Painted white, it was well-kept, an iron bell hanging from the simple eave above the front porch.

As Colt and Madison neared, a woman appeared in the doorway. She stepped out onto the front porch, shielding her eyes to see as the buggy came to a full stop. Colt jumped down and crossed the grassy yard.

Madison noticed that the woman was young and very pretty. Her hair was a soft brown, piled loosely at the top of her head. She was slim and yet quite buxom, and Madison was sure she saw the ice-blue eyes flash a look of consternation in her direction before she gave all her attention to Colt.

It seemed to Madison that Colt spoke to the woman for an eternity. She waited patiently in the buggy, trying her best not to appear interested. In truth, she was dying to know who the woman was—the funny part being that she looked peculiarly familiar. She and Colt were standing face to face, intimately close, conversing in hushed tones. The woman slanted an occasional haughty glance in Madison's direction. Sure she must look a sight, Madison attempted to straighten her hair and smooth any dirt from her face gained from the scuffle in town.

Eventually, Colt said his good-byes and returned to the buggy.

The young woman crossed her arms and casually rocked heel to toe as she watched them pull away. She waved, an unmistakably disheartened gaze settling onto Madison before she spun in a swirl of skirts and went back inside.

It began to sprinkle rain. The mountains were lost behind a wall of threatening gray storm clouds, and Madison was positive they must be nearing the outermost boundaries of the ranch. She knew Colt was still angry; hardly a word had been spoken between them the entire trip home.

Finally, Colt reached beneath the seat, bringing out a package wrapped in brown paper and handing it to her.

"What's this?" she asked, her eyes like black-fringed saucers as they lifted to meet his.

"Candy. Open it."

Madison obeyed. First she found the licorice, coyly placing a long stick of it between his teeth. A small box fell out and into her lap. She gave him a puzzled glance, his expression telling her to go ahead and open it. She did, carefully, gasping at the sight of the tiny cameo necklace.

"Ohhhh, Colt," she cried, "I love it! I do! How did you know?" She embraced him, kissing his cheek. She was certain she detected a slight blush beneath his suntanned skin.

"Mrs. Butler told me you were admiring it. Here, let me help you put it on." He loosened the reins long enough to fasten the delicate chain, planting a quick kiss at her nape.

Madison turned to face him, the smile fading from her lips. "I'm so sorry I didn't stay inside the store. There's just no excuse for what I did—I could have gotten you killed! I'm so stupid sometimes."

"I can take care of myself. You might have gotten *yourself* killed. I couldn't bear it if something were to happen to you. If it weren't for me, you wouldn't even be here. And you're not stupid."

"Yes! I am stupid! I—"

"No, you're not—"

"I am so—" she wailed.

"You're not, Madison—"

"Am so . . ."

Their eyes locked in humor, and they both broke into a gale of unrestrained laughter, the sudden pelting of huge raindrops nearly drowning out the pleasant sound.

Colt steered them onto an overgrown side road, shaking the reins to urge on the wild-eyed horses. The buggy shook, bumping and lurching in first one direction and then the other.

"Hold on," he called over the noise of the impending storm.

The sparse covering over the buggy might have been enough to protect them from a light rain, but it wasn't doing much against this downpour, Madison thought.

"Where are we going?" she called back. Squinting, she held one hand up to shield her face from the stinging drops, clinging to the seat for support with the other.

"It looks like hail. There's a line shack not far from here. We'll have to wait it out." He yelled to make himself heard over the racket of clopping hooves, the steady rumble of thunder, and the splattering rain. "There."

Colt pointed toward a rickety structure that looked to Madison as if it wouldn't make it through a sunny day, let alone a hail storm.

"What's a line shack?"

"During watch the boys sometimes use them for shelter in inclement weather. The object is to make sure the herds don't wander past this point."

By now the rain was coming down in sheets. Colt stopped as close as possible to the door, then helped Madison inside. He then unharnessed the horses, securing them beneath the safety of a lean-to roof, off to one side.

Inside, Madison turned full circle, examining her surroundings. Once her eyes adjusted to the dusky darkness, she could make out a pot-bellied stove, a small dusty mattress on a wooden pallet, some firewood, and a bale of hay, which served as a seat. A wooden crate was supplied with canned goods, a coffeepot, and a few pans. Helplessly, she glanced down at her blouse and skirt. They were sopping wet. She lifted the heaviness of the dripping cloth with a frown.

Colt burst through the door, a shower of rainwater gusting in after him. He was soaked also, water dripping from the brim of his hat. "This is a bad one," he said, out of breath, just as a clap of thunder rattled the little shack. He stopped and stared at her for a moment, then started to laugh.

Puzzled, Madison smiled back. "What are you laughing at?"

"You! You're drenched. Has anyone ever told you that you look quite fetching when you're wet?" Colt removed his holster and hat. He dropped his suspenders and proceeded to peel the wet shirt from his torso, hanging everything on a peg by the door. Opening the stove, he started to build a fire.

She felt a hot flush suffuse her cheeks, then stammered when she searched for an answer. "Well, no . . . but then, I haven't been caught in storms like this very often." Her voice evaporated into the mugginess of the confined space, her attention caught by something far more compelling.

"I'll count myself lucky then: I've seen you twice."

The flames of the new fire crackled and licked at a dry log, devouring it. A golden glow played along the perfectly sculpted lines of his arms and back, his rain-moistened skin glistening and bronze. Once again, Madison found her gaze trailing along the groove of his spine, down over his lean hips and his muscled thighs beneath the light brown denims. Fantasies of making love to him overpowered her. My God, she couldn't even trust herself any longer. She didn't even *know* herself.

Forcing her eyes away, she looked over her own clothes, realizing that the wet thinness of her blouse and chemise surely left little to his imagination. Folding her arms as a protection, she worked at distracting herself.

"Are you really acquainted with Miss Beak?"

"Who?"

"The woman who approached me inside the mercantile—the one who told me to meet you down at the livery. She said she knew you very well."

Madison saw his shoulders shake with mirth before she heard the chuckle. "So it *was* Lucy, huh? I figured as much. I suppose it doesn't surprise me that she would try to stir something up. And by the way, I intended to tell you that you did good back there. You've got backbone. I'm proud of you." He stood up, turning to face her, dusting off his hands. His chest rose and fell with his breath.

Madison casually paced the width of the shack. It didn't take long. Three steps and she was cornered when Colt came to stand behind her. "I just did what came to mind at the time. You didn't answer my question." She could feel his warm breath on her nape when he replied—the fine wisps of hair moving ever so slightly, tickling her tender skin.

"I'm flattered at your concern."

"Don't be. I'm just curious." Her retort was teasing, laced with a charming cockiness as she threw a glance back at him over her shoulder, her lashes fluttering.

Colt grinned lazily.

"Do you really think I'd have anything to do with the likes of Lucy Beak? She's got a face that would scare the ass-end off of a horse, and a disposition to match. Every time I pass through town she's all over me—like bees on honey, like scum on a pond, like flies on—"

Madison was giggling into her hand. "All right already, I think I get the point!"

She wanted to look at him but was afraid of what she would find in his eyes. She didn't have to look. She had the picture memorized: his lopsided smile, his thumbs hooked into his pants, his weight leaning on one leg, his smoky gaze burning into her, gouging at her heart. . . .

Madison bent to pull a straw from the bale, putting it between her teeth and chewing, as she had seen him do so many times. Anything to calm her rickety nerves.

His tanned fingers reached to touch the flimsy, damp material of her blouse, caressing the length of her arm. He was too close. If he were halfway around the world right now, he would still be too close. His smile faded; she knew it even though she couldn't see his face.

Madison whirled around. Could he tell? Did he see the turmoil, the revelation behind her eyes? The throbbing fullness at the pit of her stomach intensified, deep down, until she thought she might burst with the tension.

He took a step closer.

No, please, no closer! she begged silently.

His golden brown gaze smoldered, smoky as it dipped, then lifted again, holding her until her heart slammed against her ribs like a maddened thing. Madison's skin tingled; she could feel the automatic hardening of her nipples beneath the appraisal of his unabashed stare.

Slowly, his hand came up to remove the sprig of hay from her lips. Deliberately, sensually, he placed it between his, sliding the length of it along his tongue, as if hoping to glean a taste of her.

Her breath caught in her throat. Madison couldn't seem to tear her eyes from his mouth, the chiseled squareness of his jaw as he leisurely began to chew.

"Don't look at my mouth like that unless you want it on yours," he warned huskily.

Her gaze didn't waver.

Could it be *her* fingers, moving of their own accord, numbly working free the buttons of first her blouse, then her skirt, allowing them to drop into a sloshy wet pile at her feet? A shiver of warmth engulfed her, bathing her skin in a rosy flush. Her lips parted and her breath came in featherlike bursts, parching her throat. A molten fire ran through her veins. She felt an insane desire to kiss him. *Really taste him.*

Was it truly she who lunged forward, molding her body intimately to his as she pushed him to the wall, her lips blindly searching for his? The roar of blood in her ears. Deafening, pounding . . .

Colt moaned hoarsely. His strong, sinewy arms wrapped around her, encasing her tightly, locking her close to his own ramming heart. Their entire existence absorbed within a drugged kiss, Colt's tongue demanded hers, probing, mating with joyous abandon. A tormented moan tore from Madison's throat. She twined her leg around his, sliding her ankle along his calf.

He couldn't get enough of her mouth.

His hands moved over her body, burning with a searing heat through her meager cotton underclothes, exploring, seeking, cupping possessively.

Colt grasped her buttocks, lifting her, and her eager thighs limberly wrapped themselves around his waist. Her fingers clutched the hair at his nape, holding on. In one fluid movement he reversed their positions, his lips never leaving hers, imprisoning her against the wall in a crushing sweetness. Instinctively, she undulated rhythmically against his hardened loins with hungry desperation.

Madison dreamily rolled her head back and forth as his soft lips brazenly traced a scorching path along her jaw, downward, tantalizing the sensitive flesh of her neck. Was it the violence of the crashing thunder and beating hail or her own wild emotions raging inside that affected her so? The question answered itself— the storm outside the shack was nothing compared to the one unleashed within her. . . .

Colt groaned, inhaling the flowered scent of her skin, closing his eyes as he brushed his face over the soft swell of her breasts. Deftly tearing the scant material of her chemise aside with his teeth, he captured an eagerly taut peak within the warmth of his mouth, gently suckling. Madison's little whimpers were driving him wild, beyond all reason. She twisted, arching beneath the pressure of his hips, gasping, her nipple hardening like a rock under his assault.

A possessive, driving need consumed him. The fires lashed out spasmodically inside him, out of control, an irrepressible desire to brand his love into her. He boldly ground into her in slow circles, as if the cloth that separated them was no obstacle.

"Madison . . . sugar . . ."

Wildly, Colt dropped his arm, his palm sliding easily beneath her drawers, down over the petal-softness of her belly to claim the sweetness between her thighs. His fingers were enclosed in the moist, feminine folds, thrusting with firm mastery.

Madison cried out, incoherent. He dragged his mouth over her cheek to once again blend with hers, devouring in a wondrous urgency. Her long fingernails dug into the muscles of his back and shoulders, supplying a sweet agony, driving him onward.

"So wet, and ready . . ." he murmured shakily into her mouth, just as her hand lowered to free him from his pants, pressing against his pulsating hardness, her fingers circling to squeeze him deliciously.

A voice sounded from outside the shack.

Nearly drowned out by the torrents of rain that hammered onto the tiny shelter, the call came again, insistent.

Their eyes flew open, their breaths ragged.

Madison struggled to regain her composure, swiftly sliding her legs down to plant her feet firmly on the dirt floor. Still in an unbridled euphoria, her lips felt swollen and bruised.

"I heard someone!" she whispered breathlessly.

"I know," Colt responded, toiling for a shred of restraint. His eyes closed, he kept his forehead pressed to hers. He delivered another rousing kiss, nipping at her lower lip with his teeth, before reluctantly levering himself away from the wall. "Wait right there, sugar," he commanded, crossing to the door.

Chapter Twenty-Two

When Colt returned he found Madison sitting cross-legged on the mattress, cloaked in a scratchy wool blanket she had dug out of the crate. She wouldn't meet his gaze; instead she busily plucked at an array of fuzz balls on the blanket. Colt stoked the fire, then sat down beside her.

"Who was it?"

"Just one of the boys riding the line, sugar." He brushed a soft caress over her cheek with the back of his hand. "He recognized the buggy and horses" He planted a kiss on the tip of her nose. " . . . Just wanted to check and make sure all was well." He traced the delicate whorls of her ear with his tongue.

Madison fought the feelings that threatened her, promising herself she wouldn't succumb a second time. Maintaining a purely affectionate attitude, she rubbed his arm, pulling back to look at him. "Oh, no! Surely he knew what we were doing in here!"

"So? We're 'married,' remember?"

Colt slid his arms around her in a splendidly warm embrace. He smelled good, like rain, and his chest and arms were wet, glistening wet. Madison resisted, her body stiff.

"But the storm—doesn't he need shelter, too? Where will he go?"

"You worry too much. The cowboys are used to working in all

176

kinds of weather. He was dressed for it. And he's gone. Happy, hmmmmm?"

Colt's eyes glittered like hot chips of topaz, plunging seductively into hers. He smiled lazily, sensuously. She almost forgot to breathe, then labored to fill her lungs.

Slowly, his fingers loosened the soggy bow that held her braid, weaving through the mass of damp curls, fanning them over her shoulders like a silky golden veil. Madison knew she shouldn't look at him again. But she did anyway.

"C'mere."

Colt held her face steady as his mouth lowered to hers, and with a gentle thoroughness, deepening unmercifully, his tongue made tender love to the most inner recesses of her mouth, first giving, then taking. At last she was allowed to break away, breathless, quivering.

Madison's heart tripped frantically and she grappled to keep her senses intact. She felt terrible. This just couldn't go on! And it was her fault for letting it happen in the first place, for encouraging him to think she would, or even could make love to him. My God, she was the one who had practically attacked him! On top of that, she liked—no, loved—the way he felt, the way he tasted, the way he made her feel. Even more, she wanted to make him feel good, too. Madison knew in her head that it must stop, and yet her heart told her that it couldn't. It would never stop. He would haunt her for the rest of her life. Every breath she took would be for him.

His hand skimmed up and over her rib cage to cup her breast tenderly, his thumb drawing circles over her nipple. Ignoring her feeble protest, he savored another long draught from her honeyed lips, urging her back onto the downy mattress, nuzzling her neck. Colt's leg maneuvered between her thighs, establishing himself over her securely. He shackled her wrists above her head with one hand while the other roamed freely.

Despite all inclination to put a halt to this madness, Madison caught herself rocking his leg wantonly. Colt's lips sketched ticklish trails along the sensitive underside of her arm. The stubble along his jaw pricked, and delightful tremors traveled from the roots of her hair down to the tips of her toes. He stopped—just long enough to gaze down at her lovingly.

"I intend to make love to you."

It was a statement of fact, his gaze smoking, heavy lidded. Her response was an anguished moan. "Colt, no . . . I'm so sorry, but

I must be crazy. It's all my fault." She heaved against his hold with a frustrated whimper.

Colt merely grasped a stray tendril of her hair, toying with it, his brows narrowing into a frown. He didn't budge.

"First you were stupid, now you're crazy. Stop being so hard on yourself. I don't like hearing you talk that way. Madison, trust your feelings . . . trust yourself." He lowered his mouth to hers, but she turned away from his kiss.

"You don't understand; I just can't," she pleaded.

"Try me."

Madison couldn't bring herself to look at him. With her eyes clamped shut, her tears dripped rapidly to the mattress in soggy plops. She didn't want him to see her crying again.

"It's . . . it's just too complicated." She attempted to laugh, but it came out sounding like a strangled wail.

"Oh, I see. Now you think *I'm* stupid." He propped his chin in his hand, refusing to acknowledge her insistent wriggles.

"I didn't say that!" she bit out, this time looking directly at him.

"You're in love with your husband, am I right?" He released her, watching her eyes spark with anger.

"Why would you say something like that?"

"Because it's the truth?" It was a question—a question he fervently hoped she would deny, forever dispelling it from his mind.

"Well, er . . . yes, I mean no! What does he have to do with anything? He's not even my husband anymore!" She was more than a little annoyed at this turn in the conversation.

"You're hot. Is it him you think of while you're melting in my arms?" His tone was scathing, mean, and instantly he regretted it, as she looked at him with those big aqua eyes.

Colt was more than a little disappointed; he was devastated. There was doubt in her mind. This woman who had swept into his life and so thoroughly took hold of his heart was very possibly in love with another man. It was as if she had conquered his spirit, then tossed it aside with disregard. He rolled away from her with a disgruntled sigh.

The warmth of his body gone, a lonely chill coursed through her as the wind whipped at the drafty boards of the little shack. Madison knew that Colt had hit too close to home. Was it possible that she still loved Jon, to the point of not being able to give herself to another man? To a man she felt strangely connected to—a man she could fall hard for if only the circumstances were right? Worse, had Jon tarnished her ability ever to love another man as completely as she had loved him? No! She wouldn't allow herself to believe that.

Impetuously, she sat up to face him, though he continued to stare at the ceiling. "Colt! I can't be with you and then just leave, never to see you again!"

"On the other hand, we should cherish what we have. We may never have another chance."

"Don't you see?" she cried in exasperation, "I can't bear the thought of making love with you and then never, ever being able to touch you again." The words died on her lips, and she was beginning to think he might be right. She wasn't going to be able to bear not seeing him again as it was. Wouldn't it at least be better to have the memory for always?

"All of this can be remedied easily enough."

Colt tore his gaze from the ceiling, meeting her face to face, propping his head on his arm. His countenance was intense, his eyes as hard as diamonds, and Madison just looked at him in doubt. Distractedly, she played with the springy hairs across his chest. She couldn't seem to keep her hands off him. Everything about him was so beautiful.

"Be my wife. Stay. Marry me."

Rendered speechless, Madison tried to swallow, but her throat was too dry. Finally, she regained her ability to speak. "Are you joking?" she asked, her expression incredulous.

"I don't usually joke about something so serious, Madison." Didn't that beat all? Never before had Colt formally asked a woman for her hand—and now that he had, she assumed he was joking.

"Do you have any idea what you're suggesting? How can we pursue this? We're from two different worlds—literally! Besides, we've known each other for less than a week."

Despite the prohibitive words that spilled from her mouth, the urge to succumb to spontaneity, to the ultimate romantic fantasy, to fall into this man's arms, was very tempting, indeed. What kind of husband *would* he make? she wondered. Jon's indiscretions came back to her in their usual nagging way. Would she ever be able to commit to another man without reservation? Her mood plummeted again.

Colt saw the corners of her mouth droop, her eyes reflecting a faraway vacancy he didn't understand. He never should have brought up the subject of marriage. He wasn't even sure that he loved her. What was love supposed to feel like, anyway? Regardless, she was a good, strong woman, and he knew that he wanted her more than he'd ever wanted a woman before. He had bared his soul to her. It was obvious she didn't share his enthusiasm for a future together. Hell, she fully intended to return home, perfectly content with the notion of never seeing him again. What he needed to do was to wash his hands of this obsession with Madison Calloway.

"There's always a way, sugar. That is, if a person truly desires something. Here, it's not unusual for a man to meet, court, and marry a woman all in one day," he responded, but the conviction was gone from his voice. Colt got up to stoke the fire.

"You make it sound like a business arrangement."

He merely cocked a sardonic eyebrow, then dismissed her, pitching in another log. When he finished he went to sit on the straw bale, resting his ankle over his knee as he leaned back to chew on a sprig of hay.

"I mean," she added, "a man and a woman just can't get married so they can have a quick romp in the hay. It takes a little time to fall in love—"

"Does it, now?" he interrupted with a touch of sarcasm. He tapped his foot absently.

"Yes . . . and I really don't think I'm ready—"

Colt jerked a glance toward her. "Look, it was a bad idea. Forget I brought up the subject."

Madison shut up in midsentence. The trace of Irish in her blood came to the surface, flames of anger licking at her temptingly. He didn't love her. If he did, he would have said so. How could she be so naive as to fall for the first man to come along since Jon— and one well over a century old, to top it off? She let out a low chuckle at the irony of it all.

"Who was the woman at the schoolhouse?" She had to change the subject in order to cool her ire.

"Sarah Hamilton. A friend of mine."

"Oh." Madison hoped he would elaborate, and when he didn't, she said, "I take it she's the schoolteacher?"

"Hmm-mmm."

Mild amusement was beginning to dance in his heavy-lidded eyes, and Madison shook her head impatiently. "You're going to make me ask, aren't you?"

Colt hinted at a smile.

"Okay . . . You two seemed more than just friends. Are you and she . . . you know?" It struck her that Sarah was the woman who had posed next to Colt in the photograph.

Deciding to relieve her discomfort, he answered, "Yes, we were lovers. Sarah and I were never written in granite; it was more or less an understanding we had between us. When the day rolled around that I would settle down on the ranch she and I would be married. Sarah was the closest thing I'd ever found to a woman I'd consider spending a lifetime with. We think alike, most of the time. She's intelligent. She'd make a good rancher's wife." He took a deep breath. "Then I met you . . . and I think you know the rest."

Madison winced. Like a knife plunged into her heart, the pain twisted slowly with every syllable. Jealousy reared its ugly head, and she despised the feeling. The mere thought of Colt with another woman made her cringe. She tried to appear lighthearted. "Did she ask who I was?"

"Yes. I told her you were my wife."

Of course that's what he would say! Madison sensed this wonderful man would go on protecting her until the end of time. But it was so needless. After all, she would be gone soon, returned to her own time, and Colt would have to continue his life here—and all because of her it would be without Sarah. Madison had just ruined his chances for marriage!

"Colt," Madison said thoughtfully, "there are ways out of this dilemma, you know. We'll simply get a . . . a 'divorce.'" Boy, she was sure getting tired of hearing that word. "These things happen. . . . we'll tell everyone it was a mutual decision. I'll even talk to Sarah before I go back if you like."

Colt's eyes took on a deep amber hue. "It would take more than that to change Sarah's mind. She refuses to marry me as long as I carry this vendetta, and when I told her of my plans—well, to tell you the truth, she wasn't too happy." His jaw tightened in sudden revelation. "Or maybe it will ease your mind to not be remembered as my 'wife' under any circumstances."

Madison scarcely heard his last words, instead focusing on what he had said initially. "What plans are you talking about?"

Colt's heart dropped at the rebuff. Why did her response, her desires matter so much to him? He tiredly thrust his hand through his hair. "The ones I found out about today when I visited the sheriff. He was holding a telegram for me. Looks like I'll be heading down to Abilene in the next day or so."

All in one cataclysmic moment, it hit Madison full in the face. Abilene! The legend had said that Colt would be *killed* in Abilene, Kansas, in July 1878! *Killed by a sniper's bullet!* How in the world could she have forgotten? My God, she would have to warn him before the legend became fact! Deserting the bed, she jumped to her feet, spinning around to face him.

"No! Colt, you can't go!"

Madison looked quite the sight in her gauzy, damp chemise and pantalettes, complete with black ankle boots. Rosy peaks were evident beneath the transparent material, drawing his attention as her bosom heaved with her excitement. Colt reluctantly lifted his gaze to behold the gravity of her expression. Her nostrils quivered. Her eyes glittered, pressing down on him. Her hair was an untamed mass of fluff around her shoulders. Lord, she looked like a wild woman from a jungle book he had read as a child.

"What are you talking about?" he asked, frowning.

"You can't go to Abilene!" she repeated. "You'll be killed! Trust me; I know. It's in the history books, Colt!"

"Slow down. Now tell me everything."

Madison began to pace, chewing on her nail. He really wished she wouldn't do that. How was he supposed to concentrate on what she was saying when she insisted on parading her wares in front of his nose? It wasn't that he didn't enjoy it; he did, very much. The tightening in his loins proved it as he strained against his pants. He shifted positions, forcing himself to look at her face.

"After our picnic, before I came searching for you in the storm, I asked the hotel clerk about the Triple Bar C. I asked her if she knew of you. She gave me a book that recounted the history of the Jackson Hole area. Colt, you were in it! A whole chapter on the ranch. There were pictures; of you, and Garrett . . . even one of you and Sarah! Legend says you were killed in July 1878 in Abilene. Shot in the back by an unknown assailant!"

Colt stared at her, his lips parted with a mixture of disbelief and astonishment. "Are you absolutely sure?"

"*Of course I'm sure about what I read!* You can't go. That's all there is to it." She threw up her hands in exasperation.

"I have to go," he said calmly. "Bat said the rustling and bloodshed have gotten out of hand. He needs my help. I think it's Red Eagle."

"What?" Madison couldn't grasp what he had just said. "How

can you say that? Didn't you hear me? Or maybe you presume I don't know what the hell I'm talking about." Her excitement was rapidly shifting to anger. She folded her arms and tapped her toe. Then, out of the blue, she asked "Who's Bat?"

"An old friend," Colt said distractedly. "He's the Ford County Marshall. Bat Masterson is his name."

"*Bat Masterson?*" she cried, "You *know* Bat Masterson?"

"Yeah, I said he was an old friend—"

"Wow! Isn't that something?" she interrupted with a smile and a toss of her curls. "Bat Masterson is all over the history books. Why, he's as famous as Billy the Kid or Wyatt Earp."

"Do you mean to tell me that Bat made big history, and I didn't? That dirty dog . . ." He shook his head, pretending disgust.

Reminded again of the business at hand, she said, "If the legend is true, you didn't live long enough, remember? If memory serves, Bat lived well into his golden years." She fluttered her lashes smugly.

"I believe everything, Madison. You've helped me immeasurably—more than you know. But I still have to go."

His attitude was an excellent example of control. If she had just found out she was destined to die in a month's time, she would surely be a nervous wreck.

Madison couldn't bear this. If nothing else, if there were any reason for her being transported back in time, this could be it. To prevent the legend of Colt Chase from becoming fact. She had the power to do that, and yet she had no power at all. Totally out of character for her, Madison nearly flew into hysterics, gesturing dramatically as she repeated the facts again and again.

Colt simply let her rant, his eyes dropping, relishing the way her chemise inched lower, exposing her creamy cleavage and a hint of tantalizing pink crests. Madison advanced to stand before him, propping her hands on her hips. He could just make out the enticing triangular shadow between her thighs.

"Are you listening? Did you even hear a word I said?"

"Here." Colt snatched up the blanket and tossed it over her head, grinning. "Cover up before I throw you down and finish what we started. Next time we *will* finish."

She peeled the blanket from her head, her hair standing on end from the static. She hauled it around her shoulders with a grumble. "I don't understand you! How can you think of sex when I just informed you that you might die in a month's time? Men are absolutely the queerest creatures. Is this some kind of macho guy thing?" She plopped back down on the mattress, refusing to look at him.

Colt laughed. "Madison, if I *were* dead, I'd still be thinking of sex with you walking around in front of me like that." When he sobered he squatted down beside her. He cupped her face in his hands, refusing to be shrugged off by her tenacious resistance. "Sugar, thank you. You have given me a tool that no one else has. You've told me what could happen in the future. I can use that to my best advantage. Did the book say exactly where abouts in Abilene I was shot?"

Madison pondered his question, then shook her head, her eyes wide with regret.

"Not to worry. I can take precautions now. I'll make *sure* my death remains just a legend." He smiled. Colton Chase: A Legend . . . very impressive. He rather liked the ring of it.

"How can you be so sure?" she snapped.

"Because it's what I do—it's my job to be sure. I'm honored that you're so concerned with my welfare, especially since you don't have to be. After all, when you return home I'll be long dead even if I don't get killed in Abilene."

Madison rolled her eyes. "Now *that* lifts my spirits." Sighing, she drew her knees up and rested her chin. How could she ever have assumed it was her privilege to tamper with the course of history? And a legend was just a legend . . . it didn't *have* to be true, did it? At this point, she could only hope that it didn't come true.

He rose, tousling her hair as he passed. "Get dressed. The rain's stopped; I'll hitch the horses." Colt opened the door and disappeared into the humid darkness.

Chapter Twenty-Three

Madison tossed restlessly between the soft sheets, plagued with horrible nightmares of Mark and her mother mourning her death. She woke with a throttled scream, clawing at the covers, gasping for breath.

She fixed her gaze on the blackness beyond the French doors, the moon hidden behind puffs of drifting clouds, knowing Colt was sleeping out there in the dark. All alone. More than anything she wanted to ask him to come inside—to welcome him to his own bed. She wanted to be cuddled, reassured. She wanted him to tell her he loved her. As much as she feared him, she loved him. What was it that made her feel as if she had already returned home, just by looking into those golden-brown eyes?

Madison slept, then woke again with a start, tormented by a fierce thirst. She staggered from the bed, bleary-eyed, feeling through the massive armoire to find a satin dressing gown. Silently, she ventured downstairs, cursing under her breath when she reflexively groped for light switches that weren't there. Her fingertips grazed the wall for perspective as she silently padded down the staircase. The furniture resembled huge, ominous monsters lurking in the grim shadows, the lonely ticking of the clock accentuating the absolute silence.

In the kitchen she was grateful when the moon peeked from

behind a drifting cloudscape, providing a bluish light to see
by. She removed a cup from a hook beneath the cupboard and
began to pump. Crude squeaks of metal rubbing metal reverberated through the rectangular kitchen. Madison grimaced at
the unnerving racket as the cold liquid gushed forth in sporadic
spurts into the bucket. She filled her cup, then turned her hip to
rest against the counter, savoring the wet relief as it washed down
her parched throat.

A rough hand clamped her shoulder. Pinching insistently, it
caused her to nearly choke. She gulped, slopping water over the
front of her gown when she whirled around.

Madison's startled gaze met a glittering black one. Garrett's
eyes bore down on her, his expression solemn and indecipherable.
Leisurely, his foreboding gaze flickered down the length of her,
not missing a single detail.

Instinctively, she pulled the thin robe tighter about her waist,
then dabbed the moisture from her mouth with the back of her
hand. She made certain he caught her frown of displeasure at his
rudeness. She waited for him to state his intentions.

He didn't. His cold, animalistic stare continued to tear down
her composure.

"Garrett . . . you nearly scared me to death. I was just getting
a drink." Her voice was a breathy gasp in the darkness.

He smelled of stale whiskey—and lots of it. Apprehension
gripped her, and she thought to appease him with idle conversation rather than risk stirring his ire.

"Hmmmmm . . . I see," he mumbled thickly, his face a gray,
hostile mask in the eerie moonlight. "You're not really Colt's
wife, are you?" He tilted his chin up with an air of superiority,
snickering.

Garrett caught her off guard, and her intuition warned her
to beware. Many times Madison had been forced to stave off
unwanted advances from overzealous males, but never from one
so cool, so unreadable, and probably so irrational. She didn't
answer, and instead took a drink from her cup, hoping to hide
her increasing nervousness.

He still touched her with a vile heat, and she moved to shake
free of his hand.

"I don't think you are," he drawled, his lips twisting into an evil
smirk. "It doesn't stand to reason why Colt would marry without
telling a soul beforehand—especially his family."

His countenance was smug. She could see the glint of his teeth in the low light as he looked down at her.

"You're his little whore, aren't you? C'mon, you can tell me—I keep real good secrets. I won't give you away. Providing there's a little something in it for me," he said more than a little suggestively.

A hot, fleshy hand roughly caressed her silk-clad arm, and his words struck Madison like a cold, icy slap. Immediately, she jerked from his repulsive touch, backing away. Her elbow caught something unseen on the counter, sending it clattering to the floor.

"You're mistaken," she replied stiffly. "If you leave now, I'll forget any of this happened." Her voice quaked with the effort to sound braver than she really felt.

Madison turned to leave, but Garrett grabbed her arm. He swiveled her around, his mouth curling into a lascivious grin. A mirthless chuckle emanated from deep within his throat.

"Not so fast, Madison . . . if that's your real name. You tempt me in that thin gown. What treasures lie beneath it, I wonder?" He pressed closer, clenching her arm tight, his fingers digging into her flesh. His other hand dipped low to slide around her curvaceous hip.

"Don't ever touch me! I'm warning you, Garrett, I will not hesitate to tell Colt what you're trying to do," she uttered with total conviction while attempting to wrench her arm free. Rashly, she flipped the cup of water into his face.

He flinched, his brows narrowing wickedly as water dripped from the cleft in his chin. "Do you really think Colt cares . . . about a whore? Hmmmm?" Garrett tilted his head back with a chuckle at the absurdity of such a notion. "Would he favor *you* over his own brother? You're staying in *my* house. Eating *my* food. I think I deserve a little something to show your appreciation, don't you?"

He stalked her until she was backed up to the still-warm hearth. His stubby fingers slid along the side of her neck, winding through a hank of her hair, gripping it painfully. Madison shrank against the heat of the brick, her flesh crawling with revulsion. She felt the warm moisture of his breath as he panted. He stank of sour liquor and sweat.

"Ugghhhh!" she wailed her disgust, her mouth barely moving when she spoke. "I'm going to scream as loud as I can if you don't take your filthy hands off me . . . *now!*"

"Your hair is lovely hanging down like that," he rasped, ignoring her demand.

His lecherous, predatory eyes roamed over her body greedily.

"You worthless scab—you're drunk!" she spat vehemently.

Garrett snickered in a most unpleasant manner, and Madison couldn't fathom how this man could be considered a brother to Colt, true blood or otherwise. They were like night and day. Her heart felt as if it had crawled up into her throat, laying there helplessly, beating like a caged animal's. If only Colt could hear her screams.

She opened her mouth, and Garrett reacted instantly, his wet mouth clamping over hers. Madison's scream was silenced to nothing more than a garbled moan. Taking advantage, he continued with the soggy kiss, gripping her body savagely, crushing her sickeningly close to his own soft pudginess. Her eyes were wide in mute protest, and she frantically writhed within his clutches.

Mauling fingers only dug deeper into her flesh, bruising her. His mouth moved over hers, a slobbery tongue demanding entry between her tightly closed lips. One arm held her secure with its strangulating grip as the other groped over her hips, then back up to grasp her breast.

Madison willed herself to relax. Struggling was futile with a man like this; if anything, fighting would only serve to increase his pleasure. Squeezing her eyes shut in a moment's concentration, she pooled her strength. In a burst of energy, she brought her knee up to his groin with all the power she could muster.

Garrett's hold loosened, turning rubbery as his beady eyes glared wide at her in astonishment. He stumbled back, groaning, his face a ghastly purple in the soft light.

"You whoring bitch . . . !" he grit out between clenched teeth, dropping to his knees, cupping himself with both hands.

Madison froze for just a fraction of a second, amazed at what devastation a well-placed knee could bring to a man.

"You're . . . gonna regret this . . . I swear . . . bitch!"

She fled from the kitchen in a cloud of billowing satin, tearing up the stairs, tripping as she neared the top. By the time she burst into Colt's bedroom she was breathing in whimpering gasps. Her hands trembling, she made sure to turn the skeleton key that always remained in the keyhole.

Madison leaned against the door a moment to gather her wits, her chest heaving. Viciously, she swiped the back of her hand across her mouth, desperate to rid herself of the revolting remnants of Garrett's kiss.

Equanimity restored, her eyes rested on Colt's sleeping form for the longest time. His chest moved rhythmically, peacefully. Treading lightly, she went to the verandah and opened the door. She stepped out into the refreshing night air. The lonely croak of a bullfrog sounded from below.

As she stood there, she realized that she needed Colt.

God, she needed him so bad. Her eyes fluttered closed as she pressed a palm to her breast. She needed his strong arms around her, passing some of his strength on to her. She needed more than anything at this moment to hear the soothing sound of his voice, wonderful velvet words of comfort.

Madison understood their destiny was clouded, at best, but it didn't matter anymore. She opened her eyes to gaze down at him. Such a beautiful man; all bronzed and innocent in his sleep, naked down to the blanket that covered him from his hips to his toes. The masculine, angular planes of his jaw were covered with the slightest of stubble.

If only this one time, she could have him . . . have him to hold forever in her heart.

Her eyes refusing to look away from him, she slipped off her robe, absently brushing the gown's straps from her shoulders. They wafted down to pool at her feet.

Like an angel, Madison stood above him, her nakedness bathed in the silvery light of the moon, its beams extracting pale shimmers from her hair. She lowered herself. Gently, she pulled back the blanket to sit over him, the heat of his loins burning responsively into her intimate, needy flesh.

Colt stirred. Jerking his head up, his eyes popped open with a dazed frown. Then they registered first disbelief, then pure passion. Madison touched her fingers to his parted lips, her eyes plunging into his golden brown ones.

"Ohhh . . . lord . . ." he gasped, his voice husky with sleep. Sighing with exquisite awareness, his head fell back to the bedroll.

Her soft hands fluttered over him, thrilling the length of his torso, kneading his chest, toying with his nipples. All the while her body slid up and down his.

Filled with serenity, her gaze never left his handsome face, indulging blissfully in the hot-blooded arousal that was etched there. Basking in the sheer feel of him, Madison inclined her head back to wonder at the early morning sky, inky black, glistening with a million blinking stars. Colt's hands were everywhere, stimulating, searching, possessing. Grasping at the hair at her nape, he impatiently hauled her down to his lips, seizing her mouth in a desperate, hungry kiss.

In one swift plunge he took her, and pulling her lips away from his, she let out a cry as his manhood kissed her very womb. Colt bestowed on her a rousing half-smile of victory. He strained up for more.

Defeat has its pleasures, and she rode him to every one of those stars, flitting from one to the next, higher and higher—until one by one they imploded as she gasped with her own unrivaled spasms, her world bursting in a shower of scintillating sparks. . . .

Whipping her hair back, she dug her fingernails into his chest, accepting all of him, her own inner contractions stroking him to a vigorous release, surging, filling her completely. Colt let out a long guttural groan and she flung her body forward, collapsing over him, moaning, whispering into his ear as their souls merged into one.

Locked in an unrelenting embrace, their hearts racing in tempo, still joined, they floated to earth together. Colt ran a caressing hand over her hair, the other firmly cupping her buttock. Madison planted delicate kisses along his shoulder as she slowly inched off to the side, her thigh left to rest possessively over his manhood.

Temporarily sated, Colt closed his eyes and brushed his lips to her temple. His arms cradled her lovingly.

She watched his slow, even breathing as he drifted to sleep. Madison knew she couldn't tell him what had happened between her and Garrett. It wasn't right. This man had saved her life today. He had given her shelter, a bed, food when she needed it. Though he didn't speak of love, he had even claimed he wanted to marry her.

What had she done for him? She had bitched, railed in fits of anger, tried to alter the way he lived his life, even changed his marriage plans! She had followed him back through a portal of time into another century when he hadn't wanted her to; in fact, she recalled that he had demanded that she go back to Jackson that rainy afternoon. It wasn't fair that she spill her guts, likely driving a permanent wedge between the two brothers.

Her body felt as if it were filled with lead weights. Destiny would have to run its course. Sadness descended over her heart, suffocating in its murkiness.

Reluctantly, she slipped from beneath the delightful weighty possessiveness of his arm, careful not to wake him. She stood over him one last time, memorizing every feature and contour of his face and body. Then, her eyes downcast, she turned, gathered her discarded gown and robe, and went back inside.

It was time. Madison knew what she had to do.

Chapter Twenty-Four

Madison looked out over the vast expanse of the Jackson Hole Valley through swollen and red-rimmed eyes. She pulled the suede fringed jacket up around her neck, closing out the penetrating morning chill. Cinnabar snorted, tipping her head down to rip at the moist, dew-glazed grass.

It hadn't been as difficult to leave as Madison had thought it might be. Only a few hours ago she had determinedly collected her belongings, donning her own jeans, shirt, and boots before she had quietly left the house and headed for the barn. Cinnabar had been saddled with a minimum of mistakes, as she adjusted and cinched the saddle the way she had seen Colt and the other cowboys do several times.

She couldn't deny that the trip up the treacherous mountain pass had been any less than frightening. It was very dark, and if not for the brilliant moon she wouldn't have been able to see a thing. The damp and misty forest throbbed with a cacophony of night noises. Lucky for her, the vegetation was not as thick as she remembered it being in 1993, and Madison had forged on, making only one wrong turn, then backtracking in order to find the right path. She had breathed a sigh of relief upon achieving the glorious summit of a clearing just beyond the dense aspen thicket.

Dawn broke, and an eerie stillness closed in around her, as if nature was waiting for her to make her move.

Madison opened her shoulderbag and drew out the two splendidly marbled rosebuds—Colt's rosebuds. The eternally fresh petals lay limp across her palm, finally succumbing to the inevitable laws of nature. Madison felt the familiar constriction wadding deeply within her throat. She replaced the buds safely inside her purse and swung down from the horse.

Thorny vines clung to the trunk of the isolated spruce, hovering within its sacrificial refuge.

Four divinely marbled buds remained. When Madison was done there were only three.

Shocked by the magical appearance of the swirling turmoil of storm clouds low above her head, Madison remembered Colt's vivid description of the way the first storm had beset him. He hadn't exaggerated. Frowning against the sudden onslaught of pelting rain, she quickly mounted Cinnabar.

Lightning streaked across the dawn sky. Thunder clapped and the earth shook beneath them. She swallowed hard, inhaling a deep, cleansing breath before nudging the mare forward. The red horse and her golden-haired rider disappeared into the rapidly encroaching mist, downward into the valley.

Book Two

Chapter Twenty-Five

"Maddie? Is that you? I've been on pins and needles since your message—My God, where have you been? Are you okay?" Mark's voice was frantic.

"Oh, Mark! You don't know how wonderful it is to hear your voice! I'm fine," Madison answered. In her own bed, she was still fully clothed, and had been in a dead sleep when the phone on her bedside table began to ring mercilessly.

"I'm coming over—"

"No, please, I'm so tired. I was asleep when the phone rang and I've had maybe two hours' sleep in the last twenty-four. Let me rest. Come by after work. I'll fill you in then."

"Maddie, I think you'd better talk to me right now! Do you realize that you have the police in two states searching for you? Not to mention Mom. She's practically made herself sick with worry. And Lanie and Gertie haven't been able to concentrate on anything. We were all afraid you . . . well, we feared the worst when we didn't hear from you."

"I know," she sighed, "and I'm so sorry. There weren't any phones. It's hard to make someone understand who wasn't there, but I couldn't get to a phone. I took a fall from a horse . . ."

"You *what?* Are you *sure* you're okay?"

"Yeah, just fine, thanks to Colt—"

"I knew this had something to do with him," Mark interrupted heatedly.

Madison sighed into the mouthpiece, closing her eyes. What could she tell Mark that would leave her the dignity of appearing sane? Above all, she knew she couldn't bear for anyone to refer to Colt in a negative way.

"It's such a complicated story. The important thing is that I'm all right, and Colt is entirely responsible for that."

"Okay, okay," Mark cut her off just as her father used to when she had given him some feeble excuse. "I need to call the authorities and let them know you're safe—you're *sure* no one is responsible for your disappearance?" He waited for an answer.

"Mark! I'm positive."

"I'll be over in a few hours."

"All right. . . . Oh, and can you call Mom and just let her know I'm fine and I'll give her a call later? Be sure and tell Lanie and Gertie I'm okay, too."

"Sure, Mad. I'm glad you're home. I was really worried." His tone turned softly sincere.

"I knew you would be. Believe me, that bothered me most of all."

After Madison hung up she sunk back into the softness of her bed, lost in a deep sleep within a matter of minutes. She dreamt of an absolutely gorgeous cowboy in a Stetson hat with laughing, golden-brown eyes. Forever elusive, whenever she tried to reach out to him, he'd vanish into nothingness.

Mark knocked but didn't wait for an answer. He opened the screen door and stepped inside the cozy living room of the quaint Victorian house situated at the northern end of Colorado Springs.

Madison heard the knock and came sprinting up the basement stairs. She had been doing laundry. She wore faded jeans and a baggy T-shirt, her hair hanging in heavy curls down her back. She didn't look much older than fifteen.

Smiling with joy, she ran to Mark and gave him a fierce hug. He squeezed her affectionately, but then held her at arm's length. He began to smile, but his expression quickly changed to one of concern.

"Your head! What happened?" His expression was skeptical even before he heard her answer.

"The fall from my horse, remember?" She reached up to touch the fading bruise. "Leave it to my clumsiness. I fell from my horse on Sunday when I went after Colt in the storm." Madison plopped down on the couch, patting the cushion next to her. "Want something to drink? I think there's soda in the fridge."

"No, Maddie, thanks. Just tell me what happened. And I mean everything! It isn't like you to disappear without a word to anyone. I just knew something awful happened, especially when you didn't bother to check in at work. This was the week they installed the new computer system, and I knew how uneasy you were about that."

Madison's hand flew to her mouth. "Oh! I'd forgotten with all the excitement. Did they get it in all right? I wanted two extra terminals in the back office—did you remember to tell them?"

"Let's talk shop later. Don't evade the subject at hand." Mark's eyes bore down on her.

"I don't know where to start." She threw up her hands helplessly. "Last Sunday, the afternoon storm in Jackson . . . I was frightened for Colt. I knew he would be out there trying to . . ." She hesitated.

"Trying to what?"

Madison had long since accepted the fact that she wasn't going to be able to tell Mark or her mother the truth. It was a powerless feeling and now that she was faced with it, she wanted more than anything to confess everything to her brother. This was Mark—he would believe her, wouldn't he?

Madison wasn't even sure she believed herself. Now that she was back in the "real world," so to speak, with Mark in his three-piece suit, looking every inch the empowered executive, all the buildings of steel and glass, and the cars, the noise and the people, what she had given credence to in the year 1878 didn't seem so real.

" . . . Well," she continued, "he said something about riding back to his ranch, and when the storm hit I felt I needed to . . . uh . . . stop him." She smiled a little sheepishly and shrugged.

Mark frowned. "He's a grown man. Why would you need to stop him?"

"I thought he was senile, Mark." There. She said it. "But I later found out that wasn't the case."

Madison related the entire episode, careful to edit out all that would lead him to think she had lost her marbles. When she was done she took a deep breath, quite satisfied with her rendition of the whole affair.

Mark leaned into the corner of the couch, his arms folded, his ankle crossed over his knee. His expression was grave.

Finally, he said, "Maddie, I was out there. When you didn't show up for the flight home I stayed in Jackson up until yesterday to look for you. Myself and a couple of deputies were at the ranch searching half the day on Tuesday! The Triple Bar C, right? That place is a mess! You couldn't have stayed there for one night, let alone three . . . and there wasn't anyone living out there, either."

"Oh." Her mind raced. She'd known from Ernie when she returned Cinnabar that Mark and the police had looked for her, but she hadn't known they had been to the ranch. Now what could she say? She wasn't used to lying, and she wasn't very good at it. Especially with Mark. "Are you sure you went out to the Triple Bar C?" she asked sweetly.

"Maddie—I'm positive."

He was on to her. Dammit. She couldn't pull anything over on him.

"Okay. I *thought* I heard Colt call it the Triple Bar C. Actually, he took me out to the old ranch on Sunday—you remember I told you? The name of the *new* ranch is similar, but I just can't quite recall . . . But I do know that it was lovely, with a lot of cowboys. And people were definitely living there." She nodded her head in affirmation.

"And this lovely ranch didn't have a telephone?"

"Nope. They like the simple life."

"I guess. Didn't Colt suggest driving you to town to make a phone call? What about getting you to a doctor?" He paused, then cut in before she could answer. "No, wait, let me theorize— they didn't have any cars, and the doctor made house calls, right?"

Madison just smiled weakly.

"Why do I get the impression there's something you're not telling me?"

"I'm sure I've left out a lot, but I'm pretty tired."

"If it was so great there, how is it you haven't gotten any sleep in the last day or so?"

Mark grilled her relentlessly until she thought she just couldn't take it anymore. Eventually, he gave up, tired of her vague answers. He grinned at last.

"Hey, I'll leave you alone. There's something you're not telling me, but I figure you will when the time is right. You can come to me anytime, you know." He tweaked her cheek affectionately, something he knew she hated. She slapped his hand away with annoyance.

"Yeah, I know, Mark. I'm sorry to have caused so much trouble, but I'm glad you're around to care."

She hugged him again before he left, swearing that she was feeling perfectly all right to come into the office tomorrow, and that she would definitely make a doctor's appointment to check out the bruise on her head.

Later, when she sat down to call her mother, Angela Calloway was worse than Mark had been. The questions came in torrents, and Madison thought she would surely sink. After muddling through the onslaught, Madison somehow unwittingly managed to give her mother the impression that she and Colt were involved quite seriously, something she had fervently tried to avoid. The last thirty minutes was a one-sided conversation as Angela lectured Madison on the trials and tribulations of carrying on with an older man.

At last, Angela blew two kisses into the phone and told her daughter she loved her, insisting she come for dinner soon.

After she hung up, Madison felt so alone—and anxious. About what, she had no idea. She wasn't hungry, but just to have something to do she popped a TV dinner into the microwave. It was awful and she couldn't finish it. When she curled up in front of the television set the loud brashness disgusted her and she ended up turning it off, much preferring to sit quietly in the dimly lit living room. Just sit and think.

The thought of getting back into her old routine and going to the office tomorrow didn't even excite her. All she could think about was Colt, and the mess she had left him in—a man supposedly married to a missing wife, and helpless to carry on with his dreams of marrying Sarah. Then she thought of Rosannah. And Emmy. And Bud . . . then Colt again. And all she had been through, the emotions she had felt . . .

When the uproarious electrical storm had abated, leaving her wet, sick, and dizzy at the outskirts of Jackson, she had instantly been filled with an inexplicable remorse. She had been sorry it had worked. With modern-day Jackson spread out before her, she hadn't even been relieved or happy. At the time she had blamed the Godforsaken nausea.

Dispassionately, she had walked Cinnabar into town and onward to the Wild West show, in search of Ernie Hawkins. People had gawked at her disheveled appearance, but she hadn't cared.

Ernie had literally flown out of his chair when she came shuffling in looking like a drowned rat. As nice as ever and showing much concern, he had offered to do all he could for her, and that's when he had told her of the police and her brother's intense search.

When Madison had offered to donate Cinnabar back to the Wild West show, not caring if she received any money back, Ernie wouldn't hear of it. He had insisted the horse could work for her board until such time as Madison had the place to keep her. Just let him know, and Cinnabar would be waiting for her return.

Thanking him profusely, she had shaken his hand before she left, promising him she would call her brother as soon as possible.

On her way out she had stroked the red mare's soft nose, bidding her a fond yet sad good-bye. The black liquid eyes had fluttered in response, and Madison had somehow sensed that the horse had understood everything that had gone on in the past few days.

The next stop had been the Shady Oak Hotel to retrieve her luggage, and she had offered only a brief apology for her tardiness. Then it was onward to the airport, where she'd called Mark from a pay phone. He had been in the middle of an important meeting with an airline rep and, rather than interrupt, she had left a message for him to call her at home later.

Though now feeling better physically since her afternoon nap, she was still downhearted. Maybe she shouldn't go to work tomorrow morning. There were other things pressing on her mind—things she felt the need to get out of the way. Even as she thought about it, her mood soared and she began to plan her day.

A trip to Penrose Public Library was in order. She'd dig up all she could find on Colt Chase. She didn't know exactly why. What did it matter at this point? But just the thought of it filled her with anticipation, somehow making her feel closer to him.

Chapter Twenty-Six

The sun was burning into his eyelids before he even woke up. He gradually opened his eyes, and the memory of an incredibly provocative, luscious honey-blond creature looming over him, climbing into his makeshift bed, making delicious love to him, hit him full force. It had been a heaven never before conceived of; the fragrance of silky, golden curls; her satiny skin as she had sat astride him; and the sweet surrender he had detected in her trembling softness, though she tried to take control. Madison. Was it a dream, or was it really her?

Then he had held her so close, so very close, troubled by some obscure fear of losing her. Something inside had told him to hold on with every ounce of his strength—not to ever let go. But he had been so tired, so drained, and he had thought that after a few winks, he would rouse her and make love to her over and over again. He coveted her body, soul, her very being—and was going to prove it now—if she let him.

But as he looked around the verandah, there was no sign of her. Maybe she had dressed and gone downstairs. He had slept unusually late.

Bounding from the bedroll, he stalked every corner of the master suite, flinging open the wardrobe, checking for her clothes, any indication of her presence.

But he knew she was gone. It was just a feeling, the most

horrible feeling he'd ever had in his life. His strong heart was breaking and he didn't understand anything.

He jerked on a pair of faded indigo Levi's, jumping in one leg at a time. He threw on a fresh shirt and snatched up his hat and holster, tearing down the stairs and out the front door in a rush of air. He was at the barn in no time.

Cinnabar was gone, too. So was her saddle.

Damn! Why couldn't he have seen what Madison was leading up to, coming to him in the night as she had. . . . Or had she? Maybe it *was* a dream, he mused. Maybe she never really existed at all.

Wasn't it all for the best? A clean break—no tears for something that could have never been. Damn her. She could be lying in some ravine somewhere, thrown from her horse again. The horrors he had told her about on the ride up the pass were the truth—mostly. He had embellished just a little to ensure that she wouldn't try it alone. A lot of good that had done.

With a sigh and a muttered curse, he decided to ride the mountain trail just to make sure she had made it all right—for his own peace of mind, of course. He would take the fastest hell-bitch he could round up. Then he'd tuck Madison's memory away and head on down to Abilene.

With half the day wasted and his attitude just as far gone, Colt strapped on calfskin chaps. He pulled a six-shooter from its holster and was spinning the cartridge to check the ammunition when a weathered hand clapped down on his shoulder. He cast a startled look into kindly, hooded blue eyes, heavily crinkled at the corners from years of smiles.

"A little dangerous coming up behind a man loading his pistols, reckon?" Colt forced a lazy grin with more enthusiasm than he felt.

"Not in this case. A man with no spirit ain't much of a threat—he's too slow." Bud spoke in jest, but there was a serious intent in his expression.

Colt heaved the saddle to his shoulder and aimed for the corral. "No spirit, huh? Who died and made you the expert?"

Bud followed him. "Don't take no expert to see how you're beatin' yourself up, Colt. Rosie said Madison done left. No word or nothin'. Why don't you admit you're not the greatest catch this side of heaven—eat some of that pride. Quit your mopin', go get her, and bring her on back. Why you'd let your own wife take off on some feminine whim, I'll never understand. That is . . . if she *is* your wife . . ." Bud eyed him sharply, a challenge burning behind his blue eyes.

Colt's eyebrow shot up. "You don't know what you're talking about. Hell, *I* don't even know what you're talking about."

Colt vaulted over the fence and began twirling the lariat above his head. He threw. The rope flicked out like a striking snake and found its mark, the loop sizzling over the head of the most rambunctious, frisky animal he knew of. He reeled her in.

"Don't play dumb with me, boy. This is Bud standing here; I probably know you better'n you know yourself."

"First of all, I don't want any woman around who doesn't want to be around. In the second place, it's none of your damn business if we were married or not."

Colt arranged a blanket, then flung the creaky saddle over the mustang. He bent to fasten the heavy silver buckles beneath, while struggling to keep up with her prancing.

"Don't really matter if you were or not, does it?" Bud leaned over the fence. "You've shared the same heart—that's the killer, ain't it, son? Bet you never even told her your feelin's, and now you're hurtin'. You'd better git off your dead ass and go fetch 'er. Treat her right this time." Finished and satisfied, Bud turned and sauntered away, mumbling the entire way, " 'Sides, I kinda liked that girl. She had spunk."

Colt stopped what he was doing and frowned at the old man until he disappeared inside the barn. He rolled his eyes to the sky and exhaled with a grumble. "Old fart . . . God, how I hate it when you're right. But, unfortunately, it's not quite that easy."

He led the high-stepping, glossy black mustang from the corral where he mounted her skillfully, despite her exhibited disapproval, quirting her into a full gallop toward the mountain range.

Garrett sat alone at a corner table in the dimly lit saloon, the haze of smoke blurring the darkness of his expression as he silently observed the goings-on around him. It was a fairly quiet night: a peaceful card game in the center of the room and a few stinking drunks nearly passed out against the wall. The usual worn-out crib girls mingled in boredom, their eyes raised in hopes of a possible customer with every swing of the door.

They had approached him several times. But he wasn't interested, preferring to wait for Lucy. She might be uglier than a mud fence, but she knew what he liked and wasn't shy about catering to his every whim, no matter how perverse the mood.

At that moment Garrett saw Lucinda enter the back door of the saloon, the thick heels of her red satin shoes clunking loudly as she did. She wore a cheap taffeta dress in almost the same shade of red, the black lacy bodice cut far too low for her nonexistent cleavage. A ratty, shriveled-up red ostrich feather stuck out of the roll of her mousy brown hair, billowing in the breeze as she approached Garrett.

"I knew you'd be here waitin' for me, honey," she crooned as she slid into the chair next to his. "I so much look forward to Fridays, 'cause I know you'll be here with—"

"Shut up Lucy. You talk too much. What in tarnation happened to your face?" He leaned in closer to get a better look at the purplish bruise along her right cheekbone and around her eye. She had attempted to camouflage it with the pasty theatrical makeup she used, but it was only accentuated, giving her a clownish appearance.

"Oh, this?" She fluttered fingertips over her face. "Nothin' much. Pete just got a little ticked off is all."

"Three-toed Pete did *that?*" he asked incredulously.

"Yes." She eyed him flirtatiously, "Does it make you hot, honey? Are you gonna do somethin' to him, huh?" Her eyes lit up at the possibility.

"Me? Hell no, you fight your own battles, woman. I was just amazed you had a face *left* if it was actually Pete who did that. He must have been in a generous mood."

"It most certainly was Pete!" she answered indignantly, moving her finger in an imaginary cross over her chest. "Cross my heart and hope to die." Lucinda relaxed back into the chair. She pursed her lips into a wrinkled bow as she regarded him, her scheme chasing the blood through her veins in anticipation. "Not to change the subject or nothin', but I've been thinkin' . . ."

"Don't exert yourself." Garrett put the bottle to his lips, tilting his head back to guzzle a swig, the brown liquid sloshing at the bottom.

"Stop your teasin', now. I've decided to make a career change and I'd like you to be a part of it."

He glanced at her as if she'd lost her mind.

"I'm quite serious, now, honey. I've resolved to become your very own personal mistress. I would be willing to forego my successful career here to consider such an option." Lucinda glared down the length of her pointed nose, self-assurance oozing from every pore.

"You? . . . What?" He began to laugh, a little at first, then turning to uproarious guffaws.

It was the loudest noise she had ever heard him make, with the exception of the caterwauling he did while in the throes of passion. All she could do was stare at him, as her finger inched up her neck to toy casually with a loose tendril of her hair. When he calmed down she continued. "It's a very beneficial arrangement for us both, Garrett, if you'll just give me a listen. You and I get along. We're birds of a feather . . . well, wouldn't you say? Wouldn't you like to have my services available anytime, night or day, free of charge? Just take me home with you and—"

"You're crazier than a looney bird, Lucy. You think I want a goddammed woman a bitchin' and a followin' me around all the time?" He moved in close to her face, his lips forming into a thin, straight line. "Why do you think I haven't taken a woman, whore or not, home with me yet? Huh? They're not worth the trouble, and that includes the likes of you."

"No, honey, you've got it all wrong. You won't ever even so much as see me if you don't wanna. I can be real discreet like, and comfort your cowboys some, too." Garrett's gaze shot up to hers, and she wasn't sure if he was softening or not. "But if you don't want me to do that, then I'll just be all yours for the takin'. No charge. Whenever you like. However you like."

Her hand snaked up his leg until she reached his crotch, first rubbing and then giving him a few firm squeezes. His eyes darkened, their blackness shimmering like ebony marbles.

"What's in it for you? Surely you've got something up your sleeve."

"I just kinda like bein' around you, is all . . ."

He frowned, and she quickly amended her statement. "I mean, I'm not going to be all clingy or anything like that. I'm tired of this rathole, all right?" She rolled her eyes and impatiently began to rap her fingers on the wooden table.

"That's what I figured. You live up to your side of the deal, and we'll get along just fine. The first time you start asking for money, bitchin', or doing any of those other annoying woman things, you're out. Hear?" He couldn't believe he was actually uttering these words. *Yeah . . . wait 'til this whore moves in, it'll really get under Colt's skin. Just let him say something about it. And Rosie, this should set the old hag to flappin'*, Garrett mused belligerently.

"Oh! Yes! Anything you say, honey!" She had to restrain

herself just to keep from dancing on the tables. *Colt, sweetheart,* she thought—*here I come!*

"Now we're gonna start this deal out right. Get your ass upstairs. You're gonna do anything and everything I want!"

Abruptly shoving the chair back, he grabbed the whiskey bottle by the neck and headed for the stairway. Lucinda was close behind, her red heels slapping loudly on the crude planked floor.

Chapter Twenty-Seven

Madison studied the microfilm until it felt as if her eyes were welded to the tiny print on the screen. It was past dinner time; she had been at the library for over six hours and had never made it to the agency.

After all that time she hadn't even found what she was looking for. The history books were of no particular help, and microfilms of newspaper records didn't go back farther than 1892. Of course, the librarian had been more than helpful, offering to order the information she needed directly from the library in Kansas City— it would only take two weeks. . . . Two weeks! That seemed like an eternity, and the one thing Madison didn't have going for her right now was patience. What she did have was an intense hope that the legend of Colt Chase wasn't true, that contrary to what the paperback book had said, he'd lived a long and fruitful life with Sarah Hamilton and had many children. Madison sighed as she turned off the machine. Hell, even that thought depressed her. Her body was stiff from sitting so long and she knew she needed food, lest she pass out right there.

Slowly, she stood up to leave, exited the library, and then walked down Cascade Avenue toward her car, oblivious to the traffic and city noises around her. Madison felt more than disheartened. She felt crushed, as if someone very close to her had just died. Someone had. About 115 years ago. But he was alive in her heart—wasn't he? Was that enough?

After stopping to pick up her dinner of a hamburger and fries, she proceeded through town, not stopping until she reached the Broadmoor Hotel. She circled around to park by the lake.

Leaves danced in and out of the orange rays of the evening sun, fluttering shadows over the sidewalk. She strolled inside the World Arena to watch the ice skaters, then, outside again, she took a seat on a lakeside bench to eat, thinking that the hamburger tasted like sawdust. The ducks and geese were soon congregating around her in flocks. Much to their squawking and honking delight, she tossed an occasional fry or bit of bread into the sea of feathery, flappy commotion.

Madison loved to come here. It was so peaceful, a place where she and Jon had come quite frequently to feed the ducks and to walk around the lake. It didn't remind her of him, though, she thought with a satisfied smugness. No, not even Jon could ruin her enjoyment of this beautiful area.

She was thoughtfully contemplating the sublime pink towers of the hotel when she sensed a presence approach the bench to sit beside her. Turning, her eyes met well-known gray, leaden ones. They flicked over her in interest, an arrogant smile toying at the perfectly refined mouth.

Impeccably dressed in a dark suit, every brown hair in place, Jon made himself comfortable next to her, resting his arm over the back of the bench.

"Well, Maddie, what a nice surprise! Imagine seeing you here. Mark said you've been in Wyoming all week. Whatever could keep you in Wyoming for that length of time, I wonder?"

His voice was as smooth as silk, and as insincere as hell, and Madison looked away without a trace of any emotion.

"*Whoever* might be the better question—and I suppose you'll just have to keep wondering," she quipped, wadding up the paper bag her dinner had come in and tossing it into a nearby trash can.

Jon gave a polished chuckle. "Don't tell me you've found yourself some backwoods, tobacco-chewing cowboy! That's not your style."

"And just what is my 'style'? Someone like you? Someone who'll treat me like dirt and hit on anything that moves? I think not."

Madison flung him a haughty smile, batting her lashes. Jon just looked at her; he seemed to be at a loss for words for once in his life.

Then, he said, "Well, you certainly don't look too happy."

"Is that why you're here, to tell me I don't look too happy?"

"Actually, I met a client here. We just finished up a business deal a few minutes ago, and I spotted you sitting all by yourself. I just thought I'd come by and say hello."

"How nice. Planning on screwing over another poor unsuspecting bastard, huh?"

She bestowed another smile, amazed at the acerbic vitriol that was pouring from her mouth. It wasn't that she was upset, or that he bothered her. Quite the opposite—she was truly enjoying this sudden burst of self-confident power. In her mind's eye she actually thought she could see the sparkle of golden-brown eyes and a smile of courage to back her up.

Jon's jaw hung slack for only an unguarded moment, then the plastic smile was back in place. Before he could respond, Madison did.

"So when did you speak with Mark?"

"Just this morning. I called for you. Wanted to see if you'd like to have lunch. But now that the day is over, how about tomorrow?"

Madison looked at him in utter astonishment. "And what would Amanda think of that?"

Jon stumbled over his next words, and Madison found her enjoyment mounting, another naughty smile snaking to her lips.

"Well, uh . . . she wanted a separation. It's just a trial thing . . ."

She was laughing. A deep belly laugh, and it just wouldn't stop. Recovering she said, "I'm sorry, that wasn't too nice of me, was it? It looks like Amanda has more smarts than I gave her credit for. Good for her."

Jon was perturbed.

"Well? Do you want to have lunch or not?" he sighed with a grumble, cracking his knuckles as he always did when his anger was accelerating.

"Not in this life," she answered merrily, rising to leave, "and hopefully not in the next. But if we *do* happen to meet in another life, I'll be ready for you—mark my words."

Madison slung her little bag over her shoulder and turned her back on him, strutting away. She glanced back just long enough to issue an impudent wink—and of course, to fully relish the expression of utter confusion and defeat that registered on his perfect face.

God, but she was happy! She hadn't felt this good since—well, since she had been with Colt. . . .

When Madison arrived home, Mark, who had his own key, was there waiting for her.

"What's going on, little brother?" she called out as she came in the door, sliding her purse across the kitchen counter.

"Waiting for you," he pronounced, munching from a bag of chips. "These are stale." He was leaning on his side, spretched across most of the couch, the TV blaring. He tossed the bag of chips to the coffee table.

"I've been gone a week. What do you expect?"

"So where have you been all day? When you didn't show at the agency I assumed you went to the doctor. You did go like I told you to?"

Uh-oh. She had completely forgotten about that. "Well, not exactly," she confessed, not meeting his gaze. "Besides, my head feels just fine. I was at the library, then I went to the lake, and guess who I ran into?"

Mark just looked at her expectantly.

"Jon."

He sat up suddenly. "Are you okay?"

"Of course! I feel great." She slipped off her suit jacket and tossed it over the back of the couch.

Mark's eyes narrowed suspiciously. "So what happened?"

"Get a load of this. He and Amanda are separated—he wants me to go to lunch with him—and I told him, in so many words, where he could stick it. And I've never felt better in my life!" Almost, she thought with a trace of melancholy.

Mark broke into a wide grin. "That's fantastic! You've done it, Maddie! I knew you'd get over that bastard, and be a better person for it, too."

"Listen, I'm going to finish unpacking. You can hang around if you want to."

Madison rounded the corner into her bedroom, leaving Mark with the TV for company. She flipped on the radio and kicked off her heels, beginning to empty her suitcase of the final remnants. Then, shaking her head, she moved to inspect the nearly ruined leather shoulder bag, stained and stiff from having been water-logged. She dumped the contents onto the bed, being sure to empty all the zippered compartments.

An overwhelming sadness enveloped her. She extended her fingers to lift the colorful Indian beads from the pile of paraphernalia. Dangling the crude jewelry in front of her, she sucked in a gulp of air, as awareness really settled in. It had happened. She had been transported back in time. It was real.

Absently, she reached up to touch the tiny cameo around her neck, smiling sadly. Colt. Sweet Colt.

Though she tried, she couldn't seem to swallow the annoying lump in her throat. Gradually, she lowered herself to sit on the edge of the bed. That was when she spotted the three rosebuds. Blackened. Brittle. Nearly reduced to a decaying dust as they lay amid the clutter.

Her heart slammed painfully within her chest. Almost afraid, she reached out, watching in horror as a petal broke free, crumbling at her slight touch.

"I think I'll be going now."

Mark stood in the doorway, his sentence cut short when he saw her face: the hollowness. The ghostly pallor. The fear. Her round aqua eyes swimming in a sea of tears. Mark advanced automatically, his arms held open for her.

"Maddie, what's wrong?"

Clutching the beads inside a white-knuckled fist, she stood up, erupting into heart-wrenching sobs, dissolving into his arms. He held her in a bear hug, consoling, questioning, totally baffled at her sudden change in mood.

"He's gone! I . . . I left him. I'll *never* . . . *ever* see him again. Oh, Mark, what have I done?" she wailed into his neck.

"Who? What are you talking about? Maddie! Did Jon say something today?"

"Noooo!" she cried in a drawn-out whine. God, how she hated to hear herself whine. "It's Colt . . . he's dead, Mark, really dead! I'll never see him, talk to him . . ."

"Colt's dead?" Mark tried to peel her off him long enough to see her face. "You didn't tell me that!"

Frustrated, Madison reached for a tissue from the box on the nightstand, ripping it out impatiently. She bounced back onto the bed, falling to her side and rolling into the fetal position. Mark sat down beside her, rubbing her arm agitatedly.

"No. No. It's not like he died. It's a figure of speech. I just . . . I . . . think . . ." Her words withered away in a low, agonized moan.

"There is something between you two, isn't there? Level with me, Maddie! You're in love with him, aren't you?"

Her bloodshot eyes lifted to his, luminescent green in their pent-up, repressed emotion. She didn't have to answer in words.

"Does he love *you?*"

Madison attempted a nod into her pillow, sobbing. "I'm not sure," she finally admitted. "He's not the same Colt you met. He's different."

"I figured as much. Somehow I just couldn't picture you having an affair with an eightysomething-year-old man." Mark laughed feebly. "So why don't you go back to him? Is it work that's stopping you?"

She shook her head, not wanting to try to explain the impossibility of it all.

"I think if you feel this strongly, you need to let him know."

"I can't!"

"Why not?"

"I just can't!"

"You should. Is he married or something?"

"No, of course not."

"If a woman felt about me like you obviously feel about him, I sure as hell would want her to tell me."

Madison looked at him for a long time before she finally spoke. "I can't," she whispered at last, her voice a husky quiver.

Chapter Twenty-Eight

With only her shoulderbag as luggage and Colt's fringed suede jacket, Madison left Ernie Hawkins' office. The intense heat of the June sun bearing down on her shoulders, Madison rode past the outskirts of Jackson and onward to the banks of the Snake River. She followed the winding shores just as she and Colt had done exactly one week earlier, cutting off at the entrance into the lush canyon. It was so late when she had arrived in Jackson the day before, she had had to force herself to wait until early Sunday before she headed out, not wanting to be faced with the long descent down to the ranch in the dead of night. Once had been enough.

The decision to return to Jackson hadn't been that difficult. It was the only rational conclusion once she had really gotten down to the heart of the matter. Colt needed her, whether he acknowledged it or not, and she had to answer that desperate call that she didn't understand. It was a feeling, a determination like none that had ever possessed her. Damn it all, but she was sick and tired of letting life happen to her in whichever manner it pleased. It was about time she seized control.

If she couldn't prevent Colt from going to Abilene, maybe, just maybe she could be instrumental in helping him once he got there. She just might be the factor that would prevent him from being killed. Then, perhaps, she could come back with peace of mind . . . a clear conscience that Colt might pursue his life with Sarah.

That is, if she was able to come back. Something might go wrong. That possibility had crossed her mind, too, but it wasn't nearly as painful as the thought of never seeing Colt again. It had become quickly apparent to her that if she was stuck somewhere, she'd much rather it be with him than without him, regardless of where she was.

Saying good-bye to everyone had been the hardest part. Naturally, she couldn't divulge her true intentions, so her mother was left believing that Madison was off to take care of some business at Colt's ranch in Wyoming, not sure when she'd be able to return. Mark had been easier to convince, and he hadn't tried to talk her out of chasing down some rancher she'd only known for a week. There was a little trouble she needed to help Colt with, she had said. Yes, the good-byes hadn't been easy, knowing full well she might never come back. Of course, her mother and Mark hadn't known that. After locking up her little house and taking care of all pressing matters, she had left for the airport.

Madison smiled when she thought of Ernie Hawkins, his mouth hanging agape as she strolled in that morning. He probably thought she was completely cracked. He hadn't been expecting her back so soon to retrieve Cinnabar but had happily surrendered the pretty mare, wishing Madison all the luck in the world. He had also inquired as to how her grandpa was getting along. It had taken her a moment to realize that he meant Colt, and with a little laugh, Madison had assured him that Colt was as spry as ever and looking much younger these days.

Long grasses waved to and fro with the breeze as Madison and Cinnabar trudged on until the hilly crest came into view. Rounding the perimeter and ascending the hill, they came to rest in the shade of the bent spruce, her gaze quickly riveting to the curious rosebush. At her side loomed the deep, craterlike valley; a fantasy world Madison was about to enter—maybe never to return.

Everything seemed ordinary enough. The birds sang and the flies buzzed annoyingly around her horse. Madison knew that all superficial normality would change as soon as she plucked another rose. Three buds beckoned, lifted by the hardy breeze.

She swung down, almost afraid to step closer to the bush.

With a burning desire to see the man she had only known for a week's time but had felt inside her heart all her life, she grasped a marbled bud, mindful of thorns, and pulled, snapping it free. Lonelier than ever, only two buds remained on the bedraggled, thorny bush.

A cacophony of thunderous explosion sounded all around her, rocking the hills, and she cringed. Cinnabar whinnied, sidestepping with a wild toss of her silky russet mane. Madison lunged to grab at the reins, sighing with heartfelt relief when she caught them.

"Sorry, girl, but you're coming along, too."

Right before her astonished eyes, fleecy clouds turned black in unmatched fury, swirling, roiling above her head, as if acting out some primitive dance. Lightning scored charcoal skies with vehemence, reaching down with spindly, forked fingers to snap viciously at a proud fir, exploding it into white-hot flame. As if in slow motion, the tip of the tree swayed precariously, breaking, crashing to earth in a shower of sparks.

Madison screamed and held her hands to her ears, intensely aware of the electrically charged air vibrating around her. Scrambling to mount Cinnabar, she struggled to face the shying horse toward the valley. Heavy raindrops besieged her in a sudden downpour. A nudge of her heel sent the horse flying down the steep embankment, headlong into the fog, the lowering, ominous haze. . . .

The gabled roof of the pale yellow ranch house peeked from the distance over rolling hills and plateaus, welcoming. Madison's heart tripped at the sight. Stepping up the pace, Cinnabar trotted along with proud, high steps as they rounded the outermost stables, obviously sensing excitement in the air. Zak and two other cowboys stopped their work momentarily, tipping their hats as they watched her pass.

Another figure, dark and foreboding, hid in the shadows of the huge barn doors. The fire at the tip of his cheroot glowed brightly as he inhaled one last time before spewing it to the ground, crushing it with his boot. His shoulder leaning into the door, he watched the young blond woman pass, his gaze fixing on her round, feminine hips beneath her form-fitting denims.

A malevolent scorn kicked up inside him once again—and he smiled wickedly, his teeth white against the darkness of his skin. He had sworn she would pay. If the bitch was fool enough to

come back, he'd treat her to a reception she might not soon
forget. The stocky shape backed away from the double doors
and disappeared.

Like a human tornado, a scrawny rail of a woman spun out
of nowhere. She blocked Madison's path, her hands imperious-
ly propped on her hips, her bony elbows cocked oddly out-
ward. It was as if she thought she was large enough to stop
Madison's horse.

With a startled gasp, Madison jerked in on the reins and reeled
to a standstill. Lucinda Beak sashayed a bit to the side, her pale
blue eyes narrowing, her head tilted obstinately.

"You!" Madison groaned. She would have recognized that face
with the pink clown cheeks anywhere.

"Well, well, well. If this just isn't the nicest surprise. Hello
again, Matilda." Lucinda made a full circle around the horse,
stopping, her face scrunched into a frown against the assaulting
sunlight as she looked up at Madison.

"That's *Madison*. And you're Lucy, right?" Sarcasm dripped
from her voice.

"Most certainly. Whatever are you doing back here?"

"I could ask you that same question."

"I live here. What's your excuse?" She examined a fingernail
as she spoke.

"How nice. I'm sure you claim to know where Colt is; why
don't you tell me and I'll be on my way, hmmmm?" Madison
inquired acidly.

"I *always* know where Colt is, dearie. I said I live here now—
with him. Catch my drift? You're positively daft if you think I'm
going to tell *you* where he is. You'll not find him anywhere close
to here, that's for sure, and he don't want to see you, anyhow—
told me so hisself." Lucy nodded curtly.

"I think I'd like to hear that from him, thank you very much."

Putting an end to this ridiculous conversation, Madison gently
shook the reins, steering Cinnabar around the skinny roadblock.

"Don't you *ever* dismiss *me!*" Lucy screeched.

She lunged at Madison with unexpected speed, digging sharp
fingernails into her denim-clad leg, tugging at the horse's bit
with her other hand. Madison winced at the needlelike pain that
shot into her calf. Without forethought she thrust her fingers
into the stiff, greasy hair at the top of Lucy's head, gripping.
Leveraging her palm against the woman's forehead, she shoved
her back.

Off-balance, Lucy's eyes grew enormous, her spiked fingernails raking along Madison's leg for a last-chance hold as she stumbled away, gawking. Then, her arms flailing like a homely bird, she fell down, her butt landing unceremoniously in a mud puddle. Her bony knees aimed toward the heavens, her skirt blew up in the breeze.

Madison's laugh just rolled out. It was the most hilarious thing she had ever seen. Lucy seethed, muttering under her breath, her eyes shooting icy daggers.

Madison rode away at a fast trot. "I'd say we're even, wouldn't you?" she asked, still laughing at the comical scene behind her.

"You bitch!" Lucy bellowed, "I'll get you good for that! Come back here . . . !"

Lucy looked positively asinine, rolling around in a tangle of muddied skirts. When she tried to get up a long foot caught in the hem to plunge her back down, and Madison still couldn't stop laughing.

She didn't slow down until she reached the side of the ranch house, Sage and Brush yipping as they raced by her side the entire way. Her boot barely had touched dirt before Rosannah burst out of the screen door.

She wiped her hands along her apron before reaching out to her. "Madison, dear! You're back! And you've got on those godforsaken men's clothes again!" She shook her round head in gentle disapproval before sweeping Madison into a giant welcoming hug.

"It's good to be back, Rosannah!" She returned the generous embrace with touching sincerity.

"Just tell me, are you here for good? Emmy's been heartbroke since you left . . . and Colt is as sour as green apples in winter."

"I'm afraid that's up to Colt," Madison admitted.

"Don't tell me *he* was responsible for your leaving in the first place? I'll tan that boy's hide, and I don't care if he is twice my size and a man to boot!"

Madison laughed, not doubting the little woman's ability to do just that. "No, not in the way you mean. But he may not be too eager to forgive me for leaving without a word."

Rosannah shushed her, scooping her hand in between callused yet curiously soft ones. "I wouldn't worry my pretty head 'bout that," she whispered conspiratorially.

Just then Emmy rounded the corner of the porch, dropping her broom when she saw Madison. She bounded down the steps and practically fell into Madison's arms.

"You did come back!" she bubbled. "I knew you would! Didn't I tell you, Mama—she'd be back?" Emmy's wide hazel eyes leveled on her mother, and she gripped Madison's arm as if letting go would be giving permission for Madison to vanish again.

Rosannah folded her arms, smiling in assent. "Yes, dear, you told us all. Now go on and finish up with the sweeping."

"It's so good to see you, Emmy." Madison smoothed the soft brown wisps from the young girl's shiny face.

Emmy was genuinely distressed, stomping her foot and muttering about wanting to stay with Madison and letting her chores wait.

"Emmy?" Madison took hold of her hand. "Tell me where I can find Colt—then I'll come right on back and we can talk, all right?"

"Colt's gone!" she gushed in a torrent of emotion. "He won't be back now for months and months."

Madison's eyes shot over to Rosannah's, the truth confirmed with a hesitant nod.

"Another one of his missions for justice, I presume. Left this morning before dawn. I wish you would have gotten here before he left; you might have been able to stop him."

"Abilene?" Madison asked apprehensively, though she already knew the answer.

Rosannah nodded. "All he said was that he'd be back before the first snowfall."

"That's what he thinks," Madison muttered to herself, her head filling, spinning with possible solutions to this little setback.

"What was that, dear?"

"Oh, uh . . . nothing." Her jaw set with determination, Madison spun around and mounted her horse. "I'm going after him."

"Can I go . . . please, oh please . . . ?"

"Wait! You can't do that! You'll never catch him; he's got more than half a day's head start on you. He's a good rider—and fast!"

Rosannah and Emmy were talking at the same time.

Rosannah came to rest her hand possessively on Madison's knee. "It's no place for a woman out there alone. Stay here! Colt would want you to."

"I've got to go. If I don't, he might not come back." Madison knew the little woman wouldn't understand her meaning.

"Of course he will; he always does—you just have to have faith!"

"I can't take that risk. Believe me, I know what I'm talking about. Which direction did he head out in?"

"Oh my God, child . . . if you insist on doing this, let me send one of the boys with you. Colt is clever. He won't be where it's easy to find him. It'll take someone who knows his habits."

Rosannah flapped around, her ample bosom heaving, until an idea popped into her head. "Emmy! Go fetch Zak. Now, girl!" She clapped her hands until a disgruntled Emmy took off in a run toward the barn.

With a flour sack full of food, a full canteen, a bedroll, a six-shooter holstered around her waist, and an old Stetson hat that was entirely too big, Madison set out with Zak across the green foothills, the dusty plateaus, and the dry, yellow sagebrush flats, dotted with a few growth-stunted trees. Not a single cloud marred the brilliant blue sky, and in the blazing-hot heat wave the dust was choking.

They had ridden nonstop for three days at a frantic pace until her body was past the point of mere pain—she was numb. Madison had thought she had been sore before; now it was sheer hell.

By noon on the fourth day, Zak pointed at the slightest flicker of dark movement against the greenish-yellow, heat-blistered horizon. How he ever noticed that speck was beyond her. They rode slower, following a dry creek bed for just a while longer.

Sure it was Colt who rode ahead, Madison gave Zak sincere thanks for all his help. Managing a weary smile, she unfastened the sack of food and handed the rest to him for the trip home. He reversed his direction, assuring her that he would ride slow just in case she needed to catch up to him.

Madison took a deep breath, urging Cinnabar into an anxious trot, aiming toward the the haven of shade trees against the endless horizon, the lone rider ahead the only sign of life.

Colt knew he was being followed. He'd known for some time from pure instinct, but recently he'd gotten periodic glimpses of two riders. Now it was down to one rider, the other having vanished. If they were up to no good, it was always possible the second was planning on circling around to catch him in an ambush.

He had been riding the sandy creek bed for several miles. The parched terrain gave way to a lush valley, a rare spot of refuge among a bounty of shade trees. As soon as he lost sight of his pursuer, he dismounted, securing Cinder to a low, twisted branch. He pulled his rifle from the boot, double-checking the ammunition. Squatting down to his haunches behind a rotten and splintered tree trunk backed up to a steep and muddied washout, he swiped the sweat from his eyes, squinting in concentration as he waited. He rolled a long stem of grass between his teeth, every muscle tensed and ready.

At first he felt the vibration—then the actual sound of hooves pounding hard earth. Swiftly cocking, he brought the rifle to his shoulder and sighted it onto the grassy crest of the hill in front of him.

Chapter Twenty-Nine

Madison lost sight of him and brought her horse to a swift gallop. Without a thought as to where she might be going, her only concern was to catch up to Colt—at all costs. Barreling headlong over the sharp ridge of a dried-up watershed, all she saw was blue sky—then, as Cinnabar took her down the other side, a riderless gray stallion materialized before her eyes.

With the clumsy skill of an inexperienced rider, she jerked back on the reins. Dirt clods and dry grass were flung into the air, dust rising in a gritty cloud. The red mare, as startled as her rider, reared, her hooves pawing at the wind as she cut loose with a shrill whinny, her nostrils flaring. Madison screamed. Frantically, she clutched at the saddle, arching her body forward, holding on for dear life. As she held the reins taut, the flying hooves ultimately found solid ground, holding fast as the horse snorted loudly. Madison took a deep breath of relief and mentally thanked her lucky stars she was able to regain control.

Her long legs swung through the air as she slid down from the saddle with a thump. She yanked at her hat strings, flipping the hat aside, the mass of golden curls tumbling down her back. Her chest heaved with every breath, as her eyes flitted over the terrain, searching for him. The next thing she knew, she was staring down the dark barrel of a rifle, trained directly on her.

A gloved finger brushed the smooth steel of the trigger. Blinking, her eyes gradually focused on the face behind it.

"For crying out loud," he growled, shaking his head to clear his vision. Standing up, Colt lowered the rifle, slowly releasing the hammer before tossing it to the ground in a show of temper. He couldn't remember the last time he had been so angry.

It was unclear who was more confounded, as their eyes locked in an intense glare.

"I could have shot you!" he roared furiously, his eyes churning like boiling acid. He took one step forward.

At the moment that prospect didn't even bother her. No words would come, and all she could do was gaze at him rather meekly.

Colt shifted his weight, latching his thumbs into the waist of his pants. He looked worn, haggard, and was in need of a shave. Madison's first thought was that he was ill. Even so, he was the best thing she had ever seen. Cinnabar didn't hesitate to step in close to Cinder, their muzzles brushing in tender greeting.

Stiffly, Colt advanced, and she saw there were dark circles beneath his eyes. It seemed like a long time before he spoke.

"Damn," he said with a short laugh and a disbelieving shake of his head, "there for an evil second I thought I was being ambushed by Belle Starr." He took in her tousled hair, her smudged, ragamuffin face, the pistol and holster, and her dusty denims and boots. But commanding all of his attention were those enormous aqua eyes.

Madison smiled, a white flash against her brown face. And then it hit her and she couldn't stop it. Everything that had happened in the past week assailed her senses—relief, fear, happiness, sadness, and love. She began to sob—long, racking sobs originating deep within her soul. Tears streamed, creating rivers on her dusty cheeks. She wanted to touch him, but he wasn't close enough. She wanted to move toward him, but she couldn't seem to get her legs to function. They felt like awkward wooden stilts strapped to her swollen and sore body.

Before Madison knew what was happening, he was scooping her into his arms, crushing her to him with arms so powerful she thought her ribs would surely break. The tips of her boots were barely making contact with the ground. He buried his face in her hair, his eyes clamped tightly shut as he crooned softly into her ear.

Her arms automatically circled his neck, her fingers lacing through the thick hair at his nape; she held on tight, swearing never to let go. He pried her away just long enough to slide his deeply tanned hands around her neck. Supporting her head, he left a scorching path of kisses from her ear to her cheek, kissing away the tears, brushing the tip of her nose, her eyelids, her forehead, and across her cheek to the other ear.

She touched his grizzled cheek, gazing at him with the radiant glow of pure, untainted love.

"You . . . you look like hell . . ." She started to laugh in between sobs.

"Yeah? So do you, sugar—but you're still cute."

Colt grinned, his eyes crinkling at the corners, a single tear coursing down an unshaven cheek. She tenderly brushed it away.

"Why?"

His voice was raspy with emotion as he pressed his cheek next to hers. Madison wasn't sure how to answer—there was so much to tell. So much to confess, she wasn't even sure she could right now.

"Why did you come back?" he repeated.

"I couldn't . . . I couldn't stand it, Colt . . ."

He pulled back, chucking her chin with his forefinger so he could look down into those aqua eyes, the dark fringe of lashes clumped together with tears. He wasn't going to settle for that answer.

"Say it, Madison."

Her gaze probed to the depth of his soul for his meaning, even though it was right there on the surface—and she knew it.

"Trust yourself," he commanded. "Say it."

Her moist lips parted, hesitating. Amber lights flickered within his brown eyes, searching hers. He cupped her face gently.

"I love . . . you," came a breathless whisper, barely audible, "I really love you." She said it twice, her jaw quivering, reaffirming the truth she had instinctively known ever since she had first laid eyes on the old man in Jackson.

Exhaling his breath in a half-groan and a half-laugh, his mouth sought to capture hers in a fiery kiss. His tongue claimed hers with a tantalizing thoroughness, plunging them both into a passionate abyss. His arms slid possessively up her back, pulling her against his heart, pressing her trembling form hungrily against his own.

Reluctantly, he tore his lips away, brushing his mouth to her ear with a husky sigh.

"I love you, sugar. I love you, too, very much."

Madison squeezed her eyes shut, her heart threatening to burst with a joy that ran to the very core of her. It was total madness, loving this cowboy, this gunfighter, a century in the past. And yet, it was the most valid thing she had ever done in her life. Colt was so very right, all along. The voice that rose from deep inside told her so—to trust her instincts to that one everlasting love. . . . Guided by the all-powerful force that existed within, they would surely find a way.

He *loved* her. He said he *loved* her!

With a low, happy groan, she closed her eyes and smiled blissfully as she embraced him. The comforting rhythm of his thumping heart mingled with hers, his hard chest pressing against the softness of her breasts.

Colt thought of how he had walked around his entire life with everything in pieces, shards of jumbled disarray—then when Madison showed up those fragments of him had been pulled together miraculously as if by a giant magnet. She had come back to him—if he had ever doubted there was a God in heaven, he doubted no more.

Never before had he told a woman he loved her, meaning it the way he did now. In the past they were only convenient words—a means to satisfy what he thought to be some sort of basic female need. Not this time. This time those words satisfied a need within *him,* a need he never even knew existed until Madison.

Lost within each other, they stood for a very long time, holding on, rocking within each other's arms, knowing that every journey would forever lead one to the other.

Then Colt brought his fingers up through her hair, holding her head with his hands, grinning into her face, memorizing every detail.

"What?" She smiled up at him, kneading his muscular shoulders.

"Nothing. Just thinking," he murmured.

"About what?" she coyly asked.

"About how lucky I am, if you must know." He rested his lips against her forehead, placing small kisses there.

Madison giggled, "How lucky we both are. By the way, you're stabbing me. Plan on shaving soon?"

"I do now. Wouldn't want that beautiful face to get chafed . . . or any other part of you." He dropped a kiss on her lips, lingering, deepening until once again they were immersed in each other.

"You make me feel important, like I matter," she said when they parted.

"Sugar, you are all that matters," Colt murmured as he grazed his lips over her hair. "We may as well set up camp on the banks of the Platte tonight. Don't think we'd get any more travelin' in today even if we had a mind to. . . . Tomorrow we'll ride on into Laramie."

"South?" she exclaimed, shocked that he was still moving in the direction of Abilene.

"That's the way I'm going, sugar."

"Not still to Abilene . . . ?" She backed out of his arms, slanting him a sharp look.

"Still to Abilene, sugar." Colt knew full well he couldn't send her back alone. Therefore, she was going to have to go with him.

"Colt! I came back, for you! I won't let you go."

"I thought we went all through that." Colt sighed.

"We did. Before. And I didn't like the response I got then, either. When I decided to come back I swore to myself that I would stop you from going to Abilene!"

"Is that the only reason you came back, to ease your conscience? I thought you came back for me."

"I did!" she cried, her eyes widening.

"Well, let me tell you something!" His features turned to stone and he started to pace. "Abilene *is* me right now. Red Eagle is my vendetta, a murdering monster who destroyed half my family in one swipe. He's evil! He kills, tortures, and maims for the sheer pleasure of it. He's outsmarted the law for over ten years now—hell, he's outsmarted me more times than I care to admit. I'm tired of it, Madison. Sick and tired! I want it over with. I want that renegade rustler dead so I can get on with my life, raise a family—be a normal man! Abilene is my opportunity to make that happen!"

"Not if you're dead!" she challenged, turning away from him. "I thought you said I was all that mattered?" she added softly.

Colt's harsh expression softened and he stepped toward her, gently spinning her around to face him. "You are. Let me prove it to you by resolving the one force in my life that dominates my every move. With that done, and only then, I'll be free to worship you and treat you the way you deserve, the way I desire from the bottom of my heart." Colt gazed longingly into her eyes as he smoothed his thumb over the fine layer of dust on her cheek.

A smile curved his lips, "C'mon . . . let's get the horses settled, then you can have a bath."

The vision of stripping her filthy clothes off and sinking into the cool river for a bath was a little slice of heaven. She was too tired to argue and simply shrugged her shoulders when he slipped his arm about her, leading her away. Somehow she had to get him to change his mind! Originally, her thoughts had taken the form of aiding him in Abilene. Now, as reality intruded, she didn't have the foggiest idea what she could possibly do there! This life-style was so foreign to her . . . she couldn't even shoot a gun. How could she, a twentieth-century travel agent, of all people, save an experienced gunslinger from being murdered?

Chapter Thirty

There wasn't a spot on her body that didn't ache, or hadn't been rubbed raw, or wasn't bruised, and when she walked she suspected it was bowlegged. Madison waded into a tranquil cove of the Platte River, the mud squishing between her toes. It was so incredibly cold that it was a shock to her saddle-sore backside. The spreading limbs of mature elms sheltered her beneath leafy ceiling. It was dusk, and Colt remained at their campsite, not far from the riverbank.

Madison lowered herself into the gentle current of the tide, tilting her head back to douse her hair. A warm bath might have been more therapeutic, but she wasn't complaining, thrilled just to be ridding her body of the dust and grime. She only wished she had clean clothes to put on when she was done.

Colt strolled down to the river's edge to check on her, leaning against a tree with his arms folded over his chest, a roguish smile on his face. He was in a mischievous mood, threatening to steal her clothes and force her to return to camp as naked as a newborn babe. When Madison boldly replied that she had been entertaining that very idea anyway, he laughed heartily, leaving her to her own devices while he returned to warm their dinner.

Feeling rejuvenated, Madison stepped from the water to find one of Colt's clean shirts draped over a thicket. Smiling, she slipped it on, scooping her dirty things from a rock and heading back to camp.

Their encampment was set up amid the ruins of a stone cabin, long since destroyed by fire. Most of the roof was gone, but there were four standing walls and a monolithic river rock fireplace, already crackling with a pleasant blaze when she joined him. Colt's gaze skimmed over her with unconcealed approval, a sparkle in his eyes. She dumped her clothing into a pile, taking a seat on a log next to him as he stirred their dinner.

"What's for chow, cookie?" she asked eagerly.

"Beans," he replied, his attention irresistibly drawn to her bare legs. He lifted the tail of her shirt with his finger and she slapped his hand away distractedly.

"Beans . . . hmmmm, now that's different," she commented sarcastically.

"Here . . ." Colt passed her an opened tin.

"Why do you bring cans of tomatoes everywhere you go?"

"The juice is good, and it cuts the thirst much better than water. Have some; just watch the sharp edges."

Madison speared a small tomato, eating it and then drinking a little of the juice from the can. It was absolutely delicious, and she couldn't get enough.

"Go ahead," Colt said with a laugh, "eat the whole can; there's more.

"So, do you know how to use that thing?" He inclined his head in the direction of the holster she had been wearing.

"No," Madison fessed up, "but I suppose I would have learned real fast if the need arose."

"We'll have to take care of that." Colt gave her a wink and nodded his assurance. "You never told me who helped you find me. I was aware of two riders behind me for quite a spell."

"Really?" she asked with surprise. "Rosannah sent Zak with me. I was bent on finding you, but now I doubt I would have if it weren't for him."

Colt smiled, "Yeah, Zak's a good kid—good tracker, too."

He handed her a plateful of beans and she scarfed it up like there was no tomorrow. He ate his dinner directly from the pan.

"So what's the deal with Lucy living with you at the ranch? That crazy woman accosted me as I rode in."

Colt's brows drew together, his face turning momentarily black as he regarded her.

"That bitch dared to lay a hand on you?" he asked angrily, not waiting for her answer. "I ought to skin her alive! That ol' bat isn't living with me. Garrett brought her sorry ass home with him a few nights back. I swear, I don't know what's gotten into him. I told him to get rid of her." Then he chuckled, lightening up a little, "So, there was a cat fight and I missed it, huh?"

"Yes! She dug those daggers of hers into my leg and tried to pull me from my horse! She's got a thing for you, and I'm her primary competition."

"Not much of a contest. I trust you put her in her place?"

"Right directly into a mud puddle." Madison looked at him seriously, then broke into a big smile.

"That's my girl," Colt said, circling her with his arm and hugging her close. He pictured Madison hurling that little runt into the mud, and he burst into deep, full-blown laughter, Madison quickly following suit. "Don't worry, she'll not bother you anymore; I'll see to that."

"I have something I'd like for you to look at."

"What's that?" Colt tossed the empty pot aside.

Madison snatched up her bag and retrieved the well-read paperback history of Jackson Hole. She flipped it open to the correct page and handed it to him. It was a long shot, Madison had to admit, but if Colt read for himself the legend of his own death, maybe he'd have second thoughts of continuing on to Abilene.

He barely glanced at the circled paragraph before handing the book back to her. "I'm not a superstitious man, Madison, but I think it's best if I take your word for it this time." Even as he said it, a twinge of fear pricked him, warning him of the dangers of knowing too much. "You may not understand how, but this helps me immensely. I will be cautious, of that you can be sure. The only problem is," he sighed thoughtfully, "I'm not sure what to do about you. I certainly don't want you caught up in this. Then again, I don't plan on letting you out of my sight, either. Last time all I did was fall asleep and you were gone." He cast her an admonishing glance.

Madison watched him intently, her posture increasingly rigid, her arms folded across her chest. Just her luck. He wouldn't read it and seemed more determined than ever.

"Oooohhh! You beat all, do you know that?" she retorted with growing animosity. "What is it about men? You never know when to quit!"

He was only a breath away, looking at her mouth, moving ever closer, and she bounded to her feet in one lithe movement, crossing to the far side of the room. "Oh, no you don't, Romeo—you're not changing the subject by kissing me into submission. I want some questions answered! How can you risk your life after I've traveled so far to be with you? And what if I refuse to go along?" She emphasized her meaning with a light stomp to the powdery dirt floor.

"Madison . . ."

He stood up and walked toward her. She backed up a few steps.

"Don't Madison me—*Colton Chase!*—master gunfighter, cattle baron, ladies' man, challenger of fate—oh!—would you like the title of God, also?"

Her hands were balled into fists and her eyes shot fiery sparks. He had to hand it to her, she was one willful little lady when she chose to be. Though her words were meant to sting, he only heard the lilt of her voice, enjoying the pure music of it. She had come back to him and he felt like he could take on the world if he needed to.

He thought he'd lighten her mood with a little humor. "You followed me this far. I hardly think that you'd give up now. And thank you for noticing my godly qualities." He smiled lopsidedly.

She wasn't laughing . . . but she was still walking backwards. Then her foot caught on the thin, springy trunk of a sapling, sending her tumbling back, her arms flailing. Colt jumped to grab her arm but missed, and she landed on her behind with a thump. Now she was really mad.

Colt stood over her, extending his hand to help her up, "Are you hurt? You fall very gracefully," he remarked, unable to keep the grin off of his face.

"Oh, shut up." Madison pushed herself up without his assistance, her face flaming. "Why in the world is there a tree growing in the middle of a goddammed house anyway."

She was brushing the dirt from her legs when Colt took control of her hands and braced them against the rock wall, imprisoning her with his sturdy frame.

His mouth took hers in a hard kiss. He wasn't going to take no for an answer. He wasn't going to listen to *any* answer—the intention was not to let her speak at all. Madison writhed against him and he ground his pelvis to hers in response.

"Let me go," she managed a breathy gasp, struggling.

"No," he stated emphatically into her mouth, his tongue flicking to taste her lips. "I can't do that. I'm tired of your bitching—it doesn't become you."

His eyes were half-lidded, indolent, his chest undulating rhythmically, pressing into her. Roughly, his mouth lowered and he began to nibble along her jaw, moving across her neck, kissing the sensitive flesh until she moaned, tilting her head back.

Madison whimpered, wild tingles rushing through her like fire and ice. She moved under him sensuously, and his grip loosened for just a split second. She jerked free of the manacle-grasp on her wrists, coiling her arms around his neck, her legs wrapping around him, climbing up his. They strained against one another fiercely.

Colt seized another devouring kiss before lowering to bury his face between her breasts, nudging aside the baggy shirt. Then, with a fascinating slowness, he drew a lazy trail of wetness upwards with his tongue, past the pulse at the base of her throat.

He stopped abruptly, gazing down at her for the longest time. Her lips were parted, expectant. And then she got a lecture.

"We're getting married tomorrow, whether you like it or not. I'm going to Abilene, whether you like it or not. You're going *with* me, whether you like it or not. And you'll stay with a friend of mine there—*like it or not*," Colt paused, still breathing heavy. "Any questions?"

His voice was low and even, commanding. Madison bristled. She focused on his mouth, not more than an inch from hers. The feel of him was so hard to ignore. Then she realized, almost all he said were things she wanted.

"You're damn right we're getting married!" she said between gasps. "And I don't want you to go to Abilene, but if you insist, you can bet I'm going, too. They may need my help arranging your damned funeral—I bet it was a real blowout."

Their eyes locked.

Neither insinuated the slightest hint of a smile.

Like an unspent storm, their lips were all over each other again, clashing, slanting. Colt swung her up into his arms to carry her back to the fireplace. He lay her down on the bedrolls, positioning himself over her. His thigh pressed between hers, his hand gliding up and down, from an imperious grip of her hair to the soft caress and squeeze of her curvaceous, naked buttock. They simmered, squirming against one another, until Colt stopped.

He gazed down at her with the most impish expression, grinning complacently. "What's wrong . . . ?" she moaned deliriously, sliding her fingers through his hair to bring him to her, straining upward to meet his lips. He pulled back just as they touched.

"Rendezvous adjourned . . . until tomorrow," he announced, his voice raspy with unrelenting ardor. Obviously pleased with his self-discipline, he rolled away and got to his feet. Madison had ripped at the buttons of his shirt, and he pulled it off. "I think a cold dip in the river might be in order right about now." He grabbed the dirty dishes.

"What . . . are you doing?" Madison cried, lunging to her knees, her hair a disheveled mess. How could he do this? How could he *not* do this?

"I'd like nothing more than to ravish you, sugar, but let's wait until we're married."

"Since when did you become so virtuous?"

She looked so innocent, her eyes big, wide pools of aqua. "I'm not. Just in the mood for a little fun."

"*This* is fun?" she asked in disbelief. "You're driving me crazy, Colt . . ." She was whining again.

"I know," he grinned crookedly, raising his eyebrows. "Just think how crazy I'm going to make you tomorrow. That thought should sustain you. Maybe then you'll hang around through the night, and I won't wake up cold and lonely." With a devilish wink, he passed through the doorless opening.

"You're impossible, do you know that?" she called after him.

They were really getting married! Happily, she fell back to the bedroll, chewing her lip. The cogs of her mind began to spin double-time, and she decided it would be *him* begging *her* before the night was over.

Chapter Thirty-One

When Colt returned from his bath in the river Madison was waiting. The covers of the bedroll barely concealed her cleavage. Her hair was fluffed in a wild mane and her leg was outside the blanket, an indisputable invitation.

A cocksure expression playing over his face, he poked at the fire a bit before joining her—stark raving naked. She thought she might die of pleasure at the enticing warmth of his skin when he slid in next to her, radiating, saturating her very being with a reeling, urgent desire.

But Colt wouldn't honor her invitation. He simply refused to succumb to her insistent caresses, her soft, tickling lips, her tempestuous pelvic thrusts against his leg or anything else she came in contact with. Finally, he found it necessary to restrain her hands, distracting her with dizzying kisses and words of love whispered in her ear.

She was drawn out of a loving mood, just a little, when he initiated some trivial pillow talk. She almost left the bedroll in a huff when he asked her about Jon, insisting she tell him all that had happened when she had returned to her own time. He even told her it was high time he knew why they were divorced. To pacify him, Madison reluctantly related every sordid detail, and Colt managed to thaw her building ire with yet another steamy kiss, tumbling her onto her back in a rapturous embrace.

He was thrilled to the core to learn that Madison felt absolutely nothing for Jon any longer, and that her love for him was truly indesputable. At the same time, he grew to hate this ex-husband of hers, even more so than he had all along. How could anyone treat a woman like Madison the way that man had?

As Colt lay next to Madison's luscious, satiny-smooth body, he had a hard time keeping his resolution not to make love to her. It was probably the most tortuous test of willpower he had ever encountered. There were times when he thought he just might explode with the tension, thinking to hell with it all and taking her in a gushing tidal wave of lust. But he wanted their wedding night to be as special as she was. And he was going to do everything in his power to make sure it was. He didn't think Madison even knew when he left their bed to take a few more dips in the cool river water during the night.

At dawn the next morning they broke camp, heading south once again through the Medicine Bow mountains. It was a warm, sunny day, with only a few cottonball clouds floating past low peaks.

They stopped outside Laramie to water the horses, and as he had promised, Colt gave her a few lessons in the art of handling a six-shooter.

It was questionable how much she actually learned. When his arms were around her shoulders from behind to guide her in the correct procedure and position all she could think about was his masculine scent, his velvet voice, his thighs in tight denims molding to his buttocks. Apparently, he was having the same problem. He usually ended the overly short lessons with hot-blooded kisses along her neck and ears, until she was giggling for him to stop. When he spoke it was distractedly.

Colt instructed her on how to load the ammunition and insisted she practice with a few more shots while he watched. By the time she was done, she was choking from the sulfuric gray smoke, her ears were ringing, and she couldn't hear a word he said.

They munched on the last of the hardened pan biscuits, salt pork, and canned tomatoes before readying themselves to head on out. Their eyes sparkling, Madison and Colt wasted no time in mounting their horses and continuing southward. They had a very important date in Laramie that evening.

* * *

It was a sweltering four o'clock by the time they hit town. Despite her protests, Colt insisted Madison wear the suede coat, though it made her feel like Calamity Jane in comparison to the feminine figures milling along the boardwalks.

Laramie was much more of a cosmopolitan city than she had expected. It was uniquely sophisticated, while still rough around the edges. Some women sported the latest European styles, their hats adorned with ribbons and flowers perched atop their elaborate coiffures, their skirts swirling sumptuously around their legs as they walked. At least half of the men wore black frock coats, string ties, and derby hats. Obviously, eastern styles had invaded the wilds of Wyoming.

As Madison and Colt filtered through the congested traffic of pedestrians, horses and riders, carriages, wagons, and business conveyances along the wide and dusty main street, she rather enjoyed the curious stares. Female eyes were invariably drawn to Colt, and then to her, with a marked change of curious expression. Unable to resist, Madison removed her dreadful hat, tossing her shock of golden hair free. Colt frowned, then shook his head with a slow smile, while his warm gaze caressed her.

They passed freshly painted false storefronts, several eateries, at least three banks, a post office, and modern hotels—in comparison with what she had seen in South Pass City, that is. Finally, Colt stopped before an immaculate little whitewashed store, the words MADEMOISELLE PICARD'S DRESS SHOP stenciled in huge gold letters on the front window. Colt dismounted and walked around, helping her down and tethering their horses. He opened the pine, glass-paned door and motioned for her to precede him inside.

Madison couldn't prevent a ecstatic smile and a slight blush when Colt requested a suitable gown for their wedding that evening. Mademoiselle Picard, a petite brunette with vivacious eyes, clapped her delicate hands together in delight, congratulating them both.

She instructed Colt to have a seat in the front parlor while she ushered Madison off to the side. A subtly elegant ivory satin gown, screened with a simple, open-weave darker ivory lace was brought out for her inspection. It was a slim-fitting, non-cumbersome gown that could be packed to travel easily. When Colt saw it he gave a signal of approval.

The gown fit Madison perfectly, not requiring a single alteration. Mademoiselle Picard outfitted her with all of the necessary accessories, including a pair of matching kidskin high-heeled ankle boots with dainty pearl buttons. Madison politely refused the boned corset, though it was a lovely, beribboned undergarment.

Next, Colt requested Madison be fitted with a few more day dresses. Happily, Mademoiselle brought out a rose calico detailed with a simple white eyelet lace and another printed muslin with tiny teal flowers that matched her eyes perfectly.

Bundling their purchases with care, the kindly lady sent them on their way with an abundance of *merci beaucoups*. "*C'est l'amour . . .*" she sighed to herself as they left, a sentimental smile gracing her winsome face.

The couple's next stop was at the prestigious Regency Hotel to obtain a room for the evening. Madison was greatly impressed by the European decor of the lobby. Rich, darkly stained ridged wood pillars supported high ceilings ornamented with crystal chandeliers, the floors covered with plush carpet.

She had no words, though, when they were shown to their suite. The walls were cozily wallpapered in a rich forest green flowered print. There was a red brick fireplace and shiny pine floors, with a wine-colored oriental area rug. An overstuffed wine damask Victorian sidechair stood next to the mahogany dressing table. The ornately spindled brass bed took up most of the room and was romantically decorated in a fluffy white lace comforter. Heavy, multicolored tapestry curtains were tethered back from the French doors with bulky, dark green cords, fringed at the ends.

Madison left her packages on the bed and stepped to the double doors, parting the white sheers to inspect the balcony. Then she spun back around.

"Oh, Colt! It's absolutely gorgeous!" She held her arms out as if to encompass its beauty, "This is my fantasy, do you know that? These lovely clothes, this room! I've always dreamt of actually experiencing this era in style, and now I'm really doing it!"

Colt smiled with satisfaction, thoroughly enjoying her elation.

Madison dashed from one side of the room to the other, running her fingers over the smooth polished wood, touching the rich fabrics—until she passed an elegant oval mirror that hung above the dressing table.

She stopped dead in her tracks. Her jaw fell slack at the dirty, tangled mess on her head that looked more like a rat's nest than hair. It hung in lifeless, dull gold spirals past her shoulders. Her face, though attractively suntanned from the long hours on the prairie, was shiny with sweat and smudged with dirt. Her spirits sank. Some bride-to-be!

"What's wrong?"

Colt stood behind her, running his hands along her arms, squeezing. He looked as roguish as ever, peering over her shoulder, unshaven, his face just as dirt-smeared as her own. She could well imagine that face belonging to a swashbuckling pirate with a hook for a hand, a sinister patch over one eye, and nothing but vile, debauched thoughts on his mind. . . . It made a chill run down her spine and she smiled.

"Will you please let me in on this private joke you seem to be enjoying so much?"

"Certainly." She swiveled within the circle of his arms, cupping his face, his beard stabbing at her palms. "You're looking as filthy and disgusting as I feel, and I think I'm starting to like it!" She laughed until there were tears in her eyes.

Colt rolled his eyes in puzzlement. "I think you spent a little too much time in the sun, sugar."

With a kiss dropped on her lips and a pat on her butt, he pressed his hat on and walked to the door. "I'll be delivering the horses to the livery now, then I'm off to the bathhouse for a bath and a shave. I'll let the front desk know to bring up your tub. Was there anything else you needed?"

"Uhmmmm . . ." She gazed absently toward the ceiling. "Let me see . . . just you, I think."

"You'll have me, no doubt."

He hesitated, his gaze bare, raw, and very sexual. With that, he was out the door, and Madison was left alone in the rich luxury of their honeymoon suite.

Chapter Thirty-Two

Almost an hour later, Madison stood in front of that very same oval mirror, frantically fingering still-damp, heavy waves of hair in an effort to hurry the drying process. She bent over, shaking the bulk of it down in front of her, brushing fiercely.

There was a soft rap on the door and she heard Colt's voice.

"Are you ready? Can I come in?"

Madison called him in, whipping her hair back.

The first thing he laid eyes on as he walked through the door was a stunning, gold- and honey-haired vixen, exquisitely clad in shimmering ivory satin, her complexion rosy, touched by the sun. The silken hair was full and fluffed out like a gossamer cloud. Colt had never seen anything so provocative in his entire life. He blinked, awestruck.

"My very own Jezebel," he growled with a suggestive smile, advancing, "you look magnificent." The door was kicked shut. His eyes bore a scintillating sparkle. "Do you know that I would marry you tonight even if I had never seen you before in my life?"

His arm slid around her waist, snatching her to him in an unspoken demand. Madison twirled out of his gentle grasp. "Now, now, don't start something you can't finish," she chastised breathlessly.

"What makes you think I can't finish, sugar?" he teased, stalking her again, one arm remaining suspiciously behind his back.

Colt looked positively incredible himself, and she was having a hard time not staring at his freshly shaven face, a few sun-lightened strands of chestnut hair wisping over his forehead. The crisp white of the chambray linen shirt brought out the tawniness of his skin, and his lopsided white smile lit up his entire face. He wore fresh indigo denims and a butter-soft tan vest over his ever-present holster. He smelled absolutely wonderful, and she was irresistibly drawn to him, like a magnet. Giving in, she let herself be caught, rubbing her hands up the steel hardness of his chest and resting on his shoulders. His muscles hardened reflexively beneath her touch.

"I'm sorry I didn't dress for the occasion. Somehow I just couldn't picture myself in a black suit jacket with a black tie."

Madison smiled sincerely. "I'm glad. I like you just the way you are right now. You're very, very handsome, you know."

"So are you . . ." His lips grazed hers invitingly, plucking sexy kisses.

"You do realize that you're not supposed to see me before the ceremony—it's bad luck, you know."

"Did Jon see you before the ceremony?" he questioned, quite serious.

"Uhh, no . . . What does that have to do with anything?"

"And how did that union turn out? There. I rest my case."

Madison gave him a tight hug, then forced herself to continue with her toilette, almost forgetting what she needed to do, because of his intoxicating nearness. "Behave yourself, now. I still have to fix my hair."

"Your hair looks gorgeous as it is."

Colt pushed in front of her again, whipping his hand from behind his back, presenting her with a lovely bouquet of lilacs, black-eyed Susans, cornflowers, daisies, blood-red roses, buttercups, and even a few purple snapdragons. Baby's breath had been creatively interspersed throughout, all tied up neatly within a silky pink ribbon.

Madison was pleasantly shocked as she took the fragrant bunch from his hand. "Colt, thank you! They're beautiful! Where in the world did you get all these?"

He wiggled his finger for her to follow him to the window, a mischievous expression on his face. He pointed to a fenced yard two streets over that could barely be seen through the rows of buildings. It was a homey little whitewashed number with a multitude of flowers bordering its diminutive yard.

"Are you saying you picked these from *that* yard? Shame on you, Colt Chase!"

"Hey, they'll never miss 'em. It looks like a funeral home over there. Those flowers are in much happier hands with you, sugar."

"Speaking of flowers," she said softly, her playful mood suddenly turning thoughtful, "there's something I want to show you."

"What's that?"

Colt followed her to the dressing table, watching as she dug through her leather shoulderbag and removed a package wrapped in thin paper. She set it down, folding the gauzy blue paper away to expose the four perfectly formed, mauve- and ivory-marbled rosebuds. They appeared to be freshly picked—pliant, moist, and firm.

Colt's eyes lifted to hers in hesitant comprehension.

"Back in the twentieth century I went to open my purse, and Colt, it was horrible! There were three buds, then, and all of them were *black!* I touched one and one of its petals crumbled to dust! Just a while ago I ran across them again, and something compelled me to open up the tissue . . . and see! They're fresh again! These roses are everlasting—eternal! *And they can only survive if we are together!*"

Colt's attention was distracted from the immortal buds. He took her face in his hands, his thumbs caressing her silky smooth cheeks as he gazed down into her eyes. "But we've known that all along, haven't we, sugar?" he breathed with emotional conviction.

Then he kissed her; not a kiss of passion, but one of pure, unconditional, unadulterated love, a kiss that told her he would cherish her until the end of time.

"Now, get ready. I want to marry you." His voice was low, as smooth as velvet.

Without replying, Madison brushed away a tear and moved as fast as she could in the form-fitting dress toward the mirror to arrange her hair.

Finished, she stood before him for a final inspection. Colt pulled a sprig of the baby's breath from the bouquet and placed it attractively within the loose curls, piled high, shining like a crown of golden light. A delicate ruffle accentuated her slim neck, and gathered sleeves puffed out from her shoulders, narrowing at the wrist with sheer, scalloped lace.

"You look . . . fantastic," he said softly, his eyes glimmering with pride.

Colt took her hand in his and led her downstairs, where a shiny black coach with gold-painted trim awaited them. He had made arrangements with the livery stable, and the coach came fully equipped with its own driver, at their disposal for the entire evening.

"This is for us?" Madison asked, feeling giddy and lightheaded as the driver opened the door and Colt lifted her inside. "Where in the world did you find the time to hire a carriage, take a bath, and pick flowers, too?"

He slid across the cushiony, button-tufted leather seat beside her, and the driver slammed the door shut. "I have you to inspire me. I can do anything."

Colt squeezed her hand and she snuggled in as close as she could possibly get to him.

Suddenly, the miniature window at the front slid open with a grating slap. A dirty face thrust into it, wrinkling to reveal the absence of two front teeth. "Where to?" the driver asked.

"We're getting married. Take us to the classiest preacher in town," Colt answered, and the sliding window was slammed shut.

Colt glanced at Madison, the corners of his mouth curving into a helpless smile. "He was the only driver available. . . ." he explained with a shrug.

"As long as he gets us there," she responded.

"I almost completely forgot—you must be starving. Should we go eat first?"

"You're right, I'm starved. But I'm too nervous to eat. Let's wait until afterwards."

She cuddled under his arm. The ride in this large carriage was noticeably smoother than that of the buggy she had ridden in before, its springs more sophisticated, creating a lofty bounce instead of hard jolts.

Madison watched contentedly through the carriage window as horses and buggies traveled helter-skelter through the dusty streets, dodging the seemingly unconcerned pedestrians as they meandered. She wondered how many people were actually hit by passing buggies and horses, and if there were ever buggy wrecks?

While musing, she caught a glimpse of a fleeting shape scurrying up the boardwalk, hovering, weaving through the throng of people and disappearing into a saloon. He was oddly familiar, though she couldn't quite place him. She raised abruptly to lean toward the window for a better look, but the squat man was gone.

"What's wrong?" Colt asked.

"Nothing . . . I just thought I saw somebody I knew. But how could that be?" she said with a laugh, "unless it was someone from the ranch."

"I doubt that," he commented.

Just then the carriage lurched to a sudden stop, nearly throwing them both to the floor.

"Good driver," Colt muttered under his breath.

"We've arrived, mistuh!" The toothless man once again slid open the window, yelling through, as if the careening stop hadn't indicated that fact already.

Colt disembarked, lifting Madison out behind him. They stood outside a white picket fence that surrounded an immaculate pale green cottage with dark green shutters.

"Wait here for us," Colt instructed the driver, then led Madison up the front walk to the little porch. They walked beneath the branches of the huge weeping willow that sheltered the tiny front yard, giving the entire scene a fairy-tale effect.

Colt lifted a heavy brass knocker, clapping it several times. They stood, side by side, as rigid as a pair of boards, waiting silently for the door to open.

The dark green door creaked open hesitantly. A slight, balding man peeked around the corner. He regarded them suspiciously over the round wire rims of his spectacles.

"Hello. I'm Colton Chase and this is Madison Calloway. We wish to be married, sir. Would you be so kind as to do us the honor?"

The stooped man opened the door a bit wider, coughing, clearing his throat loudly. "Uggghhmmm . . . Reverend Pittman is the name. You . . . you two says you want to get married, do ya?" He adjusted his spectacles repeatedly, apparently trying to decide if he could see better over the lenses or through them.

"Yes, Reverend, we do."

"Well, uhmm, tomorrow, or Friday, both are good days for me." His watery eyes focused on the double rig only partially concealed beneath Colt's vest. Nervously, his gaze shifted to Colt's face, then back to the holster.

Colt picked up on the little man's reaction instantly. "I'm a lawman on my way to Kansas, and I'm leaving tomorrow. Sure would appreciate your marrying us before I have to leave. As soon as possible."

Madison stole a quick glance at Colt, a crooked frown on her face as she twitched her hands anxiously beneath the bouquet of flowers.

"Oh, oh, I understand." He spoke quickly, his attitude changing. "By all means, please come inside. Do you have a witness, or shall I call my wife?"

"No . . . if your wife doesn't mind, we sure do thank you for your kindness."

"Think nothing of it. Glad to be of service." He waved the concern off with a curl of his lip. "Where do you folks hail from? You a sheriff in Kansas?"

Reverend Pittman led them deep inside the stuffy, cramped house, every available space filled with an overly ornate piece of furniture or a scattering of knickknacks. He stopped at a small office at the rear of the house. A kerosene lamp burned dimly on the cluttered desk. It was the only source of light except for the dusky light that emitted from the draped window.

"Not exactly. I own the Triple Bar C, near Jackson Hole. I'm on my way to temporary employment under the Marshal of Ford County, Kansas."

The reverend shuffled into the hallway, yelling loudly for his wife. She screamed something unintelligible back and he returned, informing them that she would be down presently. "We need some pertinent information on these blank lines here." He slid a form across the desk.

Colt dipped the pen in an inkwell and began to fill in the blanks. Madison watched over his shoulder; it was the first time she had seen him write. His handwriting was slanted and very elegant. Colton glanced up at her, a question in his eyes. Madison bent down close to read what the paper said. He was stuck on her middle name, her birthdate, her birthplace, her mother and father's names . . .

Reverend Pittman was uncomfortably close, looking down on them with interest from the other side of the desk, his eyes traveling from one to the other. Madison smiled up at him, chewing her lip nervously.

"Elise . . ." She pointed to the space for her middle name. Lifting a gracious smile to the reverend, she proceeded to give Colt all the other information, making sure to fabricate an appropriate birth year. Shrugging casually, she explained, "We haven't known each other all that long."

The reverend nodded his understanding. Colt signed his name with sweeping strokes, passing the pen to Madison. Her hand shook as she dipped it into the well, metal clicking against thick glass. She signed her name, two puddles of ink settling over the letters.

"Oh dear," she apologized, "it looks as if I've messed it up."

"That's quite all right, Miss Calloway. It's still quite legible." Reverend Pittman pulled the paper away hastily, setting it aside. He stepped out from behind the immense desk, his stooped body almost dwarfed by it. "Are we ready?"

"Yes." Colt and Madison responded at the same time, exchanging glances, grinning elatedly.

"Do you realize you're marrying an 'older' woman?" she whispered stiffly out of the corner of her mouth. Reverend Pittman had once again stuck his head out in the hall to yell for his wife.

"I sure do," Colt whispered back. "It's exciting. Does it bother you?"

"No, not if you think it's exciting."

"Very . . ." He reached for her hand, clasping it warmly within his own.

Finally, the reverend reentered with his wife in tow, a round woman almost as fat as he was thin. "This is my wife, Margaret."

Colt and Madison both nodded in greeting.

"Let us begin. . . ."

The reverend began the ceremony as the bride and groom turned to face on another, their hands interlocked. He spoke the verses, droning on monotonously. Margaret stood to the side, busily chewing on a stubby fingernail.

Madison barely heard what the little man said, feeling numb and tingly at the same time. She was lost within a rich, golden brown fire—a fire that returned the warmth to her twofold, suffusing her within its glow.

Only aware of one another, they could have been surrounded by an army of raging munchkins and they wouldn't have cared. When it came time Madison heard herself say, "I do," surprised at the sound of her own voice. Then Colt's mouth moved, the low velvet, "I do" causing her heart to swell until she thought it might burst.

"I now pronounce you man and wife." The well-worn Bible slammed shut with a resounding whack! "You may kiss the bride."

The last words came far too late, Colt already having taken

Madison into his arms, capturing her parted lips in a mind-boggling kiss. It lasted perhaps a little too long for the reverend's comfort; he cleared his throat loudly.

When they parted Colt shook the reverend's hand, thanking him and his wife heartily. Margaret disappeared from the room, and Reverend Pittman insisted on making a tintype of the magic moment, explaining that they would be able to pick it up on a trip back through Laramie at any time.

Colt and Madison obediently stood before an awkward, spraddling tripod that was unveiled on the far side of the room. A brown and black square contraption was bolted to the top, a huge, thick fisheye lens at the front. The reverend dipped his head beneath a black cloth, and with a blinding *poof!* of light, it was over.

Before they knew it they were outside in the fresh air, climbing into the black-and-gold coach, as the driver snored loudly from his post on the upper deck. Colt rapped loudly at the little sliding window, and the driver sat up straight with a strangled snort. His dirty face soon appeared in the frame of the window.

"Sorry, mistuh," he mumbled tiredly, scrambling for the reins.

"That's quite all right. Just take us for the best steak in town."

The carriage pitched forward, careening in a wide U-turn as the driver began the erratic journey back up the main thoroughfare.

Madison was still in seventh heaven, toying with the object on the fourth finger of her left hand. Suddenly, she held up her hand, bewildered by the presence of a wedding ring. Now she remembered! It had all been so perfect when Colt slipped it onto her finger, and she wondered how he had come up with a ring at such short notice. Would he ever cease to amaze her? Through the coach window, the full moon caught the sparkle of a brilliant diamond, surrounded by a cluster of smaller ones, set in a rich yellow gold. Utterly enchanted, she looked up at him.

"Where in the world . . . no, *when* did you have time to get this? Colt, it's gorgeous."

He held her in a strangely intense gaze before he spoke. "It was my mother's." His brows narrowed in bewilderment. "I'm not even sure why I brought it with me. I suppose I took comfort in having it with me ever since I returned from your time, and I carried it, much like a good-luck charm." He looked at her with a pained expression, as if searching for a shred of understanding.

Madison put a hand over his. "I'll treasure it always; you know that. It was fate that brought us together, Colt. I really believe that." She lovingly caressed the firm softness of his freshly shaven cheek, then moved closer to brush his lips lightly with her own.

Something akin to an electric current traveled between them, and his arms slid around her satin and lace waist, his hands stroking the small of her back in small circles. He lifted her across his lap easily, savoring her mouth with searing kisses. Madison leaned into him, abandoning herself to the incredible fever beginning at the pit of her stomach, pervading her with its spell.

The carriage veered again sharply, rolling to an abrupt halt. Colt, prepared this time, held them both on the safety of the seat, his leg braced against the opposite side.

He sucked her lower lip into his mouth, biting gently. "We're here," he whispered.

Chapter Thirty-Three

Only being a block from the Regency Hotel, Colt sent the driver on his way with a generous tip. The happy, toothless driver slapped the reins zealously and the elegant black coach faded away into the night, pitching this way and that.

A luscious aroma of homecooking assaulted their trail-worn senses when they entered the restaurant. It was dimly lit, with thick, dripping candles. Shiny pine tables were covered with red-checkered tablecloths, reminding Madison of a cozy Italian restaurant.

They sat far away from the other diners at a tiny round table in the very rear corner. Ravenously, they gorged on the warm, crusty bread the waiter promptly set before them.

Savory steaks, soupy beans, cornbread, carrots, potatoes, boiled cabbage, and one and a half bottles of wine later, Colt and Madison sat totally engrossed in one another. They conversed animatedly and, after a generous slice of warm apple pie, Madison leaned back in her chair, patting her belly. She was woozy from all the wine and the food—and deliriously happy.

Outside the restaurant, Madison had to concentrate on every step, holding on to Colt out of need as well as want. Buoyant, they strolled up the boardwalk toward the hotel. Her world swirled around her. Though heady with wine and exhausted from traveling, sleep was really the last thing on her mind.

"You wouldn't be feeling that wine, now would you, sugar?" Colt laughed when she tripped clumsily over an uneven board.

"Whatever gave you *that* idea?" She giggled, running one hand caressingly over the expanse of his chest, the other boldly clutching his tight backside.

"Hey, you'd better watch out, young lady. You're going to start a riot behaving like that here," he teased, his eyes sparkling down at her. "I just may have to turn you over my knee."

"Ooohhh, now *that* sounds very interesting."

"I'm definitely going to have to remember to serve you wine more often."

The lobby of the hotel was deserted when Colt ushered his dizzy wife through the double front doors. And it was a lucky thing. They made enough noise to rival a tribe of rowdy Indians on the warpath. Colt scooped her into his arms halfway up the curved staircase, much to her amused delight as she turned into him, tugging away at his collar, nuzzling the scented skin of his neck with kisses. Impetuously, she flung her colorful bouquet over the banister, the flowers raining down to carpet the lobby in a medley of scented blooms.

Once inside their suite, Colt kicked shut the door and promptly locked it. He deposited her wiggling form gently onto the bed, only to have her bounce back up to pull the pins from her hair, shaking it loose with a wild toss of her head. She looked very much the wanton temptress in angel's clothing. His temptress, he thought, his eyes roaming over her appreciatively.

Colt was lighting the kerosene lamp, or trying to, as Madison's lips commanded his, stealing kisses, her hands everywhere at once. The room bathed in an intimate golden glow, he finally gave all his attention to his new wife. His expression turning serious, Colt held her close.

Their bodies swayed to the faint beat of a plunking piano, drifting through the partially open window from a saloon. He began the arduous but enjoyable task of unbuttoning the tiny pearl buttons along the back of her gown while the flame in his eyes burned, melding with her own.

Suddenly shy, Madison fumbled with the buttons of his shirt. He removed his vest and gunbelt. His strong hands then moved brazenly over her hips before he peeled the gown from her shoulders, instantly replacing the satin with his warm lips, trailing across to her neck.

The gown dropped to the floor. She sighed, tilting her head back sensuously, inviting more of his fiery kisses. A firm tug and her undergarment was gone, tossed aside, releasing her breasts.

Insatiable lust unleashed a delicious abandon within her that was entirely new. He helped her pull his shirt open, his chest bronzed by the soft touch of lamplight.

Gone for too long, his mouth found hers again in crushing urgency, and he seized her quivering body to his, the soft flesh of her full breasts tingling against the scorching heat of his skin. He captured a taut nipple within moist, velvet heat, suckling it until a raspy moan tore from her throat, pleading.

Madison's heart raced wildly. She relished the rigid muscles of his stomach and waist, her hands resting on the denim waistband before moving to pluck the buttons free.

She stroked his firm buttocks lightly—then took a step back toward the bed. Heavy-lidded aqua pools beckoned him to follow. Coquettishly, she tugged his finger.

"C'mere, cowboy . . ."

With provocative languor, she tumbled back onto the feather mattress. Colt stood over her, his chest heaving with mounting excitement. Seductively, one at a time, she lifted a delicate boot, caressing his lean thighs with her toe, hesitating suggestively at his groin.

His eyes never leaving hers, he accommodated her titillating request with verve. Unbuttoning her ivory boots just enough to slip them from her feet, he let them drop to the floor, placing a kiss on each silken arch. An alluring shimmy of her slender hips and the pantalettes were dangling from the tip of her delicately pointed toe. She tossed them into the air to land across the room.

Madison lie before his unabashed, ravishing appraisal, clad in nothing but silky ivory stockings gartered at mid-thigh. Her gold hair framed her face, glazed with passion, flowing in a riotous silken halo. This was Madison, his wife. Tempting, bewitching, responsive, warm. His soul was on fire. His blood hammered through his veins.

His boots impatiently thudded to the floor. Amber lights flashed in his eyes, smoldering, and he couldn't shed his denims fast enough. Madison's eyes lowered unashamedly, melting over every masculine line, the hard plane of his belly, the huge tumescence of his manhood. Her breath caught in her throat.

"Oh, sugar," he exhaled raggedly, lowering himself onto her, his hips grinding against her hotly, the movements more than intriguing. His mouth came down on hers, twisting, devouring. Their tongues teased, thrusting with primitive strokes.

Colt explored her body heatedly with featherlike strokes to her inner thighs, lingering expertly on the ultra-soft skin beneath the golden triangle. Madison gasped. The pleasure was delicious, and her fingernails dug into the bunched muscles of his upper arms.

Blood roared in her ears. She tossed her head, turning to him as his warm fingers pressed inside her. Her hips arched against his hand. Her arms held him tighter as a pervading need for him streaked through her.

"Do you have any idea what you do to me?" he breathed into her ear with a barely controlled huskiness, tracing his tongue along the clefts. He struggled with the overwhelming desire to take her right then. But he didn't want it that way. He wanted nothing more than to pleasure her beyond all bounds, until she could take no more, until she was thoroughly sated.

Madison's answer was an unintelligible moan from lips that were silenced by the sweet onslaught of his, rendering her quivering and helpless.

Dragging himself away from her honey-sweet lips, he kissed lower, snuggling to her breasts, flicking his tongue over the sensitive peaks. He thrilled to the smoothness of her stomach, dipping his tongue teasingly into her navel. Brushing his cheek with relish over her downy hair, he paused, looking up at her with a smoky gaze before grasping her hips and burying his face between her legs.

Madison gasped, arching her back, writhing at the raw lust that consumed her, licked at her, captured her almost instantly. Indescribably, she convulsed, nearly falling from the edge of the bed.

Colt heaved her to safety, bracing himself over her. Boldly catching her liquid eyes within the honesty of his, he held her face to receive the fierceness of his kiss, the turgid swell pressing hot and hard between her legs, seeking.

The kiss gentled, and he parted her lips, his velvet tongue lightly brushing over hers. Her eyes fluttered open, drinking in his masculine beauty. She could feel the thundering of his heart against her breast, mingling with the untamed pounding of her own.

Colt was so incredibly handsome, she thought, sliding her hand over his jaw, her fingers weaving through his soft, thick hair. Madison traced the sculpted lines of his mouth with her fingertip.

His tongue laved over it lazily before he sucked it, sending shivers through her body.

With a soft whimper she pressed her face into his neck, placing hot little bites along the corded lines. He groaned restlessly into her hair. The lusty rotation of his hips increased, becoming more insistent. Madison greedily strained her pelvis upward, yearning, opening herself, encouraging him to take her.

Colt needed no further invitation. With a robust plunge, he sheathed himself within her soft tightness, giving of himself, filling her with his strength, delving to the very core of her womanhood with firm, deep strokes. Her gasps were silenced as he claimed her mouth. Both were lost within the sheer beauty of entwined emotions. She molded her hips to his in their sensuously writhing dance, matching his movements, unwittingly driving Colt's passion into a fevered pitch as he endeavored to hold back. Deeper, he quickened, his hips circling tantalizingly.

A tempestuous whirlpool of passion inside her swirled, swelled, coaxing her to ecstatic heights. Colt murmured indistinct words of encouragement against her ear, words of love, of promise. Turbulent waves churned within her, building, crashing in a frothy mist. In a final crescendo, they broke in a gushing tidal wave, shattering her senses into shards, making her cry out against his mouth.

His sinewy muscles strained, then he let himself go with reckless abandon, matched only by her own raging spasms. With a long, low groan he drove into her, jerking convulsively over and over, his life pouring into, joining with hers. Madison tightened around the pulsing warmth within, never, ever wanting to let him go.

Still converged, Colt moved slowly. Low, satisfied growls emanated from deep inside his chest. He planted soft, adoring kisses along her neck and shoulders, up to her cheeks and nose, across the abundance of her dark lashes as she kept her eyes closed. A contented smile played across her lips.

"You exceed all of my wildest fantasies, Mrs. Chase," he crooned next to her ear in a throaty whisper.

"And you mine. . . ." She giggled softly, luxuriating in the heavenly feel of his body over hers, the rapid palpitations of her heart settling down to purr.

Colt rolled to his back, taking her with him, her curls cascading over his chest as he held her close. He tenderly brushed away the strands that clung to her damp and flushed cheeks.

The beating of his heart succeeded in lulling her into a deep relaxation, and several minutes passed before Madison stirred within the circle of his arms, her fingers toying with the hairs on his chest, tracing circles around his hardening nipples.

"What are you up to, sugar?" His tone implied suspicion, and his eyes were closed.

"Just wondering," she said softly, glancing up at him with a new admiration.

"About what?"

"Oh, it's silly." The music of her laughter drifted over the room. "I can't help but picture you lying in this position with another woman. And I wonder how many there were."

He chuckled, a deep, rich sound. "You make it sound like I have a harem awaiting me at every turn. Flattering, but not exactly true."

"I believe you said once that you had practically one in every town you passed through," she challenged.

"Actually, I think it was *you* who said that. And I let you believe it. It made me feel good."

"Well?"

Colt's eyes opened, "There were a few special ones over the years, besides Sarah, if that's what you mean."

"Only a few?"

"Do I detect a little jealousy?" He laughed readily. "Don't worry, sugar. Nobody can hold a candle to you."

Madison slid off to his side, trailing her fingertip lightly along the rigid plane of his stomach, following the tapering direction of soft brown hair. She rested her head on his shoulder. Colt watched her hand with mounting interest.

"I don't worry. I just wonder. Anyone you were in love with?" Her hand moved lower, clasping around his already hardening manhood, playing him, strumming.

He inhaled sharply, then gasped, "No . . . not like you . . . let's talk later." He turned toward her, breathing into her hair.

"No. Now." She squeezed, taunting him. "Who did you love?"

He sighed in playful exasperation. "I was only sixteen years old, Madison. Puppy love, an infatuation that I will never forget because it was the first time. As far as Sarah went, that was more of a mutual respect rather than a great love affair. Feel better?"

She gave it considerable thought, mostly to torment him, quite conscious of the subtle thrusts he was making into her hand. "I've never felt better," she said lightly, bounding to her knees to sit over him. "In fact, I feel great."

Enjoying her position of power, she dipped to brush her lips over his nipples, flicking her tongue over each, delivering sweet kisses.

She moved downward, and Colt tenderly wound a hank of her hair around his hand, bringing her gaze to his. "*Now* what are you up to?" he asked knowingly.

Madison just smiled, the sparkle in her eyes telling all. Colt lay back with a contented groan. Her lips grazed his hips. Then she lovingly caressed his swollen manhood with her cheek before welcoming him inside her mouth, alive to the pulsing beat and his masculine, earthy taste.

A hoarse groan vibrated within his chest. He clasped her face with trembling hands, bringing her mouth to his, seizing an enraptured kiss—demanding it.

Madison inched her torso over his. Colt took her with an urgent thrust. Gasping, shocked at the pleasure of feeling him inside her again, she rose above him, moving to his rhythm. His gaze smoky, his eyes locked with hers in silent communion. His hands slid over her hips, guiding, encouraging.

Madison tossed her head in wild abandon, arching back, shaking her hair until the ends beat over his thighs like thousands of charged needlepoints. She calmed, touching her fingertips tantalizingly over his inner thighs to ease his intensity.

"Be still," she whispered huskily, "don't move . . ."

Colt's chest swelled with sharp, excited breaths, his lips parting in mute protest at her impossible request. Madison's mouth curved a slow smile, her eyes closing as she dropped to drag kisses over his chin, to his mouth. He accepted her hungrily, his groans of pleasure mingling with her own.

Ever so slowly, she began to move and he filled her completely. The sensual cadence sent warm tingles of ecstasy through her until her own breath became ragged. Waves of pleasure crashed over her in delectable surges, forever giving, ebbing away . . . then reaching out to lap at her until she could stand no more.

Unable to bear the heavenly torture, Colt's body tensed in sweet agony, forging up, out of control. Gripping the brass spindles of the headboard, he strained his head back, the sinews standing out along his arms. Their worlds exploded in unison, and Madison sunk over him with a gasp, her mouth breathlessly finding his.

The fire was vanquished. Their heartbeats quieted, reconciling to a serene rhythm. After lying blissfully for a while, she felt a shiver course through her, and Colt gently slid her off, pulling the blankets around them in a plush cocoon.

During the night, Madison roused to sleepy kisses, the heat pressing into her again. She received him voraciously. They rode the waves again, reaching for the moon and the stars on their intimate journey of oneness. Their arms and legs entwined, they uttered words of love until they once again drifted into a peaceful slumber.

Chapter Thirty-Four

It might have been a noise that woke her, or maybe it was just a feeling, but Madison pushed herself up on her elbow, blinking to clear her sleep-blurred eyes. It was still dark. The lamp had burnt out and the room was bathed in the ghostly light of the moon.

Colt lay with his back to her, softly snoring. She ran her fingers over his bare shoulder, bending to kiss the tawny skin, tasting the saltiness of it.

For some unknown reason her gaze lifted to the balcony. The French doors were covered only with the pale chiffon undercurtains. It was several moments before the deadly realization hit her full force and she was able to digest the reality. Her heart slammed forcefully. There was someone there! Standing, staring at her. And she had been looking right at him!

In one second, quick enough to make her question the accuracy of what she had thought she saw, he was gone. Her eyes round with fright, she opened her mouth to speak but only managed a subdued squeak.

"Colt!" Madison shook his shoulder fiercely, never taking her eyes from the doors. He instantly rolled to face her, his arms automatically slipping around her, pulling her to him with a groggy utterance.

"No, Colt, I saw someone! There, at the door. Somebody was

257

standing there, looking in! Colt, wake up. . . ." She shook him vigorously again.

"What . . . ?"

He bounded off the bed and pulled on his Levi's. He drew a single pistol from the holster that hung from a peg beside the bed, reflexively drawing back the hammer in the same movement. The ivory of the Peacemaker's grip glowed blue in the moonlight. Barefooted, he padded quietly to the edge of the door, careful to keep out of sight, barely breathing.

"What did you see?" he whispered without looking at her.

"I'm not sure. But it sure did look like a person—just standing there! Colt . . . what are you doing? Colt . . ." she whispered back frantically, clutching the quilt to her neck.

But it was too late. He had already twisted the handle, silently opening a glass-paned door. The sheer curtains floated into the room with a fragrant gust of cool summer air. Cautiously, he crept past the portal, scanning in either direction before crossing the balcony and disappearing from sight.

Her heart hammering wildly, Madison leapt from the bed. She scooped the first available covering she could find among the clothing that lay strewn about the floor. Throwing on Colt's white shirt, she tiptoed toward the partially open door, absently fastening just a few of the buttons as she went.

A sudden, floor-vibrating thud was immediately followed by a throaty grunt, causing her instinctively to take a step backwards. Her hand flew to her breast in an attempt to calm her racing heart. She thought she detected a resonant curse, then there was a deathly quiet.

"Colt?" she hissed into the night.

No answer.

Soundlessly, her eyes darting in desperation, she advanced toward the door once again.

It was abnormally quiet and, as an afterthought, she ran back to Colt's holster and pulled the remaining pistol from it. An unearthly fear gripped her, and she tried to shove it away. Madison drew back on the steel hammer with both thumbs until it clicked. Her knuckles white with the intensity of her nervous grip, she pushed past the billowing curtains and followed Colt's trail.

"Colt! Answer me!" she grit out under her breath.

Still no response. The street below was void of any activity, the only sound being the unrelenting bark of a dog in the lonely distance.

Behind her, the balcony ended in plain sight with only a thick pottery vessel containing flaming orange geraniums. But before her the walkway extended around the corner of the brick building. Inhaling a shaky breath, her jaw set determinedly, she hugged her body to the wall and proceeded to the corner. She held the pistol with both hands, pointed downward. Very slowly, Madison leaned her body around the rough edge, and there in the dark she spotted a shadowy form lying lifelessly, bent against the wrought-iron railing.

Without thinking, she rushed forward, realizing it was Colt who lay in a crumpled heap. His chest and shoulders were spattered with a shiny dark red substance.

"Oh God, no—Colt!" It was a soft shriek as she fell to her knees at his side, sickened. She saw jagged lines of blood running over his forehead and into his closed eyes.

Suddenly, a moldy-smelling, scratchy burlap sack was hurled suffocatingly over her head from behind, a steely grip wrapping around to pin her arms as she was roughly hoisted to her feet. With a muffled scream she jerked and twisted, fighting off the unseen hands that grappled to control her.

Madison fumbled with the pistol in her hands, fighting for an optimal position to use it. In a deafening explosion it discharged— upward, into the air. Something biting was being wrapped around her body, painful, threatening to cut off her circulation. Her grip loosened, and the pistol was jolted from her unprepared grasp, clattering noisily to the wooden planked floor of the balcony. A momentary slip of the gunnysack allowed her to see it snatched up by a knobby, dirt-encrusted hand. Screaming, she began to kick out in every direction, butting her head at the hulking presence that held her.

Struck by a shattering blow, an agonizing, white-hot pain shot through the back of her skull, and everything ceased to matter. Amid the swirling darkness that enveloped her danced a million slivers of glistening light. Her knees buckled helplessly. In an odd, almost pleasant relinquishment, she slipped beneath the lure of a serene blanket of blackness.

Chapter Thirty-Five

Madison didn't want to wake up. She was so terribly tired. The constant jolting wouldn't let her rest, though, and, becoming increasingly irritated, she struggled to move her limbs. Excruciating spasms screamed through her head and down into the muscles of her neck.

She strained but could not seem to move her arms, and she felt as if she were in some sort of horrific nightmare, unable to fully awaken. She opened her eyes, but it was dark except for tiny sparkles of daylight jeering at her through microscopic holes. Madison tried to roll over, and she moaned involuntarily at the tingling ache that assaulted her arms and legs. Her hip bones were bruised and sore, and her head was throbbing ruthlessly. It was so hot. And when she breathed her nose wrinkled at the disgusting, sour smell that greeted her nostrils.

All-consuming, maddening claustrophobia engulfed her and, heedless of the pain, Madison screamed, howled, and hollered, while writhing, bucking, rolling, and throwing her restrained body. She'd do anything to obtain release. Her fear wasn't something she could control. Anxiety came in a rush of panic, waves of it washing over her with a mindless dissonance she had no power to control.

The buckboard lurched to a surprising and sudden stop.

"Ah, hell, Aussie! She's comin' 'round! Look at 'er! She's havin' some kinda fit or somethin'!"

"Bound to happen eventually, Turtle," Aussie replied evenly. "Let's get'er outta there."

Amid her thrashing, Madison felt her body being dragged and then hoisted upright to stand. Pins and needles shot from her benumbed feet to the tips of her fingers. Her struggles didn't cease, and her captors tried to subdue her.

A swirl of nausea dominated her senses. As the bindings were loosened and the sack lifted over her head, her hand flew to her mouth to stifle a dry wretch.

"She's a kickin' dame, ain't she, Aussie?" Turtle cackled with glee, licking his lips as he watched her, his quick eyes not missing a detail.

Madison stood barefoot on the hard, dry, hot earth, in the middle of nowhere, the sun beating down on her head. She clenched her hands at her sides. Her stance was wide, her chest heaving with the adrenaline that pumped through her veins in torrents. She drank in the fresh air greedily, squinting against the obnoxious glare of daylight. As her eyes focused, she saw two men, standing in a guarded position a few paces away in front of her, as if they expected her to fly into an insane rage and attack them. The idea wasn't totally preposterous.

The man on the left leered at her unashamedly, his young body stooped, distorted by a hump on his back. He clutched a bashed hat in his hand. A mop of stick-straight brown hair was cut into a wedged bowl around his head. His most prominent feature by far was the long, hook nose that protruded from his otherwise average-looking face. Her eyes narrowed. Now she remembered! This was the man she had seen on Main Street in Laramie. He had looked familiar then, and still did now. She could only surmise that possibly she had glimpsed him at the ranch. But what would someone with evil motives like his be doing at Colt's ranch?

The other man was pleasant looking, even handsome, his bright blue eyes perceptive, though partially shaded by the tight-brimmed cowboy hat. He had a full, thick mustache and the rest of his face was covered in a dark blond stubble beard. His thumbs remained hooked onto his suspenders, his head slightly cocked with curiosity.

Masculine eyes trailed over her with more than just a mild interest, making her all too painfully aware of her meager clothing and horrible situation. She shook her arms in an effort to ease the spiny tingle. Pushing her tangled curls away from her face, she looked down at her naked legs and feet. Mentally, she thanked Colt for wearing such a large-sized shirt. She abruptly became aware of the fullness of her bladder, thinking she just might wet her pants right then and there—that is, if she had had any on.

"Hey, Aussie," the hunchback said, poking the other man, "what'd ye say we have a little fun with the girl, eh? She's a lively one. We could really make her squirm, show her what a *real* man feels like? Eh?" Turtle cackled again, a grotesque sound that sent shivers up and down Madison's spine, not to mention the fear inflicted by his words.

"You heard what the boss man said. The sheila's to be delivered unharmed. Now get your brains out of your pants, mate," Aussie answered, obviously the more level-headed of the two.

Madison breathed a sigh of relief, swallowing dryly.

"Aaaahhh," Turtle snorted his opposition, "didn't say we was gonna hurt her none. Hell, dames like it just as much as men do. 'Sides, get a eyeful of them legs! Long and luscious, they is . . . whooooeeee! . . . Like nothin' I've ever seen in all my born days!" Turtle shook his head for emphasis, practically drooling.

"That's not sayin' a whole helluva lot, Turtle, considering the gems I've seen you keep company with. You just leave the lass alone—she didn't ask for none of this. Can't say I approve of all this carryin' on, anyhow. She's a respectable woman after all, not the two-bit whore I was led to believe."

They were speaking as if she weren't standing directly in front of them, hearing every word.

"Now, how would you know somethin' like 'at, huh?" Turtle interrupted. "When did you ever spend time with her?"

"I've seen her around—I can just tell these things. She's with Colt, ain't she? That says enough as far as I'm concerned."

Madison's heart thumped faster at the mention of Colt's name. A depressing awareness returned her to her senses. Her very last memory was of Colt's inert form, blood everywhere. Her stomach churned at the possibility that she must now face. Everything had happened so quickly, it had been impossible for her to tell if he were breathing or not. What if he were left for dead by these men? She couldn't bear the thought.

"I demand to know why you have kidnapped me, and where you plan to take me!" Madison was fed up with this idle chit-chat. Her sparked gaze shot from one to the other, "And what did you do to Colt?"

Both men stared back at her, shocked, as if they expected her never to utter a word. Eventually, it was the Australian who spoke. "You'll just have to wait, lassy. We've got our instructions. Just doing our job. Here . . ." Aussie passed her his canteen, " . . . wet your whistle. Don't figure we'll be passing a billabong any time soon, and the river's a good ways ahead."

Madison delivered a scathing look before she snatched the canteen from his extended hand. The idea of water was too good to ignore. She poured the lukewarm liquid into her mouth, swallowing greedily, then handed it back. Aussie picked up the rope and burlap sack, as if he were planning to tie her up again.

"No! You can't cover me with that hot, disgusting thing—I won't let you! You're holding me prisoner, right? Well, you have to treat me with dignity. It's the law; haven't you heard?" Madison was referring to prisoners of war, in the twentieth century, no less. She hoped she was convincing enough so they would fall for it and not question her any further.

The men just shrugged, looking at one another stupidly.

She decided to take the ball and run with it. "I'm warning you, if you don't treat me with the utmost respect, I'll have both your asses in a sling! Now, I need some privacy so that I . . . I . . . can relieve myself."

Madison folded her arms and waited, casually glancing about to see if there were something, anything, that might afford her some privacy.

"Ohhh," Aussie said slowly, evidently not having considered the likelihood of this particular situation. "I suppose you could walk a bit in that direction yonder," he said, pointing toward a scant patch of sagebrush in the distance.

"No, Aussie! She just might get a notion and take off!"

Turtle didn't want her going anywhere. It was obvious he would much rather have her do her business right there in front of them—for more than one reason. He licked his lips in anticipation, a lascivious gleam in his eyes.

"That's ridiculous," Madison stated with more confidence than she felt. "What am I going to do? Take off half-naked through this desolate prairie with no shoes? You could catch me easily. I'm not *that* stupid."

Thinking herself successful in reinforcing their sense of security, she didn't wait for an answer. Determinedly, and with dignity, she strode off toward the sagebrush cover, aware of their burning stares on her back.

The purplish-blue of the Wind River Range anchored the horizon majestically, and she realized it was the general direction in which they were taking her. Finished with her business and feeling a little better, with the exception of her bruised body, she headed back through the dry yellow grass, stepping lightly to avoid the biting cockleburrs that might be hidden there. The men watched with an annoying scrutiny as she approached. Aussie fumbled with the ropes again, averting his eyes when she caught him staring.

"As a prisoner, I have rights!" Madison reminded them, pointing at him, her gaze slanting in challenge.

"But . . . we have our orders, lassie. You're not to see where you're going. We have to tie you up."

At least he was trying to be reasonably kind, unlike Turtle.

"Hogshit, Aussie! Don't let her talk to us lik 'at!" Turtle interrupted. Turning to Madison, he strode toward her and leaned close to her face. "Listen here, lady, you'll do what we says, whether ya like it or not!"

"Bugger off, mate! You're a no hoper, do you know that? The sheila's right! How would you like it, huh?" he fairly snarled at the other one. Then to Madison, he said, "How about if we just blindfold you—how's that sound, lass? 'Course, we have to tie your hands 'n feet, but I'll do it loose-like."

He waited for her permission, an appeal in his sapphire-blue eyes as he anxiously toyed with the rope.

Turtle shuffled off, kicking up clouds of dust with his bulky clodhoppers. He clambered up onto the crude wagon, plopping down hard on the bare bench seat. He folded his arms like a pouting child.

Madison hesitated, "All right . . . Aussie, is it? Why are you doing this? I can't help but get the feeling you're not cut out for this type of activity. How did you get involved with whoever put you up to this?"

Aussie shifted his eyes, unable to hold her gaze. God, but she was beautiful. He didn't think he'd ever seen a more lovely sheila. And that was in her current state of dishabille. It unnerved him greatly to be standing next to her when she was barely dressed, carrying on a casual conversation. Not that he would ever take advantage of her. He couldn't hurt another person maliciously, let alone a woman.

That was exactly why he had made Turtle do the dirty work—knocking Colt Chase senseless and kidnapping his bride. Only she wasn't supposed to really be his bride; all a farce, he had been told. Wasn't the boss going to be surprised to find out the pair had actually gotten married the very night she was kidnapped?

He and Turtle had followed Colt and Madison all evening long, even waiting patiently at the saloon a few hours after the couple had left the restaurant, just so they could have a fairly decent wedding night. Turtle had griped incessantly at that, but Aussie had threatened to beat the hunchback to a pulp if he attempted to disturb them too soon. When morning neared he had given Turtle the okay to climb up to the balcony—not an easy maneuver for a hunchback, but he had managed. The distasteful operation had then begun.

Aussie hated like hell to put this poor girl in a situation like this, and hated even more handing her over to the likes of his boss. She didn't deserve that. He was beginning to despise himself for being the one to deliver her to the scoundrel in the first place. If there was any way he could abort this thing right now and let the girl go, he would. But that would mean his own ass. The boss had men everywhere, and his days would be numbered if he did something as crazy as that. Hell, but he didn't need that kind of trouble on top of everything else.

Sighing, Aussie forced himself to look into her liquid green-blue eyes.

"Well, lassie, I'm hating myself for doing this to you, if you want the entire truth." He lowered his voice, his eyes shifting up to Turtle and then back to Madison. "But I'll tell you this—mind your *P*s and *Q*s and I'll help you all I can—can't do more than that."

A glimmer of hope twinkled in the man's eyes, flashing through Madison, filling her. She sensed sincerity in his voice and took hold of his arm, "Where's Colt?" she pleaded again. "He's not dead, is he?"

"Dead as a doornail, lady, so get used to it."

The reply came from the front of the wagon, Turtle clearly having heard her question. She glanced up him, then back to Aussie, her eyes revealing her desperate need to know the truth.

Aussie shook his head once, a queer smile edging his lips as he motioned for her to bring her wrists together. Madison complied. He put a finger to his mouth to ensure her silence, letting her know it wasn't the time to be discussing Colt.

"Now get on up into that wagon, lassie, and let's be on our way."

His voice was gruff, but she was quick to detect a hasty wink in her direction before he removed his blue bandanna, blindfolding her with it.

Aussie tied her ankles, then lightly covered her legs with a filthy wool blanket that had been crushed into a corner of the wagon. It wasn't so much for warmth—the weather was scorchingly hot—but rather to protect the girl's modesty.

Madison rode in blackness, jostled painfully along the pinching planks of the buckboard. The hours bumped by, and finally she slept.

Chapter Thirty-Six

Madison came to the conclusion that this experience was the worst she had ever known. How ironic. Knowing Colt and marrying him was positively the best. It seemed as though the higher the highs, the lower the lows must be.

She felt Colt's presence all the time, knowing in her heart he was alive and probably going crazy trying to find her. And he *would* find her. Then hell's fury would be unleashed. Turtle had said Colt was dead, and Aussie had refused to elaborate, had merely shaken his head; what did that mean? It meant Colt was alive . . . didn't it?

Madison let her imagination run its course. It took her back to the warmth of Colt's powerful embrace, where nothing could harm her, his fiery caresses, the sweet taste of his mouth on hers. The way his grin was slightly crooked on one side, denting into an adorable dimple; the bend of his nose, which you had to look very closely to see, once you managed to get past his gorgeous face . . .

Then she cried and thought for sure he was dead. What if Aussie had been unwilling to tell her what could very well be the truth because he didn't want a crying, hysterical woman on his hands? Her faith plummeted to a hideous low; there was no reason to continue life if Colt wasn't going to be there to share it with her. Nothing would matter; the fire in her spirit would sputter, all but snuff out.

Madison tolerated the tortuous wagon ride for the next day and half. They stopped at dusk to rest, starting out at first light the following morning. She was only allowed to take off her blindfold when twilight enfolded them and she was unable to see anything past the circle of their small campfire.

She couldn't eat, though Aussie provided her with plenty of food heaped onto a scarred tin plate. He implored her to try something, if only a little, but all she could seem to manage was a sip of water now and then.

Late the following afternoon, the wagon ride turned rougher than usual, jolting her from her semiconscious state. They were unmistakably on an incline since she was forced to tense her legs, digging her heels into the slanted wagon bed just to keep from tumbling off. The thought that it might not be such a bad idea occurred to her. But her mind was in an increasingly befuddled state, and she failed to see how it could work. By the time she freed herself from the ropes and blindfold, she would surely be caught. No, if she was going to escape, it would have to be another way.

The wagon lurched, wheels crashing harshly over rocks and ruts in the road, and Madison thought her insides would turn to jelly. The air turned noticeably cooler, and she was forced to pull the smelly blanket closer about her shoulders for warmth. She constantly nuzzled her cheek against the collar of the shirt, for it smelled of Colt. That and her wedding ring were all she had for inner strength, and she held them dear.

The wagon stopped.

Madison tried to sit up straighter, finding it difficult since her stamina was waning by leaps and bounds. Turtle and Aussie had jumped down apparently for the wagon bounced a few times and seemed to lighten. There were voices—lots of them in the distance, along with footsteps and some commotion. She cocked her head, listening attentively, her heart beginning to race. The air smelled heavily of pine. She didn't have to be a rocket scientist to figure out that they were in the mountains.

Her insides still echoed the shakes and vibrations of the interminable wagon ride. She waited; it seemed like forever. What would happen next?

The crunch of boots upon loose gravel, the unmistakable air of a human presence nearby . . . She held her breath.

"Well, well, what have we here? So nice of you to visit my humble abode. I could use the company. I don't suppose you feel so high and mighty right about now, do you?" The mocking voice nagged on thickly, then broke into a deep chuckle.

Madison's eyes widened beneath the blindfold. Dammit! She knew that voice! Who in the world . . . ?

"Who's there? Untie me! Take this damn blindfold off!" She struggled futilely against the binding ropes. Though tied fairly loose, they were still annoyingly effective.

She was surprised when her usual abundance of energy was extinguished so quickly. Madison relaxed out of sheer necessity, her head spinning with exhaustion. The very next time food was offered she would force herself to eat. Otherwise, she wouldn't have a prayer of getting out of this mess.

"All in good time . . . *sugar*," the sardonic, syrupy voice drawled, emphasizing the loving endearment for her that was Colt's alone.

She heard him turn, spinning a heel deep in the gravel as he left her.

"Aussie! Get her inside and feed her. Keep her tied and blindfolded—I've got plans for this little angel. Hurry your lazy ass up."

"My God!" Madison muttered in disbelief, petrified at the hideous prospect, sure she must be mistaken. Her jaw quivered and she chewed her lip in extreme agitation. "It just *can't be!* . . . anyone but *him!*" she wailed under her breath, hushing when she heard the sound of another approach. Jumping and turning stiff at the warm, gentle touch, she held her blanket in place with all her might as she was lifted from the wagon and gently carried.

"Who's there?" she hissed.

"Just me, lassie."

Madison breathed easier at the familiar voice. Right now Aussie was her only chance of a possible escape. Not hesitating, she poured forth a barrage of questions, only to be stifled by his frantic words. "Shhhhh! There're too many people around now! You'll have to be patient. Trust me if you can. I'll be around when the time is right."

"Aussie! Just tell me where you've brought me! Who was that man who came up to the wagon? Pleeeaase!" She whispered as low as she possibly could.

A cool chill hit her full in the face and she was sure they had entered a structure; she felt the oppressive closeness of tight walls surrounding her. Good Lord, was he putting her in a refrigerator? It was freezing!

"Promise to button your lip if I tell you, now? You're with Red Eagle. Behave yourself. Don't provoke him, hear? Just sit tight."

Aussie sat her down carefully on the hard, cold floor. All the voices and sounds that had previously been around her were muffled, fading away.

"But . . . no! That can't be, Aussie! Red Eagle is in Kansas, isn't he?" Madison was more confused than ever. "Please, take off the blindfold."

"I can't do that, lassie."

She could sense it when he stood up to leave. The air turned remarkably more frigid and she started to shiver.

"Don't leave me here alone . . . *Aussie?!*" His name was spoken in a breathless shriek, her fright building.

"Quiet, lass. I won't be far away. We can't let on we've been talking, hear?

Madison whimpered inwardly as she listened to the bleak crunch of footsteps dwindle away to nothing. She sat rigidly, afraid to move a muscle, the cold dampness immediately seeping through her, making itself at home in her bones. Gradually, when she was sure she was totally alone, she began to explore her surroundings. The floor was fine powdery dirt and loose pebbles—very cold dirt. The wall behind her was icy rock, jagged and rough. The air smelled old, musty with a hint of sulfur.

She shuddered. Colt, help me, *please* help me. . . .

The great black stallion dashed like quicksilver through the heart of the lush green meadow, the swell of sinewy flanks rippling with each expansive stride. Its rider coaxed the animal to breakneck speed with the aid of a woven leather quirt, held steady in his left hand. Horse and rider melded in fluid grace, a vision of beauty impassioned by a worthy goal.

It was the third horse Colt had acquired since leaving Laramie. He had ridden constantly for two days and nights, without more than a brief rest. No single horse could have withstood such an ordeal.

The proud animal swerved into a skid only inches from the bottom step of the front porch. Colt dismounted in a billow of dust, flinging gravel even before the horse came to a complete stop. Three at a time, he charged up the front steps. He jerked the screen open, erupting into the serenity of the house like a tempestuous wind. The horse was lathered and blowing laboriously, its nostrils flaring in the black velvet muzzle.

"Rosannah! Rosan—" Colt bellowed, whirling about just as the little round woman scurried around the corner from the kitchen.

Dish towel in hand, her eyes were round in a face wreathed in astonishment and concern. "Colt? Whatever is going on?"

He took two long strides forward, grasping her plump shoulders between his hands, interrupting her even as her mouth formed the words. "Any word from Madison? Have you seen her? Heard from her?" He leveled his gaze with Rosannah's. A spark of hope glimmered behind the intensity of his eyes as he looked into her dark ones.

"Why, no . . . Colt? What's wrong . . . what happened to your head?" Rosannah stammered, a cold fear gripping her.

Colt spun in frustration, his fist striking the wallpapered wall, causing the wall hangings and pictures to rattle on their hooks.

Rosannah flinched, her eyes batting. "She went to find you several days ago. Zak saw to it—"

"Yeah, yeah, she found me. We got married in Laramie Thursday night." He began to pace the floor in front of her, his eyes glazed, unseeing. "During the night, I was cracked over the head. When I came to she was gone. She was kidnapped, Rosie!"

Rosannah gasped sharply, her hand flying to her mouth. "Oh, no! Who in the world would do such a thing? My God, do you have any ideas?"

"Oh, I've got plenty of ideas!" he railed, a sneer curling his lip. "The question is, which one is the *right* one? Huh? Damn! While I'm going around in circles for some kind of clue, she could be lying somewhere . . ."

"Colt, don't torture yourself like this. You've got to keep your head. Let's go get Bud," Rosannah appealed to him, wringing her hands as she watched Colt move about the parlor nervously.

"Where's Garrett?" Colt stopped abruptly. Then, his eyes spitting fire, he stalked down the hallway toward his office, his jaw set in a staunch determination.

"He's not here. Done went someplace with that whore of his, probably into town." She waved the dish towel with an air of total disgust. Her feet flew into motion behind Colt, taking two steps to his one.

"Whore? You mean Lucy?" He shook his head in angry exasperation, "Hell, what's gotten into him? Look at this mess." He leafed through the heap of paperwork scattered over the desk, stray pieces floating haphazardly to the floor. "Did he say when he'd be back?"

"Nah," Rosannah wrinkled her nose, "you know Garrett. Just said he'd be gone a few days—had some business to attend to."

"Business? With a whore in tow? I doubt that. A good asskicking is what my little brother needs."

"I told him, Colt, that that whore is not permitted anywhere near this house. I don't know what's wrong with him lately. Why can't he find a respectable girl? What do you mean, you and Madison got married? Weren't you already married?" Confusion laced her already tormented expression.

Colt dismissed the question with a wave of his hand. "I'll explain all that later. What's this?" He lifted a crumpled piece of paper from amid the jumble, smoothing his hand over the creases. He frowned, bracing his arms on the desk, leaning in close to decipher the illegible script.

Rosannah shrugged, edging in for a better look.

"Looks like a schedule of some sort—nothing like we usually keep around here," Colt muttered, more or less to himself. "All I can make out is Hole-in-the-Wall. What in the world would Garrett have to do with Hole-in-the-Wall?" His eyes darkened with calculation, then lifted to Rosannah's imploringly.

"Couldn't prove it by me. Surely Garrett wouldn't be hanging out with the likes of them law-breakers." She shook her head with conviction.

"There's a couple of names here . . . one I can't make out . . . the other, Aussie, is it? Could that be our Aussie? Is he around? Have you seen him lately?"

"No, not lately. But then, I don't hardly ever see him anyhow. Where are you going?"

Colt skirted the desk and was heading for the door, stuffing the paper into his vest pocket. "I'm going to find Bud and question some of the hands about Madison, and this, too." He patted his pocket. "If I don't show up for a while, don't worry. It just means I'm off tracking a lead."

He was out the door, leaping from the porch and onto his mount with fluid grace, galloping toward the barns like a thunderbolt.

Rosannah scuttled behind. "Good luck . . ." she called into the wind, a nervous hand brushing a strand of hair from her eyes.

*   *   *

"Hey, Colt! Certainly didn't expect you back so soon. Where's that lovely bride of yours?" Bud grinned up at the cowboy who raced around the corner of the big barn, eyeing him as he dismounted. He was bending over a damaged hoof, attempting to pry off a shoe from his favorite cow pony, a pretty little buckskin. "Rosie told me 'bout her comin' back, then trackin' ya down like she did. Damn, she's got more spirit than Little Gold, here."

Colt interrupted the older man, his face like cold, chiseled granite. "She was kidnapped, Bud. In Laramie."

Colt gazed unwaveringly into the lively blue eyes, suddenly feeling as if he'd regressed back to his youth, Bud being the closest thing to a father he'd known in ten years. A flood of emotion washed over him, his resolve weakening. His jaw twitched. Colt turned away, walking toward the corral, no longer able to face the disquiet in Bud's eyes.

Bud dropped Little Gold's leg, patting her on the rump. "That can wait." He followed Colt to stand at the fence, leaning against it next to him. "Tell me all that's happened. Is that how ya got yer head bashed up?" He motioned with a frown.

"Yep. Got an ache in my head that would kill a moose, too." He stared straight ahead for a moment before he spoke again. "We got married." Colt hesitated when he heard a snort, turning to see what Bud found so funny.

"Ahhh, for real this time?"

"Yeah, for real." He sighed. "Anyway, during the night—I don't know, it had to be pretty close to morning, near as I can figure—I got hit in the head. Next thing I know, she's gone."

"Are you absolutely positive she was kidnapped? Maybe she got antsy, up'n left again."

"No! She was abducted!" Colt shook the top rail of the fence, the storm inside him raging. "She saw somebody on the balcony and when I went out to investigate, I was caught off guard. I didn't see a thing. Don't even know what they hit me with. All her stuff was still in the room when I came to. But she was gone."

"All right." Bud waved a hand in truce. "Sounds like somebody had their eye on her. Did ya check 'round Laramie before ya left, see if'n anybody there saw anythin'?"

"Yeah; nothing much out of the ordinary. Talked to the sheriff. He was a dilly. Drunker than a skunk at eight o'clock in the morning." Colt snorted in disgust. "The only thing that sounded strange was what the barkeep at the thirst parlor across the street was able to tell me. Said a couple of strangers were keeping vigil most of the night. Up and down from their chairs to look outside—real suspicious, I guess. When they did leave it was in a hurry."

"That could be a damn good lead, Colt. Did he say anythin' else—a description of 'em?"

"Just that one was a cripple, the other a foreigner." He cast a sidelong glance at Bud, noting the deep concentration taking hold on his leathery face. The cogs were spinning for them both.

"Hmmmmm," was all Bud said, scrubbing his gray-whiskered chin thoughtfully.

"No other significant leads. Just had a feeling in my gut about the ranch; that's why I nearly rode three horses to death trying to get back here. Now that I'm back, nobody knows anything here, either. Garrett's off somewhere . . . I don't know, it was just a feeling. Maybe I shouldn't have come back in this direction. Hell, she could still be in Laramie, for all I know."

He scuffed the ground, turning his back to lean on the fence, rolling a blade of grass between his teeth as he gazed thoughtfully into the sky.

"Well, things ain't exactly hunky dory here. I don't expect that has anything to do with Madison, but that could have been the nasty feelin' ya had."

"What do you mean?" Colt's eyes shot over to Bud, squinting against the early afternoon sun.

"Ahhh, Garrett's little whore is wreaking havoc in the bunkhouse every night. Rosie's havin' herself a hissy fit over that. Can't say I blame her. It's no way to be runnin' a ranch. Garrett's just not takin' care of business like he should, lettin' things pile up, figures not comin' out right. Few more head of cattle missin' since you left."

"Yeah, I saw the condition of the office. No doubt about it, I've got to take full control just as soon as I find Madison—and give proper credit to the thugs who had the poor judgment to take her in the first place. Which reminds me, what do you make of this?" Colt pulled the wrinkled paper from his pocket and presented it to Bud.

"Where'd ya get this?"

"Found it wadded up on the desk. Can't make out most of it, but I can see where it says Hole-in-the-Wall," Colt paused, pointing, "and this here is 'Aussie.' Is he around? I'd like to ask him about it."

"Nah, he left 'bout the same time Garrett did, off on some errand, needed to pick up something—Hey! Wait just a dad-gum minute!"

"What?" Colt demanded impatiently.

"Couldn't be . . ." Bud shook his head with a grimace, holding the paper at arm's length in an effort to read it.

"What? Tell me!" Colt's voice rose. He was becoming annoyed.

"This Aussie feller, he's got an inflection to his speech, ya know."

"Yeah, I know. So he could be construed as a foreigner, is that what you're getting at?"

"Well," Bud paused, reluctant to say anything lest he be responsible for sending Colt off on some wild-goose chase. "Nah, that's a long shot. 'Sides, what purpose would he have snatching Madison, anyhow?"

"What purpose *would* he have?" Colt rolled the words off his tongue thoughtfully. "How about a cripple? Know of any?"

He straightened, searching Bud's eyes. Just a shred of knowledge was all he asked for. A rush of heat coursed through his veins, pumping raw excitement, hitting him full force, delving to his very core, fueling the deadly fire within. Colt's eyes sparkled a barbarous amber. "Think!" he prompted.

The old man shook his head. "Can't say as I do. There's a humpback feller Garrett hired on a month or so back, but I don't think—"

"Where is he? I'd like a word with him."

Zak passed with an armload of treated split rails and a spade, off to repair a weak spot on the northern side of the corral fence. Apparently he had caught part of their conversation. "Afternoon, Colt, Bud. Lookin' for somebody special?" He grinned brightly, his eyes barely visible beneath the wide, floppy brim of his hat.

"As a matter of fact we are, Zak. I didn't get to thank you for escorting Mrs. Chase most of the way to Laramie—you have my deepest gratitude on that score." Zak blushed, and Colt continued, "Right now I need to speak to the new hand—a hunchback. You know of anyone like that?"

"Sure do. That would be Turtle. He's not here, though. Mr. Chase sent him to pick up some supplies and he won't be back for another day or so." The hands were always careful to refer to Garrett as Mr. Chase, otherwise risking his peppery wrath.

Colt shot a fiery glance toward Bud, a look dripping with apprehension. Bud looked back. He was thinking exactly the same thing.

Leaving them both to stand speechless, Colt sprinted back through the barn to retrieve the black stallion. The horse had taken up temporary residence near a cool water trough.

"What'cha gonna do, boy?" Bud walked fast behind Colt.

"I'm off to Hole-in-the-Wall to knock a few heads together. When exactly did Aussie leave with Garrett?"

"Jeez, Colt—they didn't exactly leave together, just around the same time. Not long after Madison showed up . . . Sunday, it was. Garrett and the whore went by horseback. Aussie left a tad before them, on an errand for supplies he said, took the bedwagon—the one that's fallin' apart."

Colt hastily wiped his horse down, then mounted the stallion and prepared to leave, a hard resolve glinting in his eyes.

"Wait just a godderned minute now, Colt! Ya can't just mosey on up to Hole-in-the-Wall. They'll shoot ya, boy!" His voice escalating, Bud was walking fast after the trotting horse. Eventually, he broke into a slow jog, which was about as fast as he could muster.

"Don't worry, Bud. I'm heading to the west cabin. I'm sure that's the location that paper was referring to."

"That don't make no damned difference! They'll shoot ya there, too!"

"I know what I'm doing."

Colt was exhilarated, filled with more energy than he had possessed in the past two days. He spurred the stallion into a hell-bent gallop toward the purple mountainscape, the jagged peaks staring back at him in ominous challenge.

"Colton Remington Chase! Dammit! Git yer ass back here!"

Bud slowed, finally stopping the futile chase. Winded, he leaned over, resting his hands on his knees to catch his breath. "Stupid kid. Gonna git hisself killed is what he's gonna do!"

Bud whipped off his hat, slamming it to the ground with a vengeance. His gaze honed in on the lone figure riding into the horizon. Bud didn't turn to walk away until Colt had vanished into the foothills of the Wind River mountains.

Chapter Thirty-Seven

Madison dozed, her cheek pressed against the frigid stone wall. Her knuckles were white and cramped from the tense effort of clasping the wool blanket around her shoulders.

A rude jab of a booted foot into her thigh brought her around. Starting, she pushed away from the wall, fighting the fog that had governed her senses for the past two days.

"Huh?" she mumbled thickly into the darkness. "Who's there?"

The smell of food wafted past her nose. Then the clatter of something metal dropped next to her. Her mouth instantly began to water and her stomach twisted reflexively.

"Time to eat," uttered a scratchy voice.

Clumsy, rough hands tore at her blindfold, pulling a hank of hair in the process. She winced. The bandanna dropped into her lap.

A ponderous chest and the thin, grizzled beard of the man who removed it were the first things she saw. He was a mountain of a man; downright fat. A long scar creased his cheek, descending over his jaw, visible through the scraggly beard. Drab gray eyes regarded her impartially as bumbling fingers began to work loose the ropes that bound her arms and wrists. He left her ankles tied.

Madison groaned with the relief of freedom, even if it was limited. She flexed her fingers and bent her arms, inspecting her surroundings as she did so. Her eyes roamed the small cavelike chamber, over cold, gloomy, leaden rock walls, illuminated only by a single squat candle set carelessly on a slated wood crate. The words BLASTING POWDER were stenciled in red letters along the side. Madison frowned uneasily.

"Eat," the man said, plopping his overblown body down on another crate opposite her. His knees cracked with his weight. The crate creaked louder. He proceeded to stare her down, apparently intending to watch her eat.

Madison's nostrils were violated with the putrid smell of old sweat, mingling with the aroma of the questionable food placed before her.

"Eat," he repeated impassively. He brought something to his lips, tearing a stringy hunk of it away with his bared teeth, chewing noisily with his mouth open. His eyes never left her.

Madison attempted to ignore him. It wasn't easy. She wrinkled her nose at the disgusting-looking slop on the platter. Even though she hadn't eaten since the steak dinner after she and Colt were married, she honestly didn't know if she could stomach whatever filled that plate. Her eyes lifted to his in hesitation. His heavy lids widened expressively, and he inclined his head toward her food, still chewing.

Reluctantly, she picked up the tin plate. At least it was warm, easing the deadening chill from her fingers. She brought a spoonful of the brown mush to her lips, tasting cautiously. Overcooked beans. Although bland from lack of spices, it tasted better than it looked, and she polished it off within a matter of minutes. Once finished, she wiped her mouth delicately with the tips of her fingers.

The man leaned forward, passing her a nearly full bottle of amber liquid.

"Drink," he commanded.

"Could I have some water?" she croaked humbly.

He shook his head firmly, the pithy folds of skin around his neck overlapping. "Drink this."

Madison took the nondescript bottle from his callused, dirty hands. She was parched and in desperate need of some sort of liquid. The bottle went to her lips, the one consolation being that at least the alcohol would kill the germs that surely lingered there.

A breathtaking fire slid down her throat, hot tears springing forth to blur her vision. She wheezed, gasping for air. Involuntary shudders ran through her at the abominable taste. After the initial fire died down, though, the warming effect on her insides over-powered the nasty taste, and she quickly downed another swig.

Amused at her reaction, the fat man snickered, snatching the bottle back from her outstretched hand.

Madison waited for the huge man to get up and leave, but he didn't. He just sat there, scowling at her. It occurred to her that this could be Red Eagle himself, and her heart floundered at the grim revelation. My God! she thought, has Colt been after *this* grotesque monster of a man for the past ten years? The mere notion of Colt having to stand up to this man's menace was more than just a little frightening. Then again, didn't Colt say that Red Eagle was a half-breed renegade? This man certainly didn't resemble an Indian in any way, shape, or form.

Her eyes must have revealed the fearful, contemplative thoughts that were marching through her head.

"Don't worry your pretty head about him, Madison . . . he's a eunuch. Got me all riled up one day, and well, that's what happens. You may want to bear that in mind."

Madison's head snapped up in the direction in which she heard the voice. She strained her eyes into the darkness. The blood ran cold in her veins.

"Who's out there?" she squeaked, not coming across nearly as tough and confident as she would have liked. From her position she couldn't see an opening from the chamber, just several dark, recessed shadows along the wall.

The sound of slow footfalls on soft, gravel paralyzed her. The dark figure of a man in a hat crept out of the blackness, coming to stand between her and the inadequate yellow light of the candle. He was silhouetted against it, a shadow.

"The only man you need to worry about from now on, *sugar,* is me. I'm your man now. Colt's dead."

Madison cringed. Her gut lurched, and she thought she was going to be sick. He was lying. The son-of-a-bitch was *lying!* Her heart remained stoic, for she sensed that Colt was alive.

The figure began to pace. She fervently hoped he would move into the light—just enough so she could get a glimpse of his face. But she was sure she already knew who it was.

"If you want to remain healthy, and alive," he continued in the monotonous, harassing tone, "you'll do everything I say. And I do mean *everything*. You fight me, you'll feel the brunt of my temper, and I don't think you want that. I have a little treatment I use on escapees—try it and you're likely to find out what it is." He spun around, pacing in the other direction. "I heard you and Colt got married, for real this time. Isn't that sweet. Colt marrying a *whore*. I still have a hard time believing that one."

The emphasis he put on "whore" clarified everything for her. Sickeningly so. Terrifying, nightmarish chills ran down the length of her spine, creeping through her at the realization of who this man was. There was absolutely no denying it, no rationalizing at this point.

"Colt isn't dead," she hissed, the loathing evident in her voice.

For a brief instant she saw the glitter of sadistic eyes as he turned once again to pace in the other direction. There was a period of silence before he spoke. The eunuch sat between them, looking from one to the other with acute interest, smacking his lips.

"I'm speaking in terms of the final outcome. He *will* be dead when he shows up to claim you, which is part of the plan. We want him to come and pay us a visit. We're waiting. *I* want to be the one who does it. I've waited too long for this chance. He will die at my hands. He should have died ten years ago." The voice rose dramatically, as if he were performing in some cryptic Shakespearean play. "By bringing you up here, we are dictating that he follow . . . to his own death. You didn't think I would allow you to miss all the fun, hmmmmm? I'll let you witness your beloved's death. After, I get me a sweet piece of hoity-toity ass, all for my very own. Good deal, wouldn't you agree?" He laughed, low and menacing, spinning around on his heel to pause beside the flickering candle.

Madison's breath caught. She was unable to tear her eyes away from the gleam of small, black, marblelike eyes. She gasped, even though it was no surprise at all. Not really.

Garrett stood before her, the light playing shadowy tricks on his flat features. His expression was dark and brooding, his lips curling into a sneer as he assimilated her reaction with fiendish delight. Without warning, he strode from the tiny room, his footsteps echoing in the passageway long after he was gone.

"Garrett!" she cried out after him, but there was no answer. Madison turned all of her pent-up hostility toward the fat eunuch, her eyes sparking in contrast to her drawn, ashen complexion. The man had obviously enjoyed the entire exchange.

"Tell me," she spat out, "*who* is Red Eagle?"

Irritated with what he assumed to be her stupidity, he wrinkled a fleshy brow, motioning toward the exit with his thumb. Then, his knees snapping, he lifted the bulk of his frame to a standing position.

"Don't get any bright ideas about escapin'—the openings are all guarded." He scooped up her empty plate and lumbered toward the blackened doorway, turning sideways to wrench his girth through, and was gone.

Armed now with the knowledge that Colt was indeed alive, excitement began to build, as her heart pumped the blood back into her cold limbs; even her bare toes were beginning to feel like her own again. Madison's head was whirling with possible plots and maneuvers that would get her out of this predicament. She *had* to get out of here!

Though her body ached and she felt incredibly dirty, she was much more alert and positive now that she had eaten. There had to be a way she could sneak out of this place and disappear into the wilderness that she was certain lay beyond this cave. If nothing else, it was absolutely incontestable that she could outsmart every last one of these dimwitted clods. Once free—well, she would deal with that problem once they got to it.

A scraping movement echoed outside the gloomy chamber and her eyes darted expectantly toward the opening. Quickly, she ran her fingers through her hair, fluffing it, then wiped any dirt smudges from her face. She must look as alluring as possible under these circumstances. She had a plan.

Madison heard the bombardment of mumbled curses before she actually saw him. The homely hunchback entered the stuffy space, rubbing the top of his head, a pained expression on his face.

"Ow," he muttered. "Damnation, can't see a dang thing out there . . . don't ya believe in lights?" Turtle batted his buggy eyes in exaggeration, scanning the cramped room for the woman he knew was in there somewhere.

"It's not like I've got a choice, Turtle." Madison was the epitome of boredom, slumped against the wall, her chin resting on her knees.

"Ahhh-hah! There ya are! I'm not supposed to be in here, but I thought ya might be wantin' a little comp'ny. How 'bout it?"

He gave her a half-assed smile, his eyes bleary with the effects of alcohol. Stumbling back against the wall across from her, he grunted, sliding down into a sitting position, his legs wobbling like rubber.

"Wanna drink?" he offered, holding the bottle out to her, the brown, murky liquid sloshing around the bottom.

"Uhhh, no. But thank you anyway."

Madison smiled, the expression genuine once she caught a glimmer of silver strapped to his thigh. It was Colt's pistol; she was sure of it. How much of a challenge would it be to get that pistol away from him? She had long since worked free the cumbersome knot that bound her ankles, the blanket conveniently covering that fact.

As she studied the mop-headed boy-man who slouched across from her, her thoughts ran in circles. She was waiting for the right opportunity to make something happen. And she was getting nervous. Garrett could return at any moment, and he was the only one she truly feared. He was evil, his demeanor menacing. Madison had never felt comfortable around him, and now it was evident why. Colt's own brother—what would her husband do when he found out?

Turtle's eyes were focused on her breasts. Not that her baggy shirt revealed anything, but his imagination must have been working overtime. Coyly, Madison let the dirty wool blanket part, sliding down just a smidgen to reveal a creamy white thigh. She pretended ignorance of that fact. His gaze immediately lowered, a flame igniting within.

The next thing Madison knew, his lids were closed, his mouth hanging open in a yawn. This is even better, she thought smugly.

Waiting just a few more minutes to make sure he was definitely asleep, she crawled to her feet, treading lightly toward him. She was chewing her lip, her blood tingling as it raced through her veins. Every sense was attuned to her surroundings. Madison was bound and determined to get out of there.

Closer, Madison detected the soft snorts of his breathing, his hand jumping reflexively over the bottle of booze, then settling back down. She was practically on top of him when she kneeled down on all fours, extending one hand, very slowly. Her fingers closed around the ivory butt of the gun, gingerly pulling.

It wouldn't budge.

Confused, she bent her head down just a little to see what could be obstructing it, spotting a snap imbedded in leather. Pushing with her thumb, she kept her eyes trained on Turtle's face. When she unleashed the gun her hand gave an unwitting jerk—Madison gasped.

Turtle awoke with a start. His head rolled across the rock wall, first one way and then the other, his eyes crossing when he spotted her face so close to his own.

Madison cringed, cursing silently. Snatching her hand away, she leaned back on her heels as if nothing was amiss. Her heart was hammering a staccato beat, and she thought it would explode.

"I'm . . . I'm sorry I woke you," she lied, plastering a sweet smile on her lips. "I was just so . . . so cold. And you looked so . . . warm over here, I thought I would join you."

Turtle licked his lips, pushing himself erect. His eyes roamed over her hungrily.

Madison thought she might throw up.

"Oh, yeah?" he managed to grunt. "By all means, c'mere!"

He held his arms out, and she distastefully accepted the repulsive invitation, her eyes shut tight in a grimace as she snuggled within the curve of his neck. He smelled of old sweat and sour whiskey. She tried to breathe as little as humanly possible as his hands rubbed over her body, her flesh shrinking from his touch. Madison adjusted her position, snaking her arm around to try for the pistol from his other side.

Turtle quickly became irritated at her oddly restless movements. Finally, he grabbed a handful of her thick blond mane and hauled her head back, seeking her mouth with his own.

Her head caught in a vise, his lips came down wetly on hers, and she was unable to prevent her own automatic recoil. But he didn't seem to notice. Turtle only increased the pressure, pulling her closer.

Madison's fingers fluttered frantically, searching, touching, closing around the silky grip, pulling the pistol free. It was now or never.

Madison feigned fear, wrenching away from his possessive grip. "What's that?" she whispered, her eyes wide.

"I don't hear nothin'." He looked toward the passageway, then back, his eyes dark with lust. "You're hearin' things. Get back over here . . ."

He lunged for her again. She slid away, just out of his reach, the pistol concealed safely behind her back.

"There! Heard it again! You'd better check. I won't do anything unless I'm sure we won't get caught." Madison smiled prettily.

With a grumble, he pushed his deformed body up from the floor, stumbling several times before he reached the doorway.

Madison was on her feet, behind him in a trice. She raised her arm high above her head, crashing the butt of the pistol down on the back of his head with all her might, whimpering as if she were the one hit. Turtle expelled a groan with the impact, slithering to the ground in a heap. She looked at the gun in her hand. It bore an elaborate *C* engraved on the ivory handle, intertwined with roses.

Swiveling around, Madison seized her blanket from the floor and leapt over Turtle's limp form. Just as she lifted a naked leg to step through the opening, into an even darker and more ominous night, a shadowy presence blocked her exit.

Madison found herself staring into a pointed, mosquitoey face. Pale blue eyes narrowed into a suspicious glower, hands resting squarely on bony hips.

Pressing her body back against the cold rock, her eyes rolled heavenward. "I *really* don't believe this," Madison breathed, more or less to herself.

Chapter Thirty-Eight

Colt waited on the top ledge of a steep-sided cutbank, hidden within a dense thicket. Not more than thirty yards away was a plain, rundown shack, the wooden slats of the outside walls a weathered gray. The dim glow that emitted from the tiny, square window at the back had long been extinguished, the hum of voices, occasional loud curses, and raucous laughter from within dying out. A curl of smoke rose from the stone chimney. This was the notorious Hole-in-the-Wall, or at least what was considered a secondary domain, the primary one being in the central plains of the Wyoming territory. A disreputable and overrated hideout on the eastern slopes of the Wind River Range, this hovel was frequented by almost every wanted fugitive, thug, and brigand, at one time or another. Traditionally, it was a well-known retreat that connoted a measure of safety for its unsavory occupants.

No lawman in his right mind would come here to capture his prey, regardless of the circumstances; it would mean certain death for him and whoever was with him. That wasn't to imply that it hadn't been tried by many a glory-seeking sheriff or bounty hunter. But it always ended in a warlike exchange of gunfire and much bloodshed, usually with no good accomplished in the end.

Neither a lawman nor wanted outlaw, Colt's reputation as an unbested pistoleer on the trail of vengeance still barred his entrance into this shady haven, and his presence was certainly an invitation for a well-aimed bullet. Any man inside that cabin would likely shrink at the mention of his name if they stood alone. But strength came in numbers, and all of them together lent a certain boldness to their already reckless natures—and recklessness was far more dangerous than courage.

No doubt, there were probably men inside those thin walls who bore the scars of Colt's shooting talents, and would be more than happy to even the score, especially with the backing of half a dozen of their comrades. That was the problem, Colt thought, with his method of shooting to maim rather than to kill—it invariably left the instigator alive to try again; that is, if he was stupid enough.

Colt wasn't concerned with the danger. His every thought was for Madison and finding her at all costs. He would go to any lengths. Though to his knowledge he had never killed a man, he felt he could easily murder the men who had robbed him of his bride—and that was if they had treated her well. If, God forbid, she had been desecrated in any way, the fate of those responsible would be far worse.

Colt's plan was to ambush whichever unlucky soul ventured out into the night. That was precisely why he had established his post close by the outhouse—the most obvious place a man would go alone in the middle of the night.

Not only was the location malodorous, the stench wafting past on the occasional cool breeze, but his patience was running irritatingly thin. He wasn't an overly patient man as it was—he hated waiting for anything or anyone. He would much prefer to charge in, demanding what he wanted. But he was no fool. In this case, he had no choice but to wait, and that irked him.

Colt rolled onto his back, exhaling deeply, his wide-awake gaze fixed on the millions of sparkling stars in the moonless midnight sky. He had left his horse loosely tethered to a lofty pine in the valley a ways back and had traveled on foot up to this location. It was safer that way. He also left his light-colored hat with his horse, tying a bandanna around his head Indian-fashion to keep his hair and perspiration from hindering his vision.

It tortured him to think of Madison alone, at the mercy of the scum who had abducted her. Colt couldn't disregard the transparent clues that indicated that his own brother might be responsible, or at least have knowledge of what was being planned. Something wasn't right with Garrett. Colt had known it for so long now, he'd almost found himself ignoring the fact, hoping it would go away. Now, he was sorry for it. Lord, but Madison didn't deserve to be treated this way. He'd let her down. He should have protected her better. How could he have ever hoped she would be happy here, in another century with him? It wasn't logical; she had left behind all that was familiar, all her modern advancements. And for what? To be with a man who couldn't even protect her from the likes of the scoundrels who had taken her.

When he got her out of this Colt wouldn't blame her one bit if she wanted to go back to her own time. With a sickening feeling in his gut, he thought it just might be the best thing for her to do. It was the last thing in the world he wanted. But he loved her so very much, he couldn't stand it if she was unhappy. It would rip his heart out. Right then and there he decided, regardless of his own selfish desires, he would put Madison first, encourage her to do what was best for her.

The creak of dry boards swinging on worn leather hinges summoned his attention. Colt silently rolled back onto his stomach, his heart pumping rapidly, slithering slowly up the dirt embankment to watch. He inched with a crawl into a crouched position. Reaching into the top of his boot, a daunting Bowie knife was removed from its scabbard, the silver blade glinting with menace in the vague light.

A slouchy figure dressed only in crusty, baggy-crotched longjohns staggered up the slight incline toward the outhouse, a bawdy tune on his lips. His dark hair bushed out in clumps of frizz, a long handlebar mustache drooped below chubby cheeks. He was either half-asleep, drunk, or both.

With the stealth of a painted warrior, Colt moved in a low crouch, stepping silently, positioning himself flat against the side of the outhouse. As soon as he heard the warped door creak open, Colt was on him. His arm wrapped around the man's neck, pulling the bushy head roughly against his own chest. The knife was pressed firmly into the man's trembling Adam's apple.

His arms floundered helplessly, flailing back to grab at his attacker, desperate. His eyes bugged as he craned his neck to see, the glimmer of the silver blade no doubt catching his eye as it rose higher. The man stilled.

"Wha . . . what?" He tried to speak, but Colt efficiently quieted him as he dug the bare blade farther into the man's skin.

"Shut up. I'll do the talking," Colt whispered next to his ear, slow and deliberate. "I'm looking for a woman . . . blonde . . . beautiful . . . where is she?"

"No woman," he sputtered in a strained voice, still laboring to free himself.

Colt hauled his forehead back farther with a rough jerk.

The man gasped. "I . . . said I don't . . . know 'bout no woman."

"Think before you speak, friend. This knife is real slippery. It could slip just a little, like this. . . ." Colt sliced lightly against the goose-pimpled flesh, a single drop of dark blood springing forth.

The man flinched with a childish whine, his knees buckling. "Please! . . . don't! I'll do anything, just don't cut me!"

Colt loosened his grip just a tad, "You've got one more chance. Don't mess it up. A man by the name of Aussie, with an accent—along with a hunchback. They stole my wife, friend. I want to know where she is . . . *now*."

"Ain't no woman here, like I said." His eyes continued to roll up and over in an effort to see the man who had bush-whacked him.

"I'm no fool. You've heard talk. Tell me what you've heard."

Colt purposely let the man catch a glimpse of his face, and his bloodshot eyes widened dramatically with what appeared to be a combination of surprise and fright.

"Uhhhh, holy mother! You really *are* Colt Chase, ain't ya?" It was spoken as if he had first thought the wool were being pulled over his eyes.

Colt smiled without mirth, looking down on him with lazy eyes, dark and foreboding. His next words were rich with an unspoken threat, "Big mistake. Why would you assume who I was if you didn't know anything about a woman? Now tell me where she is!"

"Er . . . uh-huh, well, heard some talk, yeah . . ."

"Answer me!"

"Red Eagle has a new wom—"

"*Red Eagle!?*" Colt interrupted, the despicable name breathed through his clenched teeth.

"Yup . . . here earlier today. He said," the man winced, gagging, " . . . said she has hair like spun gold."

"That's her. Where? Tell me, dammit!" Colt yanked the man's head back again, the blade biting into his skin.

"Yessir! The old Johansson mine . . . up yonder." His arm flung up in an effort to point the direction. "Said somethin' 'bout her bein' delivered soon. Somethin' along those lines."

"Doing good, friend. Now tell me *exactly* where this mine is. And remember who you're talking to. When I come after a man, I don't miss, do I?"

"No! Nossir! Just . . . just over that south ridge, there be Blackbird Canyon. From this side, ride on through 'til ya reach a big clump of boulders—kind of a level part, that's the openin'."

"Good."

A twig snapped.

Colt's head shot back, just in time to see two burly men rounding the corner of the outhouse. They paused, apparently startled from their inebriated grogginess by the unexpected encounter. Things just might get a little tricky. At least their hesitation gave Colt the edge he needed to gain the upper hand.

Colt hustled the bushy headed man around by the grip on his head, the knife leading the way, his clumsy feet blundering across gravel.

"What the hell . . . ?" the biggest of the two blustered.

The other man, his mouth gaping, wrestled shakily for his pistol.

"Pete! Help," the hostage pleaded, his voice garbled by the pressure of the knife.

Colt hauled him backward and the man's legs kicked out, stumbling to follow.

"I wouldn't do that." Colt's eyes speared the smaller man of the two with cold steel. The man finally managed to obtain his piece, only to have it backwards in his hand, almost dropping it. He cringed visibly, freezing.

The bigger of the two advanced, his thick brows drawn together in a mean scowl, his lips a straight line across his pockmarked face. It didn't seem to worry him much that a knife was being pressed to his friend's throat. A hint of recognition flashed in his eyes.

"It's you! Kill the weasel, Jake!" he ordered with a growl, "'Twouldn't bother me a lick!"

"Damn it all to hell," Colt muttered with intense aggravation. "Three-toed Pete. This is all I need . . ."

With one lithe movement, Colt shoved the bushy-headed man into the other two, spinning to vault from the embankment. Two poorly aimed shots discharged into the air behind him. He cleared the low-rising scrub, landing on his feet, the heels of his boots digging deeply into the soft, tumbling soil. He could hear the grunt of the collision above, several grousing oaths, and then silence. They were coming after him.

In the next second he glimpsed three heads popping over the crest. Then there was another explosion, the bullet zinging past his ear. Too damn close. He dove headlong into the cover of the pine forest, rolling, coming up on his haunches with a pistol in his grip.

He took aim and squeezed off three shots successively. At least one hit its mark, effecting a beastly moan and the crunch of bushes. Another shot rang out just as he turned to retreat into the welcome darkness. A sharp pain exploded within his shoulder, hurdling him forward, extracting an involuntary groan.

The slam of a planked door, hushed voices, a few shouts, and the shuffle of footfalls on gravel filled the air above him. The little shack came to life. Colt rested behind the cover of a massive rock, but he knew he had to whip out of there, and fast. The overwhelming painful throbbing threatened to overwhelm him, reverberating throughout his entire upper body. He could feel the blood trickle down his chest and back in a wet stickiness, soaking his shirt.

Breathing heavily, he sheathed the Bowie knife and hastily faltered down the steep embankment, careful to remain within the cover of the trees at all times.

Safely gaining the distance to his horse, he collapsed into the tall grass, his head spinning, able to actually feel a bubbling from the gaping hole in his shoulder. Colt's energy was sapped. His chest heaving, his body was slick with sweat and blood.

He wasn't sure how long he had been lying there, but he knew he must force himself to get up. Grimacing, he pushed to sit up and removed his holster and shirt. With the aid of his teeth he began tearing his shirt in strips. The wound was bound as securely as he could manage alone, the provisional bandage nearly soaked with blood by the time he was finished. It was with a subdued satisfaction that he discovered that the bullet had passed completely through.

Woozy, he staggered to a nearby creek, frigid with spring runoff. He splashed his face and washed the already drying blood from his naked chest and arms.

Then Colt sat back on a rock, his head in his hands to get his bearings. When he finally rose, he slid his pistol into the waistband of his pants before mounting the black with only his right arm. He headed for the south ridge and ultimately the old Johansson mine.

Chapter Thirty-Nine

"And just where do you think you're going? Don't hurry off, we haven't had a chance to chat!" Lucy snapped sarcastically.

She was skinnier than ever, her face seeming longer and paler than usual, Madison observed.

Lucy's eyes lowered curiously to the pistol Madison held limply in her hand, but she was more concerned with the skimpy manner of the other woman's dress. Envy seethed through every pore as Lucy's gaze slid down over Madison's long, tawny legs, exposed under an oversized white shirt, clearly not her own. Damn her all to hell. Even with her hair a ratted and tousled mess and a dirty face, this blonde woman was *still* beautiful.

Madison exhaled through puffed cheeks, backed up against the stone wall, unable to retreat any further. As if with a sudden revelation, she raised the pistol, pointing it levelly at her adversary. Concentrating, she drew back on the hammer.

"Move away from the door. It's been fun—but hey, I'm leaving."

Lucy's thin lips spread into a mocking smile as she stepped sideways. She tripped over Turtle's lifeless form, glaring down with annoyance. "What's *his* problem?" she spat with disgust, jabbing him with her pointed toe.

"Drunk."

Lucy's attention reverted to Madison and the problem at hand. "You won't get very far," she taunted, "especially dressed like that. There are men posted everywhere, you know. Garrett is careful about those things."

Madison inclined her head toward the sorry specimen that lie in a heap on the floor. "Men like him?" she snorted. "I handled that jerk with no problem."

She wondered if she should tie Lucinda up. . . .

"So why are you dressed like a hussy, hmmmm? You and Colt get caught having a poke? Just between us, how was he . . . Ugghhh!"

Her sentence was never completed, as Madison's delicate, but effective, balled up fist smashed directly into Lucy's bony jaw. Her head reeled sideways and she stumbled back a few steps, slamming into the opposite wall before sinking into a neat pile next to Turtle, unconscious.

Madison's hand went to her mouth with a gasp, shocked at what she had just done. An outbreak of tingling pain bore through the offending hand and up her arm with piercing clarity. She frowned. "Ouch! Damn, that hurt . . . How in the world do men do it?"

Shrugging with the satisfaction of not having to tie Lucy up, she was quick to leave the closeness of the chamber, stepping through the timbered doorway.

The pounding of her own heartbeat seemed to ricochet from the steely walls as she made her way down the dark passageway. She blinked in an effort to see through the inky blackness, needing to feel the walls for support. She didn't even know if it was day or night outside, and she didn't care. One way or another she was going to get out and away from this horrid place.

Her feet were soundless on the hard-packed dirt. Winding through the maze of musty tunnels, she would occasionally chance upon fat candles placed for light. Unsure in which direction to go when the paths forked, she could only guess, finding several dead ends in the process.

Cautiously rounding a corner, she stubbed her toe on something cold and hard and bit back a yelp of pain. She bent down to grab her foot. Something squeaked, flapping, dive-bombing at her. Madison opened her mouth in a silent scream, waving her arms above her head frantically. Her eyes squeezed shut, she finally covered her head and dropped to her knees. A bat thumped against her several times, becoming entangled in her hair for a thankfully brief moment before disappearing in flight. Shivers of revulsion shook her.

Slowly, convinced the bat was gone, she stood up. Then, directly in the path before her, she discovered an old, corroded ore-car track. Madison followed its lead, winding around in a slight upward grade. Then the booming echo of masculine voices surrounded her. It was impossible to ascertain from which direction they came. In a panic, she sprinted toward a rusty orecar up ahead on the track and hoisted herself up and inside it. The metal insinuated its deathly coldness into her bare, exposed skin. She ducked, holding her breath, her heart racing. A rush of cool air swirled above her as two men tromped on past. Madison leapt out of her hiding spot, continuing onward.

A loud chorus of rowdy laughter and off-color conversation loomed around the next bend, and she suspected the opening to the outside was near. A lantern hung from a dowel above her head, illuminating her face in a yellow glow.

Peeking around, very slowly, she caught sight of three degenerate-looking types. They were leaning against the timbered entrance. Open darkness was beyond, fresh air and pine trees. Freedom.

What now? Madison chewed her lip thoughtfully. She frantically searched her mind for an idea, a plan to get her past those men. . . . Once outside, she felt confident she could lose herself in the wilderness. They would never be able to find her in the dead of night! She would much rather face the challenge of surviving alone in the mountains than that of spending another minute under the cruel thumb of Garrett Chase.

The pathway was littered with small rocks, and she bent to grasp one. Madison had played some fairly decent outfield as a kid, and she thought to see if her talent had persevered over the years. Pulling back her arm, she focused on the trees beyond, launching the "ball" over the men's heads. It crashed into the brush several yards from the mouth of the mine.

Madison anxiously stole a glance behind, for once again, there was that unmistakable crunching of fast-paced footsteps approaching.

The men's voices fell silent as their attention was riveted to the spot where the rock had hit. Tangled branches still swayed in the calm night air. It didn't seem as if they saw the rock, and she breathed a sigh of relief at that. But somebody was gaining on her from behind. . . .

"What the hell was that?" one guard asked in a raspy, hushed tone.

"Dunno . . . go take a look see."

"You go! Prob'ly an animal of some kind." Another pulled his piece, clicking back the hammer.

"Nothin' but a couple a yellow-bellied scaredy cats is all you two are!" the first spoke again, chuckling, but without much gaiety.

"Oh yeah?" they replied in chorus.

"*You* go see, then. Get yer skanky ass chewed by some animal. I ain't!" He thrust a finger into his chest.

"Me neither! 'Sides, may not be no animal at all. Could be that Colt feller . . ." The tone was low, cryptic, and for a moment the others didn't respond, just stared as if under some kind of spell.

Finally the first man said, "You two sure are sorry excuses for men. I'll go see. Ain't gonna let a man's legend scare *me* half ta death. If he was gonna shoot, he would have done it by now."

The man left the entrance and proceeded toward the bushes. Another followed a few steps. The third stayed put, his back toward Madison.

The footfalls were nearly upon her.

Madison tiptoed forward until she could have touched the third man. She prayed he wouldn't turn around. If he heard anything, it would have to be the wild thumping of her heart. Madison slithered softly out of the left side of the mine entrance, creeping, feeling for a position with her hands behind her.

Just then the footsteps to the rear materialized into a man, his tone ear-splitting in an angry echo.

"What the hell are you horse's asses doing?"

It was Garrett, and he was more than a little piqued.

"She's *gone,* goddammit! Find her or I'll take it out of your sorry hides myself! Do you hear me?!"

The three men, scampered back to their posts, fluttering around aimlessly, eager to do his bidding.

Madison didn't hang around to hear more. The pine needles and rocks poked and sliced at the soles of her feet. She didn't notice, determinedly scurrying down the slight incline beside the outer mine walls, off the rocky plateau and into the darkness of the woods.

Madison had no specific sense of direction, her only goal being to get as far away as possible. She would worry about where she was later. She tried to stay within the thickest part of the forest.

Yet that seemed to hamper her progress, forcing her to slow down as she assailed the rugged terrain, skirting the tangle of underbrush and saplings that were too thick to get through.

Her lungs and throat burned with exhaustion, but she refused to slow down even though she couldn't seem to draw enough breathe to run. Her heart beat uncontrollably. Charging relentlessly into a clearing, she found herself confronted by a sheer rock chasm, its drop black and bottomless. Oh God! What was she to do now? She threw her blanket down in exasperation, stomping her foot with a grumble.

Panting, Madison floundered momentarily, her eyes darting, pursuing every possible avenue of escape. She snatched up her blanket with a terrified moan. Brambles cut into her knees and fingers as she clawed her way up a narrow ravine. A muddy rock caused her to lose her footing, shooting her back down the steep grade. It was no use. She would have to backtrack a ways, possibly utilizing another fork in the natural pathway created by the trees.

Refusing to acknowledge the merciless itching stings that jabbed at the bottoms of her feet with every step, she tore back into the shelter of the trees, clutching the Peacemaker as a source of strength. Madison took solace in Colt's aura, confident in the presence of his indomitable spirit urging her onward.

An owl hooted from somewhere above, an eerie sound that bounced from tree to tree. Just then the ground began to shake with the thunder of approaching hooves.

Through the maze of trees, just parallel to the path she chose, rode a man. Cold fear gripped her, squeezing the air from her lungs. She had to stop. Dipping behind an enormous tree trunk, she trusted the low bower of limbs would conceal the whiteness of her shirt.

The rider continued on.

Madison sighed with relief, stepping away from her hiding place. But the threat of clomping hooves descended upon her again, rounding the bend in a rush. She feared whoever it was had spotted her, circling the alcove in an attempt to terrorize her into submission.

As soon as the rider passed for the second time, she waited just long enough for the sound to fade. Springing to her feet, she ran like a bat out of hell with everything she had in her. Every anger, every fear, every passion was poured into the vigor she felt at that moment.

But it wasn't quite fast enough. The horse was gaining on her, riding her heels, so close she felt the hot, snorting breath dampen the skin along her neck. Horse and rider passed, pulling up next to her. She darted to the side, into a cluster of trees. He swerved and was on her again when she exited at the opposite side. Madison cried out, refusing to look up at her pursuer.

Just as she began to change directions again, a thick, meaty arm circled roughly above her waist. Her breast was grasped brutally, the fingers digging into her ribs, hauling her up the side of the horse in a viselike grip. Madison kicked hysterically, screaming for all she was worth, lashing out—but to no avail. Seemingly with no undue effort on the part of the rider, she was easily hoisted atop the saddle, settled uncomfortably on her belly over humongous thighs. The pistol was wrested from her inflexible grip. She continued to writhe, her butt in the air, her head dangling, bouncing ruthlessly.

With a growl of frustration, she ripped at the strands of hair that dangled around her face, twisting about to see who had made the lucky catch of the day.

Madison met the plump smile of the eunuch, gazing down at her through heavy-lidded eyes, smug in his accomplishment. It was a while before Madison could catch her breath long enough to speak. She was forced to endure the bumpy gallop back to the mine in silence.

"Well," she cried out sarcastically between ragged breaths when the horse stopped, "it looks like you could be up for a promotion."

Chapter Forty

Colt's pistol was once again confiscated. It now lay atop a wooden crate in a far corner, the luster of blue steel reflecting the dim glow of the flickering candle beside it. Long shadows danced along the rock walls. Madison regarded the pistol glumly, trying her best to concentrate on Colt rather than the ridiculous situation she found herself in—again.

The fat eunuch had dumped her back into the arms of a waiting and infuriated Garrett. He now insisted she reside in the cell-like room he labeled as his own within the mine; the better to watch her, he alleged.

She was partially reclining on a slovenly pile of assorted blankets tossed into a cold, hard corner. Her wrists and ankles were bound more securely this time, the scratchy rope nipping into her skin and rubbing it raw.

Garrett and Lucy sat across from her on a rotten, holey, uncomfortable-looking wooden bench. Garrett's dark beady eyes were boring into her. He chewed nervously on his fingernails, most likely absorbed in some deranged aberration.

Lucy was rubbing her jaw, a sour look of contempt directed at Madison. She crossed her legs, swinging one continuously like a pendulum, the wilted flounce of her blue taffeta gown flapping with the movement. The three of them were alone in the fetid dampness of the chamber, its gloom cloying and depressing.

Though slightly bigger, it wasn't much different than the one Madison had occupied before.

"So, you don't appreciate the kindness your host has bestowed upon you?" Garrett broke the heavy silence, clicking his tongue mockingly. "You'll be happy to know that I've decided not to accommodate you with the special treatment I warned you about earlier. No . . . it would most likely kill your high-class ass," he paused, snickering, " . . . and I think I'd like to keep you alive a while longer. Maybe I haven't been amusing you as well as I could have? Is that it, hmmmm? It's my fault, of course. I should have provided more activities for you to pass the time." He spoke with menace, now picking his nails with a jackknife, his eyes occasionally lifting to hers.

Madison didn't reply. She merely issued a frosty glare, unaffected by his persistent needling. Ever since her recapture, Garrett had sermonized her into oblivion, his words now just antagonistic drivel that she tried to ignore. Occasionally he would touch a nerve, and fury would beat in her veins. But she would never let him see that, preferring to remain as cool as a cucumber, at least on the outside.

"I think after we're rid of Colt," Garrett babbled on, "we'll take a little ride on over to Outlaw Cave. Jesse and Frank are holed up over there. What with your charms and my genius, maybe we can get 'em to share a little of the profits from that job they pulled in Carbon. I hear it was a big one."

She closed her eyes, trying to shut him out. Frank and Jesse . . . God, wasn't that all she needed? An intimate tryst with Frank and Jesse James—what would her mother say to that?

"Do you know what I think?" Garrett placed a finger to his lips thoughtfully. "I think you need a little warming up. I think we all could use a little warming up!" His grin turned malevolent as he elbowed Lucy into action.

Madison froze at his words, slanting a narrowed glance toward the two. She would sooner die than let him see the fear in her eyes.

Lucy nearly slid to the floor at his unexpected shove. Gripping the bench for balance, she pushed herself up, standing before him in confusion.

"Well?" Garrett bellowed. "You a whore or not? Take your clothes off. Let's give Madison a little entertainment to pass the time."

Lucy went white. "I'm not in the mood," she stated glumly.

"I said, do it! Go on, Lucy, we're havin' some fun right here and now." Garrett's lip curled snidely. He took a swig of brown liquid from the slim, rectangular bottle that rested in his lap.

Lucy's mouth fell open. She widened her stance in protest, her hands on her hips. "I don't do shows, Garrett! And I ain't startin' now!"

"You will if I tell you to. Remember our deal? Now *do it!*"

Garrett's eyes shimmered, his outcry resonating from the impenetrable walls. Both women flinched.

"No!" Lucy refused to back down. That is, until he pulled his pistol, aiming at her midsection and cocking the hammer for that added touch of emphasis. Explicit worry settled on her face.

"You don't mean crap to me, woman, so don't think I won't kill your ass just for the sport of it. Better yet, you ever seen somebody gutshot? It don't kill you—not right away. A person dies real slow and painful like. How does that sound?" His gaze was cold and emotionless.

Lucy followed the barrel of the pistol with her eyes. Finally, mumbling under her breath like a spoiled child, she reluctantly slid the straps of her gown from her shoulders.

"That's more like it," Garrett continued smoothly, a lecherous blaze igniting within his black eyes.

Madison inhaled sharply. She cast a furtive glance at the woman who was disrobing at Garrett's feet. Something in the fluid sparkle of Lucy's eyes touched Madison. She actually felt sorry for the homely woman cast in Garrett's cruel shadow.

"Leave her alone," Madison hissed venomously, surprising even herself.

Garrett's smile faded. He rose from the bench slowly, drifting over to the blanket where he crouched before her. "I don't think you're in any position to be giving orders, *sugar*. Then again," he added, cramming the barrel into the soft flesh beneath her jawbone, "maybe you'd rather I started with you first, eh? I *know* you'll like my plans for you—in fact, I'm willing to bet you'll never want Colt again."

Garrett's gaze slid over her lazily, his lips spreading into a wicked smile as he dug the barrel further into her neck.

Madison's eyes were watering with the pinching pain. She tried to look away, pressing her cheek against the cool rock, coughing at the gagging reflex. Instinctively, her hands fought the confines of the rope.

Mentally, she began a lecture, convincing herself that this

wasn't going to affect her; she could detach herself from her body if she needed to, not experiencing any of the atrocities Garrett undoubtedly had in mind.

Clamping her eyes shut, she pictured Colt, pleaded with his image, begged him to find her. Please, Colt, can't you feel the beat of my heart? Follow the beat of my heart . . .

Somewhere, far, far away, she heard Garrett's voice . . . loud, yelling. Then a rough hand tore at her shirt, heaving her away from the wall. Buttons tore free, flying through the air, clicking as they hit the walls.

Madison's eyes snapped open with horror. Scratchy, hot hands with ragged fingernails were all over her breasts, squeezing hurtfully, pinching her nipples roughly between thumbs and forefingers. Garrett's flushed face loomed over hers, leering with perverted pleasure as his eyes raked in her naked beauty.

"I am married to your *brother*, for God's sake! Don't you have a shred of decency?" Madison grit out with all the loathing she felt inside, squirming away from his touch.

Garrett pinned her down, the bulk of him heavy, stifling. His eyes relaxed on her bosom, the mounting excitement evident in the rasp of his voice as he replied, "He's not my brother."

She realized Garrett was irrational. The most she might be able to accomplish would be to distract him for a few minutes. But anything was worth a try.

"You were raised together. He certainly regards you as his true brother. Colt would never do anything to hurt you. Why are you doing this?"

"You don't know what you're talking about," he grunted.

"Are you Red Eagle?" she persisted. "Did you murder your parents?"

"Shut up, bitch!" he screamed, his face contorted into a snarl.

Garrett swung his arm, backhanding her across the face. A trickle of blood oozed from her lip. Madison repressed a whimper, her watered gaze returning to him defiantly. Lucy blinked, then frowned, her eyes hardening considerably toward Garrett.

"I don't feel like discussing my life history with *you!* Understand?"

Madison could only glare at him, pity almost overshadowing her hate. But not quite. His black eyes flickered past hers and he straightened up to his knees, unbuttoning his dungarees.

"No, God, no . . ." She wasn't even sure if she voiced the words out loud. Her heart hammered, every beat a burning inside her chest, for Colt as well as herself. Her face turned away to the wall, she braced herself for what was to come, a silent prayer on her lips.

Lucy watched in horror, woodenly tugging her own clothes back on. She couldn't tear her eyes away from the man she had so willingly hooked herself up with. He was even more vile than she had originally thought! She certainly had known he was no angel—but did he really kill his own parents? Could it be that he was, indeed, the infamous Red Eagle, the very same man her beloved Colt had pursued these past years? Somehow, she'd just figured all this abduction crap was a prank that she thought mildly amusing at best. Especially when she found out that Miss Priss would be separated from Colt, giving that creampuff a good scare and a taste of the real world. Nobody was supposed to get killed—or hurt, for that matter. But Garrett was turning into a madman! Was he truly serious about killing Colt when he arrived to rescue Prissface?

The realization slapped Lucy full in the face, overpowering her, and she felt as low as low could get.

Madison's soft thighs were pried apart, extra painful due to her ankles being still bound. Garrett's coarse hands rubbed, stroking intimately as she fought back the hot tears that sprang to her eyes. Somehow angry at herself for allowing this to happen, she became overwhelmed with guilt. She shrunk into the wall, fervently wishing it would swallow her up.

With a sudden burst of energy, the battle raged again, and she fought him, her wrists straining against the ropes, toiling to close her legs. A lascivious snicker grated over her senses, making cruel fun of her futile efforts to free herself. His grasping fingers scoured, probed, and she moaned with disgust.

Madison's eyes flew open, sharply focusing on sympathetic pale blue ones. Lucy seemed to be reaching out to her with almost an understanding, a womanly camaraderie. Madison issued a silent plea for help, to make this atrocity stop! And for a moment it appeared as though Lucy moved closer, and would, if only she could . . .

Garrett grunted, positioning himself over her, his face red, his member jutting upward obscenely from its nest of black hair. As he lay heavily upon her, crushing her, revulsion swept over her in ripples. Madison couldn't stand it any longer. He would have to kill her first, she decided, just as she sunk her teeth deeply into his fleshy shoulder.

Chapter Forty-One

Knowing his black stallion was safely tethered to a tree, Colt hid behind a rock bank in the heart of Blackbird Canyon, parallel to the opening of the old Johansson mine.

It hadn't been the wisest thing to do, traveling over this rugged terrain in total blackness, without even the benefit of a decent moon. But Colt had no choice. He wasn't going to stop for any reason until he held Madison safely within his arms. The ride had been torture, as he had steadily gotten weaker. Sweat had poured off his face even though it wasn't hot, and he hurt. And he knew he was bleeding like a stuck pig.

Damn! How could he have let himself get shot? It was a stupid mistake; a mistake that could have been easily avoided. He should have drawn his pistol on the flighty one while he had a chance, blown that goddammed shooter right out of his hand. Now he was paying for his own softheartedness. Just because the man had looked like a dunce and had quaked in his boots didn't mean he couldn't shoot.

He had passed the mine maybe twice, the entrance perfectly obscured by the spiky shadows of tall pines against the night sky. Just as the canyon opened up to softer, rounder hills, he had spotted several horses and a single buckboard settled at the base, and he knew he'd found it.

Now Colt's eyes narrowed with viciousness as he imagined

Madison being carted to this place in the back of that wagon. Heaven help the men who had brought her here, for they would surely suffer for their deed. And if it was true that Red Eagle was the culprit, then years of pent up wrath would rain down on him—in torrents. Red Eagle had already robbed Colt's mother and father of their lives—the animal wasn't going to get a chance to do the same to his wife.

A couple of men were posted at the entrance to the mine, neither looking too dangerous in their current state of inebriation. One sat spraddle-legged on the ground, a whiskey bottle tottering loosely in his hand. The other stood, barely, his weight tilting against the massive timber that was embedded in the rock. He persisted with nervous glances behind him into the black opening.

Colt skirted the entrance with care, his rifle in one hand, his pistol in the other. He pressed his body flat against the rock and proceeded until he was directly around the corner from the men, his ears attuned to any conversation he might catch.

"Why don't ya relax? Sit a spell. Yer makin' me jumpy," one man said.

"Cain't. I might jus' go ta sleep if'n I sit. Red Eagle will surely have my hide if I go ta sleep. Did ya hear that scream a minute ago? I wonder what he's a doin' ta her?"

"Hell, same thing he does ta all the gals, I 'spect," the first one answered apathetically.

The tic in Colt's jaw tensed, pulsing with a raw fury. It took all the restraint he possessed not to barge around the corner and take them all by fiery storm, blowing every last one of them to kingdom come. But no, this situation required patience; he couldn't risk Madison's life that way. Red Eagle would most likely kill her without a remorseful thought.

Colt rounded the corner, his two weapons trained on the unlucky men. His eyes widening in mute alarm, the one who already stood went for his pistol; the other frantically scrambled to rise.

"You may want to try your luck with that shooter," Colt warned, his tone enough to stop them cold in their tracks; "then again, you may not."

He centered the rifle on the man who sat. Colt inclined his head, motioning for the other man to approach. Confused, wary, the man stepped closer. In one blinding movement Colt backhanded him. His head careened to the side and back, his body slapping against the rock with a sickening thump. Unconscious, he slumped across the portal.

"Whad ye go an' do that fer?" Aghast, the other man eyed his fallen partner, then Colt.

Colt merely lifted the revolver. The man gasped, cringing. With a humorless smile, Colt wiggled his forefinger, beckoning him forward.

"No! No way . . . !"

Colt shrugged, drawing the hammer back, casually aiming at the center of his forehead. The man made haste to rise. His eyes brimming with fearful anticipation, gingerly he approached, a meek whine driveling from his lips as soon as he was within range. Colt carefully let the hammer down. Then he hoisted the rifle above his head, crashing the butt directly into the second man's face. Blood splattered, sending him spinning like the first. He crumpled to the ground.

Colt wasted no time. He sprinted through the mountain opening and disappeared within its gloomy darkness. Hurriedly, but with a measure of caution, he snaked around corners, prepared for anything that might befall him. His shoulder pained him, slowly sapping his energy. But he disregarded the nagging, bone-wrenching ache, refusing to succumb to it. The emotional rage inside him was steadily mounting.

He heard a calliope of voices just around the corner. He paused, then boldly strode around the bend. Into a dimly lit corridor he appeared, confidence etched into his features, his jaw firmly set, his stance wide. His chest expanded with the roiling combustion inside. Four men inside were caught by surprise. They shuffled to their feet in a frenzy, clumsily grasping for their firearms. Nobody said a word; there wasn't time. All eyes went to the weapons Colt carried in his hands, holding them at bay, and their arms reached in cautious slowness.

"Where is she?" he grit out between his clenched teeth, a satanic amber glow glittering behind his eyes.

Suddenly, a crashing blow to the head from behind rattled Colt's senses. He whirled to meet his attacker, at the same time raising the barrel of the rifle head-level. The barrel clashed with a face, hurling the man sideways. Colt's vision blurred and he struggled to focus on the triple images of identical men dancing before his eyes. All four of the others took advantage of his temporary confusion, lunging onto his back.

He was quickly enmeshed in a tangle of limbs, grappling. Then shots were fired, ricocheting off the stone walls, and amid grunts and groans, bodies were sprawled on the floor.

A bear hug from behind loosed his rifle, knocking it to the hard-packed ground. White-hot pain shot through Colt's shoulder and he felt blood ooze and run in little rivers down his chest. With a torturous heave of his powerful arms, he broke free, whirling with a kick to the man's groin. The man went limp, crumbling to the floor moaning. Four men lay in a gruesome pile, and Colt spun around to welcome another adversary.

The cold steel of his own rifle barrel greeted his temple instead.

"Sure would like to be the man that bested Colt Chase. Yup. Surely would."

A snaggle-toothed grin hovered at his side, only inches away.

"A mighty cowardly way to do it—why don't you put the rifle away, step back, and we'll make it fair."

Colt shifted his gaze sideways to gauge his opponent. The man frowned, obviously contemplating the validity of what Colt said.

"No way in hell! You'd just kill me!" the man retorted defensively.

Colt's laugh was touched with irony. "I suppose you can't claim to have bested Colt Chase, now can you?"

"Shut yer mouth! Hand over that pistol. I'm taking ya to Red Eagle. He's expectin' ya, anyhow."

Colt obliged, slowly passing the pistol to him. The man plucked it from Colt's palm as if he were afraid he'd melt if he came into contact with Colt's flesh.

This little setback did put the advantage in Red Eagle's arena. But it wasn't anything Colt felt he couldn't handle. The downed men who lay strewn about the floor were beginning to stir, dim eyed as they watched the pair leave the room. Colt walked in front with his arms lifted.

Just outside the doorway loitered a mop-headed hunchback, trying his best to blend into the wall as Colt passed. Their eyes met. Turtle quickly averted his gaze, fleeing in the opposite direction.

"Boss? Got yer man, here!" The captor puffed his chest out arrogantly, unnecessarily jabbing Colt in the back with the rifle. They were approaching another opening off the main vein, an orange glow radiating from within.

"I've captured the Chase feller," he proudly announced again, his voice bouncing.

He nudged his prisoner through to the entryway. Colt stopped dead in his tracks. The man behind him slammed right into him, grunting as the butt of the rifle punched into his own gut. Colt's blood ran frigid—and then boiling hot. His eyes blazing, he slowly digested the activity inside the stuffy, enclosed alcove.

Chapter Forty-Two

"Damn you!"

Garrett's thundering howl of pain and the curse uttered through his clenched teeth shook the massive timbered beams of the mine chamber. Garrett's hands encircled Madison's neck in a deathly embrace, squeezing until her eyes widened in mute terror. Madison wheezed for air, watching his black marble eyes turn beastly red.

Lucy clawed at his arms viciously, "Noooo! You'll kill 'er, Garrett! Stop! Stop it!"

The mention of his brother's name resounding from the outer corridor put a halt to his barbarous actions. Rolling away from his prey, Garrett leapt to his feet, hastily buttoning his dungarees and pulling out his pistol. As an afterthought he reached up to rub his shoulder, easing the pain that Madison's teeth had so effectually inflicted.

Lucy's eyes lit up like a blue flame. Colt had arrived! Broad shoulders and all! She let her mouth drop open at the welcome appearance of the man she longed for, sighing at the glorious sight of his shirtless, virile form standing at the entrance of the cave.

Madison was prone, struggling to twist around. Snarled strands of hair clung to her face, wet from her tears. Her breath came in moaning gasps, not just because of her ordeal, but because she had heard someone announce Colt. He had found her! God, he had really found her! Her cheek pressed to the scratchy blanket, she cocked her head to see.

Her heart soared with hope, as she viewed Colt in the arched doorway—then dropped to the pit of her stomach when she realized he was at the wrong end of a gun. But the feeling of despair quickly dissipated when her eyes met his golden-brown ones. The murderous rage in his eyes melted as they reached out to her in comfort. She was aware of his gaze dipping to her indecently bared breasts and stomach and she cringed, disgusted that he should see her in this awful position. His dark brows drew together dangerously, his lips tightening into a white line—deadly. The corded muscles of his neck stood out and he flexed his fists angrily.

At last, his warm eyes found hers again, sending a message of assurance, promising. Madison swallowed dryly and examined him more closely. My God, all that blood! Dried blood streaked down his left shoulder and arm, to his glistening, dirt-smeared chest. An inadequate blood-soaked bandage dangled perilously. She knew, he was hurt by the pale, translucent look to his skin, and his face was shiny with sweat. The faded red bandanna wrapped around his head gave him the appearance of a crazed Indian. He wore his holster over just his bare skin, the sinewy muscles standing out all along his torso, swelling with every breath.

Colt's gaze shifted around the tiny room, and Madison could sense the workings of his mind as he began to devise a plan— a plan for escape.

That is, until he saw Garrett in the far corner. A pistol was aimed level with Colt's midsection and he wore a sickening smirk, taunting his older brother.

"Got yer man here, Red Eagle," the guard boasted yet again.

He tossed Colt's pistol to Garrett, and he shoved it into his waistband.

At the mention of Red Eagle, Colt's stunned eyes rapidly skimmed every nook and cranny in the cramped chamber. There was no one there except Madison, Lucy, the guard, and of course, his little brother, Garrett. So what kind of game was Garrett playing this time? Colt had been face-to-face with Red Eagle . . . This certainly wasn't him, and couldn't be the man who had killed his family.

"Heard you the first time, you moronic idiot," Garrett cried out, still angry for being interrupted. "Now get the hell out of here. Post yourself right outside the door in case I need you."

"Yessir." The snaggle-toothed one ducked out of the doorway and leaned against the jagged wall, Colt's rifle poised and ready.

At that moment Madison could only imagine the shock Colt must be feeling, the immeasurable hurt—and the confusion. That was the worst, and she could barely force herself to watch him. His face, etched in granite, turned almost soft, boyish in disbelief.

"Garrett!" he muttered vehemently.

"Come on inside, big *brother*," Garrett hissed, "time to face the truth." Garrett motioned toward the bench for Colt to be seated.

Madison unwittingly let out a little whine as she tried to use her bound arms to raise her body.

Ignoring all threat of aimed weapons, Colt instantly jumped to her aid, only to be stopped midstride, Garrett shoving in front of him.

"Just where do you think you're going?"

"Move out of my way you sonova bitch, or I swear—" Colt's fingers dug into his brother's shoulders as he made to move him aside. The cold barrel of the pistol dug threateningly into the hardened washboard muscles of his abdomen. The two men glowered at one another.

Colt heard the click of a hammer in front, the rifle cocking from behind as well.

"Sit down. *Now,* Colt! I'm calling the shots this time. Don't think I won't kill you."

Colt eyed him tensely, thinking, calculating. His grasp relaxed on Garrett's shoulders. He pushed away in disgust. Reluctantly, he sat down.

Lucy helped Madison into a sitting position, tossing a blanket over her nakedness. Madison gave the skinny woman a disconcerted glance, and Lucy's mouth tilted up into a slight smile. When Colt saw that Madison's immediate need was tended to he unwillingly and temporarily leaned back against the wall, the bench creaking under his weight.

Garrett paced, immensely enjoying his power.

Colt had never been intimidated by his little brother, and he wasn't about to start now. This show of power was doing nothing more than pushing his patience, already short, to its outer limits.

"You've got some heavy explaining to do, man. I think you'd better get started."

Colt fought to keep his temper in check. There was nothing more unsettling than what he had seen upon entering this room. His own stepbrother was attempting to rape his wife—it was difficult to tell if the act had actually been completed or was barely starting—regardless, Garrett had kidnapped her. For what evil purposes conjured within his unstable mind, Colt could only guess.

How could Garrett have gone completely insane and Colt not have noticed? It was inconceivable! Everyone had known about Garrett's eccentricities, but when did they become this malignant? What had happened? Was it something in his childhood? When did he turn so sour as to reduce himself to the life of an outlaw? Colt supposed none of that really mattered now—not now that he had taken the last step, surpassing all bounds by abducting Colt's wife. *That* was to be Garrett Chase's final, most calamitous mistake.

"*You*," Garrett grit, hunkering over, pointing a stubby finger into Colt's face, "do not tell me what to do anymore! Got that?"

Colt regarded him impassively. "So, am I to believe that you're Red Eagle? Do you really think I'm that naive?" Colt said with dry mirth, hoping to get a rise out of him.

"I am Red Eagle!" Garrett slapped his chest. "I have troops of men who are loyal to my cause. They cower in my presence. They would do anything for me, my every bidding!"

"Only because you terrorize them. Not because you're deserving of any respect."

Garrett was pacing again, stopping at Colt's acrid words long enough to shoot back an angry glance.

Feigning boredom, Colt folded his arms across his chest. He kept careful watch on the pistol Garrett carelessly shuffled from hand to hand. Colt was gripped with a horrible, debilitating sadness. The man he had grown up with and loved was evil, contriving to end the only worthwhile thing Colt had claimed in years—Madison. He somehow had always inexplicably known that Garrett teetered on the edge of sanity, so why hadn't he taken his intuition more seriously? Garrett was different; so different that after a while his behavior had been accepted as "normal."

And what about his wife? What she must have endured—and at the hands of his own brother! She must hate him as much as she did Garrett right now. Could he condemn her if she did? The dismay behind her big aqua eyes pulled at him like a giant magnet. And he hated himself for not wanting to look at her—not wanting to see the renunciation that might lurk there. Would she ever want him to touch her again?

"So what is this 'cause' you're referring to?" Colt asked.

"Money!" Garrett sputtered. "Lots of it! Anyone who joins my cause will find their own pot of gold. I promise riches and I deliver. Thousands of head of stolen cattle graze on Hole-in-the-Wall land, and the numbers will only increase. There's going to be a war, Colt. And I'm going to be on the winning side. The James gang, Big Nose George Parrott, and the Powder River gang are all banding together. No law man alive will be able to take us down. And that's a fact."

"Well, that certainly explains our cattle losses, doesn't it?" Colt replied quietly.

Garrett snorted.

"What does my wife have to do with all this? An innocent woman! I should kill you for what you've done—in fact, I probably will." His eyes hurled sparks along with the sanguinary warning.

"You're in no position to threaten, Colt. What you don't know, *brother,* is that I've been expecting you, wanting you come here. Madison was just the bait. A very pleasurable bait, I might add . . ."

Colt sprang to his feet, taking two steps toward Garrett, his look murderous.

"Sit down!" Garrett commanded, his voice quaking as the pistol jumped back up into position, but this time pointed at Madison. "If you don't give a damn about yourself, then think about her. You don't do what I say, she's the one who's going to get it!"

Garrett looked at Madison, then back to Colt, a malicious grin spreading over his face. "You were meant to die that night, did you know that?" He snickered. "But it backfired. It won't this time. And I think I'll keep Madison for myself for a while longer; that is, until I get tired of her. Besides, she owes me one, don't you, *sugar?*" He glanced in Madison's direction again, his voice cloying with a nauseating sweetness. "Remember the kitchen? I do." He laughed heartily at the vengeful look she gave him.

Colt frowned, his gaze penetrating Madison's for a clue. "What kitchen? What are you talking about?"

"Your *wife* and I had a little rendezvous a while back in the kitchen. She wasn't very receptive then—this time she will be, I guarantee." Garrett's tone was spiteful, and he raised his eyebrows at Madison.

Lucy stayed in her corner, afraid to make so much as a peep. She had never seen Garrett so vile, so inhuman. Every one of her nails were bitten to the quick.

Colt took a deep breath, becoming bored in earnest with this dramatic charade. His shoulder was paining him, and he really wasn't able to take Garrett seriously. He rubbed his face in weary exasperation. "Let's cut through the crap. What you're saying is that it was *you* who killed our folks, and you meant to kill me, too, but it didn't work out?"

"That's right, big brother. You catch on quick. It's only taken you ten years to figure it out."

"On the contrary, I believe it's taken *you* ten years to figure out a way to do me in, again," he shot back. "All bullshit, Garrett." Colt's eyes brightened, and he raised his chin in a defiant challenge. "You were only sixteen. You didn't have the balls to shoot anyone, let alone your own family. You seem to forget, I had Red Eagle in the circle of a hangman's noose once. If it hadn't been for a dozen of his cutthroat counterparts bombarding me from all sides, he would have been a dead man then. As it was, Bat and I barely escaped with our lives." His voice lowered. "I've seen and spoken to the scum, Garrett. And you're not him."

Madison was watching Colt intently, her gaze flying to Garrett in surprise. So he *wasn't* Red Eagle! Then who was?

Chapter Forty-Three

Garrett sobered, his eyes like large, round marbles. His composure was crumbling under Colt's scrutinizing gaze. He looked away, filled with frustration, wishing for once that it *had* been he who had done the filthy deed—anything that would offend Colt, wiping that pompous smirk from his face.

"*My* true family was dead. And I wanted to do in yours, believe me I did. If it hadn't been for the war your father waged on the Shoshone, my *real* family would be alive today!" His pitch rose dramatically, the guard hovering outside the doorway jumping.

Colt scowled. There was never a war waged on the Shoshone! It was an isolated incident—a small band of roving exiles out to win back their honor. Garrett knew that! Colt opened his mouth to argue but thought better of it, recognizing the wild look in those black eyes, knowing his brother was stepping over the edge, grasping at straws.

"I hooked up with Red Eagle when I was fourteen years old, Colt. He trusted me, treated me with respect!" His balled-up fist pounded his chest again. "He was like a God to me, taught me the tricks of the trade, rustling, robbing. I even went with the gang on a train robbery once—that was the time Ma and Pa claimed they were worried sick because I stayed gone for two days, remember?" Garrett gave a nostalgic laugh, scuffing the floor with the toe of his boot. "But they didn't give a rat's ass about me. I could have died at any time and they wouldn't have known the difference."

"That's where you're wrong, Garrett. Ma took you in like one of her own. There was no difference, not in their hearts."

"Shut up!" he bellowed, his voice resounding. "*You! You* were all they cared about! You were to get the ranch, everything, when they passed on. I was supposed to be their son, too, but you would have never known it."

"That's a lie. The ranch is half yours. You weren't treated any differently. You were just wilder. Matters weren't improved by your behavior."

"Red Eagle said I was crazy to put up with it! He said I could have the entire ranch if I wanted it. He worked it out. Only you weren't where you were supposed to be; you left your bedroom too quick. He messed up, couldn't find you, so he didn't kill you. . . ." Garrett trailed off softly, seeming to go within himself.

"I see." Colt chewed his lip, contemplating Garrett's words. He could kick himself for what was happening now. Somehow . . . he could have prevented all of this if he had only seen the emotional turns his brother had taken. Red Eagle had seen it and had taken advantage of it, molding Garrett to his own dastardly ways. Colt had always assumed Garrett's black moods were mostly due to their parents' murders, but he now realized the problems had begun long before that. Who could have predicted they would have resulted in something as twisted as this?

"So where is Red Eagle now?"

"Dead. Downed by a Blackfeet arrow a year ago. Shot square through the heart when he was caught stealing horses. He didn't usually join in on the fun, always had his men do the dirty work. That particular time he wanted part of the action. And he got it. . . ."

"And you carried on his legacy, is that it?" Colt finished for him, searching out the faraway look in his eyes.

Garrett nodded. "Proudly. Through me, he never died. I worshiped him, Colt . . . idolized him. He was like the father I never had."

"You had a father."

"No! Not a white man. Your father was no father to me. Red Eagle was blood of my blood. He understood me like no white man ever could."

"I'm sorry you feel that way. Our father loved you."

"Bullshit. All bullshit."

"So I've been tracking a killer all these years only to find out the key was right in my own house, with my brother?"

Colt was disgusted, mostly with himself. How could he not have acted on the vague suspicions he and Bud had harbored over the years—cattle missing, unexplained financial losses. Of course, they had never even come close to guessing at anything this devious.

"You could have killed me long before now; why haven't you?"

"It was only going to be a matter of time before you were downed by somebody else's bullet. Why incriminate myself when somebody else could take the blame? You're not God. It would have happened eventually."

Garrett smirked, taking two long strides to retrieve the whiskey bottle. He took a long swig, then dragged his mouth along his sleeve. Then, surprisingly, he flung it against the wall, shards of glass exploding into the air.

"But now, with your dear wife coming into the picture, and your wanting to settle down on the ranch—well, things are getting just a little too complicated. I need that ranch for cover, not to mention inheriting it outright once you're out of the picture. I want first pick of all your belongings. That includes Madison. Would have had all this nasty business taken care of in Abilene. Yes," he drawled with an evil grin, confirming Colt's suspicions, "my boys are rustling down in Kansas. And one of 'em had instructions to pick you off like a tin can from a fencepost when you arrived in Abilene. Only Madison put a stop to that little plan—"

"She certainly did," Colt interrupted, gazing at his wife with a wink of confidence.

Madison couldn't restrain her tongue any longer. Colt's death had been devised by his *own brother!* It was almost unthinkable!

"So it *was* you! The sniper in Abilene is working for *you?* You're despicable!" she spat. "You deserve to die just like the legend says you will, hanging from a tree for cattle rustling! No, you deserve worse than that—"

"You're delirious. Lucy, shut her up." Garrett brushed her off.

Madison wouldn't have it. Her eyes were spitting fire; it was like a new life descended over her, rejuvenating her. She straightened against the wall as best she could.

"That's right, Garrett! You've only awhile longer to live. You're going to go by way of the hangman's noose."

She could just kick herself for not having the insight to tell Colt of Garrett's supposed destiny! She had carefully recounted everything else about the legend in the history book—but somehow, Garrett's future had slipped her mind. All of this kidnapping business might have been avoided if Colt had only known and confronted Garrett earlier.

"Madison . . ." Colt was shaking his head, his brow deeply furrowed, trying desperately to get her attention. But to no avail. Her fury was unleashed, and he didn't think he could stop it even if there weren't two guns trained on him.

Garrett was eyeing her like she had completely lost her mind. "You think I'm full of it? Well, don't! I'm from the future, Garrett, the year 1993 to be exact. I know exactly what is going to happen to the entire ranch. And you, my friend, are destined for hell!" Madison bit out the last words with relish, immensely enjoying the confused expression on his face.

"What's wrong with her, Colt? What is she, some kind of witch or something? I always thought she was strange. Shut her up . . . or I will."

Colt shrugged, a queer smile lighting his face. "Can't. When she gets to going nobody can. I'd listen to her if I were you. She knows what she speaks of."

She realized that Garrett was caught off guard by her insistent and irrational tirade. His eyes were glazed and bleary with alcohol and he seemed to be losing his concentration. She spouted off endlessly, mostly to draw his attention away from Colt, aware that it was only a matter of time before he gained the advantage. Her hands were not idle beneath the concealment of the blanket, either—she had managed to work free her wrists and was at that moment manipulating the ropes that bound her ankles.

"So what now, Garrett?" Colt asked, shifting on the uncomfortable bench. Slowly, his hand was lowering inconspicuously, waiting for the proper opportunity, his fingers nearly brushing where the Bowie knife remained sheathed within his boot.

"You must die, of course," Garrett answered offhandedly with a frown, as if he were deciding what to have for dinner. "In front of your wife would be ideal."

Madison's eyes darted to Garrett, then to Colt, the cold fingers of fear clutching at her.

"We should have a little fun, first. Maybe you'd like a last request? Hmmmm?" he slurred with a chuckle. "Let me see, what would any red-blooded man like to do to his wife if he knew he were going to die? He would like to give her a poke, am I right?"

Unexpectedly, Garrett strode over to Madison, jerking her to her feet with a bruising grip to her upper arm. Madison let out a whimper, sure her arm had been pulled from its socket. Instantly, she kicked free of the loosened rope about her ankles. To her embarrassment, she lost her blanket. The baggy shirt, slit up the front, was all that covered her.

Colt leaped to his feet. The snaggle-toothed guard was right behind him. Garrett spun around, pressing the barrel of the pistol into Colt's gut.

"Easy, brother. Real excited, huh?" Garrett smiled, mistaking Colt's intentions. "Go ahead, poke your wife."

To Madison's complete astonishment, Colt sauntered slowly toward her, his eyes dark and smoky. His gaze settled over her and he took her into his arms. Madison couldn't help but bask in his incredible warmth, his tenderness, melting into him until she thought surely she'd died and gone to heaven.

"I just might do that . . ." he crooned into her ear, and her eyes shot open in surprise.

Garrett's wicked snicker could be heard directly behind them. Colt's arms were around her possessively, and he buried his face into her neck, nibbling softly. "Could we have a little privacy, Garrett?" He was breathing into her hair, his arms like steel bands crushing her to him.

Madison was at her husband's mercy, and in a quandary. What in the world did he intend to do? Certainly he wasn't serious about . . . making love to her right then and there! He felt absolutely wonderful, and there wasn't anything she wanted more than him—but not now!

"Are you joking?" Garrett tipped his head back in uproarious laughter, staggering back a few paces. "I'm no fool. This is the deal—I watch. I'll take sloppy seconds this one time, since it's going to be your last time. Mighty generous of me, don't you think?"

The guard leaned into the doorway, licking his lips in anticipation of the show, his eyes glittering brightly. Lucy had all but made herself invisible, not uttering a single word, huddled in a far corner.

Colt hesitated. Garrett hadn't fallen for his privacy suggestion. He hadn't really thought he would. His mind raced, grasping for another plan. Then, turning, his face loomed over his wife's for just a moment before his mouth crushed down on hers in a heady kiss. He trailed kisses along her neck, his lips nibbling at the soft skin of her throat.

Madison didn't comprehend what was happening. Surely Colt wasn't serious! Her hands automatically balling into fists, she pushed feebly against his chest, while his tingling kisses made her weak all over again.

"Fight me, dammit!" he whispered harshly against her ear.

"Uh, what . . . ?" she mumbled back.

"No!" he hissed. "Don't talk . . . just fight, push me away for God's sake!"

Oh, hell! He wanted her to struggle—but my Lord, what did he intend to do . . . ?!

Shaken from her lethargy, a burst of energy took hold. Frantically, she beat at his chest, screaming for him to release her, wriggling from his grasp. Fresh blood stained her hands and the front of her shirt . . . Colt's blood. He lunged for her arm in a pinching grip, yanking her back.

"Where do you think you're going, bitch?" His voice was gruff, but she didn't miss the wink just before his hand slid down to close over her buttocks, thrusting her to rub against his groin.

With another deep breath and a little screech, she twisted within his arms, accidentally butting her head against his chin. He grunted, grabbing a handful of her hair, jerking her head back to receive the kisses he was bent on delivering to her throat, moving lower.

Garrett was obviously amused. His eyes were riveted to the spectacle before him and he didn't seem to be paying attention to anything else.

In a final explosion, Colt allowed Madison to wrestle free. Clasping the front of her shirt closed, she stumbled back to the wall. He lurched for her. She ducked, slipping around him easily, her feet light as she skipped to the other side of the room.

"Feisty one, isn't she?" Garrett laughed thickly, his pistol relaxed, slumped in his hand.

The guard moved back just a little, his beady eyes roaming lecherously over Madison, then returning to Colt.

In sudden drunken revelation Garrett shouted, "Hey!" He stood up. "What the hell happened to her ropes? She was tied . . . !"

Madison shifted her course, aiming toward the forgotten gun on the crate.

Colt reached for her, purposely missing, detouring. Much to the guard's stupefaction, he snatched the rifle out of his flimsy grasp and crashed the butt directly into his face. Shock, not to mention agony, contorted his features. The guard touched his bloodied and bent nose in total amazement before he slumped to the ground.

Madison bounded for Colt's pistol, only to run right smack into Lucy. Both women gripped it tightly, neither one endeavoring to let go. Madison pulled, attempting to wrangle it free. Lucy yanked it back viciously.

Colt spun around, twirling the Henry with a rapid cocking motion, gracefully taking aim at Garrett. But his injured arm was stiffening, the soreness extending into his good arm. It took its toll, slowing him.

Chapter Forty-Four

Garrett took aim at Colt's head with his own pistol, cocking, just as the barrel of the rifle rose.

"Drop it, Colt," he breathed thickly.

He hesitated a moment, then the clatter of steel and wood struck the packed dirt floor. Madison and Lucinda, both steadfastly bent on possessing the Peacemaker, held tight. They kept their eyes riveted on Garrett, dreaded anticipation filling their eyes. The man on the floor stirred. Whiney moans filled the deadly silence of the oppressive room.

"Real tricky . . . but it didn't quite work, did it? Lucy! Get that dammed thing out of her hands!"

Garrett motioned for Colt to move away from the downed rifle. He was slurring. He wasn't thinking clearly, and it showed by the uncertainty in his eyes. It was a major mistake when he left the pistol in the open as he had.

"Give-it-to-me!" Lucy whispered, tight-lipped, her eyes wildly shifting from Madison to Colt to Garrett, then back.

"No . . . ! You let go!" Madison responded angrily with a forceful jerk.

"I'll kill her, Colt! Tell the bitch to let go of the pistol! *Tell her!*" Garrett blared, obviously fighting the befuddling effects of alcohol on his wits.

Lucinda gave the final yank, and with a gasp both women lost their balance and tumbled to the floor. A mass of entangled hair and skirts, legs and arms flailed to the beat of high-pitched shrieks. Rolling to her feet, Lucy stumbled a few steps before steadying herself against the wall, panting, the pistol in her trembling hands.

Madison climbed slowly to her feet in defeat, the shirt clutched closed in front of her. She brushed the hair from her face. Colt was eyeing her, making sure she was all right, managing a hint of a smile, and she responded in kind.

"You two are making it real hard to be civil. I have a mind to get it all over with . . . right now. Let the both of you go out of this world together." Garrett's mouth twisted cynically. "Lucy, keep the blasted gun on 'em. Do you think you can handle that? Huh? Between the two of us we *may* be able to keep them under wraps!" He shook his head disgustedly when he spotted the downed guard, conscious but leaning against the wall. His eyes were closed, mouth agape, in an effort just to breathe.

"Damn . . ." Garrett began to pace again.

Lucy watched him closely, unsure what he might be planning in that devilish head of his.

"Ohhh, to hell with all of you! I'm sick of the games! Let's just end it now!" Garrett's voice boomed. He swiveled to face them, his teeth clenched, his arms extended, taking aim.

Lucy gasped.

Madison screamed.

In the breath of a second, Colt understood Garrett's grim intention—and that he was serious. He was snapping. Looking down the dark barrel of the pistol, he watched as Garrett's stubby finger began to squeeze the trigger.

Like a flash, he threw his body blindly into Garrett's, gripping his throat, knocking him to the ground in a mélange of grunts and groans. A searing agony shot through Colt's shoulder at the reckless movement.

The pistol fired, and a bullet zinged only inches over his head as they wrestled.

Madison held her fists to her ears long after the deafening echo of the shot. Her mouth opened in a whimpering scream as she helplessly watched the two men scuffling on the floor. Blood oozed from the bandage on Colt's shoulder, running down the groove of his spine. Colt was the bigger of the two, but Garrett was heftier, thicker; it was difficult to tell if his girth was made up of muscle or fat.

Another shot was fired. Both women screamed as the bullet ricocheted around them in a threatening dance. Garrett managed to dig the barrel deeply into Colt's ribs. Now he was trying to maneuver the trigger.

Lucy squinted her eye, attempting to take aim at the two struggling combatants. Madison leaped at her to pull her arm down.

"Get back!" Lucy screeched, her eyes wild in agitation as she shook off Madison's hand with the flip of her elbow. "He's going to kill him!"

"Noooo! Lucy, please!" Madison pleaded. "Don't shoot Colt!" She touched her again and Lucy briefly turned the gun on her.

"Get away, I said! You don't know what you're talking about— just let me do what needs to be done, what should have been done a hell of a long time ago!" Her hands were shaking. She trained her sight back onto the pair, moving from side to side as they rolled, shifting.

The guard slowly pushed himself out of the doorway, crab-style, his heels digging for traction in the dirt. As far as he was concerned, this wasn't even his fight, and he'd be damned if he was going to get himself killed over it.

Another man came along just in time to take his place, one with piercing blue eyes and a bounty of dark blond bearded stubble. He hastily scooped the rifle from the floor.

A deafening blast and a yellow flash leaped from Lucy's pistol. It sent her recoiling, flat against the wall behind her.

"*Noooo!*" Madison moaned, running to drop beside the now limp forms on the floor. Her hands were instantly all over the one who rolled off to the side with a guttural groan. Her thoughts in a vigorous turmoil, she stared down into the lifeless eyes, a single clean bullethole puncturing his right temple.

Shuddering, she looked away.

Colt's hair was plastered to his face in sweat-soaked strands. A sheen of perspiration coated his body, his chest expanding with every breath. Madison pulled the bandanna from his head and began to mop the moisture from his face. He pushed himself up to sit. For a long, silent moment he stared at his brother. His elbows bent over his knees, he rested his forehead across his arms with a tortuous sigh. A mixture of emotions flooded through him: disbelief, realization, despair and, finally, exhaustion.

The six-shooter was sent clattering across the floor. Madison and Colt both shot a look at Lucy, who had plopped herself down against the wall, her legs spraddled, and was wiping a single tear from her high-boned cheek with the back of her hand.

Madison caressed his back in an offer of comfort, "Colt," she breathed, "your arm . . . it's bleeding. Are you okay?"

He nodded. "Yeah. I'm fine." He raised his head, tilting it back with a grimace, the muscles of his neck resisting with their tightness. His arms went around her and he held her close. The golden brown light in his eyes flamed when he looked at her. "What about you? Tell me the truth."

The sultry heat of his body permeated hers with such comfort that she never wanted to let him go. She reciprocated with a fervor she hadn't felt in a long while. A subtle, not unpleasant odor of sweat assaulted her senses, and she gratefully planted a kiss on his naked shoulder, savoring the salty taste of his skin.

"I'm just fine . . . now." She smiled, her eyes shining with all the gratitude and love she felt inside.

"Are you absolutely sure?" He gazed down at her intently, skeptically.

"Yes!" she insisted. "I knew you would come. That's what kept me going. I'm just worried about you." Madison's gaze flitted to Garrett's lifeless one, then back to Colt. She detected an odd spark of old remembrance in his eyes.

"He went mad, Madison . . . just berserk . . ." he trailed off to a whisper.

"I know. I'm so sorry, Colt." Madison hugged him tighter, wishing more than anything she could somehow erase the pain he must be feeling right now.

"We're not out of this mess, yet, sugar." Colt inclined his head toward the doorway, pushing his sore body up from the floor and helping her at the same time. "I lost count of how many men I scrapped with before I got to you. It's anybody's guess whether they'll let us walk out of here. Call me a pessimist, but I don't think so. And I wouldn't be surprised if they're heading this way right now."

Quickly, he gathered his weapons and reloaded. He holstered one pistol and carried the other. Taking a firm hold of Madison's elbow, Colt led her to the doorway.

She hesitated, turning to look at Lucy. The skinny woman looked so destitute, lying in a heap next to the wall.

"Wait . . . what about Lucy?"

Colt frowned, tugging her arm, "What about her?"

"She saved your life."

Colt stared at Lucy for just a moment, determining what should be done. "Lucy?" She lifted her head, focusing her red-rimmed eyes as if she had never seen the two people by the door before in her life. "You want to come with us?"

Lucy shook her head, as if it was the oddest question. Shifting her gaze downward, she again retreated into her own little world.

"Let's go. She'll be fine."

Together they left the gloomy, cell-like room, edging into the darkness of the corridor.

A figure stood just outside the door, waiting, startling them both. With lightning speed, Colt gouged the pistol into the intruder's throat, cocking it.

"Don't shoot! It's . . . it's alright! I'm not armed, mate. I believe this is yours." He backed against the wall, one hand splayed in the air, the other extended to return the rifle.

"Aussie! Is that you?" Madison sighed with intense relief, her eyes straining in the darkness.

"Yup, it's me, lassie," he replied shakily just as Colt snatched the Henry and levered it beneath his left arm. "I was just goin' to show you the best route for escape, so you don't have to meet up with all the others. Follow me?" Aussie's eyebrows shot up. He didn't want to turn his back on Colt, not caring for the yellow flare in the man's eyes.

Colt glanced at Madison in puzzlement.

"Aussie?" he addressed the man again, "Aren't you the one who abducted my wife?"

Colt's tone alone was a threat, and Aussie nodded hesitantly.

"It's okay, Colt! Really! He didn't want to. If it weren't for him, I'd be a lot worse off than I am now."

"I don't think I'm quite ready to leave," Colt announced with conviction. "I believe I'd like to pay a visit to the others, just to pass on some good cheer, if you get my meaning."

"Colt! Please, let's just get out of here!" Madison pleaded.

"The lassie's right, mate. You'd only be endangering her. I can get you out of here."

"Wait just a minute. How do I know you're not going to lead us right into a hornet's nest?" Colt wasn't the least bit convinced of the man's good intentions.

"Oh, I wouldn't do that. The rest of 'em are a'waitin' toward the front entrance. Heard the shots, they did, and I offered to go check what was happenin'. They think Garrett did away with you. . . . I'll show you another way out. Feel sorry 'bout the lass. Would like to make it all up to you." Aussie's voice died off uncertainly.

"Let's go," Colt commanded. "If you're dropping a load of crap, man, it'll be the last regret you ever have."

"Don't worry none."

Aussie broke into a brisk pace ahead of them, descending it seemed, into the bowels of hell. He snatched up a lantern, but its meager light hardly penetrated the choking darkness. At times they needed to crouch low just to squeeze through the tight, narrow passages, twisting, turning.

Madison sucked the stale, musty air into her lungs—the familiar claustrophobic feeling wrapping its oppressive arms around her. Absently, she clutched Colt's arm as she followed, stepping lightly, the sharp rocks digging painfully into her bare feet.

Little by little, it seemed brighter, until an actual glimmer of natural light beckoned to them from just ahead. Rounding a craggy corner, the mine opened wide to a breathtaking vision.

The early pinkish-gray of dawn settled over the surrounding mountains, a morning fog blanketing the tips of evergreens. The air was cool, refreshing, greeting the threesome full in the face. Greedily, they inhaled the wonderful crispness into their starving lungs.

Aussie faced them. "Red Eagle . . . is he dead?" he asked curiously.

Colt nodded, drawing Madison close with a protective arm around her waist. He holstered his pistol.

"You two might want to travel down to the base." Aussie pointed to an all-but-invisible path that wound into the cover of trees, "then around northwards is the main opening . . . just stay under cover. I best be heading back before I'm missed. I'll tell 'em the two of you are dead just to stave 'em off for a bit." Aussie ducked back into the mine.

"Wait . . ." Madison called out after him. He stopped, turning to face her. "Thank you."

"You're quite welcome, lassie. I'm just sorry you had to be here at all."

"Aussie?" It was Colt. "Would you mind doing one more thing? See that Garrett—Red Eagle—get's a proper burial, wherever you think he might like to be."

Aussie nodded his understanding. "Certainly, mate. I'll do that.

S'long!" He saluted, disappearing into the musty blackness. He was smiling, happy to no longer have to worry about Garrett now that he was dead. The man had been nothing but a thorn in his side ever since he came to work at the Triple Bar C.

Book Three

Chapter Forty-Five

Madison squatted to one knee, her hand reaching to smooth over the velvet muzzle of the new colt. Innocent, liquid brown eyes tugged at her heartstrings, regarding her warily. It shied, sidling close to its mother. She smiled in understanding.

"It's okay, baby," she spoke softly, "you don't know me too well now, but you will. We're going to be the best of friends, you'll see."

Straightening, she led the pinto out of the broodbarn and into the fenced pastureland. The colt followed obediently, its wobbly legs taking two steps for its mother's one. When Madison stopped the colt was quick to nuzzle up to its mama's flank for security. She turned the mare loose to graze. With an appreciative toss of a proud, sleek head and a snort, the horse trotted off, the colt close on her heels.

Madison folded her arms, rubbing her hands contentedly along the softness of her flannel shirt. A lump formed in her throat as she watched the incredible beauty of the two animals as they joined the other horses. The colt was the spitting image of its mother— rich cream splashed with a deep brandywine chocolate.

Colt had given her the foal as a wedding present just a week ago, not long after it was born. They had been back at the ranch for a month, and Madison felt more gratified than she ever had in her life, very much at home on the sprawling Wyoming acreage. Married life definitely agreed with her. She could think of nothing else that would make her happier—unless, possibly, if her life here with Colt could be transformed into the twentieth century. She did miss her mother and brother, and at times even longed for the hustle and bustle of the travel agency and her friends there.

The summer nights were filled with a hot passion like nothing she had ever imagined before Colt. His days consisted of ranch business, although he rarely ventured out onto the range to work now that Madison was there. Lately, he was occasionally needed to assist in the installation of the brand-new barbed wire fencing, which was a time-consuming chore, and he took Madison along for the ride whenever he could.

Her days were never boring for there were always things that needed to be done, and she was eager to learn every facet of running a ranch, even it was in the nineteenth century. It was funny, but she never had figured herself to be a ranch owner, and yet, that was essentially what she was, the wife of one of the biggest cattle barons in the Wyoming Territory.

Colt hardly mentioned Garrett anymore. Even when she tried repeatedly to tell him about Garrett's being destined for a probable hanging, he would cut her short, sometimes to the point of anger. Her persistence seemed to irritate him. He would assert himself, insisting she forget the past and live in the present—always with an ironic smile on his lips, of course.

Madison, on the other hand, felt he was repressing his feelings and wanted him to talk about it. According to her, that mask of rigid tenseness he wore at the mention of Garrett's name was actually a soft spot of vulnerability. Invariably, she ended up dropping the subject, totally frustrated. It was obvious he wasn't going to bend to her way of thinking.

Rosannah, Bud, and Emmy had been shocked, to say the least, when they learned the truth about Garrett's double life, and especially about his untimely demise. They knew he had long been a troubled man and his activities weren't normal, but had no idea they had grown so out of hand. It had been a sad time around the ranch house for a few weeks, but soon the pieces had fallen once again in place, a semblance of routine returning to their lives. All were thrilled to have Colt and Madison back together, happily married—for real this time.

Colt's shoulder was healing nicely as well. The medicinal waters at the hot springs they had stopped at on their way down from the

Johansson mine had worked wonders. And later, Rosannah had handled the injury with the know-how of a country doctor.

Emmy was springing from her shell, blossoming into a vibrant beauty. Her high peachy cheekbones highlighted her flawless complexion, and Madison told her endlessly that her classic beauty would be very much appreciated where she came from, and especially in places such as New York City. Emmy's loveliness was like a fashion model's, Madison told her.

Then one day Emmy had begun to pester Madison to take her there, her request escalating to a fervent entreaty. Madison had decided to keep her mouth shut from then on. Besides, more than a few of the ranch hands had taken notice of the young girl, and even Zak had shown a sudden interest. Now young hands from neighboring ranches dropped by, bashfully knocking on the front door with red faces and hands full of wildflower bouquets.

Emmy wasn't one to get excited, though. She was holding out for that rich, handsome rancher, one who would sweep her away to the far, exotic reaches of the globe at the drop of a hat. Madison wasn't too sure about the traveling rancher part, but she hoped Emmy would get what she wanted from life, especially when she remembered that the hotel clerk had said that Emmy had ended up a spinster.

· One day Aussie had wandered onto the ranch, his saddle over his shoulder, requesting a conference with Colt. He had uneasily turned his hat in his hand when he spoke. Colt had eyed him levelly under his straight, thick brows, his jaw taut with naturally expected suspicion. Even though this man had ultimately helped them to escape what could have become an even nastier situation, they hadn't forgotten that he had been an accomplice to Madison's abduction. And Madison had known Colt wasn't about to take any chances.

Aussie had been full of apologies, his bright blue eyes lifting to gaze sincerely into Colt's piercing brown ones. He had explained that he wanted the opportunity to make things right—to have an honest life as one of the cowboys on the Triple Bar C. It was Madison who had insisted that Colt give him another chance and Colt had finally agreed. Aussie had thanked them both at least twenty times before he took off for the bunkhouse with his tack and gear, nearly shaking Colt's arm out of its socket.

Perhaps the most unusual event of late had been the unexpected arrival of Lucinda Beak. One sunny afternoon, astride a swaybacked pack mule that definitely looked as though it had seen better days, Lucy had plodded up toward the main house, her body pitching to and fro with the mule's bumpy gait. Lucy had been in sorry shape, dehydrated and nearly starved to death. It was Madison who had insisted they nurse her back to health— at least until she could fend for herself and be on her way. Even Rosannah, though certainly not approving of the woman, had agreed that she did need some immediate doctoring.

As it turned out, Lucy had stayed on for several days. The little woman had been humbled considerably, and she and Madison had engaged in several long conversations. Madison had discovered that Lucy was really a fragile woman hiding behind a brassy exterior; after all, she had grown up with four unruly brothers, and being such a small person herself, it was all she could do just to survive. Madison had been willing to forgive her if Lucy was willing to put her best foot forward.

After profuse apologies for her hand in the whole Red Eagle mess, on the fourth day after her arrival at the ranch Lucy had been on a train heading east. She was going back to her home in repentance, hoping to make something of her life. Madison knew that even Colt had been impressed with her sincere transformation.

Happy with the way everything had turned out, Madison headed toward the house. The July heat seemed even more stifling than usual, and she was glad that dinner would be served outside in the cooler evening air.

A few hours later at the end of the meal, Colt happily announced the reinstatement of the annual ranch rodeo. The event had been banished under Garrett's management, but now that Colt was home, it was going to be restored. Madison knew from Colt and Rosannah in their discussion about ranch life that it was something everyone looked forward to during the long hot days of summer. The preparation and practice were almost as fun as the real thing, Rosannah had said, and the entire countryside would be invited, with cowboys and ranchers from neighboring spreads competing in games of skill on horseback. The rodeo would be followed by a barbecue and a rowdy barn dance, and as Colt had said, he knew only too well what benefit a function such as this could be to the morale of a work-worn cowboy.

Colt proceeded to recount some vivid and animated tall tales of past rodeos, stories that sent Madison and the others into fits of laughter. Everyone was holding their sides before he was finished, begging for mercy.

The last to leave the table, Colt pushed his chair back, rising to take Madison's hand. She took his eagerly, and they both stepped from the wraparound porch for an evening stroll. It was customary to make a routine check of the immediate surrounding area in the evenings, and Madison loved to accompany him. She blossomed in the pleasure of quiet conversation and the peaceful solitude of the ranch as it began to wind down under the watchful eye of the setting sun.

They hadn't gotten far from the house when the sound of light footsteps came from behind them. Madison turned just in time to see Rosannah passing to the side of them, her steps quick and precise as she pulled a shawl securely around her shoulders.

"Bye-bye, you two. See you in the morning."

"Good night, Rosie. Sleep well," Colt answered casually, rolling the usual blade of grass between his teeth.

Madison first looked at her husband, then at the little round woman who proceeded toward the old house. A faint light shone from the front window. That was where Bud lived ... or she *thought* he did ... Colt glanced at her once, then did a double-take, amused at the funny look on her face.

"What's wrong?" he said with a laugh.

"Where's Rosannah off to this time of night?" she asked. She became slightly annoyed when he didn't answer right away. Colt stared at her with an expression of supreme enjoyment.

"Well," he said finally, "I imagine she's off to spend a delightful evening in the company of her man—which is something you'll be doing later." He raised and lowered his brows several times.

"But I thought," she stammered with a frown, looking at the old ranch house again, "Bud lives there, right?" She felt downright silly having to ask. The knowing look on Colt's face told her everything. Then she understood. "Ohhhh, I see. When did this happen, anyway? I mean, have they always been together? Are they married? Don't look at me that way!" Madison said at last.

"So many questions." Colt smiled slyly as he slid his arm around her waist, pulling her close as they walked. "Rosannah's been a widow for about eight years now. Her husband, Emmy's father, Tom, dropped dead one day. His heart just gave out while he was working. He was the ranch blacksmith at the time. Bud, on the other hand, never married—just didn't find the right woman, he always said. It took maybe two years or so for them to finally get together."

"But the way they talk to each other—I thought . . ."

"That they hated one another?" he finished with a chuckle. "Naw, they've always been fond of each other. It was friendly at first; that's why they always pick on each other. After Tom died that fondness turned to love. I think they're truly happy together." He turned to better see her face. "Where did you think Rosie went every night? Hmmmm?"

"I don't know. . . . I didn't think she went anywhere. There are so many nooks and crannies in the main house, I just assumed she had her own room somewhere."

Madison's expression turned suddenly thoughtful as she remembered the cemetery, recalling each headstone. "It just goes to show you, there's love everywhere you turn, even if it's not always obvious to the eye."

Colt regarded her with a puzzled look, wondering why she'd suddenly turned so wistful. He stopped, moving to stand before her. He gently took hold of her face. "Listen, sugar, I need to check on some things down at the bunkhouses. Why don't you head on back to the house and I'll meet you there in no time at all."

"Yeah . . . okay."

He kissed her, deeply and quickly. Then he sprinted down the grassy incline toward the gradual unfolding of lamplight in the distance. She watched until the stalwart figure turned into a blackened silhouette against the gray twilight. Absently, she placed her palm on her stomach, a strange feeling of bittersweet sadness descending over her. Thoughts of mortality . . . and immortality.

She would tell him tonight.

Chapter Forty-Six

Not really understanding this downward turn of her mood, she slowly made her way back to the house.

By the time she mounted the staircase, her gloominess had faded just as mysteriously as it had come. Her expression turning shrewd, she smiled, quickening her pace. Once in their bedroom she hastily stripped off her gown and underclothes, tying her hair up as she sank gratefully into the hot tub that routinely awaited her each evening at this time. *Thank you, Zak,* she thought.

Tonight she didn't linger. Smoothing lavender-scented soap over her skin, then rinsing quickly, she was out within a matter of minutes. Drying off, she shook her hair loose and brushed it furiously until it swirled around her naked shoulders in a lofty cloud of golden curls. Her mouth tilted into a positively wicked smile.

She jerked open the heavy wardrobe doors, fishing for one of Colt's bandannas and tying it artfully around her neck. Next, she retrieved the extra Stetson from the peg by the door. Standing before the mirror, she positioned the hat on her head, first one way and then the other, until she was totally satisfied with the look.

The lamplight was lowered and she sat in the big, green leather easy chair, sinking within its cushy center. Her long legs dangled provocatively over the thick arms just right, so Colt would have the most optimal view of her when he entered the dimly lit room. Fluffing her hair, she leaned back and waited.

It wasn't long before the sound of a door slamming came from the distance and boots on the stairs echoed in the hallway. She could barely suppress the giggle of anticipation that bubbled in her throat. She just loved his expression when she did this sort of thing. That was the best part. Well, almost.

The crystal doorknob turned, then clicked. The door swung open and Colt strode into the room. Madison watched him open his mouth to speak, then look once—then again, all words lost, forgotten. He stopped midstride. His expression was briefly one of shock, then awareness, then one of smoky, dark, pure unbridled lust. A slow, devilish grin spread over his face.

Madison lowered her eyes, her dark-fringed lashes fanning over her cheeks demurely. When she looked up at him flirtatiously Colt felt as if he was being drawn into bottomless pools of aqua light. She ran her tongue over her lips.

"Have I ever told you how good you look in a hat?" he drawled lazily.

"Never," she retorted in a breathy whisper. "How good?"

His hat spun toward the row of pegs that lined the wall behind him—and missed. He didn't bother to pick it up. He bent over and struggled with his boots, hopping in place a few times before they thumped to the floor. His pants and shirt followed.

Before Madison knew what was happening, he was on her, all over her, scooping her up into his arms. He ripped off her hat with a toss. Lips and hands were everywhere at once, and she was his captive, powerfully secured within his embrace.

The lovers collapsed onto the plush down coverlets of the bed, twisting, straining against one another, becoming one quickly, passionately. In a gushing surge of heat, it was over.

Entwined in the throbbing aftermath of their spent passion, their rapid breathing began to slow. A light sheen of moisture glistened over their bodies.

"I'm sorry, I wanted to take it slower. I'll make it up to you, I promise."

"I like it fast—sometimes," she said coyly.

"I'll have to remember that," he spoke softly, smiling.

Blissfully sated—for the moment anyway—Colt kissed her possessively before he rolled over with a husky groan. He rubbed his eyes with the palms of his hands.

"God," he moaned, "one of these days you're going to kill me."

"You seem to be in perfectly good health to me," she observed, grazing her fingernails over his chest, moving up to caress his square jaw. The stubble prickled beneath her fingertips—she loved the feeling.

His hand joined hers. "I need a shave. Would you do the honors, sugar?"

"Sure," she purred contentedly.

"I wonder if your bath is still warm." He staggered from the tangle of bedclothes, dipping his hand into the lukewarm water to check. "Good enough." He stepped in, immediately sinking in over his head and coming up with a splash.

Madison slipped into a sheer dressing gown. She promptly pulled up a stool and slapped the foamy shaving brush to his cheek, swishing it back and forth. Then she reached for the straight razor.

Colt frowned, watching the troublesome expression on her face as she examined the long razor blade. She was looking at it like she'd never seen one before. "You *do* know how to use that . . . don't you?" he questioned worriedly.

"Of course. I use it on my legs all the time," she replied matter-of-factly. Chewing her lower lip in intense concentration, she tilted his chin back and brought the blade near his neck. "Relax . . ."

He pushed himself up abruptly. "Your legs?"

"Yes, and if you keep moving like that, your face will look as hacked up as my legs do." She scowled. That hadn't quite come out the way she intended.

"Uhmmm . . . how about if you hold the mirror and I do the shaving, all right?"

Madison smiled, placing the razor in his hand. "Chicken, huh? Suit yourself."

Shifting the stool to the side of the brass tub, she held the mirror up to his view. For a few moments the scraping of the silver blade over rough whiskers was the only sound.

"Colt?"

"Hmmmm?"

"I'm pregnant." She said it so nonchalantly that it could have just as easily been the weather she was talking about.

The scraping stopped. Dead silence.

His golden brown eyes flickered up to hers, then down to rest on her stomach. "Don't look at my stomach, silly!" She pushed at his shoulder playfully. "It doesn't show yet!"

Pregnant? He didn't know what to think, let alone say. A giddy feeling of happiness started at the pit of his stomach, teeming upward. Strange, but he felt like laughing! Not a little, but one of those long, deep, hysterical laughs that brought tears to one's eyes. He resisted, thinking she might not understand. He certainly didn't want to hurt her feelings. A baby?

"Are you sure?" He raised his eyebrows.

"Well, I don't have a pregnancy test to use, but I'm at least two weeks late."

"Oh. They have tests where you come from?"

"Gee, you make it sound like I'm from another planet. Yeah, they have real quick tests. If the stick turns blue, you're pregnant. If it stays white, you're not—that type of thing."

Casually, she began to suds up his hair with the bar of soap, smoothing the creamy lather over his shoulders and arms. He just sat there, like a big stump.

Occasionally, she stole a glance at his face; his eyes stared past her, seemingly into oblivion. "Are you going to finish shaving or just walk around with half a beard?"

"Huh? Oh, yeah, sure . . ."

He swished the blade and moved it slowly to his face. She held the mirror up again. She watched him finish shaving and then lather the rest of his body and dunk to rinse his hair. When he stood she handed him a cloth. While shaving and washing himself, he had never once looked at her.

Madison's heart began to thump unpleasantly, almost painfully. A pregnancy was the last thing she had expected, but she was ecstatically happy. She hadn't even thought she *could* conceive, and now so soon after they were married, it had happened! That was it. It was too soon. He didn't want a baby this soon. Oh, why had she said it so bluntly? She should have worked up to it. The familiar heat crept up her face, the burning behind her eyes. God, but she didn't want to cry . . . not now.

Colt briskly rubbed the excess moisture from his hair, dropping the cloth to the floor. Madison moved away, her dressing gown floating out behind her as she headed for the bed. He caught her arm, twirling her around to face him. The tear that streaked down her cheek tore at his heart like a dagger. He drew her to him, maybe a little too roughly in his urgency. The dressing gown parted. He squeezed her warm, soft nakedness to his. She sighed heavily, or was it a sob?

"I'm sorry, sugar . . . so sorry. I've hurt your feelings." His hands made big circles over her back, his fingers running deep into her hair, pressing her close. "Forgive me. I love you. I'm very happy. So happy that I just don't know what to say. Ever since I was a kid I've dreamed of the day when I would have my own family . . . my own sons."

Madison looked up, her lashes clumped together in a glitter of tears. "You're happy? Really? Are you sure?"

"The only other time I've been this sure about anything was the night we got married."

His eyes were infinitely penetrating, and the burdensome weight that had smothered her heart was suddenly lifted. She felt as light as a feather, her spirit soaring. She hugged him to her with all her might. "I love you so much. But what if it's a girl?"

"All the better," he said, low and husky. "She'll be the image of you." He backed her slowly to the bed and lowered her gently into its softness.

A sigh melted into the air as his warm flesh pressed hers. The lovemaking, gentle, masterful, exalting, continued into the early morning hours. Sated to the point of exhaustion, they slept. The only sound beyond the evenness of their breathing was the peaceful pitter-patter of a cleansing summer rainfall on the roof.

Chapter Forty-Seven

Her expression melancholy, she stared right past him. They were alone in the barn. It was past midnight and most of the guests had gone home. Remnants of the festivities lingered, but the cleanup would have to be orchestrated tomorrow—everyone was just too tired now. All the lanterns had burnt out except for one, and it radiated a lonely orange glow in a far corner of the barn.

Half the countryside had attended the annual Triple Bar C barbecue and rodeo, and the busy day had been filled with a bounteous banquet of food, celebration, and rowdy competition. Later, cowboys, farmers, townspeople, young and old, had kicked up their heels at the barn dance. In fact, Madison had noticed that Emmy shared quite a few dances with one gentleman in particular—a nice-looking fellow from farther down south along the Green River, an influential rancher, or so she had heard mention.

The party had been a complete success, and things couldn't have gone any better, unless maybe if Madison hadn't gotten sick at the end. But what did she expect? She now thought about it defiantly. She was pregnant and had morning sickness—all the time. But that wasn't all that was on her mind.

At some point, Colt had bestowed on her a tantalizing kiss, lowering her to the cushion of hay where they now lay together. Madison placed a hand over her abdomen, deep in thought. Her white cotton gypsy-style gown fit uncomfortably tight and her stomach seemed to be enlarging abnormally fast. At least it seemed abnormal. How could she be sure? She'd never been pregnant before. How soon was a woman supposed to show when she was expecting a baby? As near as she could figure, she couldn't possibly be more than two months along.

On top of that, a couple of times she had bled—oh, just slightly and very pale, but nonetheless it was worrisome. Well, she might be naive about pregnancy, but she was intelligent enough to know that wasn't normal. And the sickness—my God, she'd never been so sick in all her born days. She was ravenous all the time, and yet the thought, appearance, or smell of food made her want to retch. Her stomach cramped frequently, too, in regular intervals. What she wouldn't give for a few of those twentieth-century pregnancy manuals right about now.

Madison hadn't told Colt about her concerns. She didn't want to, either. It would only worry him, and he'd insist on calling a doctor. She was fairly sure that she knew more about the situation than a nineteenth-century doctor did.

Colt brushed a strand of hair away from her cheek. "Something wrong?" He tilted his head to catch her gaze.

"Nothing much," she replied absently.

"Nothing much? But something. Feeling sick again?"

"No, not really, I've just been a little . . . blue lately. I can't really pinpoint it. It must be the pregnancy. Hormones and all. I'm just sorry I ruined your evening." She smiled weakly.

"Don't be foolish! You couldn't ruin anything if you tried. Whatever a hormone is, I'm not convinced. What's on your mind? Tell me."

"A hormone is what makes a woman a woman and a man a man," Madison explained.

"Sounds interesting to me . . ." Unable to ignore her position, he leaned in closer, pressing his thigh gently between hers, brushing his lips over her forehead.

She inhaled deeply, searching for the right words, wondering if it was possible to make him understand the minute shred of loneliness that persistently gnawed at her insides. More importantly, could he comprehend her fear? There was no place she'd rather be than with Colt, and yet the feeling lingered. She was certain it was all brought on by her condition—everything was exaggerated: her sense of smell, appetite, emotions . . .

Madison tried to disregard the tenacious little nibbles on her earlobe, the tickle of warm breath in her ear.

"It's just that I long to pick up a telephone and tell my mom and Mark that I'm pregnant. But the long-distance bill would be atrocious." She gave an uneasy little chuckle.

His lips were on her neck, his hand stroking her arm, squeezing. So warm. Shivers vibrated through her, and it felt wonderful. . . . But not now! She wanted him to *listen* to her now.

"Colt . . . I'm afraid."

"There's nothing to be afraid of. I'm here," he said softly, molding his body to hers, searching for her mouth.

"You don't understand." No, he didn't. And she was so fearful he wouldn't. Ever. "I'm afraid of giving birth, here, with no doctor, no hospital. No painkillers. I'm afraid something is going to go wrong and I'll lose the baby."

Colt pulled back to look at her. Madison's voice rose with urgency.

"I guess you could say I'm a wimp. But I'm not like all those frontier women who were here today! This life, this century, that's all they know! They don't know that in a hundred years or so, their children would almost always survive, and that they could go through childbirth with virtually no pain. They could even choose *not* to have any more children if that's what they wanted! Here, they have to lie in a sweaty bed and suffer when they give birth—that's just a part of life. There's a very good chance a child won't survive past his first year. But not in 1993, Colt! And that's what I'm afraid of! I'm afraid of losing our baby!"

Colt's face hardened, his body turning rigid. His heart thundered against his ribs, and he pushed himself up, waiting for her to continue.

Madison sat up, clutching a handful of hay and tossing it down in frustration. She knew she was venting her hostilities on him. It wasn't his fault, and yet she wanted to lay blame, right now needing somebody to yell at.

"Do you realize that if there's a complication with my pregnancy or delivery I could die? Or the baby could die? In 1993 most complications are detected and corrected before they happen."

Madison jumped up, her chest rising with every agitated breath. She was consumed by this stormy upheaval of worry, and it took control.

Colt's hard gaze followed her as she paced back and forth over the packed dirt floor. Nothing short of a lighting bolt through the roof of the barn could have stunned him more. Dammit, he'd thought she was happy. Of course, he couldn't know all the advanced concepts of the future—only she knew that because she had lived it. But he certainly wasn't a dimwitted idiot who had no capability of understanding or learning!

"I'm sorry you feel that I'm too stupid to comprehend the sophistication of the twentieth century. Throughout the passage of time mankind has continued to progress and make steady advancements. It only stands to reason that 1993 would be superior to 1878. I can only provide for you the best my day and age has to offer. I can give you a midwife, a doctor, creature comforts, my love and support, but I can't do any more than that, Madison! Oh, there is one more thing—I can help you go back. Is that what you want? To take my baby and go back to the twentieth century?"

His jaw was set firm, his lips in a straight line as his eyes drilled holes through her.

Madison threw her arms up with a grumble. "I knew you wouldn't understand. I didn't mean that at all!"

"I thought you made a conscious choice to live here with me."

"I did . . . but that was before I got pregnant."

"You mean you expected to go through our marriage without having a baby?"

His tone turned incisive, his eyes glinting like cutting slivers of topaz and she looked away.

"I've never been able to get pregnant before. I suppose I didn't give it much thought. . . . Besides, that's really not the point," she stammered, her heart pounding.

She couldn't seem to catch her breath. He was intimidating her, and she couldn't think straight! He had it all wrong! How could he think that she would just flippantly want to leave him like that? That wasn't what she had meant at all. And she really hadn't given any serious thought to returning—not until now.

" . . . unless," she added with a pause.

"Unless what?" He frowned.

"You come back with me! We could go together." The words came out so soft, she barely heard them herself. Her eyes became wide, searching his.

Colt was on his feet, snatching his hat from the post of a stall, pressing it onto his head angrily. He took long strides toward the big double doors. Madison gasped. He spun around.

"I figured as much," he growled. "You know I can't do that! Why would you even mention it? Just being polite? Considerate, maybe? My going really makes no difference, does it? Your mind is made up, whether you know it or not."

Colt dismissed her, jerking open the tall door and heading out.

"Why not? Why can't you go?" she cried after him, running to his side, skipping to keep up with him. "I wouldn't go without you. You know that!"

"Do I?"

He stopped dead in his tracks to look down at her again, his expression mocking. Madison knew that he was thinking of the time she had left before, disappearing without a word.

"I would be like a fish out of water in your time," he continued. "What else do I know but ranching? How would we live? Oh, I almost forgot . . . I could sling a fancy pistol at the Wild West show; *that* would make a fine living for us. Or, better yet, you could support us with your agency!"

The words bit at her, slicing her to the quick.

"Forget your pride for a minute, all right?" she slung right back. "There are ranches in 1993, too! We can make it work together. We love each other; nothing else matters but that and our baby. I'll sell the agency. We'll buy a spread somewhere . . . either Wyoming or Colorado!" She tossed her hands in the air, ideas popping into her head randomly. Quite good ideas, she thought.

"Are you sure I've got the brains to run a ranch in the future, huh? There are so many advancements, you know," he jeered.

Colt felt so utterly helpless that it infuriated him. How could he ever hope to measure up to this woman's expectations when she was accustomed to so much more? Damn, but women were such fickle creatures. As an afterthought he spun around and went back inside the barn to retrieve his saddle.

Madison watched in astonishment as he brushed past her again, tossing the saddle carelessly over the fence and clicking his tongue several times. Cinder cleared the rise a moment later, heeling up in an energetic cantor, snorting. Colt vaulted over the fence and threw first the blanket and then the saddle over the stallion's back.

Angry turmoil festered within her, increasing with each passing second. Madison struggled to keep from exploding, and to top it off, her mind felt like mush. She couldn't seem to think of a single worthwhile retort.

"Stop it!" she finally cried out, stamping her foot. "I told you I didn't mean it that way! The quality of life in 1993 *is* so much better, if you would just give it a chance. Sure, there are many modern concepts to learn, but it wouldn't take long. What's keeping you here, anyway? There's no family left!"

"Rosie, Bud, and Emmy are my family," he gritted without bothering to look at her, jerking a tight cinch in the saddle.

"They'll be fine on their own. They have each other just like we do. Or at least I thought we did. Funny how you left me out of your list of family."

"What makes you think we could even go forward again? It wasn't a normal thing. A fluke is all it was. And you seem to be forgetting that I was an old man in 1993—could you handle being married to an old man, sugar?" He swung up to his mount.

The moon was round, unnaturally yellow. It hovered low over the mountainous horizon, contouring his face in its taunting brightness, making it impossible to see his features clearly. He veered and slapped the reins.

"Don't ride away from me, dammit!" she called, jogging along the side of the fence. "You were only perceived as old; you weren't *really!* I was able to see you as you truly were. Wait—we need to talk! *Colton!*"

"There are some things that need tending to," he said, his voice thick, dispassionate. "I trust you can make it back to the house on your own."

"At midnight? What needs checking on that's more important than us?" she ventured loudly.

He didn't look at her. Even if he had, it was too dark to see his expression, the scowl . . . the hurt. Why had this come as such a blow? Wasn't this what he had promised himself, that he would do right by her, allow her to make the ultimate decision as to what was best? It seemed so long ago when he had first came to that conclusion. Back when he had let her down so intolerably, allowing for her abduction right beneath his very nose. But things had changed. Her love hadn't faltered as he had feared it might; and now she was pregnant with his child—how was he supposed to let her go away with his child? She possessed all that mattered to him in this world, not excluding his soul. If she walked away, he would deflate, wither away to nothing.

Yet even if it were possible, how could he leave a substantial ranching empire such as this and enter a new world with the responsibilities of a wife and child? The thought daunted him, a terrifying reality that reached out to tease him unmercifully. How could he face Madison each day knowing it was her capability alone that would see them through another day, while he stupidly floundered in feeble attempts to learn new concepts of life, to fit in?

"Go get your rose, sugar," he challenged softly, sarcastically, easily, with no hint, no trace of any feeling, "the storm awaits."

Madison cringed, the burning in her chest unbearable. His words were torture, reaching out to scratch at her with fingernails laced in an acrimonious acid.

But he didn't notice her pain. He raced away, not even pausing, quirting the great horse into a sleek, graceful leap over the corral fence, then vanishing over the rise.

"Damn you to hell, Colt Chase! Can't you think past yourself for a minute?" Madison cried out into the night, unheeded, a tear streaking down her cheek. Whirling around, she kicked at the fence post furiously. It hurt. She wailed in rage as well as pain. She thought she had broken her toe, but at the moment she didn't even care.

Madison was left alone with the big yellow moon and a chilly throb in her heart. A tempestuous wind swirled out of nowhere, tearing at her skirts, whipping strands from her long braid as she slowly limped her way through the grass toward the desolate darkness of the house.

Chapter Forty-Eight

As she sat on the perfectly white painted bench in the rose garden, she heard the resonanting chime of the tall clock. In full bloom and in every color of the spectrum, but mostly red, the roses enveloped her, masking her misery with their thick, cloyingly sweet smell.

Even in the dead of night, the heat in their upstairs bedroom was oppressive. But it was the chilly atmosphere in that room that had prompted her tonight to seek the fresh air in the garden. Except for necessary conversation, she and Colt had hardly spoken to each other this past week—and not from her lack of effort. Countless times she had tried to goad him to talk to her with no favorable results, and finally she had given up.

A trillion stars watched down over her from their perch in the vastness of the sky. When she looked up, scanning the heavens, it was so painfully obvious how microscopic a human being really was. Even though her problem seemed monumental to her now, in comparison to the great scope of creation it was minute indeed.

Madison stood up, sighing. Shrugging off an unwarranted shimmer, she smoothed her hands down the silken material of her dressing gown. She moved inside the gazebo, occupying her mind with the intricate weavings of the thorny vines, forever struggling, working their way up along the lattice walls. How beautiful and deceivingly innocent. She brushed a soft fingertip over the velvet petals of a single blood-red bud—such elegant crimson perfection. The heavy perfume hung like a cloud, assaulting her overly sensitive nose, causing the familiar nausea to churn in the pit of her stomach.

Madison's condition had also worsened in the past week. Unable to stomach a full meal, she found it was easier to munch little by little on bland foods. Rosannah, having had three children herself, had sympathized fully with her situation and had insisted that she needn't even occupy a chair at the nightly meal. Instead, Madison walked, and walked, and walked some more.

What was worse than the nausea was the cramping, and Madison felt sure it wasn't normal. At least the bleeding had stopped. The threat of a miscarriage still loomed foremost in her mind. Colt didn't seem the least bit aware of the break in her routine. He didn't even care.

The past two days she had managed to talk Zak into letting her take Cinnabar out for a ride. Judging by his look of consternation, he hadn't been thrilled with the idea, particularly since Colt had issued specific instructions that she wasn't to ride.

But that had been before he wanted her to go back. And it was obvious he did. He expected her to.

In response to Colt's telegraphed instructions, Cinnabar and Cinder had been fetched from down south by the cowboys who were driving the longhorns up from Texas. Madison had missed her horse, and as soon as the mare was delivered she wanted to ride her. She had fervently promised Zak that she would be extra careful.

Madison couldn't deny that a desire to defy Colt's orders played a large part in her eagerness to ride. His demeanor was so cool and aloof since their argument, it drove her crazy—although she would never let him know that. At this point, she wanted to do just about anything that would elicit his attention. Unfavorable attention was better than none at all and she had tried that earlier that day.

She had ridden out as far as the line shack where she and Colt had escaped the thunderstorm for much-needed solitude. She needed the time to think, but instead she had jumped up at every noise to see if it was Colt, wishing he would show up, searching for her. Yes, he would be angry at first, because she had ridden out so far alone—and then because she had ridden in the first place. But Madison much preferred his wrath to the stilted, lukewarm, polite conversation of the past week.

It was nearly dark when she'd returned from her ride, and Colt hadn't appeared to notice. All he did lately was work, she thought, remembering the light that had emanated from beneath his office door earlier that evening. After having soaked in a hot bath she was in bed, though not asleep, when he had come up to their room.

Why did Colt clam up like this, retreating within himself with anger? She thought, frustrated. Why couldn't he respond to her prodding, discuss the problem instead of stewing in a pit of bitterness. It was all so pointless. The thought was pushed back because it terrified her—but what if he weren't "stewing" at all? What if he had just decided he no longer cared enough about her to put forth the effort? Maybe he didn't even want her around! As far as she was concerned, it wasn't an option to attempt a trip into the future without him, but if she was so inclined, it was evident that he wouldn't try to stop her. He claimed he loved her. How could his mind have changed so drastically to the point of dismissing his own unborn child?

Even out here in the serenity of the rose garden, the unanswered questions haunted her, invaded her sanity. Unwelcome tears sprang to her eyes. No, she wasn't going forward in time again. This was her home now—and she was here to stay whether he liked it or not.

Slowly, she reached out for the long stem of a flawless red bud. Mindful of hidden thorns, she pinched it free with her thumbnail, pressing it to her nose, her eyes fluttering closed.

Colt rolled to his back with a huff. Exhaling in frustration, he pressed his palms to his forehead in an attempt to ease the throbbing that intensified with every heartbeat. The thin sheets were damp with sweat, the room stifling even though the French doors stood wide open. A three-quarter moon filtered through the room, illuminating everything inside within a ghostly gray cast.

Nothing unusual. He couldn't sleep. Hadn't had a worthwhile night's sleep since the rodeo. Thoughts of Madison were foremost in his mind; and the pain of the knowledge that she wanted to leave him. Wanted to go home.

Home. The ranch wasn't where she considered home—that thought alone ground the torment even further into his soul, unbearably. How could their happiness have disintegrated right before his eyes, so quickly, before it had even truly begun? God knew he was happy—he had never known such contentment as that which he felt when she was in his arms, when the lovemaking was through.

Then she told him she was going to have a child. He wouldn't have thought it possible, but the woman had managed to make him even happier.

The facts gnawed at his insides day and night. His greatest fear was of losing Madison and the child. He had faced that fact head on throughout the past week. Thinking about letting her return to her time was one thing. Letting her actually do it was another matter, entirely.

Life would certainly be easier in the twentieth century, judging by what he had observed himself, and by what Madison had told him. It was just this huge swell of pride that consumed him, held him at bay. He was a proud man! And with reason; he was remarkably skilled, competent, well-known, feared, and respected by exactly the right people.

What kind of a person would he be in 1993? An unknown face. An expert shootist in an era where they no longer existed. A cattle baron with no ranch. Skills that were a century and a half passé.

Every day he would have to face the woman who meant the most to him in the world—unable to offer anything, relying on her for his mere existence. To Colt, it sounded like a life of total embarrassment.

As if all this turmoil inside weren't enough to occupy his mind, he'd discovered a glitch in the accounting records. The books weren't even close to balancing. So far, he'd traced them back six years, tapping into the same series of clever patterns. There could be no doubt as to Garrett's intentions—thousands upon thousands of dollars had seemingly vanished every year that Colt had studied so far. The question remained: What had happened to the money? Had Garrett pocketed it gradually, squandering it during his drinking, gambling, and womanizing sprees in South Pass and who knows where else—or had something else been done with it?

It was a question that might never have an answer.

Hell, but he was tired of not touching Madison, disgusted with himself for punishing her for his own feelings of inadequacy. How could he have disregarded her feelings so totally? She had told him of her sickness—why hadn't he listened? Something could be horribly wrong! He was her husband. What kind of man was he to let her walk out of his life without a fight? And that was exactly what was going to happen if he didn't get his priorities straight. She was carrying his child, for God's sake!

Abruptly, he rolled toward Madison's side of the bed, his arms sliding across the coolness of bare linen. He lifted his aching head in confusion, focusing his tired eyes on an empty pillow. She was gone!

"Madison?!" he called out, a little more gruffly than he intended.

The covers were flipped aside as he bounded from the bed, groaning as the incessant throbbing increased twofold. He jerked into his blue jeans, hopping simultaneously toward the door. His voice echoed her name, two, maybe three times before he hit the front door. He was on the front porch, stalking the length of it, his eyes searching frantically for a sign of her.

A cold dread settled like a dead weight in the center of his gut. His breathing was labored, coming in slow gasps as his pace broadened, determinedly circling around to the back. He muttered, chastising himself bitterly for being so utterly apathetic to her feelings!

She couldn't have left!

He couldn't blame her if she had.

It was at that moment he knew precisely what needed to be done, if, God forbid, she hadn't done it already.

Chapter Forty-Nine

Despite the comfortably cool air, a nervous sweat broke out on Colt's brow. He cursed himself over and over for being such a hard-headed fool. He didn't deserve her! He sucked in a dry, painful breath between his clenched teeth.

"Mad—"

His call was cut short just as he spotted an angelic figure inside the gazebo. A soft breeze caught the white satin of her gown, pressing its flowing lines translucently against her slim form. The moonlight pulled the silver lights from her hair in radiant shimmers.

He didn't waste a moment's time. His bare feet were silent along the path of flat, smooth stepping stones his mother had meticulously laid so many years ago. Colt stood behind his wife. He hesitated only briefly, his hand reaching out to touch her shoulder, sliding lightly over the satin. He squeezed gently.

"Madison."

She gasped, starting at the caress, spinning around. The rose dropped to the wooden floor of the gazebo, but not without first pricking her fingertip with the jagged tip of a thorn. She brought her injured finger to her lips, sucking at a droplet of blood that instantly formed there. Madison's eyes lifted to warm, golden brown ones, those very ones that haunted her every thought.

They held for the longest time.

Colt's strong arms grasped her to him, enclosing, crushing her against the sturdiness of his body. He filled her to the core with an exquisite vibration, the power of pure, unconditional love. She drank it up, quenching a thirst she didn't even know she possessed until then. She melted into him, dripping like warm honey, the steady thump of his heartbeat comforting beneath her cheek.

"I was afraid you left without me," he murmured into her hair, his hands kneading the tightness from her shoulders.

The tension of a million years evaporated with his ministrations, a tingle washing through her. "I'm not going anywhere, Colt, I told you that. Never . . ." she purred persuasively against his chest.

"Yes—yes, you are. You're going back if we can make it work again."

"Huh?" She drew back to look up at him, her heart tripping erratically—a cold fear gripped her at what she thought he meant! "I'm not leaving you, Colt!" she replied adamantly. "I don't care if you don't want me to stay. You're not going to get rid of me that easily! You married me, remember?" Her voice cracked with emotion and apprehension.

"You think I want to be rid of you?" he said, incredulous. Mirth laced his voice. He was amazed that she would actually believe such a thing, but very pleased with her decision to stay. Colt tilted his head back with a low chuckle. "Madison Chase . . . how I love you! You've made me such a happy man, do you know that?" He held her tightly within his arms for all he was worth.

She frowned, her eyes mirroring intense confusion. "Happy, you say? You sure have an odd way of showing it. You haven't spoken to me in a week. You have a stubborn streak in you a mile long!"

"I know," he sighed, "my mother must have said that to me a thousand and one times." He marveled at how she succeeded to become more beautiful each time he looked at her.

"Smart woman," she replied tightly.

"I'm sorry I put you through that. I'm done wallowing in my own self-pity, sugar. All I've done this past week is worry about myself and wonder how in the hell I'd ever get by without you."

"I never had any intention of leaving! That was your interpretation!" Madison hastily interrupted.

"Now let me finish." He pressed a finger to her lips.

Madison calmed, letting him continue.

"You were absolutely right about living in the twentieth century—if for no other reason than the health and quality of life for our baby. So, that leaves only one thing to do." Colt looked at her squarely, willing her to understand what she must do even though it wasn't what they wanted.

Madison chewed her lip, mostly to keep it from trembling. Disconcerted, she didn't want to hear what he had to say. She was deathly afraid to have him elaborate, for fear it was exactly what she was thinking. No! She wasn't going to let him send her back alone!

"If you're thinking of sending me back, you've got another think coming! I never meant to deride you or the ranch, or this century. I was just anxious—something that happens quite frequently to pregnant women. It passed, just as quickly as it may descend on me again with no warning. I seem to be on an emotional roller coaster lately, and you'll just have to put up with me for a while! I love this ranch, Colt! It's like a paradise to me. The tranquility, the simplicity—I couldn't ask for more. I don't want you to think for a minute that I'm unhappy. You make me very happy, Colt," she gushed on and on. And on some more.

He gazed deeply into those glistening pools of aqua, his expression changing from one of profound consternation to mild amusement, and then back again.

"Whoa, there! Slow down. I understand and I believe you. And no, I'm not sending you back alone . . . well, not exactly." He stammered only slightly at the last words.

Madison caught his hesitation and became wary. "What do you mean . . . not exactly?" Her eyes narrowed.

"I'm going with you." He sought to alleviate her fears, but it was a delicate situation and irritatingly he was at a loss for the right words.

"Good."

"Just not at the same time is all."

His brown eyes left hers, flickering downward while he continued to rub her arms.

"That's ridiculous! Why not?" she cried in alarm.

"Because . . . It's imperative that you return for medical care, for the baby's sake. You said yourself things weren't going well." Colt paused. He didn't know a hill of beans about the nurturing of a pregnancy and delivery, unless one happened to be a horse or a cow.

"I'm sure what I'm experiencing is practically normal. I can certainly wait until you can come with me!"

"There are several loose ends I must tie up before I can leave, Madison. Time-consuming tasks that have to be handled." He cleared his throat, his eyes searching hers imploringly, "There's no reason or need for you to be here. Not when you can safely wait in your time. Especially not when our baby's life is in jeopardy. I'll only be a few weeks behind you."

"No!" she protested vehemently, pushing at his chest without even realizing it. "I won't go without you! I'll just wait, that's all. . . . I've been here this long, another few weeks won't matter."

"That's true, Madison, but the problem is . . . I won't be here."

Madison frowned, not at all liking where this conversation was leading. He was being too evasive. Either he was subtly trying to get rid of her or he was deliberately not giving her the whole story.

"Where will you be?" she asked softly.

Colt sighed, as if something was troubling him deeply. "I need time to secure our future."

"I don't understand. What could you possibly do?"

"I have a plan. I don't know if there's any merit to it, but there's only one way to find out. If it works, we'll have everything we've ever dreamed of—and in the twentieth century, sugar."

"I don't care about any of that! All I want is you at my side! What if something goes wrong and you're not able to come forward? No, I won't go without you!"

"If it works for you, of course it will work again for me," Colt replied, with more confidence than he actually felt. "You're worrying needlessly."

"But I do worry! What if I go to 1993, then something happens and you can't follow? Then again, maybe neither one of us will be able to go."

"This is life and anything's possible, right? We've proved that. That's where faith and trust come into the picture. You do trust me, don't you?"

"Of course I do. . . . But what is so important that it keeps you here another few weeks?" she asked, truly baffled.

"It has to do with some legalities, some of Garrett's shenanigans, to be specific. I'll need to make at least one trip into South Pass, possibly farther. My little brother was embezzling funds from his own ranch. He was doing it for many years. I found out when I began pouring through all of the old records. It took some figuring, but I finally came up with his method. He must have skimmed literally tens of thousands of dollars over the years, Madison."

She let out a little gasp, "What did he do with it all?"

"I'm not sure. But I aim to find out. I plan to uncover a few more things, too, before I say good-bye to 1878."

"What does it matter now, Colt? It's over." Madison moved away from him, slowly sitting on the white planked wood-and-wrought-iron bench. Colt sat down beside her.

"Not quite. If my strategy works, we'll be set for life. The ranch will come off that auction block and our children will grow up to inherit one of the biggest spreads in Wyoming. Now tell me that wouldn't be something in 1993, huh?"

"And if it doesn't work?" she challenged, by far not convinced.

"Then we'll be no worse off than we would have been if I just dropped everything and followed you."

"Unless we're separated," she added grimly.

"That won't happen. Have faith, remember?"

"You're not going back up to that Hole-in-the-Wall place, are you?" Madison slanted him another skeptical glance.

"No . . . nothing that dangerous, I assure you. It's really quite simple. I'll be traveling over some pretty rough country, something you definitely don't need to be doing in your condition. I want you safe in a doctor's care while I'm getting things in order."

Colt slipped his arm around her shoulders, pulling her close. Raising his brows with a final decisiveness, he chucked her playfully under the chin for emphasis. Then he took her hand and rose, leading her out behind the gazebo and into the lushness of the garden.

Madison suddenly stopped. "Colt . . . you really *have* decided to go to the twentieth century, haven't you? I mean, this isn't just a ploy to get me to do something for my own good?" She laughed uneasily.

Madison regarded him with a sparkle in her eyes. Her laughter tinkled softly on the mild gusts of wind that began to pick up around them. An odd gush of familiarity washed over him. He frowned, just a little, pondering. The déjà vu left as quickly as it had come. Then he couldn't help but be amazed at how incredibly sexy she made every word she uttered sound.

"Yes, Madison. I'll not be far behind. You can trust me with every fiber of your being."

A squeak escaped her throat as his arm impetuously slid beneath her knees, scooping her briskly into his arms.

"Would it be possible to continue this discussion in the morning?" he asked. "I'm tired. At least, too tired for words. Although there is something I'd like to say to you. . . ." Colt winked, breaking into a lopsided grin as his gaze slowly lowered to rest on her lips.

"Well," she hesitated, "if you insist." She sighed with a big smile, curling her body into his, kissing the warm, scented skin of his neck. "But I don't like it. Not at all."

Colt didn't either. He held back the words of comfort that sprang to his lips for fear his own uncertainty would bleed through, too easily recognizable. The last thing in the world he wanted was to send her off without him—but the alternative could prove disastrous in the long run. If something were to happen to him, Madison would be alone here, in a world she was unfamiliar with, without his guidance. It would be nightmare enough to leave her and their child alone in her own time—but at least there, if he weren't by her side, he felt confident she could manage well enough without him within her own familiar surroundings. After all, she had her family. If only he could leave with her. . . . But her safety was paramount. And he must be allowed the chance to make a life for them.

Colt walked into a cozy grove at the edge of the garden, where the tightly knit webbing of rosebushes met the beginnings of pines and poplars. The floor was a spongy mat of cool grass. He loosened his hold gradually, letting Madison slide slowly to touch her toes on the emerald grass.

"You know," he said in a husky whisper, "I've had this fantasy since I was a long-legged, rangy kid who was just discovering that girls weren't so bad after all—in fact, they could be rather fun."

"Oh yeah?" Madison replied, her fingertip caressing the fullness of his lower lip, "And who were you discovering this with, hmmmmm?"

"Her name was Beth. She was the daughter of a grub cook we used to have many years ago. I was maybe fifteen, she was two years older. My first love, and just as curious as I was."

"Ahhh, I see . . ." Madison's eyes glittered, her brows tapering with inquisitiveness. "And what did this Beth look like?"

"A *woman* would ask that question," he said with a laugh. "Well, let me see—not nearly as gorgeous as you."

"Naturally." Madison didn't bat an eye.

"Naturally," he agreed with a sly wink. "But she was quite well-endowed, if I remember correctly." His hand slid to grasp her soft breast gently, squeezing suggestively.

Madison couldn't resist his infectious grin. "And so . . . what was this fantasy of yours?"

His mouth lowered to mere inches from hers, his voice smooth velvet. "To make love to the most tantalizingly luscious creature this side of heaven . . . right here, in the rose garden, on a soft bed of grass, the sweet perfume of roses filling our heads." He paused, brushing a stray curl from her cheek. " . . . With the glow of the moon reflected in the passion of her aqua eyes."

Madison forgot to breath. She watched his mouth, hypnotized, taking in a ragged gulp of air before she was able to speak.

"Oh. Were you able to fulfill this fantasy?" she asked softly, rubbing her hands up the hardness of his chest, gliding over the slight sheen of perspiration.

"No, but I think I'm going to now."

Colt's mouth descended, slowly, brushing hers, his lips slightly parted for just a taste of the sweetness she offered. Madison melted, and his composure crumbled. Urgently, he gathered her warmth to his, devouring any protestations she might possibly have left. His tongue engaged hers, plunging in a wildly suggestive rhythm. With every ounce of the hot-blooded passion that pounded through his veins, he made love to her mouth. Clasping her buttocks, he brought her close, grinding his hardened arousal against her.

The fly in his jeans was already open, and Madison wedged her fingers inside. Colt groaned, not hesitating to free himself, kicking the jeans aside. Madison's gown was hastily slipped off her shoulders, floating to the ground, and she clutched at him, suddenly finding herself lowered to the pungent sweetness of earth and green grass.

"Oh, Colt . . . you feel so good. I won't leave without you. You know that," she whispered against his mouth.

"Yes, you will. You must understand that it's the best way. I'll be right behind you and we'll be together forever."

"But . . ."

"Shhhh, tomorrow, sugar . . ." His mouth played upon hers with a tormenting thoroughness. Her wiggling body beneath his drove him on, stirring a vigor within that wouldn't be thwarted.

"Should we be doing this? I don't want to hurt you, or the little one." He eased his weight slightly off to the side. "You know, there are other ways that are equally enjoyable."

His voice was husky in her ear, his delicious tongue lazily tracing each fold while his thumb toyed with her nipple. Madison strained against his hard thigh, pulling him as close as she possibly could.

"No, please . . . I want you *now*. Just be gentle."

An ardent yet tender immersion brought forth a mingling of soft, breathy gasps, their private world rocking in a union of joyous bliss. Bathed in a river of moonlight, the lovers were oblivious to all else but their own endless horizons.

Chapter Fifty

Madison tossed and turned, first yanking the covers tight beneath her chin, then kicking the tangled mess away. She was so hot, sweaty. She dreamt of Colt. And of Emmy, Rosannah, Bud . . . even Zak. Then, when she dreamed of the little chocolate cream colt, its legs wobbling so innocently, struggling so hard to keep up with its agile mother, she woke up sobbing until she didn't think another tear could be manufactured by her weary eyes.

Another apparition had floated past her in the night, twice so far since she'd returned. It wasn't anything she could make sense of easily, as most dreams tended to be, but still it bothered her—she couldn't imagine its significance. In her dream masses of bodies undulated rhythmically in waves, like an angry sea of animals, flesh, and dust—snorting, roaring. Were they animalistic bellows, or was it the carnage of the earth beneath an assault of thousands of hooves?

Cows. Of course. A logical dream, considering she had just spent several months on a ranch—but raging, angry cows? Why?

Madison had ridden through the stormy portal of time almost a week before, returning to her little Victorian cottage on the north end of Colorado Springs. By far the worst part of leaving had been the good-byes. She alone understood that it was forever—at least where Rosannah, Emmy, and Bud were concerned. A story

360

had been concocted for their benefit, justifying Madison's need for a hasty departure. The family was told of the failing health of Madison's mother, and of fear for her unborn child's health. Well, at least half of it was true. In view of that, the couple would be returning to Colorado Springs to live, Madison first, and Colt following soon after. Bud would run the ranch with a free hand to hire a foreman if necessary. It had been especially difficult because, naturally, Rosannah, Bud, and Emmy would be expecting periodic visits.

Emmy had clutched Madison close, almost refusing to let her go. She had bawled in earnest, begging Madison not to leave until finally, relenting at the sea of tears, she had been able to pacify the young girl with a feeble promise that Emmy could come visit them often in Colorado Springs. Afterward, Madison had despised herself for the blatant lie.

With Colt, she had refused to let herself dwell on the idea of forever, fearing it might be so with him, also. He had called her crazy for even allowing the thought. He must have sworn a million times that nothing could keep him from finding her. And yet how could he be so sure? He was only human . . . and this whole thing was a supernatural, immortal phenomenon beyond their complete comprehension.

Madison hated the circumstances that had forced her to transcend this barrier without Colt—at the same time loving his child more than anything in the world. It was all so bittersweet.

Another marbled rose had been severed from its life-giving, thorny ligament. And when she had been forced to kiss Colt good-bye, the storm clouds had danced, heckling from above, as if a monumental chapter of her life was coming to a final, memorable close. Madison had gripped his shirt for all she was worth, clinging to him, anguished and infuriated at the same time—abhorring him for making her do this and loving him at the same time, more than anything, more than life itself.

Madison had cried, imploring Colt for a better way. But when the deafening squall had surrounded them, sweeping her appeals away in its fury, he helped her to mount Cinnabar. Colt had kissed her hard, squeezed her hand tight. He had promised, over and over, confirming their rendezvous in two weeks at that very meadow in the Jackson Hole valley. He had ordered her to hold on fiercely, with all her might, and then slapped Cinnabar on the rear flank, sending her galloping away from him and into the storm.

Madison had screamed. No! She didn't want this! And his eyes, oh God, even now she couldn't get his eyes out of her head. Soft golden brown, liquid with unspent emotion, forever branding her with his everlasting love.

Then it was over. She was alone—and impassive. Ernie Hawkins had been quick to accept Cinnabar as a temporary "employee" for the next two weeks, working the show for her board. Madison had assured him it wouldn't be any longer than that. And she had prayed she was telling the truth.

Madison had made an appointment with an obstetrician as soon as she returned to the Springs. He was an older doctor whom her mother knew and recommended. Angela was tickled pink to be able finally to anticipate the arrival of her first grandchild, even though she still hadn't had the pleasure of meeting the unborn child's father. Angela had been quick to remind Madison of that fact, over and over again.

"When you took off for Wyoming I thought you said this wasn't a romance," Angela had said, her reading glasses perched on the end of her nose.

"I said it wasn't your *average* romance," Madison answered matter-of-factly, "and I was right. We were married eleven days after we met."

"I just don't understand what the big secret is. When are we going to meet this Colt fellow?"

"Mom, he's not a 'Colt fellow.' He's my husband. And I said I will be going back to Jackson to pick him up in two weeks."

Whenever Madison said those words, even though she'd never been overly superstitious, she was anxious to knock on wood, toss salt over her shoulder, and anything else she could think of, all with her fingers crossed. She felt a little silly—no, actually, she felt moronic, but she knew this world wasn't necessarily exactly as one always perceived. And she was willing to try anything to add that extra measure of security for Colt's safe arrival into her century.

"Are you going to have another wedding?" Angela had persisted.

"Why? We're already married." Madison frowned, her words trailing off. Were they married? Come to think of it, probably not! At least not considering modern standards and legalities. She didn't like that notion at all.

"Yes, but you should have a *real* wedding, dear, even if it is your second time around. You need a ceremony befitting that elegant antique ring you're wearing! Maybe something small and quaint, with just a few friends, here at my house if you like."

"You'll be the first to be forewarned if we decide to do that," Madison assured her, "and I'll even let you handle all the planning. How does that sound?"

"Wonderful! I'd be delighted. Speaking of marriages, Jon's been calling at least once a week since you left. Why don't you give him a buzz, show him that ring, and tell him where to go." Angela rattled on, her brows slanting at her words. She didn't skip a stitch in her needlepoint.

Madison laughed. "Now that sounds like a wonderful idea to me! So, can you really tell this is an antique just by looking at it?" she questioned, fluttering her finger under Angela's nose. Of course, Madison knew it was, but her mother's confirmation seemed to ground her, reinforcing Colt's true existence. Sometimes it still scared her to think, in some obscure way, that she might have dreamt the entire episode.

"I told you it was." Angela sighed, adjusting her glasses to see it better. "It's obvious, dear. The gold is twenty-four karat. See how it's worn thin at the bottom? And you can tell by the design of the setting and the stones. You'll want to get it strengthened if you're going to be wearing it all the time."

Madison had clutched the ring tightly when her mother said that, almost sure she could feel Colt's vibration just by wearing it.

Angela had insisted on accompanying her daughter to the obstetrician. Dr. Metzger was a kindly, older gentleman who also wore his glasses perched on the end of his rather large nose. Madison marveled at how he even kind of *looked* like her mother! He was soft-spoken and had a wonderful bedside manner, but Madison had been careful to affirm that he probably wouldn't be delivering the baby. Instead, she had told him of her plans to deliver in Wyoming—funny, she wasn't even sure what city; Colt had been vague about the ultimate scheme of things.

Dr. Metzger had been very helpful, assuring her that he would recommend another physician at her request. For now he insisted on running a few tests. That had alarmed her, especially since Madison already feared a potential problem. Her abdomen was growing by leaps and bounds. Madison knew of friends who went to their fifth or sixth month before making the change into maternity clothes. But from the looks of things, she would be wearing them by her third. The doctor had been concerned about the very same thing. But he had calmly assured her that everything appeared to be fine, and that the tests were merely routine. He had scheduled the ultrasound for five days later.

Now, Madison stumbled to the bathroom with the early morning dry heaves. Her appointment for the ultrasound wasn't for another four hours, but she couldn't sleep, not with thoughts of Colt plaguing her constantly.

Since there were things she could be accomplishing, she decided to get ready and go into work early. Mark was going to the hospital with her since her mother had made a prior commitment. Though she had tried to get out of it, Angela was obligated to help a friend with a booth at the monthly antiques show at the city auditorium.

When she arrived at the travel agency, Madison lost herself in her work. It was the only way she could get her mind off her apprehensions. She was happy that since her return she had fallen right back into the groove with her old clients, continuing on as if she had never left.

She knew her employees were glad to have her back. In fact, Lanie and Gertie had arranged a coming-home party, complete with a cake her first day back in the office. To them, she was still Madison Calloway, and she preferred to keep it that way for a while longer. Mark and her mother were the only ones who knew of the marriage and pregnancy. But in the very near future it wasn't going to be too difficult for Lanie and Gertie to guess her condition—they had already commented on her apparent weight gain.

Madison had to pee so bad she thought sure she was going to explode. In fact, it would actually be a *pleasure* to explode right about now. Anything to relieve this pressure!

She lay uncomfortably on the hard steel table, insufficiently covered with a thin mattress. The hospital technician expertly slid a metal wand through globs of clear goop squirted over the slight mound of her tummy. The woman stared at the fleeting image, giving forth several experienced oohs and aahs. She nodded her head thoughtfully, finally giving a professional response to the erratic, fuzzy, gray-and-black picture on the little TV screen at Madison's side.

"Well," the technician finally commented in words, "there's definitely two in there. Congratulations Mr. and Mrs. Chase! You're going to have twins!"

"Ohhh, no, I'm not Mr. Chase . . . I'm her broth—" Mark stopped in midsentence. He gaped at the technician, then shot a look of utter shock toward Madison. Then he started laughing hysterically.

Madison's head jerked up from the flat pillow, dazed, her eyes wide, illuminated in stunned disbelief.

"Twins?" they both repeated.

Chapter Fifty-One

The screen door slapped against the house and Colt strode into the kitchen, little dust clouds released into the air with every labored step. His exhilaration of a few moments before was still burning like wildfire through his veins as he aimed his sights for the coffeepot, pouring himself a steaming mug of the bracing brew.

"I heard the shots! Colt?—what on earth happened? What's going on?" Rosannah burst into the kitchen like a little round whirlwind, her eyes wide with fright. As Colt shuffled around to face her, coffee cup in hand, she expelled a gasp of surprise. Good Lord, he looked like a dirt monster with eyes! He was covered with a thick coating of yellow-brown dust from head to foot, the line of white below his eyes an indication of where his bandanna had protected his nose and mouth. He stood with a peculiar lean against the pantry.

Colt's eyes sparkled and he smiled, recalling the tense situation he'd been in only moments before. The utter rush bombarded his senses as he strived to put Rosannah's mind at ease.

"The longhorns took to runnin'—" he drawled a little too slowly for Rosannah's liking.

"Oh my God!" she gasped again, pressing her hand over her mouth. "Where's Bud? Was anyone hurt?" Profound worry misted her dark eyes.

"Don't worry, Rosie, Bud's fine. It was one hell of a stampede, but we got 'em stopped all right. I think they've worn themselves out enough for one day." Colt gave a weary little chuckle before he shuffled toward the table, his gait wobbly and stiff as he obviously favored his left leg.

Rosannah frowned at his odd movement.

He lowered himself gingerly into a chair. "I heard the shots and got to camp as fast as I could. By that time, those crazed cattle were headed right for the gorge. I thought we'd all but lost 'em, but I had to give it a try. Lucky for me, I was riding Bluebell—she's one of the best cow ponies we have. I made it up to the leaders, fired a few shots to startle 'em . . . and damn if they didn't turn away from the gorge and begin to circle. It was a beautiful sight—until the lightning." Colt shook his head at the rotten turn of events. "The storm got 'em started again— right toward Cookie and the chuckwagon."

"Oh, my! You're hurt . . . what about your leg?" It was difficult to see the extent of the injury for all the dirt and grime, but she could tell by his awkward manner that all wasn't well. She moved to sit across from him at the table.

Colt glanced downward with a little shrug. His eyes slipped closed for a moment and he took a deep breath to chase away the fog that wanted to settle inside his head. He continued, "We got the chuckwagon moved. There were a few scary moments up on top of the ridge when I didn't think they were gonna stop. Spread some salt . . . that seemed . . . seemed to . . . do the trick. Got 'em stopped . . . all right." His speech slowed dramatically. It seemed like it took forever to get the coffee cup to his lips, and when he did it was as if he didn't have the energy to drink. He was so very tired all of a sudden. And his leg was beginning to pain him more with each passing second.

Colt lifted his eyes one last time before the cup slipped from his grasp and everything went black.

With a yelp and a scream for Emmy, Rosannah leapt out of her chair and was at Colt's slumped form in a flash. With horror, she noticed the pooling of blood beneath his chair.

Colt slept for two days, but it wasn't a restful sleep. It was fitful, with waking spells of irrational or despondent behavior. Emmy and Rosannah treated his bruised arm with a liniment, wrapping it in brown paper and vinegar. But his leg was a different story. They bathed it as best as they could. Luckily for him, it was a clean puncture wound in his thigh with a minor amount of tearing, the work of a well-aimed horn. It required several stitches. Emmy prepared the needles, thread, and cloth for bandages for Rosannah, who performed the actual handiwork.

Colt seemed unaware of their ministrations, except for an occasional toss of his head and a sleep-drugged groan. Afterward, mutton tallow was applied to reduce the swelling and inflammation, followed by a beefsteak poultice.

In intermittent spurts, Colt broke out into spasms of gut-wrenching coughs—and when he wasn't coughing, he was sneezing. Emmy sat vigil by his bed, wrapped in the oppressive heat of the upstairs bedroom. She mopped the sweat from his face and neck with a cool cloth, adjusted the bedclothes, and encouraged him to take drinks of water. When he stirred she spoke soothing words of comfort. The others came and went, endeavoring to pass on a little good cheer of their own.

Rosannah made frequent checks, usually with a hot mug of ginger tea or a concoction consisting of turpentine and lard to smooth on his chest for the congestion. By noon the third day he was coming around, and Rosannah and Emmy were joyous—at first.

Then it became sadly apparent that he was burning with fever and completely delirious. He would mumble jibberish, about nothing that made any sense, to no one in particular. He didn't even seem to know where he was. He referred to Emmy as Sarah, and he stared right through Rosannah as if she weren't there.

Doc Richards was summoned from South Pass City. He arrived in the evening, and Rosannah led him to Colt's room, putting a candle to the kerosene lamp for light. Colt tossed his head on the damp pillow, the words he uttered incoherent. After a careful examination, Doc Richards's face was bleak. He adjusted his square spectacles, then yanked a huge white handkerchief from his pocket and blew his nose loudly.

"Rosannah, Miss Emmy . . . I don't know how to put it pleasantly, so I'll just hash it out like it is. Colt's leg needs to come off."

The room was deathly quiet. Rosannah and Emmy exchanged horrified glances, their hands flying to their mouths in shock. Emmy let out a wail of despair.

"Surely there must be something else we can try first," Rosannah said, her eyes pleading with the doctor.

"We're dealing with a time factor here. If the infection gets any worse, this man will die. I recommend that it be done right away. If you like, I'll stay the night and do the surgery first thing in the morning."

Rosannah waited, then gave a curt little nod, her dark eyes swimming with moisture. Emmy dashed from the room in a flurry of tears. Doc Richards proceeded to medicate Colt with a dose of laudanum and left him to rest until morning.

Morning light was filtered through a dense covering of thick, gray rain clouds, the weather gloomy and humid, befitting the grim task ahead. The doctor was up early and readying himself for the surgery. The nightstand beside Colt's bed was well supplied with morphine, a sharpened saw, gunpowder for cauterizing, and plenty of sheets and bandages.

Emmy, her eyes red from crying most of the night, begged the good doctor to reconsider. When it was explained that there were no other alternatives she ran from the room once again, blubbering hysterically. She only hoped that Colt would have the strength to draw the pistol she had told him was under his pillow. She had placed it there last night before she had gone to bed.

Rosannah and Bud entered the room and Doc shuffled toward the bed. He fiddled with the instruments inside his black leather bag, then organized them on the bedside table.

When he finally pivoted to face Colt, he found himself looking down the dark barrel of a Colt Peacemaker. It was held by a shaky hand, but there was no question as to the aim. Shaky or not, if it was fired, it would hit its mark.

The doctor gasped, faltering back a step. Rosannah and Bud leaped forward, but then stopped, open-mouthed, when the pistol veered, leveling on them.

Colt struggled to lift his head from the pillow. He was pale, his face beaded with perspiration. His bloodshot eyes drifted in and out of focus.

All Doc Richards saw was the fiery amber orbs searing right through him.

Colt's brows drew together in fierce resolve before he spoke. "I don't believe you'll be using that saw today, Doc," he rasped.

Chapter Fifty-Two

It had been six days since Madison first discovered she was carrying twins, and there was only one day to go until her scheduled rendezvous with Colt.

Madison sat in her office, busily whipping through the airline schedules on her computer. She scrolled through pages and pages, and still found no available flight for a family of four to Kauai over Christmas. It wasn't at all unusual—just frustrating as hell, as one of her most valued clients was involved. The last vacation the family took in Cancun over spring break had been a disaster. Upon their arrival they had discovered their hotel was overbooked and couldn't accommodate them. It had taken some fancy footwork, a quick tongue, phone calls and a telex, but Madison had managed to secure them even nicer accommodations at a neighboring hotel at the same cost. All the same, she wanted and *needed* for this particular trip to come off without a hitch for herself as well as for them.

She sighed, rubbing her forehead as she leaned back in the chair. All at the same time, three agents barged through her office door and lined up before the desk.

"Maddie, I've got a lady who needs to get to London for a funeral but doesn't have a passport. What do I tell her?" Lanie was first in line for help.

"We'll have to do an overnight to San Francisco. Have her

fill out the paperwork. There're applications in the filing cabinet. Where's Mark?" Madison asked.

"Lunch," the women answered in unison.

"All right. Tell him when he gets back to do the passport first thing."

Lanie smiled, briskly proceeding to the files.

"Maddie," Gertie said, "I can't get the computer to give me the right price on this ticket." She slapped her ruined example on the desk for Madison's inspection. "When I print it I get a higher fare."

"Are you sure it should be lower? Did you call the airline?"

"Yup. It's a popular fare. They don't understand why it won't price, either."

"Okay . . . leave this here and I'll give the rep a call."

"Thanks, Maddie." Gertie left.

There was one to go, a new agent by the name of Barb whom Mark had hired to start this morning.

"I'm sorry to bother you." She smiled pleasantly. "I'm not quite sure when I should be going to lunch."

Maddie laughed with relief. "Now, that's my kind of problem—an easy one! If it's not busy, go now. We'll get a regular lunch hour set up by tomorrow."

"Sure thing. Thanks!" Barb exited, squeezing past Mark, who was rushing in.

"Maddie—"

"Mark—"

They both spoke at the same time, then laughed, Mark indicating for her to go first as he took a seat.

"Lanie needs some help with a rush on a passport."

"Oh, no problem. Be with you in a second." Mark grinned at Lanie, who was still rummaging through the files.

"As I was going to say," he continued, "Mom called right before I left for lunch, while you were on the phone. She said she has some things for the babies—a double stroller or something. And she picked up your vitamins from the doctor today."

"Why is she doing all this? I was going to run by his office and pick them up after work!" Madison groaned with a little laugh. "And a stroller? Are you kidding me? Isn't it a little soon?"

Madison couldn't believe her mother's excitement. On second thought, she could. It was just her mother's endearing way—in fact, she had already started purchasing the newborns' layette! Not to mention the color scheme, wallpaper and all, that she had picked out for the nursery decor. Madison had explained to her that perhaps it was a good idea to wait until she had a definite place to live before she started decorating a nursery.

Ever since Madison had found out she was carrying twins, life had been a three-ring circus. She had become an instant celebrity, and it was virtually impossible to keep the wonderful news out of the office. Madison had elected to inform everyone at work, which had turned out to be a relief. Now she didn't have to worry about concealing her pregnancy, which was a hopeless task anyway.

Her employees still considered her name as Calloway, although the consensus of the grapevine was that she had married Colt Chase's grandson, who also had the same name. Madison had supposedly met him through his grandfather, and it had been a whirlwind romance. Confusing—although partially true, it seemed to be a story that had more or less fabricated itself, and Madison didn't even have to fib.

"Now, Maddie, don't get mad, but I couldn't resist getting the babies a little something myself." Mark tossed a couple of kid-sized baseball caps on her desk. The emblem read Skysox. Madison snatched them up and broke into a fit of giggles.

Lanie finished her business and left the office. Madison hadn't missed the look she had exchanged with Mark in passing. There was something going on there; Madison was absolutely positive. And she thought it was great.

"These are terrific!" Madison said, holding up the caps. "But I think they'll be in college by the time they grow into them! Thanks. You're going to be a great uncle."

Mark smiled, "I know. So when do I get to meet their great dad? Have you been able to get a hold of him with the good news?"

Madison hesitated, the smile fading from her face. Her heart thumped. Whenever she thought of Colt she got a heavy feeling in her stomach. It was just nerves, she kept telling herself, all due to the fact that she hadn't seen him in thirteen days, which seemed like forever. With every passing day the anxiety had worsened, her anticipation mounting as the rendezvous date approached. She was so excited she could hardly stand it. So why in the world wouldn't this awful feeling go away?

"Er . . . no, I haven't," she stammered, "but that's not unusual; he's hard to get a hold of. I'm flying out tonight to pick him up."

"Will you be coming back here right away?"

"Actually, I'm not sure what his plans will be. I think so."

Mark frowned. It bothered him the way Maddie was so evasive about her new husband. Something wasn't right about her story. Though he could think of no reason for her behavior, he still had a notion there was something she wasn't telling him. It crossed his mind that maybe she wasn't married at all—maybe she had fallen in love with Colt and he hadn't share her feelings, leaving her high and dry. And now she was expecting twins . . .

"Well, okay," Mark sighed at last. "Don't worry about anything here. Call me as soon as you get back."

"I will. Thanks, Mark."

Mark got up and left. Madison chewed her lip, checking her watch. Her flight to Jackson was due to leave Colorado Springs in less than three hours. A lump formed in her throat and she thought she might cry. Why? There was no excuse . . . just a feeling.

It had to be those dreams—or rather, nightmares—she'd been having since she got home. The one about the herd of raging cows was the most puzzling. A good night's sleep was practically nonexistent for her as an even worse nightmare had plagued her the past two nights. It involved a man with mussed gray hair and a saw—similar to the kind used to cut down trees. His eyes were beady behind crooked spectacles and he looked down at her sternly, then started approaching with that damned saw. . . . It was terrifying!

Madison brushed the unpleasant thoughts away. She tidied up her desk and grabbed her purse. On her way out, she paused at Lanie's desk and gave her the assignment of finding a flight for four to Kauai. She asked Mark to take care of a few other loose ends.

After a quick trip home to pack a small carry-on bag, she dropped by her mother's to pick up the vitamins and then went on to the airport.

Colt wasn't there.

Madison's palms were clammy. Nerves, *she* thought, as she rubbed them down her pants legs. She sat on her haunches beneath the spruce and stared at the marbled rosebush as if the concentration of her gaze could somehow make a difference, change the wheels of destiny.

He was just late. That had to be it. He had sworn he would ride up to Jackson Hole that very day, and the day wasn't over yet.

Madison wouldn't chance horseback riding any longer, so she had rented a Jeep at the airport to make the trek up to the meadow.

It had involved a little creativity as far as finding the correct four-wheel drive trail, and she had needed to park and hike a ways besides that. But it had been an easy hike and the weather was fine.

Damn, but she wished the weather was awful! She wanted a storm, a horrible storm—because that would bring him back to her! There was only one bud left on the straggly, thorny bush. One! Once it was gone, it was over—wasn't it? Madison was filled with a myriad of sparring emotions. If he didn't come to her, she would go to him. Simple. That's all there was to it. Yes, it would undoubtedly be a one-way trip, but compared to the alternative of never seeing him again, it was not that bad an option.

One thing she knew to be the absolute truth: She couldn't live her life without Colt Chase. And she wasn't going to allow their innocent babies to grow up without knowing such a wonderful father!

Madison pushed herself up, impatiently treading through the thick tangle of grass to stand at the crest of the ridge. The wind blew at her baggy cotton maternity pants and top. They were huge and she felt like a professional clown. All she needed now were size 20 shoes. Dr. Metzger had told her to be sure and buy roomy maternity clothes, because whether she believed it or not now, she'd grow into them eventually.

The sun was warm, casting everything golden that was lucky enough to be touched by its rays, and Madison waited until the sun disappeared. The air turned bitingly cool as twilight settled in. She knew she should eat, but she had no appetite, forcing herself to munch on the raisins she had thrown into her purse as an afterthought.

Finally, with a great reluctance, her limbs feeling as heavy as lead weights, she slowly made her way back to where the Jeep was parked. Every so often she swiveled around to check—just to see if maybe, just *maybe*, every dream and desire she'd ever possessed had been fulfilled and there would be a regal gray stallion mounted by the most handsome cowboy she'd ever laid eyes on. . . .

Madison didn't crumble until she arrived at her hotel in Jackson, locking the solid oak door behind her. Then she fell down onto the soft bed, buried her face, and had a good, long cry.

Colt? Where are you? How could any God in heaven be so utterly cruel? She had lost him! It was just as she had feared all along. She had warned him repeatedly! If she came forward in time alone, they would lose one another. And her worst apprehensions had come true. Her heart felt as if it were being crushed in a giant, unrelenting press. Madison didn't think she could feel any worse than she did right then.

But she did—the following day, and the day after that. Her routine of endless waiting in the sunny meadow didn't change. Nor did the plaguing questions. Should she pluck the last rose? Cinnabar wasn't here. Maybe it wouldn't work without being on horseback, the speed of galloping through the eye of the eerie storm a necessary element for her return. What if, in her attempts to go to him, she unwittingly destroyed that last rose, destroying all chance of Colt ever joining her in this century? The memory of the other immortal buds, blackened once again since her recent return, haunted her—and she began to sob.

Until finally, her devastation complete, inconsolable, she left their beautiful meadow, alone, and headed back to Colorado Springs. What else could she do?

Chapter Fifty-Three

Colt's dire situation had improved the day the doctor left. The burning fever had broken the next day, and it had been a slow but downhill trek from there. His leg had pained him dreadfully, and he kept a bottle of whiskey by his bedside at all times. The combination of tonics, bitters, and laudanum, along with the liquor, had made the agony a little more bearable.

The morning Colt had pulled the pistol on old Doc Richards was the morning the old man had packed his bag with a shake of his bushy head, sympathetically leaving behind any applicable medicines for the dying man before riding away in his black one-horse buggy. The doctor was certain Colt would die if the leg was not amputated.

Colt had proven him wrong, with the help of Rosannah, Emmy, and Bud. Now in his second week of convalescence, he was walking with the assistance of a wooden cane fashioned from sturdy oak by Zak, a carving of a horse's head improvised as a handle. He exercised and ate as much as he could possibly stomach, realizing the urgent need to build up his strength. An effort had been made by Rosannah to contact Madison through her mother in Colorado, but so far no response had been received.

Colt was very much aware of the date. The time had come and passed for him to tie up loose ends and go to his beloved wife. *Oh, Madison! What must you be thinking?* He had sworn to her that he would meet with her in that meadow—their meadow. He had failed through no fault of his own. But nonetheless it was a gross default. There was so much to be done! And he hadn't even begun yet.

One good thing about his plight—with all this bed rest, there was plenty of time to think. To plan. It was all very simple, the whole scheme prepared for skillful orchestration as soon as he was able . . . very soon. And then he would transcend the barriers of time to join his lovely wife and their baby, forever.

By the end of the fourth week Colt was well enough to limp, with the aid of his cane, down to the barns, where he saddled up Cinder and headed into the foothills of the Wind River mountains. Armed with a pick ax and several empty saddlebags, he scaled the western slopes well below Atlantic City. There, exactly as he remembered, was the childhood lair where he and Garrett had frequently passed their time—that is, during those times when it hadn't been occupied by something bigger and hairier than they were.

Colt had been haunted by this instinct, since he had discovered Garrett's absconding of the ranch's money. If Garrett had hidden the missing cash somewhere, possibly it was here, the cave being more of a favorite of Garrett's than his.

Checking first for any current wild inhabitants, Colt lit a tinderbox candle and made his way inside the craggy black hole. Whitened animal bones were littered across the entry way and Colt smiled. That was a trick Garrett had frequently used to scare two-legged intruders away—no doubt they were planted for that very purpose now.

Advancing entirely by memory, he located the precise aperture he was searching for, only penetrable by squeezing his body in sideways. Within the gloomy dankness he discovered the familiar old wooden dome trunk in the chipped and faded colors of salmon and sea green. With a scraping hiss and a puff of dust, it opened. A long, low whistle escaped his lips.

Amazing! Wads of bills, some bound, others loose, in both small and large denominations. The bottom of the trunk was full of gold and silver coins, even a few choice pieces of jewelry and a couple of gold pocketwatches. The trunk was so heavy, it could barely be moved, let alone lifted.

Colt felt extremely lucky, indeed. This was much better than his wildest imaginings, and he wondered at the origin of this cache.

There was too much money to have come from the ranch alone—possibly another source was part of its unsavory history, such as a bank or train robbery.

It took a while in his condition, but he managed to stuff the saddlebags as full as was practical. Then he mounted Cinder for the trip back down the mountain.

The following morning Colt was worn out and still weak from the trip to the cave. It was too soon for all this activity; he knew that. He also knew his leg was far from well—there was still plenty of swollen flesh, which attested to a sizable infection brewing inside, one that sent agonizing pains shooting through his leg whenever it was bumped or touched.

Despite his questionable condition, he had to finish the tasks at hand and get to Madison—for more than one reason. Yes, he was dying to be with her, but it was also imperative that his leg receive medical attention. If Madison was right about the medical advancements of the twentieth century—and he had no doubt she was—then he would seek them out. Because if he didn't, the leg would have to go—or the blasted infection would surely take his life.

Despite his infirmity, Colt traveled to South Pass City that day, his saddlebags full, armed to the teeth. He visited the law office of Beckett & Sons, then went to the most reputable bank in town and made a very impressive deposit. It was slow going. He didn't get home until evening because of the stiffness in his leg; it was becoming increasingly more difficult to mount his horse.

That night in his room, by the yellow glow of lamplight, he composed two letters. His affairs well in order and the envelopes sealed, he retired for the evening.

He awoke to a resplendently sunny day and to one of the most upsetting duties left to perform—saying good-bye. Cinder was tacked and tethered at the front of the house. With the aid of his cane, Colt hobbled through the main house to deliver his farewells. Emmy. Bud. And Rosannah. They didn't know on this second day of September that it was forever. But he did. Careful to keep a smile on his face and any stray tears in check, he pressed the envelopes into Rosannah's hand, along with his instructions. He was trusting her—and Emmy—with his very life and future.

Then he was gone. Astride Cinder, he headed up the winding mountain pass, destined for the Jackson Hole valley, the little chocolate brown paint pony in tow.

Chapter Fifty-Four

As was characteristic of her during the past few weeks, Madison
sat at her desk with a mountain of paperwork looming before her.
Mark was worried as he watched her through the glass windows of
her office. She had come back from Jackson without Colt, refusing
to discuss it and depressed as hell. And it wasn't getting any better. She worked all the time—sometimes twelve or fourteen hours
a day. Her tan long since faded, she looked pale and worn out.

All this couldn't be healthy for her, or for the babies, and the
most disturbing part to Mark was that she didn't smile anymore.
That charm that radiated her own brand of contagious cheer wherever she went was gone. Her eyes were droopy and lackluster,
accented by the perpetual presence of dark circles. Mark knew
in his heart that Colt was responsible, and he felt like killing the
man for what he had done to his sister.

He was distracted from his murderous thoughts as he watched
Lanie pass his office and head for Madison's.

"Maddie?" Lanie stuck her head inside the big glass door.
"There's a gentleman out front who would like to see you."

"I really don't feel like seeing anyone right now." Madison
sighed. "I'm getting ready to leave. Did he have an appointment?"

"No . . . but he says it's very important."

"Oh, all right. Send him in."

Madison smoothed a few stray curls and straightened her desk. She really didn't have the time to dawdle. Her flight left in an hour and a half. It had taken a little while to work up the courage, but Madison had decided once and for all what she must do.

When Colt hadn't shown up as promised she could only conclude that something had gone terribly wrong. She trusted him enough to know that as the absolute truth. These past few weeks had been sheer torture, but she felt that she had needed the time to prepare herself for the journey back—the final journey of the marbled rose. Besides, there had been the remote chance that Colt would still show up, and she had wanted to give him a decent opportunity to do just that. Now it was painfully obvious he wasn't coming. So Madison was going to him.

A few moments later, a very refined gentleman in an immaculately tailored navy-blue pinstripe suit entered her office. He was quite distinguished, his salt-and-pepper hair accented by perfectly trimmed silver sideburns.

"Mrs. Chase?" he inquired politely.

Madison started. People rarely called her Mrs. Chase, especially at the office. "Yes?" she stammered just a little, frowning.

"My name is William Bancroft, of Bancroft, Childs and Lambert. We're a law firm in Jackson, Wyoming." His eyebrows shot up, his voice smooth.

For a moment, Madison could only gape in wonder. A law firm in Jackson? What was happening?—was she being sued? Had she done something wrong? Traveling back in time without a license, maybe? A smile laced with a touch of her old ironic humor curved her lips.

"May I sit down?" he asked pleasantly.

"Oh, yes! Forgive my rudeness. Please, have a seat." Madison smiled more brightly than she had in weeks, gesturing toward the brown leather chair in front of her desk. For some reason her heart was racing at an incredible rate.

Mr. Bancroft sat down, positioning an expensive black leather briefcase in his lap. He opened it to remove a thick manila envelope. He passed it across the desk to her. Madison took it haltingly, a question in her eyes as they lifted to his.

"Mrs. Chase . . . this is quite an unusual circumstance for my firm. It's been a mystery to myself as well as to my colleagues. I don't understand it completely myself. A client of my father's, Emily Bartlett Stockton—"

Madison gasped involuntarily at the sound of the name, her hand climbing to her lips.

"She passed on many years ago, in 1968, to be exact. She was the owner of the Triple Bar C ranch near Jackson. Perhaps you're familiar with it?"

Madison was agog. "Yes! Yes, I am."

"Well, Mrs. Chase, congratulations! You are the new owner of that spread. It's one of the biggest in Wyoming, you know. You were named in her will as the sole inheritor—you and your child. But, for reasons I haven't been made aware of, possession wasn't to take effect until September 1993."

He took a deep breath and continued, obviously embarrassed, "I must apologize, but over the years there were resignations and deaths at our firm and Mrs. Stockton's file was misplaced. We've only recently recovered it, and as a result the conditions of the will were not carried through. I'm here to try and make restitution. Of course, the first thing I did was to stop the ranch from being auctioned, and I've taken the liberty of hiring ranch hands and a construction crew to refurbish the entire spread to the condition it was in prior to Mrs. Stockton's death. Again, I apologize on behalf of the firm. We're prepared to do everything in our power to correct this grave error.

"In her will there were instructions for this envelope to be delivered to you here, on this particular date." Mr. Bancroft indicated the envelope Madison still held in her palm. "I'm confident there are further explanations inside. Did you know Mrs. Stockton well?"

"What?" she gasped, her mind spinning, unable to comprehend all she had heard. "I'm sorry! This is just so . . . unexpected. No, I didn't know her real well, but we did become friends when she was a young girl—"

Mr. Bancroft frowned, opening his mouth as if to speak, but nothing came out.

"Oh . . ." Madison laughed off her blunder, "what I mean is . . . when *I* was a young girl."

"Of course. I see." He smiled, nodding.

Madison held the envelope up to regard it more closely. The name Madison Calloway Chase was typed professionally on the front. She glanced at Mr. Bancroft, smiling awkwardly as she ripped it open. With her hands trembling as they were, it wasn't the easiest task.

Mr. Bancroft softly closed his briefcase and stood up. "I'm

certain we can remedy any error to your satisfaction. I'll leave you to your privacy, Mrs. Chase. Here's my card." He placed it on the corner of her desk. "Contact me whenever you like and we'll set up a meeting to tie up loose ends. There will be some papers for you to sign."

Madison nodded, thanking him profusely. Taken aback by this sudden event, she felt as if she were floating on air as she walked him to the door. When Mr. Bancroft was gone she left instructions not to be disturbed, then sat down and began to read the letter:

Dearest Madison,

I'm confident you must be quite confused by this point. Let me assure you, you're not alone. I have spent the better part of my life baffled by this strange circumstance. I'm an old woman now, Madison, but I never forgot you. Had it not been for your kind spirit and loving nature, I might not have flourished in this life as I did. You taught me more than I can put into simple words. When you departed the ranch that summer of 1878, I was devastated, and later crushed when I never heard from you.

When I was in my 25th year, Mama was stricken with a horrid case of pleurisy and lay on her death bed. She entrusted with me a tattered envelope. Imagine my surprise to find it contained the paperwork to a large savings account in my name. More importantly, a letter with my name on it was also contained within. It was from the man I loved with all my heart, a man who had earned my deepest respect—Colton Chase.

Yes, I loved him, Madison. More than you can ever know, in a way even to this day I don't fully understand. It was an innocent love, but no less powerful because of that. I nursed him back to health after he had been gored during a dreadful cattle stampede that killed two of the hands. If it hadn't been for the pistol I placed under Colt's pillow, that doctor would have taken his leg. I couldn't let that happen! I felt deep within my heart Colt was reaching out for my help.

Oh, Madison, I hated you so when you first arrived at the ranch. You were my worst nightmare. You were there to take my beloved Colt. But you cultivated that putrid hatred into a love of the purest kind, and I came to realize what a lucky man Colt was to have found a woman such as you.

You became the sister I never had.

Thank you for your treasured gifts. I was ahead of my time throughout my entire life. A person couldn't call me shy. I was envied. I traveled the world in style—a style you helped to create. I was one of the lucky survivors of the S.S. Titanic. My life has been rich and full, but it nears a close now, and I must explain my purpose.

I made several promises to Colt. The first was that I bequeath my precious Triple Bar C to you and your children. Second, I was asked to use the money in the savings account to open a trust for maintenance of the ranch after my death, until the year 1993. Naturally, you can understand my skepticism. Thirdly, Colt urged me to have utter faith in him, to believe, and for that he would be eternally grateful. He requested I write this letter of explanation, and to specify delivery to you on this exact date to your travel agency in Colorado Springs. He also entrusted me with another letter from him to you, which I have enclosed. It is for your eyes alone, penned by his own hand the day he left the ranch, never to return.

So you see, I've possessed these instructions my entire adult life, but whether to act on them was the question. No, there was never a question. My beloved Colt asked it of me—and for him, I would do most anything.

Farewell my dear Madison—there are things in this world we don't understand, but have faith and maybe we shall meet again.

> Yours forever,
> Emmy

Her teeth were painfully imbedded in Madison's fist as she fought to hold back her tears. So many questions!

Swiping a stray tear from her cheek, Madison hurriedly ripped open the second, smaller envelope. Colt's elegant, slanted script leaped out at her from the ancient, yellowed envelope bearing her name. She held her breath despite herself, terrified of the unknown that awaited her, praying. It read:

My Sweet Madison,

Sugar, I miss you so, and despise myself for breaking our rendezvous. There was a stampede the day I sent you home. Yes, the longhorns. We lost two of the hands, something I didn't even realize until much later. I nearly lost my leg, and lay in a delirious stupor for days. I expect I gave Rosannah, Emmy, and Bud quite a scare. In truth, if it hadn't been for them, I might not have survived the grievous ordeal.

I love you more than life itself. And if I should fail you in the physical aspect of this bewildering life, do not fear that I shall ever fail you in the spiritual. I will always be by your side, for all eternity.

I am at this moment preparing for my final journey to you. It is September 2, 1878, and I am leaving for Jackson Hole to pick me another rose. The ranch is yours and our child's—should something happen and I don't make it. Always know of my true love, sugar. Meet you at the Triple Bar C . . .

All my love, Colt

Tears were flowing in torrents. The dreams she'd been having were of a stampede on the ranch! Colt had been hurt and he had needed her! Madison was shaking so badly, she could barely function to fold the letters and slip them safely into her purse. She was numb, unaware of anything that was going on around her.

The office was swarming with clients, every agent occupied with a customer, but Madison didn't notice. Without saying so much as a fleeting good-bye to anyone, she was out the front door.

Mark chased her out the door, alarmed by the abruptness of her departure. He was forced to abort his pursuit, though, when she beat him to her car, ignoring his shouts for her to stop, then speeding out of the parking lot.

"Who was that man in Maddie's office a few minutes ago?" Mark asked Lanie as he strode back inside.

She shrugged, ruffling through the pile of papers on her desk. "Oh, here it is . . . a Mr. Bancroft. An attorney from Jackson, Wyoming, I believe he said."

A thousand possibilities raced through Mark's mind at that moment. He had no idea what had happened or what, if anything, he should do to help his sister.

Madison's flight landed in Jackson just before dinner. For the second time she rented a Jeep, winding down the two-lane mountain highway en route to the Triple Bar C ranch. What would she find there? A dilapidated mess as before? Mr. Bancroft had said they'd already begun to renovate. . . . She could only guess—the suspense was an absolute killer. Her heart had been thumping so hard, she felt as if her chest was actually sore from the erratic palpitations.

My God! she thought. Could it be true? Was Colt coming home to her?

As the Jeep bumped and bounced along the dirt road, Madison chewed her lip nervously, terrified of what might greet her, begging silently for what she fervently hoped would come. The peaked roof of the ranch house emerged in the far distance, partially hidden by the generous foliage of giant trees. She was forced to stop at the white arched gateway. It was closed.

Madison got out, racing around to pull at the gates, a huge padlock securing it. She kept on tugging, more out of frustration than anything.

"Excuse me, ma'am. May I help you?"

Madison jumped, overwrought. Her hand flew to calm the rapid expansion of her chest. She could only stare at the man on horseback, positioned casually on the other side of the whitewashed fence. How long had he been there? He leaned, his arms folded over the saddle horn, a bemused smile creasing his deeply tanned face as he looked down at her. He poked the underside brim of his hat, pushing it up, revealing just a hint of silvery hair and a weathered brow.

Madison gasped. Good Lord! He was the spitting image of Bud.

Chapter Fifty-Five

"You wouldn't happen to be Madison Chase, would you?" the rider asked with a warm, knowing grin.

"Yes, I am," she stammered, "and you . . . ?"

"The foreman, Buck Epson. Pleased to meet you. They told me to be expecting you."

"They?"

"The attorneys," he clarified.

She thought she was surely losing her mind this time. After all she'd been through these past couple of months, one would assume she'd be immune to this sort of occurrence. Madison could have sworn he'd said his name was Bud! . . . No, of course, she knew he had introduced himself as Buck, but the resemblance to the other man was absolutely uncanny. She still gawked. He must think she was a total nitwit!

"Oh! Yes, of course . . ." She gave a little laugh. "Nice to meet you, Buck."

He swung down from the pretty little bay. Taking a huge silver ring of keys from his belt, he proceeded to unlock the gates, rattling on in idle conversation, his ice-blue eyes sparkling. He swung the gates open in a wide sweep.

"I'm sorry for staring," she apologized, "but you remind me of someone. A foreman a long time ago . . ." Her words dwindled at the pleasant memory.

Buck laughed, a rich sound, "Ain't that somethin' how us cowpokes all seem to look alike?"

"Yeah . . . it's something, all right." Madison slowly backed toward the driver's side of the Jeep, preparing to get in.

"You go right on up to the house and take a look around. I'll be working around the main barn should you need me." Buck nodded curtly, with a touch to the brim of his hat. He waited patiently for her to drive through.

"Thanks, Buck," Madison called as she drove by. Through the rear-view mirror she saw him close the gates, then mount his horse to ride away. Astounding, she mused, shaking her head.

The Jeep bounded toward the crest of the hill until the stately ranch house burst into view. Madison slammed on the brakes, consumed with awe. From every corner as far as she could see were men working: a scaffolding hung at the second story, where workers put finishing touches on the pale yellow paint; stacks of lumber and construction equipment littered the yard; the porch was being completely reconstructed. The sounds of hammers and electric saws mingled with the voices of the workmen, creating an air of chaotic harmony. A moving van was backed up for easy access to the front door.

Slowly, Madison pulled the Jeep up as close as she could get, and then got out and headed for the porch. Carefully, she avoided the construction scrap piles and miscellaneous tools. Her eyes wide with pure pleasure, she drank in the sight of what was being formed from the old mess. It was spectacular! The house would be even better than it had been in 1878. Nearly gone was the old, broken-down ranch house she had first seen the day of the picnic, with Colt, the old man . . . so long ago. With a burst of energy, she skipped up the newly constructed front steps with unbridled enthusiasm, twirling to survey the panorama of the surrounding land.

Her breath caught. Herds of grazing cattle milled over vast spreads of endless pastures. The barns and other outbuildings,— both old and the more modern steel ones—were being redone, with yet more construction crews at work. Everything was so beautiful, and it all brought forth such a rush of satisfying memories, she thought she would start crying all over again.

Madison forced her attention from the mesmerizing view and stepped inside the partially open front door, to be greeted by movers who scooted by her on their way to fetch another load. Like a child in a candy store, she stood perfectly still, awed.

A rush of sweetly scented air swept past her nose, reminiscent of cinnamon potpourri mixed with lemon furniture polish. She gasped with utter delight.

She began rushing through the maze of rooms. It was positively incredible. Though most of the house hadn't been totally renovated, smatterings of the furnishings she remembered were stacked in rooms that had been completed.

Hurriedly, she ran from item to item. Dashing into the dining room, she ran her fingertips across the cherrywood hutch. This would display her own collection of flow blue china beautifully!

Still unable to comprehend this drastic change, this miracle, she sprinted upstairs. She burst into Colt's bedroom, *their* bedroom, sighing with a bittersweet tangle of emotions that welled inside her. She was besieged with a flood of memories—from the first moment she had seen this room, the time she had thrown her boot at Colt, to the days when they had shared it as husband and wife. . . .

The four-poster bed was definitely the original. It looked much older, the dark polished mahogany dull and scarred. Everything was stark, still unfinished, the walls freshly covered in new wallpaper of blue, green, and rose flowers. The big green chair was sitting in the middle of the room, still wrapped in a protective cloth. Madison lifted a corner to peer underneath. Though much older and very worn, it promised as much comfort as before.

Mr. Bancroft had certainly kept his word about rectifying everything, and Madison made a mental note to ask him how he had managed to track down some of the ranch's original furnishings.

Tears of gratitude to him rolled down her cheeks, and she swiped at them impatiently. There was more to see, and she headed downstairs straight for the kitchen. She marveled at the wonderfully modern conveniences. The kitchen was almost finished. It was twice as big as the old one. *Oh, Rosannah! If only you could see your haven now!*

Madison impetuously ran back outside, a nagging feeling pushing away all other thoughts, dominating, calling her away.

Colt! Where was Colt? She walked the immediate grounds, casting expectant glances in a northerly direction, toward the ridge. Every breath was seized in her throat, twisting in expectation and apprehension each time her eyes lifted.

Good God, where *was* he? Madison felt as if she were sweating bullets. She wiped her palms along the front of her dress. She hadn't bothered to change clothes before she caught the plane to Jackson and was still wearing the navy-blue-and-white tent dress she had worn to the office. She imagined she looked very inappropriate wading through the tall, swaying grasses in her maternity dress, stockings, and low heels. But she didn't give a damn what anyone thought. This journey was for Colt; he was all that mattered right now.

Finally, she pulled the letters from her purse, reading them again for the zillionth time, as she had done in the airplane on her way here. Satisfied that she had studied every word, she folded and put the letters away. Yes, he would be here, any time now. She paced, until the incessant late-summer wind had nearly torn every hair from the professionally neat coil she had fashioned that morning. They drifted in weary wisps around her expectant, luminous face.

Were her eyes playing tricks? Was that movement beyond the far slope? Then her heart stopped. Her breath stopped. But her legs were moving like a bat out of hell.

There on the pine-sprinkled rim was a rider, poised proud in the saddle, a tan-colored Stetson on his head. The huge, mottled gray stallion trotted purposefully down the near side of the saged plateau, the rider leading a wiry, chocolate-splashed paint pony behind him.

Madison was running, charging through the tall grass, puffing until she couldn't seem to supply enough air to fill her greedy lungs. At last she was forced to stop in exhaustion, clutching at her swollen stomach, unable to keep the tears at bay or the brilliant smile from consuming her face.

Colt smiled brightly, too, white against the bronze of his face. When he was near enough he lifted a leg over the saddle, easing himself carefully to the ground. He retrieved a cane from the saddle boot, dropping the reins. Even with a broken gait, he strode toward her with determination.

Before any words of concern escaped her lips, she was scooped within his arms, captured against the solidity of his warm body. He welcomed the sight of her with unequaled fervor, giving forth a long growl of utter gratification that originated deep inside him. Madison's arms entwined around Colt's neck, clutching in a powerful lock. She buried her face with an anguished cry, inhaling his ever intoxicating scent. They were kissing and talking at the same time. The music of mingled laughter wafted over the hillside.

"Madison . . . my sweet, sweet Madison . . ."

"Oh, Colt! I was so terrified," she cried, leaning back to beam up at him. "Your leg—"

"Don't worry about that. I'm here now, sugar, and it'll be a cold day in hell before you manage to get rid of me again." He sealed the promise with a kiss.

Laughing, she tossed his hat aside, thrusting her fingers through the thick chestnut hair. It hadn't been cut since that fateful episode when she had performed the honors, and it was charmingly shaggy, the length gaining on his broad shoulders. He looked downright scampish.

"You're not *old,* Colt! Isn't that wonderful?" she giggled with happiness.

"Everyone else may not see me the way you do," he reminded her.

"Who cares?" Positively giddy, she kissed him again. "Colt, I missed you so much. I was afraid I'd never see you again."

"Me, too," he confessed.

Colt's hand snaked down, his fingers spreading gently over the swell of her stomach. His expression was one of joy tinged with surprise. "You're getting fat, sugar. Been eating a little too much while I was away, huh?" he teased softly.

"Oh, Colt!" she uttered in a half-laugh, half-sob, nearly forgetting her big news. "I *have* to eat a lot—I'm feeding *three!* We're having *twins!*"

Colt's gaze was suddenly deep, fixing on her with such profound emotion, Madison thought sure she would dissolve right then and there. Then he hugged her, clutching her tighter still, until she felt the dampness of his tears on the curve of her neck.

"I love you, sugar," he breathed huskily.

"I love you, too, soul of my soul . . . more than you'll ever know. So much more . . ."

Epilogue

Madison sat by the edge of the swollen creek, watching the two babies play. They looked very much alike from afar, tight ringlets crowning their heads, shimmering like golden halos. With supreme concentration, they grasped at pebbles with their fat fingers, tossing them into the rushing water with no small amount of theatrics. Synchronized giggles bubbled into the sun-washed air.

Madison clapped her hands together, smiling brightly at their antics. "That was very good, Charlie! Now let's see if your sister has as good a pitching arm as her mother. C'mon, Katherine, let 'er rip!"

The chubby two-year-old scooped a handful for herself and promptly splashed them into the water, her corkscrew curls bouncing gaily as she did. She screamed wondrously at her own newfound abilities, her eyes bright in amazement. Madison smiled, clapping for her daughter, pushing to stand up when she heard the approach of a vehicle.

Just as she expected, the black pick-up truck bounded up the dirt driveway, splashing purposefully through every mud puddle, skidding to a gravel-slinging halt. Colt leapt out of the cab, striding to meet her, a blazing smile lighting his face. His muscular arm circled possessively about her shoulders. He bestowed on Madison a lingering kiss before kneeling to greet the two toddlers.

391

They ran, their arms swinging at a much faster tempo than their legs, directly for him.

"Hey, I thought I made it perfectly clear that I wouldn't teach you to drive if you didn't do so responsibly?" Madison chastised, wagging her finger in his face.

Colt grinned. "And as I always say . . . you take the bull by the horns, sugar, you're bound to get stuck." He winked.

Madison backhanded him playfully across the shoulder.

Colt drew his two children into a great bear hug, growling loudly, much to their giggling amusement. He lifted both squirmy children, one on each arm, and held them close as he headed for the house. Madison slid her arm around his waist and walked slowly beside him.

Madison marveled at how Colt's leg was practically like new. It was next to impossible to notice the limp any longer, thanks to the prompt administration of modern medicine.

Colt and Madison were now legally married in the twentieth century, thanks to Angela's insistent prodding. The wedding had been a fantasy conceived only in heaven itself. A small, very romantic affair, it had been performed within the newly contucted gazebo, overseen by tangles of vibrantly hued roses, their perfume filling the air.

The weather had been a perfect combination of Indian summer and the golden foliage of fall. Very pregnant, Madison had still managed to fit into her original wedding gown from Laramie, with expert alterations by a seamstress, that is. And, unbelievably, Colt had looked even handsomer than he had at their first wedding. Naturally, he had worn all western clothing, right down to a brand-new dashing ivory Stetson.

Mark had given the bride away, and Angela had cried profusely. Buck had been quick to provide a clean handkerchief, not at all shy about demonstrating a growing admiration for the silver-haired woman.

But the thing that pleased Madison the most was the fact that Colt had retained his youth on the last journey forward. Everyone saw him as the age he truly was—and to her, that symbolized much more than met the eye. It was a sign that Colt was meant to be there for good, hers for all time.

"So what happened in town?" Madison asked her husband as they mounted the porch steps.

He set the wiggling children down and they scurried away, one chasing the other.

"Mr. Kilroy, the man who called last week, is a gun authority. Wants my Peacemakers for his antique collection. After careful examination he came to the conclusion that my pistols are definitely authentic. He was very knowledgeable about the legend of Colt Chase. Imagine that." Colt shook his head in mock amazement, winking before stealing another heady kiss from his lovely wife.

"So what did he offer you?" Madison laughed.

"A lot. One hell of a lot."

"And . . . what did you say?" she coaxed, becoming very impatient at his vagueness.

"I said . . . hell yes! Don't expect I'll be needing them anymore. Plus, they'll be displayed at that museum up in Jackson. It'll be nice visiting my old pals on occasion. We've survived quite a few hairy adventures together, you know."

"I know. Boy, do I know," she purred.

Madison smiled contentedly, slipping her arm through his and around his waist to embrace him in a tight hug. She gazed wondrously up into his face, absorbing the indescribable love she found there, pulling it into her heart where she would cherish it for all time.

Cupping her face, Colt entrusted a meaningful kiss to her lips before they parted just long enough to get through the doorway, arm in arm. The twins bounced gleefully behind them, squeezing in through their legs.

LOVE SPELL

THE MAGIC OF ROMANCE
PAST, PRESENT, AND FUTURE....

Dorchester Publishing Co., Inc., the leader in romantic fiction, is pleased to unveil its newest line—Love Spell. Every month, beginning in August 1993, Love Spell will publish one book in each of four categories:

1) *Timeswept Romance*—Modern-day heroines travel to the past to find the men who fulfill their hearts' desires.

2) *Futuristic Romance*—Love on distant worlds where passion is the lifeblood of every man and woman.

3) *Historical Romance*—Full of desire, adventure and intrigue, these stories will thrill readers everywhere.

4) *Contemporary Romance*—With novels by Lori Copeland, Heather Graham, and Jayne Ann Krentz, Love Spell's line of contemporary romance is first-rate.

Exploding with soaring passion and fiery sensuality, Love Spell romances are destined to take you to dazzling new heights of ecstasy.

FROM LOVE SPELL
FUTURISTIC ROMANCE
NO OTHER LOVE
Flora Speer
Bestselling Author of *A Time To Love Again*

Only Herne sees the woman. To the other explorers of the ruined city she remains unseen, unknown. But after an illicit joining she is gone, and Herne finds he cannot forget his beautiful seductress, or ignore her uncanny resemblance to another member of the exploration party. Determined to unravel the puzzle, Herne begins a seduction of his own—one that will unleash a whirlwind of danger and desire.

_51916-X $4.99 US/$5.99 CAN

TIMESWEPT ROMANCE
LOVE'S TIMELESS DANCE
Vivian Knight-Jenkins

Although the pressure from her company's upcoming show is driving Leeanne Sullivan crazy, she refuses to believe she can be dancing in her studio one minute—and with a seventeenth-century Highlander the next. A liberated woman like Leeanne will have no problem teaching virile Iain MacBride a new step or two, and soon she'll have him begging for lessons in love.

_51917-8 $4.99 US/$5.99 CAN

FROM LOVE SPELL
HISTORICAL ROMANCE
THE PASSIONATE REBEL
Helene Lehr

A beautiful American patriot, Gillian Winthrop is horrified to learn that her grandmother means her to wed a traitor to the American Revolution. Her body yearns for Philip Meredith's masterful touch, but she is determined not to give her hand—or any other part of herself—to the handsome Tory, until he convinces her that he too is a passionate rebel.

_51918-6 $4.99 US/$5.99 CAN

CONTEMPORARY ROMANCE
THE TAWNY GOLD MAN
Amii Lorin

Bestselling Author Of More Than 5 Million Books In Print!

Long ago, in a moment of wild, rioting ecstasy, Jud Cammeron vowed to love her always. Now, as Anne Moore looks at her stepbrother, she sees a total stranger, a man who plans to take control of his father's estate and everyone on it. Anne knows things are different—she is a grown woman with a fiance—but something tells her she still belongs to the tawny gold man.

_51919-4
                                             $4.99 US/$5.99 CAN

AN HISTORICAL ROMANCE
GILDED SPLENDOR
By Elizabeth Parker

Bound for the London stage, sheltered Amanda Prescott has no idea that fate has already cast her first role as a rakehell's true love. But while visiting Patrick Winter's country estate, she succumbs to the dashing peer's burning desire. Amid the glittering milieu of wealth and glamour, Amanda and Patrick banish forever their harsh past and make all their fantasies a passionate reality.

__51914-3 $4.99 US/$5.99 CAN

A CONTEMPORARY ROMANCE
MADE FOR EACH OTHER/RAVISHED
By Parris Afton Bonds
Bestselling Author of *The Captive*

In *Made for Each Other*, reporter Julie Dever thinks she knows everything about Senator Nicholas Raffer—until he rescues her from a car wreck and shares with her a passion she never dared hope for. And in *Ravished*, a Mexican vacation changes nurse Nelli Walzchak's life when she is kidnapped by a handsome stranger who needs more than her professional help.

__51915-1 $4.99 US/$5.99 CAN

LEISURE BOOKS
ATTN: Order Department
276 5th Avenue, New York, NY 10001

Please add $1.50 for shipping and handling for the first book and $.35 for each book thereafter. PA., N.Y.S. and N.Y.C. residents, please add appropriate sales tax. No cash, stamps, or C.O.D.s. All orders shipped within 6 weeks via postal service book rate. Canadian orders require $2.00 extra postage and must be paid in U.S. dollars through a U.S. banking facility.

Name _____

Address _____

City _____ State _____ Zip _____

I have enclosed $_____ in payment for the checked book(s).

Payment <u>must</u> accompany all orders.☐ Please send a free catalog.

TIMESWEPT ROMANCE

A TIME-TRAVEL CHRISTMAS
By Megan Daniel, Vivian Knight-Jenkins, Eugenia Riley, and Flora Speer

In these four passionate time-travel historical romance stories, modern-day heroines journey everywhere from Dickens's London to a medieval castle as they fulfill their deepest desires on Christmases past.

___51912-7 $4.99 US/$5.99 CAN

A FUTURISTIC ROMANCE

MOON OF DESIRE
By Pam Rock

Future leader of his order, Logan has vanquished enemies, so he expects no trouble when a sinister plot brings a mere woman to him. But as the three moons of the planet Thurlow move into alignment, Logan and Calla head for a collision of heavenly bodies that will bring them ecstasy—or utter devastation.

___51913-5 $4.99 US/$5.99 CAN

FUTURISTIC ROMANCE
FIRESTAR
Kathleen Morgan
Bestselling Author of *The Knowing Crystal*

From the moment Meriel lays eyes on the virile slave chosen to breed with her, the heir to the Tenuan throne is loath to perform her imperial duty and produce a child. Yet despite her resolve, Meriel soon succumbs to Gage Bardwin—the one man who can save her planet.

__0-505-51908-9 $4.99 US/$5.99 CAN

TIMESWEPT ROMANCE
ALL THE TIME WE NEED
Megan Daniel

Nearly drowned after trying to save a client, musical agent Charli Stewart wakes up in New Orleans's finest brothel—run by the mother of the city's most virile man—on the eve of the Civil War. Unsure if she'll ever return to her own era, Charli gambles her heart on a love that might end as quickly as it began.

__0-505-51909-7 $4.99 US/$5.99 CAN

LEISURE BOOKS
ATTN: Order Department
276 5th Avenue, New York, NY 10001

Please add $1.50 for shipping and handling for the first book and $.35 for each book thereafter. PA., N.Y.S. and N.Y.C. residents, please add appropriate sales tax. No cash, stamps, or C.O.D.s. All orders shipped within 6 weeks via postal service book rate. Canadian orders require $2.00 extra postage and must be paid in U.S. dollars through a U.S. banking facility.

Name _____

Address _____

City _____ State _____ Zip _____

I have enclosed $_____in payment for the checked book(s).

Payment <u>must</u> accompany all orders.☐ Please send a free catalog.